The Cats
of Savone

Novels by David-Michael Harding

How Angels Die

Cherokee Talisman

Available at Amazon, Smashwords, and Barnes & Noble

Find free reading excerpts, preview upcoming
novels, and check out the author's blog at -

DavidMichaelHarding.com

Completely Abridged – Vol. 1

The Cats of Savone

8 Short Novels for Busy People

BY

DAVID-MICHAEL HARDING

The Cats of Savone

A
Q&CY
BOOK

Cover : Sculpture by Linda Brenner from *Ghost Cats*, an installation at Eastern State Penitentiary Historic Site, Philadelphia, Pennsylvania.

Cover Photograph by Bill Christensen

Photograph of the author by William Tillis and Harold Hutchinson

Cover by William Tillis and Kerwin Designs

DavidMichaelHarding.com

Printed in the United States of America
November 2013
First Edition

1 3 5 7 9 10 8 6 4 2

ISBN 10: 0985728515
ISBN 13: 978-0-9857285-1-9
Library of Congress Catalog Number: 2013916043

The Stories

The Cats of Savone

The wall is thirty feet high and ten feet thick. It surrounds Savone Correctional Facility, a maximum security prison where I live. Its presence creates a solid atmosphere of stone and white cement that separates my world from another. The inner and outer sides of the monster wall are halved, conflicted twins of protection and separation. Perversion of normal ferments inside and slips through the hands of sanity scarcely under control. Outside spins the causal chaos of life. Intimidation is the only shared definition visible from either side. For Johnny Cash, Merle Haggard, and a dozen others, prison walls are memories bent to rhymes. The lyrics play tricks and hide the poet's pain. Minds seldom pause to wonder if the words had been gleaned from skid bids, short stays in county lock-up, or from scars that still bleed after aching years of blind-hard state time. Either way, the sentiments are as accurate as can be compressed in the space of a song. Telling the whole story would fill volumes no one would or could read. Page after page would be totally void of the titillating drama and violence of Hollywood or real-life prison. Instead, you would find it inked with the painful boredom of high anxiety, symbolized by blank pages running to empty chapters on to entire books void of letters, words, motion, or even thought. This is the reality on my side of the wall.

It's said the monster goes fifteen feet into the ground to discourage prisoners from tunneling their way to freedom. I don't know if that is true. It is but one of many rumors that surround the prison – rumors that have grown – some from fact, some from fiction, as though it mattered. One thing that is known is that no one has ever escaped over or under that wall. The only thing that can get through Savone's wall is prayer.

I recall one rumor that had enough legs to move to the level of unsubstantiated fact. The story centers on the gymnasium. Like all good tales the real story isn't in the first blush. In fact it has damned little to do with the current gym at all. The gym was only the whitewash that covered up an ugly page of the prison's first hundred years on up to about 1970. It is documented that the prison was built with inmate labor. Originally the inmates were somewhat trusted men who could work long hard hours. That inaugural rendition of Savone Correctional was a few buildings that housed the men at night, chained. At dawn the shackles were removed and the men taken to local coal mines to split rock. The free labor didn't sit well with local miners who were trying to eek a living out from beneath a black mountain and eventually forced the State to retreat from its attempt at a job training program ala 1870. The inmates stopped mining and built the wall instead. In short order, two thousand of their closest friends moved in and the prison became the largest maximum security facility in the state.

In those early days an inmate cemetery took shape out of necessity. Coal mining always will be dangerous work, but even more so in the mid-19th Century. Men were killed or just up and died for causes natural and otherwise. Unclaimed dead, and there were plenty, especially during war years when death was so common, had to be buried and there generally wasn't anyone standing in line to collect a dead convict. The county mortuary profited for a time until an enterprising warden decided to pocket the two dollars a head allowance the state coughed up for the unceremonious hauling off of the dearly departed. His option included unmarked graves at the end of F Block, behind the tractor barn. This proved real convenient when a nightstick came down too hard and skulls cracked like dry wood. The wall's broad back blocked any witnesses except for men already in chains and no one was going to listen to them anyway.

After the Attica riot jumped off and reform stripped the word "Prison" off the wall above the main gate, replaced by the words "Correctional Facility," though the faded outline of the original title could still be read twenty-five years later, the liberals decided to build a nice new basketball and handball gym at Savone. This was a dozen wardens removed from the two dollar man, but when plans came in for the new building it was hastily decided the best place to pour ninety yards of concrete sixteen inches thick would be at the end of F Block on the site of the old tractor barn. Some of the graves weren't that old when the excavation equipment rolled in. It's said the Buildings & Grounds head man stood there with a big ratty ledger and directed nearly every shovel full of dirt as the footers were dug. When the concrete stood ready to pour, the current superintendant – no longer called warden as another result of Attica, along with correction officer or C.O. for guard, and inmate for prisoner – stood there with some other suits to commemorate the event. From the highest tiers on cell block F, many men said the superintendant tossed that same beat up ledger under the concrete flow. Now it and that cemetery lay forever out of reach beneath where the new gym stands.

Closely related to the cemetery story is another tale that is absolute fact. This comes from any sane man with senses intact, understanding that sanity and senses, each dulled beyond repair from lack of use, can be in short supply in Savone. The story is centered on the ghosts of hundreds of prisoners and at least two guards who have died on my side of the wall. These ghosts prowl the halls day and night, serving a sentence beyond life, constantly looking for the front gate or perhaps a different type of pardon.

Some jailhouse rumors are born, live, and die in a very short time while others, like the ghosts, impact more deeply and more often. For instance, there is a cell in D Block no one wants. Too many have died there and some remain, wandering through the bars in death like they wish they could have done in life. These ghosts are real. Even the cats that prowl the hallways of the 150-year old prison searching for mice, have been seen to arch their backs, hiss, and screech away from Deadman's Curve, frightened by the many unseen dead that linger there. I myself have felt a chill as I've walked through that long curved hallway. Deadman's Curve is the result of an architectural mistake when the construction of a cellblock didn't line up with what should have been a straight hall. As a result, the long narrow bend is invisible to officers stationed at either end. Somewhere in the middle, where the chill comes on, blood has covered the floor more times than anyone can remember. When I walk that curve a dread comes over me as it must the cats, but I can't run and hide as they do.

The ghosts may be dismissed by the uninitiated as rumors and even the cemetery as legend, but the cats of Savone and how they came to be cannot. It has nothing to do with legend and everything to do with legacy – a legacy that began in 1971 when in a convoluted role something tried to get in the prison rather than out.

On the prison side of Savone's wall, in the huge open corner where the north and west walls meet beneath the big gun tower is a mammoth recreation area known simply as "the yard." A sand covered field as big as a gridiron and often used as one runs a hundred yards along the base of a gentle slope that grows uphill to the north wall.

At the east end of the sandbox are two concrete basketball courts. The concrete is so rough and ragged that Savone's brand of basketball is strictly a passing game. The Harlem Globetrotters couldn't dribble on that concrete. New jacks – new inmates – or transfers from other prisons learn quickly that a dribbled ball will rocket off the unfinished surface to curses and laughter of equal proportions split between the offense and defense. The jagged concrete and the often net-less, loose, bent rims that rattle with each shot, are called "the sixth man" in Savone. The Sixth Man at Savone is by far the finest defensive player ever to play the game.

The unique brand of basketball behind the wall pales to what exists in the yard on the slope above the sand. One hundred years ago the gentle grade proved the perfect undefined grandstand for the no equipment, few-rules-version of football played at Savone. As with any Friday night high school game in the free world, friends clustered with friends. On the slope in Savone Prison, miniature neighborhoods formed. Men gravitated to their own kind – distinguished by relation, home town or city, age, interest, race, or crime. The microcosm of society, though filtered by crime, formed in small patches of ground about fifteen feet square, separated by streets – pathways between the little dirt courts. There were very few fights over the land, but again, much like the free world, a group from one court and its larger neighborhood shied away from walking the dirt path streets in another neighborhood. If you didn't belong there, you had no business there. The courts themselves were much tighter. Almost like a man's cell, the courts were an extension of a prisoner's house. If you weren't invited, a misplaced step on someone's court could result in a crack in the mouth or worse. It was trespassing – a high crime behind the wall.

Prisoners began to bring what food they had and sat on the hillside watching the games, gambling with tobacco, and eating bologna. When the bologna grew tiresome or had been replaced by a gruel that tried to pass for oatmeal – breakfast, lunch, and dinner in the prison mess hall seldom distinguishable from each other – the prisoners launched some of the very first tailgate parties in the country with food smuggled or stolen from the chow hall or gifts from visitors. Lacking tailgates, they used wooden boxes for tables. The boxes held crude concrete filled coffee cans that served for dumbbells or scrap wood for shanty town type small fires. In a place of deprivation, anything that could be pressed into multiple uses was valuable. Storage boxes became tables and chairs. Additional crates materialized until all manner of boxes were collected as stools in disjointed circles around the small fires which became cooking pits in the sand. Of course all of this was a violation of regulations and Savone survived on regulations.

As quickly as the tiny neighborhoods formed, the guards saw the scraps of turf become sources of pride. Gardens and lawns, if only manicured weeds, cropped up. Though real vegetables were in short supply, if a half-rotten and mushy tomato or melon passed through the kitchen, you could guarantee its seeds were in the black marketplace of Savone by that night and sprouting in the sand in ten days. And because the courts were desired, they became tools to leverage good behavior. If a prisoner caused a problem he'd lose access to his court. Losing the ability to collect with his friends in a place more or less their own in a wild screaming world of two thousand convicts was a big deal. The guards and the administration saw the good that came from the squares of dirt, not for the intrinsic rewards for the prisoners, but their own selfish maintenance of control. Either way, it served the purpose of both groups, so the courts remained, flourished, and evolved until in time some even had rickety picket fences made from of pieces of wood lath snuck into the yard one piece at a time over the course of months.

Other courts were not so elaborate, but still revered. Much of this was attributable to the resourcefulness and access to materials of the men who took up part-time residence there. Each court eventually was provided at least one box, more or less three feet square to protect cooking utensils and firewood from the weather and easy, though very risky, theft. For men that would wile away the days and their lives in the yard, the small courts became the stoop of a brownstone, a bench in the park, or a quiet back porch. Often the smells of fried chicken or ribs filled the air and coaxed the convicts who belonged onto the courts for the food and safety found in numbers. Back in 1971 that same temptation drifted over the wall like a free man and caught the sensitive nose of another drifter, a pregnant cat with no name.

On a court, where halves of chicken were sizzling just above the sand, a steady hand was tending the rough stove. Charlie Dennis had been on this court for twenty-three years. For twenty-three years he had tended the cooking fire as the names and faces of those around him on the court slowly changed. Some had been paroled. Others became ghosts in the halls. And while the names changed, the faces always held the same look that comes when liberty goes.

Charlie's eyes were the same as others, but in the corner was a spark of kindness. He kept it hidden, for in prison, kindness is taken as weakness. Rather than decency, a show of humanity or thoughtfulness is seen as a fault, a vulnerability to be exploited. As such, Charlie kept it tucked away, out of sight, like the crude knife that lay hidden in the sand just beneath the storage box.

Being found in possession of a knife, a homemade shank really, would lead an inmate directly to a cell called 'the box' which was a stripped down cell for long term isolation. However, not possessing a shank when one was needed could easily land a man in a wooden box, destined for another anonymous potential gym site. Charlie's shank was a simple sixteen penny nail set in a wooden handle. Several handles had rotted away over the years, but the rusty steel remained, and with it, a comforting presence. He felt his eyes drawn to its secret hiding place for a dose of reassurance each day. If trouble was floating through the prison Charlie carried his shank, but that hadn't happened to him in years so it stayed hidden in the yard.

Other prisoners had different types of protection. They carried slicing shanks made from stolen razor blades melted into toothbrush handles, or carried the bare blades on the roofs of their mouths where they could spit them into their hands, slice a man, and return the bloody blade to their mouths in a second. Others fashioned bits of wire, pieces of bed frames, or even cigarette filters melted together and sharpened on the concrete floor of cells to make nice fiberglass blades that wouldn't ring. To ring meant setting off the multitude of metal detectors prisoners passed through as they moved down Savone's old dark brick hallways and to ring was a clear invitation to being locked down in your cell or worse. Clandestine handoffs, skullduggery, chicanery, or drops were often in order to move any metal through the prison.

Charlie had a sturdy frame, muscular when he was younger, and a round face with deep crow's feet set in a tanned face from daily visits outside to the court. His hands were tanned as well and showed the first signs of arthritis as the knuckles were swollen and stiffening with time. He was somewhere in his sixties now and only remembered his birth date when a prison guard or administrator pressed him for identification. Even then it was just an automatic response and was forgotten again until he needed to recall it for a C.O. When his birthday did come, it went without remembrance, no cards or letters, and certainly no fanfare. His walk was a bit stooped from carrying sixty plus years on his back, but apart from gray thinning hair, he was in decent condition despite having spent more than half his life behind bars. He looked the same as the other men in the yard, always dressed in drab prison issue green from head to toe. The guards wore bright blue shirts and dark blue pants. It was an easy distinction for the eye. Yet the officers, whether they knew it or not, were themselves doing twenty-five year sentences until retirement – their own parole from Savone – but their sentences were served eight hours at a time.

Above his green, Charlie always wore a dark green knit wool hat. It was worn in place of the hair that had receded over the years until only a few white tuffs remained over his weathered ears. The sight of Mickey, ambling across the yard under his own long hair, made

Charlie reach up and tug his few strands and shake his head at what once had been.

Mickey was everything Charlie was no longer. He was young, maybe thirty, tall, and powerfully built. His blackish hair hung in a tangled mane around his shoulders. Not unlike Charlie's hat, Mickey always wore a pair of old wool gloves, the fingers of which had been worn away over his six years in Savone. Why he wore them was a mystery, but Mickey's gloves were never challenged. He took them off when he ate and kept them clean. Beyond the wall it would have been different, but on this side, that was enough.

His step hindered by a bad hip, the result of a stab wound three years before that left him with a limp, Mickey shuffled up the hill to Charlie and the court. As he moved, Mickey thought of little. There were no plans in his head today or ever. For Mickey, the cooking chicken was as far as he could see or wanted to. This inability to look ahead further than such things as grilling chicken had caused him to be the subject of several criminal investigations, the last one of which had deposited him in Savone where, according to legal papers he never fully understood, he would live for at least the next fifteen years. Whenever Mickey told anyone how much time he had to do, he always said, "Fifteen to life, or whichever comes first." With his quick temper stacked on strong arms, it was easy to conceive that "life" might indeed win out before the state could get its minimum out of Mickey.

Charlie stood over the makeshift grill and prodded the chicken as though they needed it. Behind him, the last two members of the court mused over a chess match. Doc G, ten years younger than Charlie, and with a slight, round build and look, maneuvered the black pieces. G could spout philosophy and calculus theories, but struggled with people and the dynamics of conflict. His opponent, Frankie, moved the white pieces, but that was all he could do. Frankie was the smallest man on the court and one of the smallest in the prison. He was built and looked like he was sixteen – waif thin – with skinny adolescent arms and legs and a bony face that would crack under any blow. Yet, if there was trouble, Frankie would wade into an ass kicking and take his lumps to help his friends and mentors on the court. Apart from his loyalty, Frankie could be counted on to broker valuable information back to the court through several powerful conduits. His slight build made him no physical threat so he could approach anyone, but his primary source was the homosexuals – pragmatic, closeted, or flaming, – whose network was more expansive than the narcotic dealers and gamblers.

Though older, Charlie and Doc G would throw down with anybody to protect the court or maintain respect. They never sought out trouble. They stayed out of drugs, gambling, and sex – the big three which led to fights and stabbings. However, each juggled. Juggling was providing an item, usually food or cigarettes as a two for one. If you wanted a pack of smokes today, you could get them via 'the juggle,' but next week you had to pay back two packs. It was a living for the haves over the have-nots – a form of interest not unlike usury practices outside the wall. Charlie and G could also rely on their contacts in Savone to come by food, wood, paint from the shops, and almost anything else. Other cons came to them when they needed things and paid according to a strict timetable and hefty vig. If there was any delay in payment, that's where Mickey stepped in. Other prisoners understood that Charlie's court was respectful and trustworthy, but if crossed, someone was going to be hurt bad. With this understanding, business was generally conducted without problems.

The one-sided chess match continued as the chicken sizzled in the background. The black knights danced at G's command while Frankie's white king ran for his life.

"Check," Doc said as if half asleep.

"Where?"

"Queen's bishop to queen's rook five."

"Huh?"

"Here," G pointed. "You've only got one move."

"I know. I know," Frankie said before a lengthy pause. "Where?"

"Your king's rook to king's knight three to block."

"Where's king's knight whatever?"

"King's knight three. Right here. You must get serious about your game if you're ever to advance, Franklin."

"Keep it up, old man, and I'll advance your ass right down the hill!"

G ignored the toothless threat and set in motion his deadly black knight.

"Well put, Franklin. That's check... and mate. Have a pleasant day."

Frankie stared at the board. "This game sucks, man."

Charlie turned from the smoking chicken. "Another clinic, G?"

"Yes, Sir Charles, another clinic."

Mickey stepped onto the court, glanced at the chess board then turned his attention to the chicken.

"Let's go boys," Charlie said in answer to Mickey's unspoken question. "Get 'em while they're hot."

As the men ate, the saucy smell of the chicken barbeque drifted on an unnoticed breeze up and over the wall and down to the soon-to-be mother cat that paced between resting under the cars of the guards. Despite her distended stomach, she moved with the light gait unique to cats. She paused and put a foot on the wall as if to test it. Her nails came out on demand, but bristled at the hard concrete. Even had it been a carpeted plank, she would have had trouble ascending the thirty feet with the extra weight of her unborn babies. She hesitated a moment longer then moved off on tired padded feet.

The scent trail she followed had begun to fade when the cat came to the north gate. The huge gate was twenty feet wide and as high as the wall, but more importantly, it was about four inches off the ground. She lowered her head and peered beneath the ton and a half of metal. On the other side she saw fences, a wire gate, razor wire, and a truck. She could also see soft clouds of smoke rising from a gentle hillside. The trail was stronger here and caused a darting tongue to brush her twitching whiskers.

Suddenly the truck started with a roar and there was a tremendous racket above her head. The cat's reflexes made her run as the gate gave chase or so she thought. She scampered into the street and slipped beneath the safety of a parked car. From behind a tire, anxious and wide eyes watched as the gate slid open and the truck rolled out and away. The gate resisted a change of direction, clanging and banging until it returned to where it had been when she first came to it.

Her paws came up under her heavy body as she settled in for a wait while the same patient eyes that had many times followed meals of fluttering birds and timid mice watched the quiet gate. The car had been driven recently and although the summer weather needed little help, the engine's heat felt good on her tired back. She lowered her head and let her eyes drop to slits. All that kept her from a deep sleep was the increasingly frequent movements inside her.

"Attention in the yard. Attention in the yard. The yard is closed. Line it up."

The amplified voice drifted over the wall much like the smell of Charlie's chicken had earlier in the day. It woke the cat with a bit of a start. The babies had been taking a toll and she was uncomfortable and tired. Her eyes opened to darkness. She stood awkwardly and stretched before moving again toward the wall. On the other side, Charlie, Mickey, and countless others moved in the opposite direction. The inmates trudged along reluctantly, funneling down into a single line before disappearing into the dark brick building that housed their cages. As the men, heads bowed, not out of reverence but rather worn despair, stepped into the block, the cat, head ducked as well, slipped beneath the north gate, through the fence and into the yard.

In the blocks beyond Deadman's Curve, gates were crashing shut on the cells signaling the end of another day in an endless blur. From the end of the block, the cells all looked the same – like company row houses built next to a rail yard, a foundry, or a mill. Like people, it was what was inside that spelled the difference. Outside, where company policy kept the houses all the same, the houses were indistinguishable, like the cells. Behind the cell's barred sliding door, personality might show. Some were neat and clean, others far less so. Some had a clothesline of shoe laces tied for laundry fresh from the sink. There were decorations of sorts that consisted of cards stuck to the pale green painted steel walls or "short eyes" – porn pictures – clipped from magazines and taped above the gate. Simple religious symbols were in many, but almost none displayed photographs from the street. Photos of family were tucked away for days when dark clouds swept into a man's cell and brought a feverishly cold, painful rain. Then the brutishly tough and the meek alike thought hard about an escape – the midnight express that would roll down the company walkway in front of their gate – when a slit wrist in a bucket of warm water granted the Grim Reaper's version of parole. Many of the ghosts in the prison had been lifers with no release date while others were on a skid bid. Savone made no distinction between weak and strong, short or long. It broke most every man in one way or another and no one left without its scar. Men who didn't change were still not the same.

Frankie shut his gate and locked himself in for the night. It was a routine that often struck him as strangely funny. He was his own jailer. There was no key and the guards controlled the opening of the gates from the end of the company, but if you didn't step in and close your gate, the consequences would be uncomfortable at best, painful at worst. A thousand times a day in a prison as large as Savone, convicts like Frankie were their own jailers as they locked themselves in their cells, though very few saw any laughter in it. Frankie's humor hid the sigh of relief that was embraced by the safety of a locked gate between him and the rest of the prison. No one could touch him. There would be no misunderstanding in a line, no confusion over a word or show of respect. No trouble. No blood.

Frankie tried yet again, to write a letter – a kite – to send out and wait for an answer that may never come. This attempt, like others before, ended after two lines on a crumpled paper, not dramatically thrown across his cell, but pushed into a battered folder. He could use the same two lines tomorrow or the next day or the day after that. Nothing would have changed anyway.

Instead of laboring over words that wouldn't come, Frankie pulled out the plastic jug from beneath his bed. The peach slices, chunks of apple, raisins, and sugar had settled nicely. He drained off a plastic cup of his special brew and waited for a coaxed sleep to overtake him.

Several cells away, Doc G was kneeling on his prayer rug, deep in conversation with Allah. After several quiet minutes he crept up off aching knees, solemnly rolled up his rug and went to bed without a sound.

Mickey's cell was Spartan. The toilet bowl was rusty and dust balls jumped into the corners as he whipped back the single tattered blanket of his bed. He stretched out and quickly masturbated into a ragged towel. With the calming release and nothing on his mind to hinder the descent, Mickey dropped off to sleep without a struggle.

Charlie's sleep wouldn't come so readily. Following a tradition he had started years before, he sat on the edge of the small metal bed and reached for his diary. As he perused the day's events in his head, he lowered himself onto his beat up mattress. After a half hour he sat up, scribbled briefly in the book and undressed.

Outside, the cat had found the Court of Barbeque Chicken. Unfortunately for her, the men had been tidy for fear of drawing the very prey she sought in lieu of a discarded scrap, but perhaps the aroma, pushed to the ground by the settling dew, would lure mice as it had her. She crept into a crevice between the box and a stone chair and waited. It was only a few minutes before the first hard pains came. She adjusted her position again and again until cat sized tears welled up in her eyes and blurred the sight of the moon above.

In his cell, tears of his own trickled down Charlie's cheeks as he tried to edge himself into the reluctant arms of sleep. It was part of the same tradition that brought out the diary. He would eventually sleep, but not without returning to close the book. In it he had written, "No rain. Chicken smelled good today. Nothing else." Then he slept, surrounded by the uneasy breathing, plentiful coughs, banging gates, and occasional screams that were the sounds of the night in Savone.

The morning light saw six hundred men and four new-born kittens come into the yard. While the men, some of the most violent in the state, moved all around them, the kittens sought out their mother's milk with blind eyes. They were full and the day well warmed when Mickey stepped onto the court. He plopped down on a stone seat and pulled out his package of tobacco. As he creased his paper and started tapping the cheap tobacco into it, a slight noise, a hiss, brought his attention to the edge of the box. The cat, smoky gray on her own and made darker by the shadow of the box, looked like a huge rat. Another hiss caused Mickey to jump and spill his smoke. Still holding his now empty rolling paper, Mickey leaned in toward the cat's nursery. The cat peered back and spit at the interloper. Mickey jumped again, dropped his paper, and quickly — quickly for him and his game hip — made his way down the hill. After each few bouncing, hobbled steps he looked back at the court, the box, and the cat.

Charlie was walking the worn path around the perimeter of the yard, head down as usual. In front and behind, inmates were stretched out like an uncoordinated freight train, each carrying their own unique baggage. Mickey caught up to his friend and grabbed his arm.

"Charlie!" Mickey nearly yelled before collecting himself and speaking in a whisper. "Charlie, there's something wrong on the court."

"What, somebody steal something again?" Charlie said without breaking his slow stride.

"No, Charlie. Listen. There ain't nothing missing. There's something been added."

Charlie thought a great deal of the much younger Mickey. Undoubtedly there was a father-son bond that had fashioned itself behind the wall. Charlie had no son and though Mickey had a father somewhere, he never knew him. The quiet demeanor Charlie reflected to the world was the balance to Mickey's unchecked and rudderless emotions. Charlie felt pride from the gift of giving and teaching by example and gentle lecture. Most of the time Mickey only knew Charlie's advice had kept him out of solitary confinement, lockdown, or that hell-hole of a strip cell in the hospital ward. But the teachings, no matter how well they may have worked at times, couldn't gain permanent roots in Mickey's mind. They needed Charlie's constant, daily, often hourly, cultivation or Mickey was soon cuffed and taken to the strip cells.

Charlie's face gave away his annoyance. "What's up, Mick? Somebody throw their garbage on it?"

"No, Charlie. There's a cat next to the box. It's making stupid noises."

"Have you been drinking Frankie's shine?"

"Not this morning... Not yet. I'm telling you, it's a cat."

"Maybe a rat."

"No. It's a cat. C-A-T. Cat."

"A cat?" Charlie said as he eased to a stop and looked at his struggling apprentice.

"A cat," Mickey said proudly.

Charlie paced off toward the court. "Let's see."

As the two men neared the court they unintentionally picked up Doc and Frankie. "Morning, gentlemen," G began. "It's a beautiful day to—"

"No time, G. There's a cat on the court," Mickey whispered.

Charlie said a curt good morning and moved on his way with Mickey hobbling along behind. Frankie and G fell into place, staring at each other and muttering. "A cat?"

When the quartet neared their court the pace dropped off and they approached the box with a mixture of caution and curiosity. They all heard the hiss of the cat.

"See.   I told you," Mickey said as he sat down.   Charlie motioned for him to be quiet then crouched down in front of bared fangs. He backed up and the cat retreated.

"Wow, some pissed, huh, Charlie?" Frankie said from the safety of Doc G's back.

"Perhaps it's ill, Charles," G said, himself trying to get aging eyes to pierce the shadow.

"No, I don't think so," Charlie said thoughtfully as he and the others found seats around the court, Frankie moving twice before he was satisfied with his view.

"What's wrong with him?" Mickey asked.

"Nothing, Mick. And it's not a him. It's a her."

"How do you know that?"

"Listen..."

The yard was suddenly as quiet as a church mouse. It was as if the sound had been shut off on a movie the court was set in. Despite the hundreds of men wandering in the yard – the basketball, weightlifting clanging, wheeling and dealing of gamblers, dopers, dreamers, and drama queens – movement also seemed to stop. In that frozen moment of silent stillness a faint whine, a pitched squeak, came from the shadow of the box.

"She has kittens."

G relaxed while Mickey look puzzled.

Frankie smiled. "Cool, man. Very cool."

The small group watched the anxious cat for a long time. Occasionally one of the kittens would cry and when its whine was contented, almost fatherly smiles came to the faces of the human members on the court.

After an hour, G made a suggestion. "I've got a tuna fish sandwich here. Perhaps she's hungry after her ordeal." He slipped carefully toward the cat, pulling out his sandwich as he did. "Take it easy my little friend."

The cat spit as before until her nose caught the smell of the fish. Instinct to protect and hunger waged a short battle as G carefully tossed a chunk of tuna into the shadow. Razor claws cut into the fish and held it while needle sharp teeth bit deep, in part out of hunger, in part out of fear. Eventually the men took turns throwing pieces of G's snack. It was Mickey's misguided effort that brought the cat into the open.

The group stood slowly to block the view of others in the yard. From his vantage point, Charlie could see into the cat's lair. There were three little bodies piled haphazardly atop one another. A fourth, clearly dead, lay off to the side. Charlie held up three fingers to his friends. The cat picked up the morsel and returned to her kittens and the convicts went back to their seats.

"How do they look, Charles?"

"One's dead, but there's two tiger colored ones and a third one that's mostly white with a little color, sorta calico. It looks pretty tiny next to the tigers."

"Awww shit," Mickey said. "One's dead already?"

"Yea, Mick. Mighta been born dead."

"Can we bury it?"

"No way, man," Frankie spouted. "The mothers eat 'em."

G turned to Mickey to erase the childlike fear he knew would be on his companion's rugged face. "No. I don't believe she'd eat the deceased kitten. When she allows us, we'll slip it away from her and bury it here on the court."

Mickey was relieved and Frankie pleasantly disappointed he was wrong.

The remaining hours were consumed by the men and the cat eyeing each other amid talk of how to keep her hidden from the guards. After a quick day, the announcement came that the yard was closed. Despite their intentions and the tuna, the cat had not let the men near the kittens.

Once back in their cells, the evening rituals began. Doc G however, found himself saying a prayer for the kittens' health and safety. Frankie wrote a letter and shared the news of the find. Mickey had trouble falling asleep for the first time in years as he fretted over the kittens and wondered why the one had died.

In the confines of his cell, Charlie's pen labored furiously at the diary. When he tired, he looked back at his work and surprised himself when he counted five full pages. Later, he clicked off his bare bulb and went to sleep like the others – thinking of the kittens, and smiling.

In the yard, the cat stirred and pawed her sleeping brood. She paid no attention to the dead kitten and little to the tiny calico. The same teeth that had threatened Charlie closed gently around the neck of a tiger as she picked it up and strolled off the court. She traveled only a short distance down the hill before she tucked the kitten in a stand of weeds. Energized by a sense of urgency from an unknown source, the cat returned to the court and carried off the second tiger. Slower now, she repeated her steps for the weak calico.

For a few moments, the new mother rested over her three babies and watched the nighttime of the yard. Then, with a tiger in her mouth, she jogged across the expanse to the north gate. She carried her cargo through the fences and under the huge silent door. In seconds, she had disappeared into the darkness.

The last two kittens remained unattended for several minutes until their mother returned without a sound. The cat sniffed the still calico then roughly pushed it aside as the selective mother mouthed the second tiger. Without looking back, she shot across the yard and beneath the gate for the last time. To her, the last of her babies was dangling below her chin.

At the lineup for yard next morning, Charlie had a towel, an intended bed for the kittens, wrapped secretively around his waist under his shirt. G and Frankie had brought food. Mickey, further back in line, had carried his last gulp of milk back from the chow hall in his mouth and spit it into a small plastic bag. When he hit the yard, the others were already some distance in front of him. By the time he arrived at the court, they were sitting dejectedly, staring blankly at their dirt floor.

Frankie wanted to deliver the bad news. "They're gone, man. They're all gone except the dead one."

Mickey, like the others before him, went to the box and looked for himself. "Sonofabitch! Where'd they go?"

Charlie touched his friend's arm. "She probably didn't think they'd be safe here. They do that sometimes, Mickey."

"Bullshit! We weren't gonna hurt them kitties! I'd kill the first mother fucker that touched them cats."

"I know that, Mick, but she didn't."

Mickey sat down, as disillusioned as the rest. In time he dug a small hole with the heal of his boot and watched as Doc G laid the dead kitten in the shallow grave. It wasn't much of a ceremony. Mickey said he was a good kitty and Frankie started to snicker. He couldn't help himself, but neither could Mickey.

After the funeral it occurred to Charlie that while the cat had moved her family, perhaps they were still in the yard. A minute after imparting his theory on the others, they were searching. Mickey held his little bag of milk as if it were a talisman as he discreetly poked through the islands of weeds that dotted the hillside.

It was Charlie who discovered the kitten. He bent as if to tie his shoe so no one noticed him slip the limp furry ball into his pocket. He sauntered back to the court and motioned discreetly for the rest of the searchers. As they collected, Charlie laid the unmoving kitten by the fresh grave of the other. Mickey looked down as he walked onto the court. "God damn it! Why they all dying?"

"I don't know, Mick," Charlie said as he toed out another grave. As he continued to dig, a tiny sneeze, scarcely detectable, came from the kitten. The scene that followed would have been equally at home in either a hospital emergency room or a Marx Brother's movie. Charlie cuddled the baby, picking pieces of dead grass from its fur. Doc G said a prayer and Frankie stomped the new grave closed. It was Mickey though who saved the kitten's life. He pinched a small hole in his bag of milk and held it as Charlie force fed the newest member of the court.

Charlie smuggled the kitten into the block that night and wasn't seen for the next several days. He stayed in his cell and nursed the baby with milk smuggled from the chow hall. Within a week the kitten was much improved and living comfortably in a cardboard box beneath Charlie's bed. Within three weeks however, Gretchen, named after Charlie's mother, had already outgrown her temporary home and was pirated back to the yard.

Her return to the court and the next few weeks passed without any major incidents. Still, word of a cat living in Charlie's box was spreading. Though it was overlooked when Mickey carried milk back to his cell in his mouth, the same conduct by the revered Doc G and Charlie was garnering suspicious looks. What concerned Charlie the most was that if the other cons saw these things and learned of Gretchen, it was only a matter of time before the guards did too.

At the only door from the prison to the yard stood a small shack not much larger than the convicts' dirt courts. It housed the guards' coffee pot, raincoats, and riot gear. For five days out of every seven, Officer Johns stood in the doorway of the shack as the inmates filed in and out of what he referred to as, "My yard." Johns was a barrel-chested fifty-year old man with the beginnings of a paunch hanging over his tight belt. His thick arms completely filled the sleeves of his blue uniform shirt above a faded tattoo on his right forearm. His face was unwrinkled and tight, belying his age. The haircut was the same as he had received when he reported for military service thirty years earlier. On his hip swung a chipped and battered black nightstick.

Officer Johns was the picture of what a guard was meant to be – big, strong, strict, but fair and honest. The rumors of Savone had him placing several wayward inmates in the ground beneath the new gym back in the days when such things were done. Now Johns was older. He was about to take a cozy job in a gun tower on top of the wall, far above the day to day bustle and noise, and finish his career as a gatekeeper.

When he was dressed in bright blue, Johns always had two things with him – his stick and a cup of buttermilk. Twenty-three years of voluntary imprisonment had given him a sour stomach which the buttermilk soothed. As he walked the yard he sipped his tonic and paced the same eroded trail as the prisoners. On this particular day, Johns was circling Charlie's court. With each pass the circle grew tighter, like a shark circling its victim. After several near misses, Johns stepped uninvited onto the court and addressed no one in particular with more of a declaration than a question and never made eye contact with anyone present. "What's goin' on, fellas?"

Charlie spoke up. "Not a thing, Officer Johns, sir."

Johns slowly drew his nightstick and walked around the court, using the stick to flip over stones and part clumps of weeds. "Oh, I don't know about that," Johns snorted. "Something's going on. I don't know quite what yet, but I'm going to find out. Guaran-fuckin'-teed."

The members of the court secretly traded worried looks as Johns jammed his stick under the lid of their box and pried it up. He held the top up with the nightstick and leaned over to see inside. Following a tense few seconds, he stepped back and lowered the lid. Johns made one more sweep around the court then walked off, still muttering. "I'll figure it out all right..."

Mickey was anxious to see into the box himself, wondering like the rest if Gretchen had hidden or escaped. Charlie bid him to wait, but driven, Mickey reached over, lifted the lid, peeked inside, then gently set the lid down and leaned back with a blank look on his face.

"Well?" Frankie questioned. "She there?"

"Hell yes, she's there. I don't see how he coulda missed her. She's just sitting there. Looking all cute and shit."

"Perhaps she was under a pan or something," G suggested.

Charlie stood up anxiously. "This isn't gonna work, boys. Our luck, and Gretchen's, ain't gonna last."

"Any suggestions, Charles?"

"Not a damn one."

"Well, we better think of something. Johns is headed back this way."

Sure enough, Johns was walking toward them. Mickey got up from his chair and sat on the box while Charlie returned to his stone seat to wait out the inevitable. As Johns came onto the court, he spoke to Charlie. "Request permission to come aboard, Captain."

"It's your world, Officer Johns."

The guard grunted over a sip of buttermilk, drew his nightstick again, and sat on a stone bench next to Charlie. The buttermilk rested on the stone between the two men as Johns doodled in the dirt with his stick. "You know, Dennis, not much can go on in a place like this that a couple of old timers like us don't know about, is there?"

"No, sir. I don't imagine not."

Johns softly echoed Charlie's answer. "No, sir. I don't imagine not..."

The men sat in silence for another long minute. Johns then abruptly rose and started to leave. Charlie noticed the cup of buttermilk on the stone and held it out. "Officer Johns, sir? You forgot your buttermilk."

Johns never stopped walking. "No, I didn't. Your friend in the box looks a little thirsty."

"Damn," was the best anyone could muster as the tough guard ambled away.

About a month later, when Gretchen had become impossible to conceal, Johns returned to the court. Without a word, he opened the box, picked her up, and shut the lid. He petted her then set her on the ground. She immediately bounced onto the box and surveyed what was to become her new world. As Johns walked away he left a half cup of buttermilk on the box, as he would five out of seven days thereafter. That night Frankie wrote another letter, G gave thanks for an answered prayer, Mickey couldn't sleep, and Charlie filled six pages of his diary.

With her freedom assured by Officer Johns, Gretchen quickly conquered the entire yard and everyone in it, everyone except one. While the hardest criminal or the most deranged sociopath would smile when Gretchen came near, Alejundro Benerize would clench his decaying teeth at the sight of her. Benerize didn't hate her for something as simple as being a cat. He hated her because everyone else loved her. His pleasure had always come at the expense of the weak and vulnerable, but it wasn't always the immediate pain that gave him satisfaction. He was a man who relished the suffering of those that were witness as he pulled the wings off life. There was a perverse power in impacting so many with one single act.

With nothing except deals of trafficking, gambling, and extortion – so normal for him both inside the wall and out that it was becoming boring – Alejundro needed to cause greater pain. Lost amid the smiles Gretchen brought the bent hands who gave her gentle pats and rubs, Benerize felt only a wish to extinguish the one light in Savone's desolate yard. Though his scarred knuckles and prison tattoos made him look formidable, his resentment of Gretchen was no match for the pleasure she brought the other men, so he kept quiet, biding his time.

It wasn't easy for Benerize to keep his rage in check. In the street it lived at the surface, as much a daily part of him as his breathing. Four years ago his anger landed him in Savone. A convenience store attendant had embarrassed him when Benerize couldn't find the release latch for the hood of his car. Easily goaded on by his cronies, Benerize picked a fight with the teenager, lost control, and pummeled the kid to death by repeatedly bashing his head against the concrete curbing surrounding the gas island. There had been a dozen witnesses. Before that arrest, he had done two skid bids for assault and possession. Since he'd arrived at Savone, Benerize had done little better. The last month had seen his release from a year in solitary for striking an officer. That incident could have been worse as he had tried to cut the guard with a sharpened can lid. Quick reflexes by the officer saved his own life and saved Benerize a lifetime in the box though he did pick up extra charges, as though it mattered in a twenty-five to life bid. But he was back in Savone's general population now and had a new weapon in his boot and a new victim – Gretchen.

In time, Gretchen walked brazenly past officer John's shack on Charlie's heels and into the belly of Savone. Once she was acclimated to the damp dark and the noise, she became Her Majesty-in-Residence, playmate, silent listener, and the bane of rodents. Day and night she roamed at will. Locked gates were nothing as she stepped through the bars. Even closed doors were only minor inconveniences as one meow brought guards with keys rattling as quickly as had one of their number been knocking – probably quicker – as no C.O. could resist those green eyes as Gretchen sat at a locked door looking up. She rubbed everyone's pant leg – scent marking both blue and green with no distinction – until almost everyone inside Savone was duly hers and she theirs. Men benefited and mice suffered. She profited from the convicts in return. If a lazy mouse showed itself beneath a steam radiator and Gretchen was in that cellblock, a snappy call of "Kitty kitty kitty," brought her nearby with ears forward on the hunt. When the chase was over, cheers went up as Gretchen carried the mouse up and down the long company, up flights of stairs and down other tiers of cells, showing off her prize to her many friends.

As the winter solstice approached, Gretchen became acquainted with snow. Soon she was frolicking about, playing with the other residents of Savone, several of which had built a ramshackle ski jump down the main street in the middle of their small hill. Gretchen sat on inmates' laps and, with a constantly twitching calico tail, watched the skiers try to ride their wooden slats and makeshift toboggans. Mickey carried her down on one jump, much to Charlie's chagrin, but a few yards from takeoff she bailed with a powerful leap of her own. Her jump so upset Mickey's balance that he tumbled out of control and crashed harmlessly into a snow bank. For her part in the wreck, Gretchen was rewarded with an avalanche of pats, rubs, and ear scratches as laughter rained down on the pile of snow and flailing limbs that had been Mickey.

Off to the side of the ski jump, Benerize dipped his hand into the snow. As he packed it tight, Gretchen strode defiantly to the center of the takeoff ramp. It was apparent that she knew the next jumper would wait for her to move despite his shouts. The men laughed and were looking back and forth from Gretchen to the skier. No one saw the incoming ice ball. With a resounding thud it crashed into Gretchen's hip and blasted her off the ramp. Her instincts caught her and, as expected, she landed on all four feet. Those same instincts told her to run for the safety of the court, but she had to do it on three legs. The fourth, badly bruised, was dragged along on the snow.

Benerize gave himself away with a broad smile and a wicked cackle, both of which drew several inmates, including an infuriated Mickey, in his direction. Other prisoners collected and traded insults with Benerize, while Mickey, who hadn't the intellect for words, rammed through the crowd. A hard right hook hit its target flush on the jaw with a crack that was still echoing across the yard as Benerize slumped down into the snow. As Mickey cocked his shabby boots for the kicks that would keep Benerize down, Officer Johns grabbed him from behind. Johns knew who he had collared, but never looked at Mickey. Instead, he jerked him backward into the crowd. By the time Johns looked down at the semi-conscious Benerize then turned to the group of agitated cons, Mickey had been successfully swallowed up, just as Johns knew he would.

"Break it up! Show's over!" Johns barked.

Frankie was standing on the innermost edge of the crowd. He looked up the hill to the court where Charlie and others were giving Gretchen a crude examination. "Yo, Officer Johns–" Frankie began as he pointed to Gretchen.

Johns had his stick in his hand in a fraction of a second. In the latter half of that fraction, it was in Frankie's chest. "You hear me, flaco? I ain't saying it again. Move out!"

The crowd broke up beneath an umbrella of low murmurs. Benerize stumbled through the snow, touching his aching jaw and easing it from side to side as on the court, Gretchen tested her hip. She wasn't hurt badly, but for the rest of the winter she limped slightly. While she soon became accustomed to her tender leg, her limp was a constant reminder to others.

Johns realized that this cat had brought changes to his yard. The most noticeable was in Mickey. He became Gretchen's guardian. As she moved from court to court and pranced across the yard in search of food or fun, Mickey was always nearby. She would limp along lightly on her rounds while Mickey sluggishly followed on his own game hip. In Mickey's uncluttered mind their common handicap had formed an unbreakable bond. To Johns, this devotion signaled consequences for a misplaced step or another snowball, even an accidental one.

The snow was eventually replaced by warmer days which sped the healing of Gretchen's injury. As her body healed her leg, it also signaled in her a drive a million years old. When she disappeared for two days in April, a massive search was begun. Benerize would have been severely questioned or beaten outright had he not been serving thirty days locked down in his cell at the time.

When Gretchen appeared back on the court there was a huge sigh of relief from prisoners and guards. In the days that followed, things in the yard settled in as if nothing had happened. Several weeks later however, it became clear that something indeed had. Gretchen was pregnant.

"Pregnant, huh?" Doc G said with the look of a disapproving father. "Are you certain, Charles?"

"I'm sure. Look at her. She's getting wider than the broadside of a barn."

Gretchen strutted around atop the box as if on stage.

"Damn!" Frankie said excitedly. "Gretch got hers, man!"

Mickey petted her affectionately, but had a cross look on his face as he spoke. "Where the hell's the father?"

Frankie laughed. "That boy is gone! Did the deed and jetted, man!"

"Well, whatever happened, I think we can take care of her," Charlie smiled. "Even without a husband."

Mickey gently lifted Gretchen off the box and handed her to Doc G. "We'll take care of her okay," Mickey said gruffly as he retrieved a can of tuna fish from the box. As he opened it, each stab of his can opener punctuated the words of his next sentence. "And if I ever catch that other cat, I'll take care... of... him... too."

The following weeks saw Gretchen grow bigger and her coarse, but caring nannies more anxious. The preceding fall, a hole had mysteriously been cut in the box to allow Gretchen to come and go as she pleased. Now an extra blanket appeared on the court, along with a tell-tale cup of buttermilk. By the time the second litter of four kittens was born in Savone, Gretchen's box had become a cozy nursery. Though everyone tried not to disturb the new family, the lid of the box was lifted and lowered countless times a day. Men who were paroled came to say goodbye as often as new jacks came to say hello.

Johns watched all of this from his new post in the watch tower over the north gate. When things were quiet, he scanned the yard through his binoculars until he located Gretchen and her playful offspring. Sometimes he watched the yard through the powerful rifle scope attached to his Springfield. This practice had no effect on the cats, but served to keep the lid down tight on the yard, something the cats seemed to be able to do from inside the pot.

When summer was in full swing, an innocent act of clumsiness led to two killings. Frankie had just sat down in the chow hall next to a new jack. The inmate, with his freshly shaved head and stiff green clothes, was nervous. As he ate he accidentally tipped over his milk. The splash landed on Frankie's pants.

"Yo! Yo! Yo!" Frankie hollered as he jumped up. "What the hell, man?"

In an instant, the new man had to decide which way to fall. He could be apologetic and run the risk of being taken for weak, or be a tough guy and deal with the consequences. He looked at the diminutive Frankie and opted for the latter.

"Shut your face."

Frankie noticed the closing guards. He sat down and whispered his final remark. "Make sure you're on the list for the yard, bitch."

"Whatever, asshole," came the reply of a nervous man.

As the chow hall crowd filed out after breakfast Charlie and Mickey slid in behind the new jack.

"Son?" Charlie began. "Generally when there's an accident like that back there, you would offer to wash the man's pants for him or pick him up something in the commissary for his trouble. Saves a lot of problems."

"That's real sweet, but I don't wash nobody's clothes."

"Have it your way. Big mistake though. It's not worth it."

The new inmate turned around. "Look, old man. It don't cost a dime to stay outa mine. Step off!"

Mickey put his hand on Charlie's shoulder and leaned his hulking frame toward the new jack. "Hey!" he snapped. "Don't let your mouth write a check your ass can't cash. Know what I mean?"

The fresh green prisoner silently turned around and continued on his way as Charlie shook his head approvingly. "Well put, Mick. Very well put." Mickey just grunted.

As soon as the new jack's untried boots hit the dirt of the yard, Frankie cornered him. "Yo, bitch! You wanna do my wash or do you wanna get your punk ass handed to you?"

"You want a wash woman, go find a dike."

"I got one. You! You doing the right thing, or do I bust your bitch ass outa the frame?"

Mickey was confused by all the talking. "Set it off, Frankie! Crash the sonofabitch!"

Someone yelled from the other side of the growing crowd. "Frankie ain't crashing nothing! He couldn't crash a car if he was drunk!"

The combination of encouragement and embarrassment sent Frankie into the new jack. Everyone, including the tower guards, watched as the pair exchanged mostly misguided punches. The officers moved in slowly, content to let the bad blood be cleared. Everywhere in the yard, inmates were running to see the fight. Benerize was no exception. As he trotted along the base of the hill, a movement out of the corner of his eye caught his attention. It was Gretchen coming down from her court. Benerize slowed and let other men pass him as he neared the spot where Gretchen's path would cross his. He thought about the shank in his boot, but there wasn't time. Instead, he knelt down swiftly as the two paths intersected.

Gretchen saw him only as another man in green. By the time Benerize's hands tightened around her face and throat it was too late. Instinct drove the claws from all four feet into his hands as she struggled to break fee, but her attacker was too strong and too quick. Benerize dropped a knee on her side and crushed her down into the tall weeds as he violently twisted her head completely around in a single vicious snap. Gretchen's body went limp. The killer stood up quickly and jogged on toward the fight.

It had only taken seconds. Frankie was still swinging, Officer Johns was still watching the fight through his rifle scope, and the kittens were still playing on the court. In her grave of weeds, a single paw twitched a few times then stopped. Gretchen's muscles relaxed as death's grip tightened.

Frankie's fight ended with both men leaning on their knees exhausted. The guards descended and led the tired fighters inside where a lackluster inquiry was conducted by disinterested officers. There were no weapons and everyone knew the cause and the necessity. Each man had to stand his ground once the first words were said. It was just the way it was done.

Though anti-climactic, the scuffle was the topic of discussion around the yard. No one noticed Gretchen was missing. It wasn't until the second day that her absence became an issue and then it happened only because of the evidence she left behind.

" 'Cuse me, Meester Charlie?"

Charlie, Mickey, and Doc G looked up from their sizzling grill to see Estefan standing nervously at the edge of the court. Estefan was a small time burglar with no solid attachment to any particular court. His English was poor and he was poor – on both sides of the wall. He would sometimes get a piece of chicken for shoveling snow off the court or carrying firewood for the fires, but when he'd been paid he was told to leave the court in no uncertain terms.

Mickey ignored him and looked back to the grill. G nodded hello, but didn't speak. Charlie however, spoke graciously. "Good morning, Estefan. Come on in. How are you doing today?"

"Not good today."

Charlie prompted his visitor as he tended the darkening chicken. "What's the trouble?"

Estefan stepped onto the court, but continued to eye his dirty sneakers.

"C'mon now, Estefan," Charlie said. "Spit it out. You're among friends here."

Mickey looked from the chicken to Doc G and rolled his eyes, which caused Estefan to speak tentatively. "Someone is missings from ch-your court."

Mickey jumped menacingly around G and Charlie and rammed a pointed finger in Estefan's chest. "Look shithead! Just because

Frankie's locked up for a couple a days, don't think you can just show up and make off with his chicken!"

Estefan was backing up under pressure from Mickey's index. "I no want Meester Frankie's cheekins! It is ch-your friend, the cat. She is missings!"

Mickey stomped back to the grill. "She'll be back in a couple a days too. So you ain't gettin' her 'cheekins' neither!"

Charlie couldn't conceal his smile at Mickey's comments and busied himself with the chicken, quietly dismissing the would-be beggar. Doc G however, had heard something different in the visitor's voice and walked toward him.

"Estefan," G began, "what do you mean, the cat is missing?"

"She is gone, si?"

"Yes, but there's every indication she will return shortly. She enjoys a sojourn beyond the monster from time to time."

"I hopes are you right, Meester G."

"What makes you believe I may not be?"

"I seen something yesterday that made me worry for ch-your friend the cat."

Charlie turned to hear Estefan better as Mickey protectively knelt down among the swarming kittens.

"What did you see, Estefan?" G asked hesitantly.

"Scratches. Deep scratches. Like a cat make when she fight or is hurt."

"Where, Estefan? Where did you see these, ah... scratches?"

Charlie, carrying his baster, and Mickey, carrying a kitten, moved up beside G to hear the answer. Estefan's eyes darted back and forth between the three men as his words came out in a near whisper. "On Benerize."

Mickey clutched his precious cargo and turned to Charlie for help.

Charlie ignored him and concentrated on Estefan. "Come sit down, friend. Now tell us again. What's this about scratches?"

Estefan rather nervously related his story. "I was going by hez house yesterday and he was leaning on the bars. When I pass, I see big scratches on hez hands. Like dez." Estefan made a claw out of one hand and dragged the bent fingers across the back of the other.

The members of the court were quiet as Estefan's news settled in. Then Charlie remembered the grill. "Mickey, tend to the chicken.

When it's done, you give Estefan here a good big chunk. And stay here with him. Doc, come with me please."

As the two elder statesmen of the yard made their way down the hill, G spoke his thoughts out loud.

"It occurs to me, Charles, that Mr. Benerize has not been in the yard for several days. Nor, as I consider it, has he been in the chow hall."

"I was thinking the same thing. We'd better send someone to give Benerize a look see. Make sure he's okay."

"But of course."

The men walked across the yard hatching a plan that would confirm or lay to waste Estefan's story and the unspoken allegations that sprouted from it. Doc G talked briefly with a trusted confidant about a proposed visit to Benerize's cell and passed him a pack of cigarettes while Charlie considered the options available. He decided it would all hinge on the clandestine peek at Benerize and whether Gretchen could be found.

As G returned, it was decided that a covert search of the yard would have to be done. They picked up Mickey and Estefan and began their search, but not without first agreeing that should they find Gretchen, and she was dead, they would leave her where she was. If Benerize was responsible, the uproar created by finding her would prevent him from ever leaving his cell again. As it was, Charlie was already thinking how to pull Benerize to the yard if it came to that.

Mickey quickly paced around the yard. His thinking was that if he didn't see anything, it wouldn't be. As he walked, he carried a kitten and spoke to it constantly. Estefan walked the streets between the many courts, just as he would on any day, but looked through the men for Gretchen. G meandered around the outer edge of the yard looking carefully and quietly through the weeds. Charlie was canvassing the bottom of the hill. He thought back to when he had searched in similar fashion and had found the nearly dead calico kitten. And as before, first there was a hint of something – a splash of fur – then the recognition of a leg until a cat could be seen lying in the tall grass.

This time there would be no last minute miracles. If the gathering flies weren't indication enough, Gretchen's mouth, agape between her shoulder blades, told Charlie what he had feared from the moment Estefan had mentioned those damn scratches. He struggled back to the court and sat undisturbed until G and Mickey saw him there and joined him.

"What's up, Charlie?" Mickey said as he traded one kitten for another. "We done? I knew she wasn't here. Old Gretch is just off somewhere. I'll bet she—"

A wave of G's hand stopped Mickey in mid-sentence. Charlie's ashen face had already betrayed the bad news.

"Where is she, Charles?"

Charlie looked up through watery eyes. "At the bottom of the hill there..." His words were weak and trailed off badly. G sat beside his friend and patted him on the knee.

Mickey sat the kitten down slowly then stood before them both with clenched fists and veins that were showing in his neck. "Maybe she ain't dead. Remember? She done that when she was a baby, remember?"

"Mickey...," Charlie said softly. "She's dead."

"How the hell do you know, man? You ain't no doctor!"

"Mick, her head is twisted completely around. Somebody snapped her neck." Charlie dropped his head.

"Somebody? Weren't no somebody at all. It was that fuckin' Benerize! That's who done it. That's who killed her." Mickey bent down and scooped up one of the kittens. As he petted it, he scanned the yard. "Okay, mother fucker. Let's see how you look with your head on backwards."

"Take it easy now, Mickey," G suggested to deaf ears. "We don't know for sure if—"

"Bullshit!" Mickey shouted as he stormed off the court and headed up the hill. "I know plenty!"

Mickey sat down on the top of the hill near the base of the wall in a patch of weeds far from anyone. He sat there until the yard was closed – cradling the kitten and checking the yard.

G looked up at Mickey then back to Charlie who had yet to lift his head. "Charles, you'll have to talk to him. He's going to kill Benerize."

"Hmm hmm."

Doc G looked at the kittens batting each other's tails on the court then back up the hill to Mickey.

"What will you say, Charles? Mickey is a shallow well, I'm afraid."

"Hmm hmm."

"That doesn't ring of reassurance."

"Hmm hmm."

"You're not considering leaving him to his own limited devices, are you?"

"Why?"

"Why? Because Mickey is going to murder a man over a cat."

"Right now, G, that sounds like reason enough to me. In fact, if Mickey don't kill Benerize, I will."

"Charles! Listen to what you're saying! You're talking about killing a man because he killed an animal, maybe! There are millions of cats just like Gretchen outside the wall. For God's sake, Charlie! What are you thinking?"

"You wanna know what I'm thinking? I'm thinking you're right. There are a million other cats out there. But guess what? There's also a million men like Benerize out there too. Hell, there's two thousand of them on this side of the wall alone."

There were a few still moments as G arranged his words.

"Yes, Charles, but listen carefully, please. Gretchen was just a cat."

Charlie finally looked up. His eyes were red and his cheeks held tracks of tears. "Oh, so because Gretchen was just a stupid cat, she don't count for shit. Is that what you're saying?"

"Not exactly Charles, but—"

"Well, does she count or not?"

"It's not like you're positioning. It—"

"God damnit G! Does she count or not?"

"No! She doesn't count! She doesn't count. Not against the life of a human being."

Charlie pointed with enthusiasm to the tall grass at the bottom of the hill. "That cat never hurt anybody. And more than that, she made people happy. She made all us happy. Two thousand pieces of shit criminals and she made them happy. Who'd Benerize ever make happy, huh G? Not that gas station kid or his folks, that's for sure. His girl? The kids he never got to have? Who, G? Tell me, who?"

Now it was G's turn to bow his head. "I don't know, but I know it's not right to kill a man over a cat."

Charlie got up and stood in front of his friend. "When is it right? When is it all right to kill somebody? Ever? Never? To protect your family? For revenge? For money? For a hundred bucks? This yard is full of men who've killed for less."

G snapped his head up and the two friends faced off. "That doesn't make it right. You don't kill a man for a cat!"

"But you fuckin' kill him for thirty dollars, don't you, G? Isn't that how much was in the till when you hit that hotel lobby? Thirty bucks? And boom! That clerk went down, didn't he G? For thirty dollars..."

Doc G was burning at his friend for the memory. His jaw twitched and his eyes tightened, but it was Charlie who released his eye's hold, looked away, stepped into the small swarm of kittens, and knelt down. He playfully rolled the kittens in his hands and brought each one to his face in turns for a rub and a kiss.

After several silent minutes Charlie stood up with two kittens in his hands. His knees were aching from kneeling and there was a tightness in his chest. He went back to G and sat beside him. He handed him one of the kittens in atonement for bringing up the past and compensation for the questions to follow. The little one in Charlie's lap walked in a tiny circle twice then lay down and began to purr. The kitten on G's lap fidgeted and cried.

"G? What did you do with that thirty bucks?"

"I... I don't really recall... Scored a rock probably. Smoked it while the world ended."

"I'm sorry G. But don't you think Gretchen was worth more than thirty bucks?"

"Yes, she was," G said slowly, his head down further as he concentrated on the kitten. "But it's still not right. Killing isn't right. Not for thirty dollars, not for a million dollars. And certainly not for a cat."

"Maybe. I don't know. But I do know this. If Benerize has Gretchen's claw marks on him, come this time tomorrow, he'll be a dead man."

Without looking at him, Charlie addressed his friend for the last time. "You in or out, G?"

Doc G looked out over the yard and at the wall beyond it. He blinked hard and rubbed his face as if waking from sleep then gave a slight sigh as he slipped the kitten onto Charlie's lap.

"I guess I'm out Charles. I guess I'm out." G rose and slid his hand along the box as he shuffled off the court for what he knew would be the last time. Charlie kept his eyes on the kittens and contemplated the loss of two friends in one day.

Despite the heaviness on his heart and mind, Charlie knew there was a good deal to be done before the sun appeared over the wall in the morning. First, he leveraged twenty years of contacts behind the wall to learn everything he could about Benerize and his latest reluctance to show himself in the yard, chow, or elsewhere. Cons like to be out of their cells – moving with the flow of the prison. The flow gives them their income, access to information, and as much freedom as some will ever see.

There were times for every man when the comparative quiet, comfort, and security of his house is preferred over the noise and hustle, but they were generally rare and not without cause. A 'Dear John' letter or no letter at all could drive a man underground. Everyone had different fracture points when the weight of the years caused them to curl up in their bunk at all hours in the hopes of sleeping and dreaming their sentence away. Or perhaps lay there inflicting punishment through a disjointed mind, hoping it would serve as reparation for past sins and aid in relaying remorse and a contrite heart to the parole board or God. Whatever the reason, self-imposed lockdown was accepted and understood. But not this time, and not with a man like Benerize.

While Charlie's network channeled back information on Benerize, he sent a kite to Frankie, who would be released from lockdown for his fight the following morning. The kite said simply that Frankie should be prepared to fight the new jack again. He was to look for Charlie as soon as his boots hit the yard.

Word soon trickled across the yard that an inmate named Gustavo was deep in debt to Benerize for cigarettes – the prison's currency – as a result of Gustavo's gambling, drugs, and use of the juggle. Through a long, convoluted, and untraceable line of men, word was sent to Benerize that Gustavo was prepared to pay the next morning. This would lure Benerize into the open. Word was also passed to Gustavo not to come to the yard.

Lastly, there was Mickey. He was still sitting on the top of the hill with the purring kitten. Charlie walked up casually and stood beside him. He looked straight ahead while Mickey's attention stayed riveted on Gretchen's baby.

"Benerize will be out in the morning," Charlie said stoically. "You be close to me."

Mickey never looked up.

Charlie returned to the court where he watched the yard until it closed. Then he, like the others in both green and blue, filed into the prison for the night.

The sun was high above the wall the next day when the convicts reclaimed the yard. Charlie came out with Mickey as usual, but Mick went directly to the court. Charlie waited in the sand near the officer's shack at the door while the other players – some knowing small pieces of the puzzle and others totally unaware – spilled out of Savone's bricks. The new jack stepped cautiously into the yard for just his second time. Frankie was a few men behind him, looking for Charlie. When their eyes met, Charlie motioned for him to be patient.

Meanwhile, Mickey hopped onto the court as the kittens came filing out of their box. He squatted down near the opening as the babies circled him and tested their tiny claws in his green pants as they stretched the welcoming of a new day. Each received a vigorous good morning rub compliments of Mickey's left hand while his right plunged into the cool sand beneath the box for Charlie's shank.

Charlie was still watching for the young man who was to have checked on Benerize. As he waited, Mickey came up beside him holding a kitten. The kitten was tugging at Mickey's gloves and trying to wrestle with the hard wooden handle Mickey held gently against the little one's stomach.

Benerize had been flushed out. He was some distance away, looking through the crowd for Gustavo. Charlie noted him then allowed his eyes to run through the crowd behind Benerize's, still looking for the messenger. Not seeing him, Charlie shifted his gaze back to the doorway. Off to one side he saw Doc G standing alone. As their eyes caught one another's, G's left hand slipped from its pocket and moved up to his chest. His left lay stretched out flat while his right came up slowly and became a tight claw. G pulled his curled fingers across the back of his left hand and nodded a prolonged yes. Once the message had been relayed, G's arms dropped limply to his sides and he walked away. Charlie turned to Mickey, but he had already moved off. He, the kitten, and the shank, were closing in on Benerize.

Frankie was nervously watching Charlie from across the yard. When the deliberate nod came, Frankie knew it was no mistake. He ran over to the new jack, traded obligatory insults, and started swinging. The crowd gathered as if it was part of the script. Benerize too played his part and was soon absorbed by the cheering tide of green.

In the north tower, Johns' attention was also drawn to the fight. He grumbled as he slid a thick arm through his rifle's sling and brought the powerful scope into position for his eye. When Johns saw it was Frankie and the new jack again, he slipped his finger off the trigger and started to scan the spectators. He soon found Benerize and centered the cross hairs on his face. Benerize looked bored, but was following the fight with hundreds of others who were cheering or offering encouragement and advice to the inexperienced fighters. The noise was that dull roar created by space. Though the officer's ears were at the mercy of distance, Johns' vision was pulled in close by the magnification of the rifle scope. The con's head and shoulders filled the powerful lens. In a voice that was barely audible Johns spoke to Benerize, one hundred and fifty yards away.

"Why don't you try something, shithead? Give me a half a reason and I'll splatter what brains you've got all over my yard."

Benerize turned his head to the side and unknowingly lined up his temple under the cross hairs.

"Perfect," Johns said softly.

A rush of movement shot into John's tight view. It was a shank! Benerize abruptly turned and faced Johns again. His eyes were wide beneath the crosshairs, but lifeless. Then he slumped to the ground. Johns tried to see into the crowd, but it had become a mass of scattering humanity. Men, Frankie and the new jack included, were running anywhere and everywhere as long as it was away from Benerize.

Charlie had gone to the court when the fight first jumped off. On it he found Doc G. Neither had spoken. Rather, G played with the kittens while Charlie started a small fire. In a moment, Mickey would join them, but for now he was merely part of the hurriedly disbanding crowd.

The wooden handle of the shank was still beneath the kitten. Mickey was cradling the baby like a football as he hustled across the sand toward the courts. In one quick move only seconds before, he slammed the shank into the fleshy spot at the base of Benerize's skull and saw the rusty nail vanish. Then he snapped the handle off, leaving the spike buried in the brain of Gretchen's killer.

Mickey stepped onto court and set the kitten down. Charlie held out his hand without a word. As the broken handle passed from Mickey through Charlie to the fire, G kept his eyes down on the kittens. On top of the prison, the siren began to scream as if Savone were in pain. Anyone still standing sat down wherever they were. Simultaneously an army of blue shirted guards began pouring into the yard and Officer Johns, fresh from his tower, began stalking through the maelstrom.

Johns went to the body, where a dozen guards had already gathered. One was crouched down next to Benerize's neck and pointed to the head of the spike.

"Drove a nail right into the sonofabitch's head."

"Didn't even need a hammer."

"I guess you could say somebody nailed him."

"Awww, man. That's lame."

"Still pretty funny."

"Don't quit your day job just yet."

"Who's the lump of shit sleeping in the dirt?"

"This fine upstanding citizen is Alejundro Benerize," Johns said. "He's a banger, gambler, a little dope if he can score it, juggles. He caught a body a few years ago and made the big time. What else you got?"

"There's a little piece of wood left on the shank. Could match it up I bet."

"All right," Johns directed. "Let's get on with this. Start patting the bastards down and running them inside. Lock the place down."

"Are we stripping them?"

"No need. Anything we're looking for has already been buried somewhere in this litter box. If you could see it, these shitheads have just done more digging than a prairie dog town. You can poke in the sand around some of the heavy hitters if you want, but even if you find something they'll never go for it. They'll say someone else buried it months before. We'll spring a cavity search on them in a couple of days when things have calmed down and they think it's safe to dig up their shit."

Johns spun around and headed into the heart of the yard. All around him his C.O.s were picking up inmates in ones and twos and searching them. Despite all the effort, two hours later the only thing the officers had to show for it was a short length of a thin guitar E string destined to be sold as a needle for a cell-made tattoo gun. It had been taped to an inmate's forearm. When discovered, the con said his shirt must have come back from the laundry with the wire caught in it. He had never seen it before.

As Johns walked through the searches in the yard he replayed the murder he had witnessed through his rifle scope. His voice replayed the scene in his mind's eye.

"There was Benerize," he thought. "The shank. And the hand. Something about the hand... It had a glove on it. Or did it? The fingers... I could see the fingers, but not the hand. Like half a glove. Half a glove... Fingerless gloves. Fingerless gloves! Mickey."

Johns changed direction and headed for Charlie Dennis' court.

From behind his fire, Charlie saw Johns coming. He handed Mickey his wooden poker as he made the decision to meet Johns halfway. Charlie moved fast to the bottom of the hill and into the sand as Johns approached.

"What's up, Dennis?"

"Don't know, C.O."

"Well, I figured that," Johns said with a smile. "Where's Mickey?"

Charlie didn't say anything yet turned and looked up to the court.

"How long's he been there?"

"Long time."

Johns painfully repeated. "Sure. Long time..." Then he stepped around Charlie and headed again toward the court. "Gotta have a talk with him, Dennis."

Charlie was walking beside the officer with his head down. "He doesn't know anything."

"No one ever does, do they? But I do."

The unlikely pair took a few more steps when Charlie realized they were next to the tall grass that held Gretchen's distorted body. "C.O.? Could I show you something?"

"You got piss poor timing. Later."

Charlie couldn't stop himself from reaching out and gently cupping the guard's arm. Johns froze except for his free hand which instinctively reached for his stick. He didn't pull it however and instead stared coldly at Charlie's hand as it held his sleeve. Charlie let his now trembling hand fall away.

"That could get you six months in the box and a helluva beat down, Dennis."

"Yes, sir, and I'll take it if you'd just look at something first."

Johns never said yes, but as Charlie took a few short steps to the tall grass, Johns followed. The burly guard was looking firmly at Charlie until the old convict pointed into the weeds. Johns gracefully slid his scarred stick from its ring and parted the grass, inadvertently disturbing the flies that had discovered Gretchen.

The veteran officer stood for several minutes examining the dead cat. He could see her disjointed neck clearly. Occasionally his eyes rose to Charlie, but inside they ran to Benerize. When Johns had seen enough, and thought enough, he withdrew the nightstick and let the weeds spring back to conceal Gretchen's body. Then he looked long and hard at Charlie, who met his eyes stare for stare. Johns suddenly broke it off, slid the stick into its place on his hip, and stepped once more in the direction of the court.

Charlie's eyes widened as he fell in behind the guard. "Officer Johns?" he said anxiously.

"I did what you asked me to, Dennis. Now I gotta talk to Mickey."

G was still petting the kittens and Mickey was stoking the small fire when Johns came onto the court. Frankie had arrived and was sitting behind G, trying to look small. Johns walked to the fire and gently took the fire tempered wooden poker out of Mickey's gloved hand and began turning over pieces of burning wood. His eyes took turns looking at the fire and reading the young man's face.

"Nice little fire you got here, Mickey. Nice little fire."

A minute or more passed as the burning wood snapped over the soft cries of the kittens playing.

Mickey didn't look up until he felt Johns nudge him to take the poker back. Johns then turned and looked at Doc G who was caressing the babies.

"Been quite a day, ain't it, Doc?"

"Can't really say, C.O. It's just beginning."

Johns motioned toward the stretcher that was carrying Benerize out of the yard. "Oh, I don't know. It already ended for some."

No one spoke. G absently petted the kittens with as much vigor as Mickey tended the fire. Charlie was just standing in the middle of the court where Frankie continued being small. Johns knelt down in Charlie's shadow and stroked the kittens for a minute then quickly stood up.

"Frankie," Johns said. "That little fight of yours is gonna cost you thirty days lockdown. Let's go."

"Awww, man, Officer Johns...," Frankie whined. "You don't wanna go and do all that. It was just—"

A piercing stare from Charlie cut him off.

"There a problem with that, Frankie?" Johns demanded.

"Uhh..., no sir."

"Good. Then get your ass down there by the gate."

Frankie slumped his shoulders and made his way off the court. Johns began to follow, but stopped by Mickey and his fire once again. He stood there quietly, looking out over the prison complex from the hill.

After a few moments Johns spoke. "This is my yard, but it's your world. I don't have to live here, you men do. Don't you, Mickey?"

Mickey continued looking into the fire. "Yes, sir. We do."

Johns muttered as he stepped away from the crackling fire. "Yes, sir. We do..."

The C.O. hesitated another minute as he looked down at the frolicking kittens.

"Mickey?" Johns said.

"Yes, sir, Officer Johns?"

"Go bury your cat."

Gretchen was buried in the same spot where Charlie had toed out a tiny grave back on the day he had first found her. Other than complaining about missing the funeral, Frankie served his thirty days without a whimper and the following year was sent home on work release. Estefan and the new jack occasionally ate on the court, but never really belonged.

Officer Johns finished out his last two years dropping off buttermilk and gazing out of his tower. When he retired, Mickey gave him a calico kitten as a present. After being rejected four times by the parole board, both Mickey and Doc G were returned to the street. Charlie eventually became a ghost in the halls of Savone. Only the cats can sense him and when they do, they're not afraid.

ABOUT THE COVER : The photograph was taken at Eastern State Penitentiary Historic Site, Philadelphia, Pennsylvania. When Eastern State Penitentiary closed in 1971, a city worker, Dan "The Cat Man" McCloud, cared for the prison's cats for 28 years. The cat casting is by Linda Brenner from her installation, *Ghost Cats*, arranged within the prison walls. *Ghost Cats* reflects just one of countless fascinating stories associated with the facility.

Learn more about Eastern State Penitentiary (opened in 1829) and its worldwide influence and significance in prison history as well as its notable prisoners such as Al Capone and "Slick" Willie Sutton at, **easternstate.org** or visit the historic site at 2027 Fairmount Ave., Philadelphia, PA 19130.

"Ssscree-baa."

My Boo Radley

Mrs. Talada, my junior high school English teacher, assigned <u>To Kill A Mockingbird</u>. I never read it. Instead, on test day my wandering hazel eyes became practical periscopes and searched the papers of my nearby friends and returned to me with a seventy something. It wasn't until years later that I followed Harper Lee's Jim and Scout around during that hot summer in Macom County as they played and grew in the shadow of their misunderstood neighbor and guardian, Boo Radley. By then my Boo Radley was gone, and a part of me too for that matter. But the part that remained carried a special memory that would last the rest of my life. I wasn't the first to not follow the cue of an English teacher and there were many times before and after that Mrs. Talada pulled back an empty hand as she reached for my work, but if I'd read that story I'm certain things would have been different somehow, though I'm not certain what that somehow would have been.

Back when English assignments were left undone, my house was the Mecca of activity and misadventures for me and my friends. It was in the middle of the neighborhood and close enough to the school to overhear the discussions, debates, and the myriad suggestions of things my friends and I should do and those we shouldn't – the latter generally received with much more enthusiasm. But what made my house so inviting was that the high school's baseball diamond was right across the street.

When the varsity, or the junior varsity for that matter, had a home game, a group of us boys would be in the small stands. Calling the five rows of stacked and staggered runs of rough plank seats bolted to angle iron, "stands," might be a bit generous, but they were wonderful. Every spring Mr. Joe Cummings, head of the one-man Recreation Department, who we affectionately called the Commissioner of Baseball, could be seen putting on a fresh coat of dark forest green paint. Everything associated with the Recreation Department that required painting was dark forest green. Somewhere Mr. Cummings must have had a fifty-five gallon barrel of the stuff. There were so many layers of green paint on the bolts and boards of the bleachers you couldn't have scratched yourself if you tried. Splinters didn't stand a chance. The best part was the terrific noise ten eleven-year-olds could make stomping their feet on those green planks to rattle opposing players. It was heaven.

So we'd collect well prior to the first pitch from a seventeen-year-old who we thought could throw lightening strikes. We'd be there rain or shine watching with the umpires and managers up at the sky on humid early summer afternoons. I can still recall the disappointment when a game was called for rain. It made no sense to any of us. Playing any game in the rain only made for more excitement. When you're eleven years old, you're as happy wet as dry, probably happier. Puddles are magnets for boys. It's been that way since the invention of rain.

"Play ball!" was a call to arms. We'd stop our bat-less pepper game and scramble across the planks to the top row. From the best seats in the park, we'd ogle the dreamy crisp red and white uniforms of our high school and cheer for all we were worth. Nestled between the screams for the good guys and the raspberries for the bad, we learned about the game. I watched the pitchers mostly – scrutinizing each subtle move in their delivery. Then I'd go to the little league field right next door to practice my exaggerated kick and throw against the backstop fence until the streetlights came on.

Three houses away from mine, yet still within sight of the ball fields, was a tired old house where the E-Man lived. The house was dark and looked abandoned most of the time. However, in the spring and summer, when the teams took to the fields, the house gave up a twinkle of life. Then, if you looked close, you could see a curtain pulled back in the lone front window. At the time I never considered that the E-Man was watching the games, same as me. He remained a non-entity, a non-person, near monster really, or so a group of pre-teen boys thought. And though it was us who threw the eggs on Halloween and dared each other to step on his uncut grass, I would guess it was a misplaced word by an adult some years before us that had created the mysterious E-Man. Otherwise the house on the corner would have stayed just that. One day a parent must have said something as they drove by the weary house about the disfigured man inside or the accident that made him. Then fertile young imaginations took over.

Part of our stories about the E-Man – shortened from the Elephant Man after we had learned about him when someone tried to buy his remains – was closer to the truth than we would liked to have known at the time. The E-Man was hideous looking. Forty years earlier, before much was done with reconstructive surgery and little concern was given to cosmetics, a fiery car crash had taken one of his eyes, his nose, and parts of both ears. He lips had been replaced by scar tissue. His scars, the hidden ones as well, had eventually forced him under. Now the E-Man peered out from behind his curtain on game days. What he did on the others days I don't know, but he didn't come out, which was good for us kids and I supposed for him too.

There was a time, pre-accident, when it wasn't this way. The person beneath the E-Man's very real mask had a childhood, a teen-age hood, and a few short years beyond – each full of baseball. The E-Man had been a player back in the days when they wore coarse wool uniforms instead of triple knit poly. His abbreviated career was spent barnstorming the country pitching for a semi-pro club. It wasn't quite the big leagues, but it was close. He might have made the jump in another year or two, but a late night crash and a flash of fire created one of those "we'll never know" endings.

With the E-Man's background and my growing baseball card collection, it was only right that my first encounter with him should come on the heels of an errant throw. I don't remember if it came off my skinny arm or someone else's, but I do remember seeing my special Roberto Clemente Autograph Model hardball sail through the already shattered window of the E-Man's dilapidated garage. Our initial reaction, and the one we followed, was to run, fearful that somehow the ball would awaken a sleeping Frankenstein. Later on we went back, after dark believe it or not. While my anxious friends waited nearby, I opened the creaking door and stepped inside the Lost Garage of the Damned. Under the dim light of my dad's flashlight – the worst flashlight ever to swallow batteries as it paid no attention to the switch and came on and went off of its own accord when you least expected or wanted it to – I discovered that my ball was gone. As this realization sank in through my eyes another hit my ears. Someone or something had just opened the E-Man's squeaky back door screen. My feet flew from the garage, positive it was a trap, and fortunately brought the rest of my body with them. Once we all piled onto the safety of my back porch a discussion ensued about the missing ball. In the end it was decided that the E-Man probably ate it. Perhaps it was just as well, someone suggested. After it was on the E-Man's property we shouldn't touch it anyway. I whined that it was a Roberto Clemente Autograph Model, but by the next day we had moved on to our next misadventure. I didn't cross paths again with the E-Man for five years.

One spring evening as my junior high school catcher and I were sitting on my back porch discussing our first tryout for the varsity, we heard a familiar sound coming from a strange place. A couple of houses away there was a heavy thump, then a light thump of a bounce, and the rolling noise of a baseball coming down a roof. Thump, thump, roll. Thump, thump, roll. We recognized the sound as solitary baseball, a game we had grown up with. Our games became innings in which the roll was actually a hit coming off Don Mattingly's bat. If you caught it clean he was out. I usually made myself spin around once after the ball came off the roof in order to give the Yankee's slugging first baseman a chance. Everyone had their own rules – balls and strikes, innings and outs – but this particular game was coming from the E-Man's garage. Even though were sixteen now we still looked at each other in wonder. Who would dare play solitary there?

We crept through backyards until we were stationed at the corner of a neighbor's house where we could just make out Mattingly's fielder. It was the E-Man. He threw the ball smoothly and listened for the roll to guide his steps to the ball, but he couldn't catch. The falling darkness and his dead eye were ganging up on him. The ball would shoot off the roof and in and out of his tiny battered glove which could have passed as a relic in a Cooperstown showcase.

As we watched the E-Man's game progress, one of us hatched a devilish scheme. Whoever thought of it I don't remember, but I was the one who threw the stone on the garage roof. The E-Man's throw and mine arrived at the same time. We could see him weaving back and forth, confused by the two rolling sounds. He followed the script of the prank exactly and reached for the stone as it came off the roof. Even in the dark we could see it hit him in the face as the ball dropped to the ground nearby. The battery mates who would come to dominate high school baseball in my state, turned and ran away laughing as the E-Man stumbled and held his cheek. We had no way of knowing, and perhaps at sixteen wouldn't have cared, but his only eye teared up – not at the pain – but at the lost ability to catch a stone or a baseball and discern one from the other.

I guess it was about a week later as I was taking out the garbage one evening when I heard the sound again. Thump, thump, roll. Thump, thump, roll. I was alone now, less mischievous and more nervous, yet still drawn to the garage. As I watched the E-Man play solitary, one ball seemed to jump off the roof faster than the others. He stabbed at it with this ragged glove, but only succeeded in knocking the ball higher in the air.

The arc of a live baseball in play can take strange hops. This one bounced and rolled until it came to a stop just a few feet in front of me. Instinctively, I reached down and picked it up. It was a worn out Roberto Clemente Autograph Model. After all these years, I had my ball back. A part of me was ready to run, but a bigger part looked through the gathering darkness at the E-Man, forty feet away. I stood there holding the ball. My ball. His ball. Then he held his glove up.

The antique mitt was speaking in the international silent language of the game, "I'm ready. Throw the ball." I threw an easy sidearm toss at the shadowy figure I knew was the monster. He caught it cleanly, scooped the ball out of his glove, and threw it back. I tossed it again, softly, like you'd throw to a child. The E-Man snatched it out of the air and quickly whipped it back hard. I caught it, but the battered horsehide punished my naked hands. I put the ball under my arm and rubbed my hands together. If I could have seen his scarred lips, I would have detected a smile as he recalled the stone that rolled off the garage roof. I threw the ball one last time, held up my hands to wave him off then turned and raced across the back lawns to my house as if something were chasing me.

Taking the garbage out wasn't so much of a chore after that night. I'd wander out and listen for the sounds of solitary baseball. When I heard them, I'd sneak my glove out of the house and head to the E-Man's ballpark. It wasn't all that often, maybe just a few times now that I think back, but when I went, I went drawn by some combination of adventure, curiosity, and fear. It was like getting on a scary ride at an amusement park.

One spring afternoon as the Majors were beginning training, I heard the sounds early. It was still daylight. I hesitated in going because someone might see me. I wasn't forbidden from going to the E-Man's, not by my parents anyway. I think it was me that forbid it, hastened on by what I knew the reaction of my friends would be. Regardless, on this afternoon I snuck over looking for another roller coaster ride. When I got within sight of the E-Man, he seemed to sense me and turned around. He watched me walking toward him, his eye renewing my fears as it measured my steps. When I was about sixty feet away he held up his hand and stopped me. We were farther apart than before, but it was lighter too. I considered that the light had prevented him from wanting to be closer. As it was, I could see the scarring that covered his face. A picture of Freddy Kruger came to mind and fed the fear that was being held down by my glove.

Then the E-Man raised his leg, kicked somewhat stiffly, and pitched. The ball rocketed into my glove belt high – a fastball, right down the pipe. I threw the ball back and crouched in the unusual position of the catcher. He moved his head slowly from side to side, lining up his good eye I imagined, brought his leg up and fired. Another fastball, low and away, but it caught the corner of the plate. Strike two. I tossed the ball from the crouch. Another windup and throw. I saw the ball breaking as cleanly as if it had been in a dream. It was a stunning curve that stayed down. Swing and a miss. "Strike three. Go sit down chump." I would have liked to thrown the ball around the horn, but since there was only the E-Man and me, I tossed it back to him with a knowing nod and a smile.

With the ball in his hand hidden behind his back, the E-Man bent over with his mitt on his knee as if he were looking in for me to call a pitch. I laughed a little and shook two fingers at him on my left thigh, our team's sign for a curve. He shook it off! I flashed him a one that said, "How 'bout a fastball?" He shook his head no. What else? I improvised a new call as I laid three fingers against the inside of my right thigh and tapped twice. He nodded and went into his delivery. It looked from his motion to be another curve. I was looking for it, but it didn't come. Instead the ball broke in the other direction, spinning away like a reverse curve. I never saw a pitch like that and was lucky to get my glove on it. After looking with disbelief at the old ball, I threw it back.

The E-Man looked in for another sign. I wanted to see that pitch again. I tapped three fingers twice against my leg. He wound up and sent that same reverse curve. This time I stood up, goaded by a keen interest in the funny pitch. As I tossed the ball back, I spoke to him for the first time. "Hey, how'd you do that?"

The E-Man took a few steps toward me. It was slowly getting gray around us and the sight of the E-Man coming in my direction made me wish I hadn't asked about the pitch. Then he did something that I was very thankful for. He stopped, put his glove under his arm, and reached into his pocket. From it he pulled a black eye patch, like a pirate's I thought, and put it over the spot where his lost eye should have been. Next, he took a hanky, one of those big red ones like a farmer might carry, out of his back pocket and tied it around his face like Jesse James.

He moved toward me again. As he got closer, I could see the E-Man well for the first time in my life. Even with his disguise, he was frightening. I thought his hair was long for an old man, but I guess it helped cover his tattered ears. What I could see of his face was nothing but bright pink scar tissue. I started to back away, perhaps unknowingly, but back away from the neighborhood monster just the same. He stopped. I stopped. He started to move again and I felt as if someone had pushed my chest as I leaned backwards. He stopped again. We stood there like that for nearly a full minute — he in his disguise and me in my fear.

After a time, the E-Man's hand, as pink and scarred as his face, came up and held the ball out to me. He was less than ten feet away. As I watched with wide eyes, he deftly moved the ball around between his fingers until they came to rest with his index finger covering a seam. He moved his arm forward slowly, twisted his wrist to the inside with a snap, and pushed down with that index finger – the opposite of how you threw a curve. The E-Man repeated the grip and motion several times as I watched intently. Then he spoke, well, sort of spoke. The voice was more like a raspy whisper – low, gravelly, and very spooky.

"Ssscree-baa."

I tried to hide it, but I'm sure he saw me cringe at the sound that came from his fire damaged throat.

"Ssscree-baa," he said again as he continued demonstrating the motion. Then he took a deliberate step toward me and thrust the ball into my glove. He smelled like some kind of ointment, sort of like Ben-Gay, but not. As he stood beside me, I concentrated on the ball like never before, working hard at keeping my eyes and my mind off my new pitching coach. I had my Roberto Clemente Autograph Model resting in my usual curveball grip. Behind his mask, the E-Man nodded as he held out his empty hand and mocked that reverse twist. Without the ball, his hand trembled slightly. I tried the release, but it wasn't right. He reached down and gently touched my hand. I'm ashamed of it now, but I jerked back. He shook his head in a slow yes and reached for my hand again. His touch was icy but incredibly soft. The shaking was more pronounced now or was it me? As he held my hand around the ball I tried to look away, but gentle maneuvering by fingers that knew what they were doing called me back. He set my index finger over the seam and moved my wrist repeatedly in the convoluted inside motion.

"Ssscree-baa," he said again as he twisted my hand. "Ssscree-baa."

"I can't... I don't understand you."

He said it slower. "Sssscrree-baaa."

It didn't help. I shook my head no. The E-Man dropped my hand and walked away.

I called after him. "I'm sorry. I just don't–"

He turned back to me and motioned for me to wait as he tossed his glove aside and disappeared into his garage. When he came out he was carrying a weathered bushel basket and an old wooden box. He sat the box against the garage then laid the basket on its side on top of it. When he was finished he came back to me. I saw him pull something from his pocket as he got closer. I held out my hand to meet his and was given a small wood screw. He took the ball from my glove and made the same delivery motion while pointing to the screw with his free hand. "Ssscree-baa," his burned throat whispered.

"Screwball?"

"Ssscree-baa," he said as he nodded yes and his body relaxed.

"Screwball. Cool," I said as I mimicked his twisting motion.

Then the E-Man pointed to his garage and shook his finger at the basket. "Ssscree-baa."

I tested my twist again as I adjusted my grip. He didn't speak, but held his hand out and repeated the twisting motion. I wound up and delivered. I missed the basket, but at least hit the side of the building. There was no break on the ball. A couple of more throws brought the pitch closer to the basket and put a slight action on the ball. I ran the ball down after each throw and hustled back to the E-Man. He gently showed me what I had done wrong and pointed again to the basket. After countless attempts the ball started to break and one of my new pitches bounced off the box – low in the strike zone, but getting closer. I threw a few more times as night settled in around us. We were on the dark side of twilight now and with his eye patch and mask the E-Man looked really scary. I handed him the ball and started backing away. "Thanks for the lesson," I said as I continued backing up. "I'll keep practicing."

The E-Man nodded politely then turned toward the basket. He kicked and after a quick reverse curve I heard the "Ssscree-baa" smack into the basket. That was the last time I saw him.

The next day I began to tell my friends about the E-Man. No sooner had I begun then they started in on me.

"You nuts? Don't go near that crazy bastard!"

"Don't you know that if he touches you, you'll catch what he's got?"

"Yeah, your skin will flake off and everything!"

"I heard he tries to kidnap people, kills 'em and takes their skin off to put on himself!"

"Nooo…"

"Yes! My dad says they've been trying to get him in a hospital for the criminally insane for years."

"Oh, man, he didn't touch you, did he? If he did, get away from me. I don't want no disease."

"No, he–"

"You didn't really go over there, did you?"

"No, I–"

"I didn't think so. You're such a liar."

"Good. That old sonofabitch will kill you, man. We need you alive if we're gonna take the title."

"Right. If he don't kill you, we will.

"C'mon, let's go."

At practice I tried out the new pitch a few times. One cut away so hard my catcher missed it and caught it with his knee instead.

"Keep it over the plate, will you? Damn it. That hurt like hell."

"It was over. Coach! Sit in on a few and call them for me. My catcher's gone blind."

My coaches were impressed. I already had a good balance of pitches, but nothing like the screwball. I showed it off and they had our best hitters step in. They all whiffed on straight pitches. I worked hard to perfect the screwball, but never mentioned the E-Man. In fact, I never spoke of him again until I was out of high school. On Halloween nights I managed to steer everyone's eggs away from his dark house, but that was the best I could do. In truth, it was all I tried to do.

That spring I made the varsity at sixteen on the strength of a 75 mph fastball, a good change-up, a curve I had to fight to keep down, and of course the screwball. Two years later as a senior, my arm was strong and lively. The fast ball moved up dramatically to near 90 and my curve was staying low in the strike zone. I had a deceiving changeup, a good cutter, and the screwball was breaking off hard, baffling batters all over the state. Though I never returned to the E-Man's, I always looked for the pulled back curtain when I walked to the mound for the first pitch. Often I would look beyond the bleachers, loaded with family, friends, and scouts, to his house and wonder about my onetime coach. When the year ended, I turned down a minor league contract to pitch college ball for Southern California's Trojans.

At college practice, when the screw was slapping my catcher's glove after passing over, under, and around my new teammates' bats,

I told them the story of the E-Man and how I happened to learn the screwball.

"That's pretty cool."

"Yeah, a little weird, but all right. Helluva pitch."

"That's a wild story, man. Back in Oakland I used to stop and see this old guy, right? He said he was a bomber pilot in World War II. Wicked cool guy. Told mad crazy stories."

"I had a crazy uncle like that. Everybody thought he was a nut case, but he was the sharpest guy in the whole family."

"Hey, what other pitches did he teach you?"

I dropped my head and told them none as I wandered off to the mound. The bright sun made the sixty feet six inches to home plate glow as I scowled and focused. What a fool I had been. An immature fool. Then and there I vowed to go see the E-Man on my next trip home and do the things I should have done before and say the things I should have said. It was time to give something back for that pitch. I wound up, kicked hard, and threw my first 90 mph plus fastball across an empty plate into the backstop.

Months later when I finally drove up my street I looked out over my high school field and thought of the contrast with the stadiums I saw with the Trojans. Then there was my house, looking smaller now, and further up the street, the E-Man's. As I rolled closer I noticed a large truck in front of the dilapidated place and men carrying furniture down the broken concrete sidewalk. I passed my house and stopped behind the truck. As I got out and walked up the sidewalk, two men carried a dusty and faded armchair by me. I let my pitching hand run the length of its worn arm as a man in a suit stepped onto the porch from inside the house.

"Hey," he said. "Aren't you Curt Vernicki?"

"Yes, sir. I live right over there."

"Yes, I know. I read you turned down that minor league contract. Smart move. Get your education first. I thought you'd be in California."

"Yeah, I was. We're on break. Hey, where's the old guy that lives here?"

"Doesn't live here anymore. He died a couple of months ago. Hey, who do you think is going to take the American League East? The Yankees are strong as ever, but I think that Boston—"

"What'd you say?"

"Huh? Oh, the East. I think it's Boston all the way. With their pitching they–"

"No. Before that. The old man. He died?"

"Been dead awhile. No estate or anything really, but I've got to clear things up here. Hey! It's funny you should stop by. Don't get excited, it isn't any money, but he left something for you. Hold on a minute. I'll get it."

I followed him onto the rickety porch and waited there looking at the dusty peeling paint and the dirty window where I imagined the E-Man watched the ball fields. But I was looking in and he would have looked out. It was a difference I could never fully appreciate. Behind this glass prison wall he bore the pranks and taunts of my friends and I, and those that came before and after, both young and old, some of whom whispered in passing cars, not bothering to stop, while others threw stones on the roof of an old garage. And he endured it alone. It would be a long time before I could fully grasp all this. For now, on the E-Man's porch, his death was beginning to register. In an instant, the man in the suit returned and broke the spell.

"Here you go," he said as he handed me an old scrapbook. "It's probably just junk, but the law's the law. It says I've got to turn it over to you."

I opened the book and found a few ancient newspaper clippings about a Brooklyn Trolley Dodgers farm club strangely called the Pirates, and a Thomas Kouterick, a *"hard throwing British immigrant who's bent on riding a vicious screwball into the Majors."* On the remaining pages there were reams of articles about my playing. In the beginning there were tiny clippings from Little League with my name circled in faded red pencil. I ran quickly through the pages, somehow not wanting the uncaring attorney to see my inheritance. The pages flipped by as if they were in an antique movie machine. I witnessed a boy move through Little League, the teenage Babe Ruth and American Legion teams, and into high school. The articles grew longer and there was an occasional picture held in with brittle yellowed tape. At the back of the book were articles about the minor league contract and USC. One had a single word highlighted in its headline – "Screwball Hurler Opts for College." I closed the book.

"Oh, yeah," the man said. "I nearly forgot. This was supposed to go to you too." He reached into a bulging suit coat pocket and pulled out a baseball – a worn out Roberto Clemente Autograph Model. "Here you go. I guess the old guy was a bit of a strange one. Never met him myself, but I hear he was a mess to look at."

I slowly took the baseball from his hand and caressed it until my fingers found the screwball grip. "No, he wasn't that bad. And he wasn't strange at all... He taught me a lot."

"I didn't mean it like that. I guess with all those clippings, you two must have been real close. I'm really sorry."

"I'm sorry, too."

I stepped off the porch and headed home. My fingers ran over the seams and flicked at the cuts in the discolored, stained, and dirty baseball while I cradled the E-Man's gift under my arm. I felt sick. I had taken the pitch and ran, never giving anything back when I easily could have. I could have stopped by, should have stopped by, once in a while. Stopped and talked about his pitching, my pitching. But I didn't. I felt the weight of the book begin to slip beneath my arm. I pulled it out and began looking through it again, slowly this time. I don't know how long I'd been sitting on my back porch before my dad found me there. I told him the story of the screwball and the friend I never knew and now never would. He slipped a strong arm around my shoulders as I buried my face in his chest and remembered how to cry.

When my tear ducts were empty we sat side by side, me holding the old baseball and our laps sharing the load of memories the E-Man had captured. My dad and I relived several games, especially the older ones, and found the treasures of the past pressed in the brittle pages. Halfway through dad put his hands flat out on both pages.

"You didn't leave him empty-handed, Curt. Just look at this book. Look at what you were able to bring into his world through the game of baseball. Who else could have done that? No one. Baseball was his life and he was able to live it through you. Through you and that pitch."

I nearly started to cry again as I considered it. Dad was right as dads usually are. Somewhere in the distance I heard the sounds of solitary baseball.

Today I'm still pitching. I'm putting them across for the Columbus Clippers. It's not the big leagues yet, but it's close. I reach back for the screwball now and again, usually when I'm in a jam, and I remember the E-Man. In return I think he puts a little extra English on it for me. English. And I'm still reminded. Mrs. Talada. <u>To Kill a Mockingbird</u>. I wish I'd read that book.

The underground railroad didn't take tickets. Just courage.

Black Men in Bright Blue

Rachel Justice saw the black men in bright blue in her dreams. Being ten years old lent itself to dreams, but being a young white girl in 1863, especially in South Carolina, the first state to secede from the Union, the presence of the black men bid her keep her dreams within herself. Yet to Rachel the dreams were much more vivid than just playful specters dancing across the nightscape of her mind. And still, the thoughts – real, dream, or otherwise – may have given cause for punishment or even The Treatment and rightly so she considered for the black men in bright blue had no place in her world. It was best they stay in the cloudy land of dreamy short lived visions that crowd a young girl's head.

Setting aside her concerns and the dreams themselves, the men had been real or nearly so, she thought. Rachel was quite certain she had seen them, but always after night had come. She was so certain of it that night's arrival at Providence, her father's plantation, did not necessarily bring with it friend Sleep. Rather than sleep, darkness brought an urge to pursue the dream. So Rachel would often leave the sanctuary of her bedroom within the main house and creep around the sprawling farm usually pretending to be a spy for General

Stonewall Jackson. It was during episodes like this, when she would steal her way to the cabins of the field hands, magically transformed into a Union camp, that she would see the black men in bright blue passing beneath shadowed gables as silently as ghosts.

The row of small houses was on a makeshift dirt road. It was hardly a road at all as there wasn't a wagon or even a horse in the thirty-some-odd house shanty town. The cabins were below simple — one room laid-up rough log squares with clapboard roofs. Behind the swinging burlap that doubled as window pane and curtain, dim light bounced about and reached out to paint slow moving shadows on the dusty ground. As a rule, Rachel wasn't allowed down there during the day and after dark even her father seldom visited. Only the night, the dream, and General Jackson thought her being there permissible.

She made her first daylight visit to the town only recently when she accompanied her mother as they delivered a large bundle to one of the shacks. That day Rachel waited on the wagon seat as Colonel, their old cart horse, stood on three feet, resting the fourth and lazily swished his tail out of worn habit. While the old horse dozed behind drooping eyelids Rachel's eyes darted all around her. There were so many things they hadn't seen before. As it was with most new sights, each picture generated an abundance of questions which she was certain to press on someone. Far too quickly for Rachel's eyes and inquisitive mind, her mother returned to the wagon followed by an elderly black woman who walked beneath the stoop of a slightly bent back and lagged badly. Ahead of her, Rachel's mother, Mrs. Martha Justice, covered the ground as if her steps were water gliding over a smooth rock. Even her footprints in the dust seemed elegantly placed.

"And to be sure, Carol Anne," Mrs. Justice said sternly as she climbed aboard the wagon and sat next to Rachel. "Three."

The movement behind him stirred Colonel and he placed all his feet beneath him in anticipation of moving on.

"Yes, 'am, Miss Justice," the black woman answered. "Three it is."

"Very good then. Best be busying yourself. The day is short already." With that, Mrs. Justice chirped to Colonel. He leaned against his harness and the wagon moved up and away from Carol Anne, whose words trailed off behind.

"Yes, 'am. Three. Gots to get three ready. Praise be Lord Jesus. Three! Amen. Three."

As Carol Anne neared her small house, she began to sing triumphantly. Rachel, who had been staring at her, looked from the black woman to her mother.

"Mother, why does Carol Anne live in such a tiny house?"

"That is all she requires. Her needs are few."

Rachel considered this for a moment. "Well, why does she live down here and not someplace else?"

Her mother paused before answering. "Because she works for your father."

"Then why doesn't she save her money and make a nicer house?"

This time the pause was longer and more awkward. "Carol Anne works at Providence and is given food, clothes, and a place to live in return for her labors."

Rachel came back with the quickness of a child's mind that sees the world in a simple light. "Does Carol Anne work hard, mother?"

"Yes she does."

"Then father should give her a nicer house. I shall ask father to give Carol Anne a nicer house."

Mrs. Justice didn't respond, but snapped the reins down on Colonel's rump. He snorted and the wagon lurched forward past two black men carrying garden tools toward the main house. Rachel turned in her seat as the wagon passed and watched the men until they vanished below the crest of a small hill which stood above the slave quarters.

Turning again to her mother she asked, "Do those men work for food and a tiny house too?"

"Yes," Mrs. Justice said without looking at her only child.

Rachel pointed to the bent backs of laborers some distance away in the fields. "And those folks there. They all work for free too?"

"Well, yes, but it's not exactly for free. They each get meals and—"

"Do they get paid money? Like when I do something for PaPa he sometimes gives me a penny. Do they get pennies?"

"No. They do not get pennies."

"Then why would they all stay here? I don't think I would stay without getting pennies. Why do they stay? I don't think I would stay."

"They must stay."

"But why? I don't think—"

Mrs. Justice pulled in Colonel's steps and the wagon stopped. She turned in her seat and looked closely at her daughter. "Rachel, do you know what a slave is?"

"A slave?"

"Yes. A slave."

"No."

"Rachel," Mrs. Justice said mechanically, "a slave is a colored man or woman, maybe an Indian, who belongs to another person."

Rachel looked back, but her eyes gave away her lack of understanding.

"Listen to me closely," her mother continued. "The people who live here and work for your father are his slaves. They belong to him, like the fields and the cotton, tobacco plants, the peach orchard, and this wagon. And Colonel here. Your father owns Colonel so he takes care of him. Colonel cannot just wander up the road to the Jenson's place because he belongs to your father. If your father let him go off wherever he wanted, we wouldn't have a horse to pull our wagon, would we? And if we allowed the slaves to leave, we wouldn't have anyone to tend the crops. See? These people you see around the plantation are like Colonel in many respects. They are taken care of in exchange for their work, just like Colonel is fed for pulling this wagon. Understand?"

Rachel nodded yes, though she didn't completely. Her mother, wanting to put some distance between herself and the conversation, spoke to Colonel and the wagon moved again.

They were nearing the main house before Rachel spoke. "Mother, is Carol Anne a slave?"

"Yes she is."

"Does she like being a slave?"

"I don't...," Mrs. Justice hesitated before continuing. "Rachel, there are a great many things you do not understand as yet." She looked away and frowned to herself. "There are a great many things I don't understand."

Another moment and she turned her attention back to her daughter. "Slaves – slavery – is such a thing, darling. I can't say I'm completely comfortable with it myself, but I am a woman of means and as such accept my station in God's world."

"Slavery. Mother, should I like slavery?"

"You should do as you are told and do what is expected of you throughout the majority of your life," Mrs. Justice replied.

Rachel bowed her head as though she'd been scolded. "Yes, ma'am."

Her mother suddenly reined in the confused horse once again. She slipped an arm around Rachel's shoulders and spoke in a soft voice. "But there are times, my precious, when you must listen to another voice, one that comes from inside. From your heart. Often it speaks loudest of all, but we pretend not to hear. That is the voice we should listen to." Mrs. Justice accented her words with a vigorous hug. "We should listen to our hearts."

Rachel's face became a smile as she moved tightly into the comforting fold of a mother's arms. She loved it when her mother was like this — open, smiling, warm, and full of hugs. Often in the house she became someone else, someone cool and distant.

After another moment, the hug relaxed. Mrs. Justice spoke again and the baffled Colonel drew himself up to the main house. A stable boy approached with head down and silently took hold of the old horse's bridle. Mother and daughter disembarked and headed into their expansive home. Rachel hesitated in the doorway and looked with a combination of wonder and sadness back at the boy, no bigger than her, as he led the big horse and empty wagon to the nearby carriage house. This notion of slavery was churning in her mind and raising a quiet tone in the young girl's ears, but her mother's voice called from inside the house and broke the spell.

"Rachel, come inside. The Daughters of the Confederacy will meet this evening. Be assured of having yourself prepared for our trip in proper fashion."

"Yes, ma'am," Rachel answered as she closed the door on her picture of the boy and the horse.

As the Carolina sun methodically relinquished its hold on the day, the field hands made their way to their shantytown. Night sounds began to echo across the fields as the smells of simple meals drifted out from the ramshackle houses. In the main house, Rachel was finishing her own dinner alone in the kitchen. Her parents ate separately in the formal dining room. A slave maid had prepared the meal, but was nowhere to be seen. Miraculously she would reappear each night and clear Rachel's table just as she finished. Normally Rachel left the table with the dishes, but tonight she lingered and watched as black hands cleaned up after her. She was full of questions, but could not force them out onto her silent and unknowing teacher. Still, she watched and thought of work and food, pennies, and Carol Anne's rickety home.

Night had a firm grip on the plantation as Mrs. Justice primped Rachel's dress in the large foyer of the house. "There. You are the absolute picture of a fine southern lady. Remember to hold your head erect as you greet the ladies in attendance this evening. You are a Justice and of proper breeding. I expect you to demonstrate as much."

Rachel resisted the urge to struggle against her mother's preening. Mrs. Justice could be very firm and even harsh in her role as matron of the plantation. Many times Rachel had witnessed her mother chide one of the maids to tears for an act or omission. But as Rachel stood in the hallway watching her mother's hands caress the bow on the front of her dress, it occurred to her that she had seen those same hands dole out huge bundles of food and clothes to many more slaves than had ever been lectured. It was peculiar, Rachel thought, that her mother was often like two people. One was aristocratic and cool and the other warm and giving, like the lady in the wagon who had explained voices of the heart to her that afternoon. That was the mother Rachel loved the most, as hard as it could be to find her.

Straight away the pair was walking across the front lawn to the carriage house with Rachel carrying a basket with her mother's contributions to the buffet for the meeting and two corn muffins for the short trip. Colonel had been hitched to the wagon some time before, probably by that same young boy, Rachel mused. She looked for him, but he wasn't to be found. A shadowy figure began to stir near the stable and approached the wagon just as Mrs. Justice and Rachel dropped onto the wooden seat. It was Mr. Calloway, the plantation foreman.

Rachel didn't like Mr. Calloway. He was always grouchy. Whenever he looked at her he snorted like a bull. Worst of all, he was never without a black leather whip which he carried neatly coiled and tucked under his belt. The whip had a name around Providence.

It was called The Treatment. Though she had never seen him use it, she had once heard it cracking above the cries of a grown man. She had run from the sound of the whip and had fought to keep as much distance as possible between herself and Calloway ever since.

"Mrs. Justice, ma'am, you ought'n to be trapsin' around here in the dark."

Rachel's mother was startled by his sudden appearance, but recovered so quickly that neither Rachel nor Calloway took notice.

"My dear Mr. Calloway," she quipped with as much sarcasm as she could fit in next to her own drawl. "I am hardly trapsin'."

"No, ma'am. What I means is, you ought to be sportin' a light."

"I shouldn't think a light necessary. And since you brought it up, what is it that has you out here wandering about at all hours? Tell me that, my Mr. Calloway?"

"I thought you should be carryin' a lantern, especially on the road."

"Colonel knows the way quite well, thank you. And you haven't answered my question. Why are you out here meandering about in the shadows mimicking a highwayman or some wayward ghoul?"

"Just doin' my job, Mrs. Justice."

"Your job is to tend to the needs of this plantation and I don't believe skulking about in the dark is one of your primary duties."

"No, ma'am, but we been havin' a lot a runaways and Mr. Justice, he said—"

"Mr. Calloway, are you suggesting that my husband instructed you to hide in the shadows, sneaking about like a prowler, with designs to leap out to frighten his only child here?"

Rachel took her cue perfectly and quickly painted on a pouting face and widened her eyes in the moon's dim light.

"Well, no ma'am, but—"

"I should certainly hope not. Now, move along to your own quarters for the duration of the evening."

Providence's matriarch waved her hand condescendingly toward Calloway as though he smelled badly. "Go on. Get along with yourself."

"Yes'am, Mrs. Justice."

Calloway's figure was quickly swallowed by the darkness. Rachel was glad to see him go, but happier yet that she had witnessed her mother dress him down so.

Mrs. Justice shifted repeatedly on the seat and brushed at her dress as if to remove something Rachel was certain wasn't there. As the elder justice fingered Colonel's reins, she spoke in a voice that quivered with a nervousness that hadn't been there just moments before.

"Well, there now. We're shed of him. Aren't we, Rachel? Now I suppose we can get on to our meeting in peace."

There was a pause that should have been followed by the sound of the reins colliding with Colonel's rump, but the sound didn't come. The gap was so pronounced that Rachel actually leaned forward in anticipation of the lurch of the wagon, but nothing happened. Rather, Mrs. Justice resumed her uneasy banter and brushing until a rustling noise behind them drew both Rachel's and her mother's attention to the rear of the wagon. Though it was so dark she couldn't see much further than just behind her own seat Rachel began to pivot quickly toward the noise. For her part, Mrs. Justice was unnerved. In fact, she became the picture of resolve that had a moment before summarily dismissed Calloway. With a firm and steady grip, Mrs. Justice grasped Rachel's thin arm and squelched her effort to peer into the darkness of the wagon bed.

"Let's be on our way." With that the reins clapped and Colonel began his walk to the meeting.

"But mother, I heard something behind the wagon."

"I'm sure it was nothing, dear."

"No, mother. I heard something." Then in a whisper, "I think there was someone behind the wagon."

Her mother laughed at her quiet fear. "Oh, my darling Rachel. It's just the dark. Just the dark playing tricks on you. Let's have no more talk about it. Now tell me, what have you in your basket to nibble on during our journey?"

Soon the calming rhythm of the road and the taste of fresh corn muffins began to eradicate the recent memory of strange sounds in the dark. By the time Colonel stood at the hitching rail outside of the Jenson home, Rachel had all but forgotten it entirely.

The meetings of the Daughters of the Confederacy were loosely conducted over tea and around the pleasant conversation of southern ladies. Grace flooded the room with each wave of the guests' flowing dresses. The women wore simple gowns designed for traveling, but each attendee had given their dress a little something extra — an additional row of pleats, a touch of lace, a contrasting color — to set its wearer apart and to proclaim, "Here is distinction!" It was expected and recognized by everyone.

As was generally the case there were about fifteen pictures of fashion present. Rachel knew most as being local women, with an occasional daughter as a traveling companion like herself. A few were unknown to her which made Rachel think they must be from far away as she knew everyone who lived within a day's ride of Providence.

To Rachel these meetings were little more than organized gossip sessions, a theory both supported and promulgated by her father's comments concerning the D.O.C. In fact, Rachel seldom recognized a meeting taking place at all. Her mother made the customary rounds between all the guests, alternating between listening and telling stories, trading compliments on the dress selected, the weather, and of course, the war. These conversations were often punctuated by subtle whispers in perfumed ears.

Talk of the war was something Rachel listened intently for. She couldn't remember a time when there hadn't been talk of war. The greatest extent of what knowledge she had on the conflict had been gained by eavesdropping on her father. Whenever he entertained a guest in his study, Rachel crept to the closed door and put her ear to the floor and listened at the threshold. It was here on the floor that she first conceived her game of spy. She would listen though she understood little and scamper away when the sound of creaking leather boots signaled an approach.

Between whiffs of pungent cigar smoke, Rachel learned the names of the players in the war. The war itself was referred to as many things. Her father chiefly called it, "the fight for independence." As with so many things, "independence" lacked a clear definition for her, but the names of the warriors did not. Talk often centered around the exploits of a general named Lee, "a truly great man," and a "scoundrel" named Grant, or "that sonofabitch Sherman." Having no experience with the word, it was almost a year before Rachel realized that "sonofabitch" was not General Sherman's first name. Even after she learned otherwise, William Tecumseh Sherman was always called "Sonofabitch Sherman" in her late night campaigns around the plantation.

The greatest general though, was a man on a gray horse. Rachel knew the horse to be gray from a painting on the business side of her father's study door. And she knew the rider to be Thomas J. "Stonewall" Jackson. Mr. Justice explained that the painting was dated. "Now," her father had told her, "General Jackson has more stars on his shoulders and a sorrel horse under his rump." But when Rachel closed her eyes she saw the general as painted with no mind to number of stars and colors of horses.

She had heard the story of how Jackson came to be called "Stonewall" several times and though the story often changed dramatically her admiration did not. He was the leader who spearheaded tremendous charges against overwhelming odds, battled tirelessly to make the Confederate States of America free, and above all else was a courageous and loyal soldier. Stonewall Jackson became her gallant general on a gray horse and came often to ride with her on Rachel's evening forays over the battlegrounds of Providence for their beloved Confederacy.

Rachel's excursions to enemy lines were set aside for the moment however, as she shuffled among the Daughters of the Confederacy with a tray bearing a miraculous selection of tiny cookies and finger cakes. In her travels between parlor and kitchen she paused only long enough to dispense her load unless the conversation turned to "the fight for independence."

"Oh, dear no," Mrs. Jenson was saying. "You never want to mix nutmeg with cinnamon, even in a dusting. Why one taste just cancels the..."

A dropped off treat or two and Rachel moved away.

"...and well, she claims there was nothing between them, but mind you, if you had seen the look in his eyes! Well, I never..."

Boring.

"So I told her, I never did say such a thing, but if I wanted to, by heaven I would! But to tell the truth..."

Slim pickings tonight. Just ladies talking ladies' things. Nothing of interest to a burgeoning spy.

"...and your three makes seven. That's the largest ever."

"Yes. A group that size will be difficult, but there were many concerns."

"Certainly, but the concern should be with continuing our work, not increasing the risk of exposure."

"You needn't remind me of our intentions. As I said—"

"But, Martha. You had an allotment of one. And yet you bring three. Then there's all this talk of concerns!"

"Keep your voice down."

"We haven't room for Martha's concerns. We haven't room—"

"For a family? Is that what you're saying? One would have destroyed a family. I apologize, but there was no other way."

Rachel's expression did little to cloak her interest and confusion at this strange conversation. Stranger still was the fact that one of its primary contributors was her own mother.

"Obviously it's too late now," another woman moaned. "We'll have to manage, but Martha, in the future, please consider the longer range terms of our mission."

"That is exactly what I was considering," Rachel heard her mother say. Then Mrs. Justice politely excused herself and stepped away from the small cluster of women. Rachel followed closely, but said nothing about the unusual conversation then or throughout the ride home.

Several days passed without incident. Rachel ventured out a few nights to reconnoiter with General Jackson and to check the whereabouts of the Army of the Potomac, but sunlight would find things quiet and unaffected by the scouting. On the morning following one such excursion, Rachel's mother summoned her to the kitchen. She arrived to a beehive of activity. Mrs. Justice was flittering from pillar to post doling out instructions on the fly. Her servants responded quickly and departed on fleet bare soles, intonations of "Yes, 'am," echoing after them.

"Rachel, come here, dear," her mother called as she whirled. In her arms was a brown paper wrapped package of considerable heft. "Hold your arms out and see if you can carry this. Easy now, it's rather stout."

Rachel obeyed and felt the weight of the plain brown paper bundle fill her arms. She gave only slightly then deftly adjusted the package with a tiny heave. "I've got it, mother."

"Excellent, dear. Now, you know Carol Anne, correct?"

"Yes, ma'am."

"And you recall where she lives – toward the fields?"

"Yes, ma'am."

"Fine. Do you think you could manage this parcel all the way down to her?"

"I think so," Rachel said as her arms and eyes again tested the weight. "Yes, ma'am, I can do it."

"That's a good girl! I am just simply overrun here. We have a meeting of the D.O.C. tonight and your father has stepped out and invited the corresponding husbands to Providence for the evening. Some sort of meeting he claims. No doubt we will find all the brandy gone, replaced by a house full of the smell of cigars on our return."

Rachel nodded in agreement above the bundle, but secretly longed to stay at home and listen at doorways. Certainly there would be talk of the war. There'd be discussions of letters coming in from the front, of battles and strategy, troop movements, and generals.

"Now off with you to Carol Anne's. And don't return until you've done as I've directed."

Rachel's thoughts turned from battle to the back door of the kitchen. Just as she hastily left the bustle of the kitchen behind her, her mother's voice caught up with her again.

"Tell Carol Anne, two! There's a shiny penny for you when you've finished."

Thoughts of the penny put new strength in her arms as she headed for the shantytown. Unfortunately, the strength was short lived. Before she had cleared the out buildings that buttressed the main house, Rachel had to set the bundle down and rest. In a minute she was up and going, but soon the scene repeated itself as her skinny arms began to fumble the clumsy package. Several times she stopped and started. After a time her arms gave out entirely and the bundle dropped to the ground, tearing as it hit. Bright blue denim peeked out from the slight tear.

Rachel sat on the ground beside her resting burden and gently tweaked the coarse blue material between her fingers. She was so consumed by the cloth that she didn't notice the young stable boy approach.

"Miss Rachel. Is you sick or sumptin'?"

Rachel turned with a start and shading her eyes, squinted up from the dirt at her interviewer. "No. Not exactly. See," she said as she stood awkwardly and wiped the dust off her hands. "I was resting. Me and this dumb old package was headed for Miss Carol Anne's and it's kind of heavy. My arms are tired out."

The boy leaned down to pick up the bundle. "Maybe I's can tote it fo' you."

"Oh, that would be splendid!" Rachel replied as she bent to help her new assistant. As the unlikely pair hoisted the parcel together, the boy noticed the tear and the bright blue denim inside.

"The blue!" he exclaimed then just as quickly threw a blanket over his excitement and lowered his wide eyes.

"What's so special about blue?" Rachel asked.

"I dunno," the boy answered as he watched his bare toes squish through the dust beneath his feet.

"Haven't you seen blue cloth before?"

"I seen it afore."

"Then what'd you get all fluffed up about? Only denim, right?"

"Yes, ma'am."

"You don't have to call me ma'am. Call me Rachel, like you did before."

"Okay, Miss Rachel."

"And what's your name?"

"Nathaniel Job. But 'erybody call me Joby."

"Job. That's a fine Christian name," Rachel said in an excellent impression of her mother.

"Yes, 'am. Thank you, Miss Rachel."

With formalities accomplished the duo set out with purposeful steps, but as they approached the crest of the knoll they were both sweating and breathing heavy. They exchanged anxious glances before Rachel suggested they rest for a minute. Both sat in the dirt road measuring off the remaining distance between the package and Carol Anne's, now about fifty yards away.

"You know what, Joby? My mother said she'd give me a shiny penny for delivering this parcel." Rachel accented her declaration by kicking at the package with a dirty toe.

"A whole penny? Jus' fo' fetchin' this here bundle?" Joby said in disbelief.

"That's right, a whole penny. And a shiny one at that."

"Land o' Goshen. I could fetch a hundredt bundles a day fo' a penny a piece."

"That would be a hundred pennies. Then how much would you have?"

Joby stared at her blankly.

"A hundred pennies, silly," Rachel said again. "How much is

that?"

Joby concentrated hard. "I s'pose it be's a hundredt.

"No, no. It'd be a dollar. A hundred pennies is a dollar. Everybody knows that, Joby. A hundred pennies is a dollar."

Joby lowered his head. Rachel twisted down and around until she could see his face. "Aww, don't be ashamed of forgetting. Everybody forgets things. You did just forget, didn't you, Joby?"

The boy kept up his admiration of the dirt around him and said nothing.

"Why, Joby, don't you know how to 'cipher?"

Joby's head waved the answer.

"Do you know any arithmetic?"

Joby's head was still swaying and didn't stop at this new question.

"Golly, Joby, how come? Don't you go to school?"

The boy looked up at Rachel and though his eyes were dry they were full of despair.

Rachel continued, though with greater tenderness. "Can you at least read and write?"

Joby spoke for the first time in several minutes. "No, Miss Rachel. I dunno how to do no learnin' things."

Rachel sat quietly for a moment then fairly leaped to her knees and began smoothing the dirt in front of her. Joby sat up on his knees by her side and watched as Rachel's hand mimicked an eraser on a blackboard.

"Now watch, Joby. This is a J," Rachel said as she traced the letter in the fine dust. "Now, O. Then B. And Y. There. J-O-B-Y. That spells Joby."

She pointed excitedly as Joby stared at his name in the dirt, seeing it for the first time. Rachel carefully retraced each letter and said them slowly as Joby followed the tip of her finger with his eyes. "J-O-B-and-Y. Joby. Now you try."

The young boy's hand was trembling slightly as he pushed his work scarred dirty finger into the dirt. He drew it slowly through the dust as his eyes darted back and forth repeatedly from Rachel's JOBY to his own scrawling. Rachel noticed the poor attempt and covered his hand with her own and provided gentle guidance. She sounded out the letters and Joby mouthed them after. When they finished Rachel encouraged him to try again and again. After several tries Joby was printing his name and saying the letters plainly.

"That's terrific, Joby. You never have to be embarrassed again. You can now write your own name."

Joby was smiling broadly as he etched his name, erased it, and then quickly repeated the lesson. "J-O-B-Y. Joby. Joby."

Rachel got to her feet and her student followed. "We'd better get this parcel delivered or we'll both get The Treatment," she laughed.

They continued on to Carol Anne's, with Joby looking often over his shoulder to the spot where his name was carved in dirt. As expected, the remainder of the short trip was filled with echoes of J's and O's and the others.

When they reached Carol Anne's door, the tired house was very quiet. Rachel bravely knocked on the battered wood, causing the entire door to shake beneath her light raps. Carol Anne answered directly. Her surprise was clearly evident by the look of wonder and amazement on her face.

"It's me, Miss Carol Anne. Rachel."

"Why yes. Yes it is." Then the aging seamstress noticed the splash of blue spilling out of the bundle. "Oh my. And you've brought me a little sumptin', I see."

Carol reverently touched the blue material then looked beyond it and took notice of Joby. "And you've picked up a helper 'long the way."

"Yes, 'am. My name's Joby. J-O-B-Y. Joby."

There was an instant look of concern on Carol Anne's face at the sounding of the letters, but she smiled, albeit cautiously. "I know who you are Joby," she said as she took the package from their arms. "You two wait here. I've got a honey biscuit for your trouble."

The children looked at each other and nodded their appreciation. Rachel covered her mouth to stifle a giggle as Carol Anne retrieved two hot biscuits from a pan atop a wood stove and brought them to the youngsters. "Here you go. Now mind you they are fresh as the morning and hot as the noon-day sun."

The pair tossed their treats from hand to hand to avoid the burn as they thanked her and headed back toward the main house and the stables. As they began to scurry away Carol Anne called after them.

"Missy Rachel! Did Miss Justice give ya'll a number for me?"

"Oh, gracious. Yes. She said, two!"

"Alright, childrens. Run on now."

Carol Anne was singing again before the door closed. Hearing her, Rachel stopped in the dusty road and looked back at the tiny cabin. Joby stopped with her.

"Joby, why is Miss Carol Anne singing now? I wonder why she likes sewing so much when she doesn't get paid for it?"

"It the blue. She always take to singin' when she sew the blue."

"But why?" Rachel questioned as her eyes moved from Carol Anne's cabin to the fields beyond. "Look. Nobody wears what she makes. Why would she commence to singing when no one wears what she makes?"

Joby turned away and started to walk back to where his letters waited in the dirt. "Them's travelin' clothes."

Rachel ran to catch up with her new friend. "Traveling clothes? What are traveling clothes? Who's traveling? Where they going?"

Joby had reached his dusty chalkboard and sat down beside it. "I dunno."

Rachel stood above him and scowled. "Whatdaya mean, you don't know? You knew they were traveling clothes all right. Now, who's leaving and where they going?"

"I dunno, Missy Rachel," Joby answered as he lazily drew in the dirt.

"Awful funny how folks know some things, but not others," Rachel demanded as her voice rose. "You listen here, Nathaniel Job. I showed you how to write your stupid name, now you tell me about traveling clothes, this instant!"

Joby looked up with a face held gently in the hands of sadness. "But I cain't, Missy Rachel. I jus' cain't."

Rachel stomped her feet through his dirt letters and ran off toward the house.

"You're just a dumb old slave. That's all you are. Can't even read and write his own name." Then she began singing her taunts as she skipped, looking over her shoulder. "Joby can't read! Joby can't write! Joby can't read! Joby can't write!"

For his part Joby sat in the dirt and watched through teary eyes as his short lived friendship faded. The tears trickled down his cheeks and fell on the dusty 'J' beside him. "Can so write my name," he cried softly as he again traced 'JOBY' between his feet.

Rachel had stopped near the house and was spying on the crying writer. Behind Joby, coming up the hill from the shanty town, Rachel saw a dirty hat appear, then a head beneath it. In a moment shoulders followed as the walker ascended the slope behind the unsuspecting boy. As Rachel continued watching from behind the safety of a peach tree she saw that the man was Calloway and he was pulling the Treatment from his belt.

She edged through the orchard toward the dirt road and Joby. As she came to the edge of the orchard Rachel saw Calloway lay the whip out behind him, uncoiling the black snake for a strike. She wanted to scream a warning, but was frozen. The whip snapped toward Joby and cracked sharply just inches above his head. Both children jumped. Joby spun in the dirt as his heels and palms tried to back pedal away from the advancing task master.

"Get back here, boy!" Calloway screamed.

Joby froze while his friend melted enough to move out from the safety of the trees. Calloway was now towering above Joby as he recoiled the whip in his filthy hands.

"What are you doing, boy?"

Joby looked down. "Nothin', Mas'er Calloway, sir."

Calloway's eyes caught the letters in the dusty road. "What the hell? This here yourn, boy?"

Joby didn't answer until Calloway's dirt caked boot prompted him. "Yes, sir. Mas'er Calloway, sir."

Rachel felt the kick herself and was now walking toward Calloway and her friend.

"Where you been learning this shit, boy?"

"I dunno, Mas'er Calloway, sir," Joby called up from the ground as he began to immeasurably inch away.

Calloway noticed Rachel creeping slowly toward them, though she was still a considerable distance away. "Bullshit you don't!" Calloway screamed. "You's a lying niggra, boy. And now I'm gonna give you some more learnin'. Learnin' what happens to niggra boys what lie!"

The Treatment spit out with practiced authority. The first lash ripped over Joby's up stretched arms and Rachel began to run. By the second strike, Joby had curled into a dusty ball on his dirt chalkboard. The third lash lay over his skinny back, ripping easily thru his thin worn simple cotton shirt and biting deep into his flesh. And while the leather tore at his skin, the tip of The Treatment struck the ground and snapped up Joby's name from him.

Meanwhile, Rachel was headed pell-mell down the road. Her momentum outran her legs and she fell in the dirt. She was screaming as she scrambled to get her feet beneath her. "Stop it! Stop it!"

Below the whipping a monstrous black man lumbered out from the shadows of the cabin row and stepped tentatively toward Joby and Calloway, but Rachel would reach them first. Her lanky body was dirty and tired, but her voice still carried her mother's jurisdiction. "Stop that! Stop that this instant!"

Carol Anne appeared behind the huge slave and took hold of his arm. As she did she motioned toward Rachel who was descending on Calloway with the Furies behind her.

"What are doing?" Rachel yelled. "He didn't do nothing!"

"That's just it!" Calloway hollered back. "He ain't doing nothing and he's supposed to be workin'."

The exchange gave Joby a chance to unwind his bleeding body and take to his feet. Calloway started to move after him, but Rachel reached out and grabbed the end of his whip.

"RUN, JOBY!"

Carol Anne and the black man discreetly moved back into the shadows of her house as Calloway started in on Rachel who, like Joby, had started to run.

"Okay for you, Missy! But it'll mean the Treatment for the both of ya. I'll be bringing this to your father. Then you'll run! And you'll stop playin' with niggra boys. And you! Run, boy! But you can't outrun the whip! I'll find you and then you'll reckon the devil hisself has got holt of you!"

Rachel dashed around the back of the house, but Joby was nowhere to be found. She looked for a minute then fearful of Calloway, crashed through the screen door into the kitchen. She was panting hard with streaks of tears in the dust on her flushed cheeks. Her mother saw the sight and crouched down in front of her.

"What in the name of heaven have you been doing? You had best have seen to your task before you began this silliness. You are a fright."

Rachel was trying to get her story out between gasps. "Mr... Calloway... the Treatment... Just spelling... and—"

"Oh, Rachel. I've told you a hundred times to steer clear of Mr. Calloway. That whip has given you nightmares as long as I can remember."

"No... There was a boy..."

"That's quite enough," her mother directed as she stood to her full height and buried her hands in the pockets of her apron. "Go upstairs and get yourself presentable. I have a great deal to do to prepare Providence for your father's meeting. Hmmph! Meeting, my left foot. Just an excuse for drinking, smoking, and loose talk. That's what it is."

Mrs. Justice was already back to her duties as mistress over many.

Rachel crept close to her, looking for a shoulder, an ear, or at least a hug. Instead a shiny penny was pushed into her hand as Mrs. Jenson strode unannounced into the kitchen.

"Martha. I'm so sorry to pop in so, but we simply must talk."

Out of habit, the slave maids and housekeepers silently disappeared into the farthest reaches of the house. Rachel greeted Mrs. Jenson politely, but her disheveled look garnered only a disapproving nod. With the curt greeting tucked away, Rachel followed on the heels of the servants, but held up just outside the kitchen door. From within, her mother and the unexpected guest spoke in whispers.

"Martha, there's been a problem to the south," Mrs. Jenson began. "Several travelers were intercepted last night. I don't have all the particulars, but I do know there's been a lynching."

Rachel heard her mother sigh deeply. "Oh, no."

"It's a poor consequence," Mrs. Jenson continued. "But there's now ample room available."

"Oh, I don't know. Times here are very strained. And there are so few hours left in the day. I don't believe arrangements could be made."

"Regardless, I wanted you to know. You agonize so over these decisions. I thought the extra room might ease your burden."

"Thank you, Maudie, but I believe tonight is already set. There's no time for changes at this late hour."

"Ah, no time for your famous blue coveralls?"

Rachel jumped – her eyes as wide as saucers!

"You know," Mrs. Jensen stated with an air of pride. "I understand they're quite popular to the north. They seem to give the travelers confidence and also invites confidence in employers. With your blue on their backs, your travelers fit in well in the coal mines of Pennsylvania, the factories of Detroit, along the docks in New York City, wherever. It's a wonderful thing you do by that, Martha. The others may soon follow suit."

Mrs. Jenson paused and looked about the kitchen. "I see you're preparing for the men folk to descend. The old fools. Just an excuse to drink up your husband's bourbon."

"My thoughts exactly," Mrs. Justice said absentmindedly.

"Well, dear, I'm off. See you this evening, Martha." Mrs. Jenson pivoted and bolted out the swinging kitchen door. Rachel just managed to duck away from the door's assault. Mrs. Jenson strutted by within inches, but never noticed Rachel crouching on the floor as the door swung back to place.

Inside the kitchen, Mrs. Justice was still talking. "Yes. And thank you. Lord, another lynching."

Rachel staggered away from the kitchen surrounded by a thousand thoughts, one of which occupied her mind so completely she dropped her shiny penny. It bounced off the polished hardwood floor until it found its edge and began to roll. She chased it down and dove on it with both hands, like a cat capturing a mouse, until the sounds of voices perked her ears. The penny had brought her to her father's study doorway.

Inside, Mr. Justice was having a very deliberate conversation with Calloway.

"Certainly I agree, Mr. Calloway. I can hardly afford any more losses, but I'm pressed as to what to do. I try to treat them well and yet they still run."

"You treat 'em too well. They understand the whip better'n kindness."

"Oh, I don't know about that."

"Well sir, it's your place, but if'n you keep a goin' like you are by next spring there won't be a hand left to till the fields. Then what, Mr. Justice? Then what'll you do?"

Rachel listened to the silence as her father thought.

After a few minutes, he spoke slowly. "You've made a valid argument, Mr. Calloway. All right then. I agree. Post your guards at the river, along the edge of the shacks and the stable."

"Now you're talkin', sir. It's a hard way, well I know," Calloway offered with counterfeit sympathy. "But if'n you gotta kill one or two to keep the rest to home, well then that's what you do. It was them what forced you into it."

Rachel silently picked up her penny.

"Yes, I suppose you're right," Mr. Justice said carefully. "It's a damn shame to have to do any killing."

"It's for the best, sir. You drop one of 'em and the rest'll stay put."

"Yes, I trust you are correct."

Rachel ran away from the study like a shot. She dashed up the stairs to her room and flopped down hard on the bed. She put her hands, one of which still clutched the shiny penny, to her ears and shook her head. "What's going on here?" she said out loud to no one but herself. In her mind she replayed the conversation of her mother and Mrs. Jenson. And then the one between her father and Calloway. And the eavesdropping at the D.O.C. meeting. And the noise in the wagon. And the bright blue denim. Always the bright blue.

An hour later still found Rachel on her bed. Her thoughts had turned to General Jackson. He was fighting for her father's right to independence. That much she had learned from closed study doors. And he was fighting for her, right? Oh, how she loved the general on the gray horse. She had spied for him. But something was wrong and the wrong was welling up inside her. She could feel it. And the something was soon summed up by a newly spelled word. JOBY.

Rachel jumped off her bed and flew out of the room and down the stairs. In seconds she cleared the mansion and the wide green lawn. As she ran she thought as best she could of what to do and what to say. She sprinted through the dusty school where Joby had felt the whip, down the hill, and beyond to Miss Carol Anne's door.

Rachel didn't knock. She burst through the door and bolted straight to a plain wooden table where Carol Anne stood wringing out a threadbare towel in a large pan of water. On the corner of the table sat two freshly stitched pair of bright blue overalls.

Scraps of the magic material lay scattered around the basin. Rachel snatched up a small piece and held it up to Carol Anne as she fought to catch her breath.

"This... This, Miss Carol Anne! I know... I know! You... You have to make one more. A small one about my size."

Then Rachel's eyes caught sight of the water in the large bowl. It was pink.

Carol Anne's face held none of the pleasantness of earlier in the day. She didn't even acknowledge what Rachel had said. Rather, she turned to the side and looked toward the back of the one room cabin where a small group of slaves were standing around an old handmade, quilt covered bed.

Rachel left the table and walked slowly toward the bed. At its head was the huge black man who had earlier stepped from the shadows. Rachel locked eyes with him and he helped her draw near. When she had, the man shifted his gaze to the bed and Rachel's own eyes obeyed. Stretched out before her was Joby, but he was scarcely the same boy who had helped her with the package only hours before. His face was swollen everywhere. Both of his eyes were pressed tightly closed. There were lumps on his bleeding scalp and his jaw wasn't aligned properly. His breathing was slow and laborious. Rachel started to cry and most of the attendants moved away from the bed. Carol Anne replaced them and dabbed the blood from Joby's battered face.

"Joby? Missy Rachel here to see you," Carol Anne whispered.

Rachel's lower lip trembled and pumped tears down her cheeks. "Hey, Joby," she called, sensing he couldn't see her.

Joby raised a dirty hand and Rachel took it into her own along with the piece of blue denim she still held. The shaking in Rachel's lip spread throughout her entire body. Her shoulders began to heave as she fought to maintain her composure. With each of Joby's dwindling breaths, Rachel lost another battle with her emotions. Joby tried to talk, but couldn't. Instead, he weakly pried open Rachel's hand and faintly pressed a dirty finger into her pale white palm. On it he began to spell his name. He struggled to say the letters, but couldn't speak so Rachel said the letters as he wrote them in her hand.

"J... O... B... Y..."

When he finished, Joby's hand quivered slightly and collapsed in Rachel's still open palm. Carol Anne slipped beside the crying girl and eased Joby's lifeless arm from her trembling grip and returned it to the quilt. Everyone turned from the bed except the man at the head who reverently pulled a white handkerchief from his pocket and spread it over Joby's puffy face. Rachel looked up at Carol Anne who was wiping the tears from the only white face in the shack.

"Wh-what h-happened?" she stuttered as she gulped for air between crying heaves.

Carol Anne didn't speak, but someone else muttered, "Calloway."

Rachel began to cry all the harder and buried her face in Carol Anne's waist.

"It's my fault. It's all my fault..."

"Nonsense, Missy Rachel," Carol Anne soothed as she gently maneuvered Rachel back to the table. A chair was pulled out for her and as she sat, she pulled the distraught girl up on her lap and began to rock her. "Ain't your fault, child. Ain't no one's fault but one man alone."

Someone behind them spoke in a murderous tone. "Damn white folk!" And a murmur of agreement rippled over the tiny throng.

Then a young man pushed through to the table where Carol Anne was seated with Rachel. "Get that white girl outa here!" he shouted.

"Hush, Teo!" Carol Anne scolded.

"No, damn it! She right. She the one what done it. Get her 'way from this poor boy."

"Teo! I said that's enough!"

Teo snatched Rachel's arm and tried to wrench her off Carol Anne's lap.

"TEO, NO!"

From out of nowhere, two mammoth black hands grabbed Teo from behind and effortlessly pinned his arms to his sides. Teo's legs buckled under the immense pressure as the huge man spoke in a calm, but powerful voice. "Leave go o' that child whilst you got arms that still can."

Rachel's arm instantly floated free and Carol Anne shuffled her to the door.

"You best run along to home, Missy Rachel. I'll tend to Joby."

Rachel looked back into the room behind Carol Anne. The big man was still holding a subdued Teo. The faces around them were taut with sadness. Some were angry, but none were dry. Further into the room lay Joby. Rachel looked at the white square on his face then turned and ran into the dusk of early evening. She ran for her mother. She wanted, needed, to be held and hear the mother's voice who had spoken so gently to her on the wagon not so long ago. That's the woman she craved as Rachel stumbled and fell again and again as she scrambled up the hill through the orchard to the back door of the kitchen.

Surprisingly, the kitchen was empty. Rachel streamed through the lower rooms of the house and found no one. The slaves had returned to their homes, collecting there to begin the simple funeral preparations for Joby. Even the women that were supposed to remain at the house to put the finishing touches on Mr. Justice's meeting were absent. Eventually Rachel's search led her to the bottom of the stairs where her mother spotted her from an upper landing.

"Good Lord, child! What have you done with yourself?" Mrs. Justice swooped down the stairs to Rachel who tried to collapse into her mother's arms, but was grabbed and held out for a harsh inspection instead. "Rachel. Now you listen to me and listen well. Get yourself up those stairs and made presentable. Immediately! We should be leaving within the hour."

"But mother, it's terrible! Just awful."

"I won't hear another word."

"Mother, please. Joby. Joby's–"

Her mother shook her sternly. "That is quite enough! This is a very important trip tonight and I sh'ant be late on your account. Now go!"

Rachel was crying again, adding new tears to Joby's, which still skated beneath her chin. "Oh, mommy! I–"

The next words were jerked inaudibly from Rachel's mouth as her mother spun her sideways and swatted her hard on her bottom. "Now git!"

Rachel was jolted by the spanking, but clamored up the stairs until she reached the mid-point landing. She turned and through blurry eyes saw her mother standing with hands on hips at the base of the stairs.

Mrs. Justice critically prodded her daughter on. "Go! I've got too much to do to be bothered with your foolishness! Nonexistent battles and such. Nonsense. You cannot possibly understand how important it is that we depart in a timely manner. There are many other people to be considered in this world beyond yourself and your imaginary playmates. Now, get yourself in order or there'll be more of the same. Move!"

Rachel's fists were clenched at her side. Though she still felt the sting of her mother's hand she had stopped crying. Her face was red from anger now rather than tears. For the first time in her young life she confronted the woman at the bottom of the stairs. "I want my MOTHER!" she screamed uncontrollably before turning and running to her room.

The scene was a near repeat of earlier in the day. Rachel flung herself on the bed, literally wrenching from anguish. So much had happened today and she was alone to deal with it. She cried for want of her mother, not the lady at the stairs who had now dropped her hands and was staring at the empty landing, but the soft mother who explained things so well, the only one who could make sense of this terrible day. But Rachel couldn't find her, couldn't reach her.

It took several minutes before her breath was her own and the tears to subside. Rachel rubbed her red eyes. They itched. Only then did she realize her hand still clutched the patch of blue denim from Carol Anne's table. Its magic brushed her cheek and brought a look of resolve to the young face. Joby was gone and she ached deeply, knowing she had a hand in his death. But no one else had to die. Or at least she could try to save a life to make up for the one that was lost.

The gray horse pranced to the front of Rachel's battle, vainly trying to rally. Rachel eyed Jackson hard in her mind then dismissed him with a wave of her hand. "No, General. Not today. This is wrong." And the gray rider vanished.

Hurriedly and with eyes brimming with determination instead of tears, Rachel quickly washed and dressed for the Jenson's. In minutes she was ready. As she checked her look in a full length mirror, the tiny swatch of blue called to her from the bed. She gently picked it up. On it was the dust and blood from Joby's hand as well as her own tears. Without hesitating she turned up the collar of her blouse and pinned the snip of bright blue to it. Carefully she massaged the collar flat again and with the blue hidden, headed quickly to the door.

She cracked it open and discreetly peered up and down the hall. There was no one within sight or sound. Out she went. The site of the recent screaming bout was empty as well, so she descended the stairs in a flurry and darted out the front door.

The manicured lawn was dark. It was getting late and she knew her mother would soon collect her for their trip. Rachel's spying games were paying dividends as she expertly snuck around the house. From the hedges she could see men with lanterns collecting near the stable. They milled around kicking at nothing in the dirt then began to move away in a variety of directions. All were carrying guns.

Rachel moved on. She traveled quickly around the edge of the orchard and was nearing the other side when she faintly heard her mother's voice call in the house.

"Rachel. We will be leaving in a scant ten minutes. Bring yourself down."

Rachel allowed herself a slight smile at the notion that her mother thought her upstairs. As quickly as it came however, the smile faded and she moved on toward the shanty town.

In a few moments Rachel was perched at the corner of the nearest building in the slaves' quarters. Carol Anne's lay twenty-five yards beyond. She watched intently for what she thought would come. In another moment, it did. Two shadows, one looking monstrously big, moved surreptitiously along the side of Carol Anne's shack. The moonlight was not exceptionally brilliant, but still Rachel could see the color that surrounded the travelers and set them softly aglow. It was the magical halo of bright blue.

The travelers moved like ghosts, ever silent. In the gathered darkness their feet seemed never to touch the ground. Rather, their garments carried them like wings of sapphire. Rachel watched with knowing amazement at the sight she had witnessed before, but never believed. Now she believed because she understood. The black men in bright blue were real. And they were headed straight for the stable and the waiting guns.

Her hand absently reached beneath her collar and tugged at the blue talisman pinned there. Its relationship to the bright blue that now moved toward the guns sent courage to her heart and energy to her feet. She scurried away. Thirty seconds later she had run a course that would intercept the travelers on the back side of the small hill. She waited in the shadows of a small grove for the ghosts to arrive.

Soon they came – floating breathlessly up the hill. The pair of specters moved from one stand of trees to the next. In seconds they had drifted to within range of Rachel's whispered voice.

"Travelers, please don't move."

She stepped out from behind a skinny tree that had completely hidden her slight frame. The men were afraid and began to back away, not certain if Rachel herself was a ghost or perhaps worse yet, a player in some devilish trap. She moved in on them and was quickly recognized.

"Missy Rachel!" the big man whispered. "What you doin' out here?"

"There isn't time to explain, but there's guns waiting for you just over that knoll not a hundred feet from here."

"Oh, Lordy," the smaller man moaned. "We's dead fo' sure now. C'mon. We's gots to get back to the river."

Both men started to move, but Rachel clutched the bright blue of the big man's pant leg. "No, wait. There's guns there too. I heard them talking. There's only one safe way. You have to come with me."

The men eyed each other in the darkness as well as the little white girl pleading before them. The big man remembered her grabbing the dangerous whip to defend Joby and knew this child had courage.

"Alright, Missy Rachel. Where do we go?"

"Through the orchard. I know a path there. It isn't far, but we've got to hurry."

"The orchard?" the big man said. "Ain't they no other way?"

"No. Please, we must go now!" Rachel's tiny hand reached for the huge black mitt that hung near her face. The man's thumb was as big as her wrist, but she wormed her way inside. Gently the hand closed and swallowed Rachel's hand, wrist, and most of her forearm. Secured to her charge, Rachel glanced around and started back in the direction she had come.

The men's gait was crippled, hampered by the tiny steps of their leader. With a gentle boost Rachel was suddenly airborne, gliding over the ground at tremendous speed toward the orchard. Now she was certain that these ghosts or men or whatever, could fly. Never had she moved so fast.

Just inside the orchard Rachel was softly returned to earth. On another day she might have asked for another ride as part of some game, but this wasn't play. The guns around this encampment were real. They had to hurry. Rachel took a step deeper into the orchard, pulling again at the big hand. This time the hand resisted and brought her springing back.

"We must hurry!" she ordered.

The big man crouched down on his knees. Still he was much taller than his little general.

"Missy Rachel, you ever seen a dead man?"

The question was lost on her, but she answered as fast as possible. "Yes. Yes. Plenty. There's a war about you know." In truth, Joby was the only dead person she'd ever seen, apart from some old man in a funeral procession lost someplace in her memory.

The big man shifted his bulk and spoke again. "Missy Rachel, they a dead man yonder in that orchard. It don't look like they's much way 'round it. You 'fraid, Missy Rachel?"

"No..."

"Then we best be movin' on."

Rachel led the way, but found herself clinging closer to her monstrous friend with each step. Halfway through the grove she was by his side, clinging to his muscled arm with both hands. The man caught sight of the body first and cradled Rachel closer, covering her head and eyes with his free hand. The dead man had been hung, or at least eventually hung. His hands weren't tied and dangled freely as his body twisted in the night air. A strange and ancient drive made Rachel peek through the huge fingers that covered her face and she looked at the corpse. She watched it spin slowly toward her in the moonlight as she walked by. When it had turned completely, she saw the distorted face above the stretched neck. It was Calloway. And he was hanging by his own whip.

Rachel shuddered. Her protector felt the quiver and scooped her up to his chest again and began running among the peach trees. In no time they emerged on the other side near a shallow ravine and Rachel's feet found the ground by the rocky edge.

"There," she said as she pointed down into the darkness. "Get down there. You can't see the bottom now, but it isn't maybe fifteen feet deep. I've crawled down this bank. You can easy. There's a little creek down there. Follow it upstream about a mile. You'll come up under a small bridge. Wait 'till you hear a wagon stop on that bridge. Then get in."

The smaller man was already over the edge, but the big man knelt again in front of the little girl. "Looky here, Missy Rachel. You go 'round the outside of the orchard goin' on back. T'ain't nothin' to be 'fraid of and I's know you a brave girl, but if'n you would, jus' skirt the orchard, alright?"

"Yes. Yes. Just git a going and mind you watch for that sonofabitch Sherman," Rachel offered with a tiny smile. "Of course, in those blues you'll probably be taken for Union anyway."

"Yes, ma'am. I reckon so," her big friend smiled back.

"Look," Rachel said excitedly as she turned up her collar and stretched her neck to expose the secret patch of blue. "I suppose I'm Union now too. Do you imagine General Jackson will understand?"

"Yes'am, Missy Rachel. I's sure he will." With that, the hulk slid into the gully and out of sight.

Rachel turned back and faced the orchard. Her fingers again sought out the charm pinned to her collar. "I sure do hope the general forgives me," she said as she stepped into the trees. Her plan to slink the long way around the edge of the grove was suddenly changed by a voice in the distance.

"Rachel. Rachel? Let's go."

Her mother's voice was faint, but sought her out among the peach blossoms. She was out of time. She'd have to go straight through the orchard or run the risk of another whipping. Her spindly chest heaved in a preparation breath and she dove hard into the dark peach trees.

She knew the way well even at night, but now it seemed much different. It was darker than it had been just a few minutes before.

She changed direction to avoid the body, ran on some and changed direction again. The orchard was pitch black now and Rachel's eyes were widening and she was beginning to shake and sweat, but she ran on feeling more lost and alone with each stride.

The trees around her were coming to life. They reached out for her, trying to snatch her up into the branches and hang her like Calloway. "They hang traitors!" her mind taunted, and she was a traitor to the Confederacy. She would hang for it! Now she cried and ran all the harder, clawing to escape her fate. On and on through the snatching black forest that seemed to have no end. Spinning. Lashing at the limbs that tried to grab her. The whole orchard was moving and tipping now. Every branch held the whip and every bough was Calloway's swinging corpse lunging for her.

Rachel was faint and dizzy. She leaned forward on her knees, gasping for breath as she cried out, "I'm sorry, General! I had to. It just isn't right. Forgive me. Please!"

As she sobbed, the fingertip of a soft glow of light touched her chin and brought her face up. In the distance, on the far side of the orchard, a soft gray light summoned her from her delirium. She stepped toward it. Soon she could make out the silhouette of a rider on horseback through the trees. Each successive step brought an increased brilliance to the gray light and as it intensified, Rachel began to see the horse and rider clearly. It was a gray rider, but more, it was General Stonewall Jackson, just as he appeared in her father's painting.

"He's come to execute the traitor," Rachel heard her voice say.

She watched helplessly as the General drew his sword. The swish of the steel resounded as the heavy blade came to life and flashed in the strange glow. The gray horse abruptly snorted and plumes of steam shot from its nostrils. The powerful animal pawed the ground unmercifully, tearing up clumps of sod and causing the earth to quake beneath Rachel's feet. The arms of the trees fell back. She thought surely she would die, but walked on stoically through the grove to her betrayed idol.

After a testing prance, the gray horse reared magnificently. Rachel stopped dead in her tracks, legs shaking as she stared up at the ghostly horse and rider. From high atop his mount, Jackson pointed his gleaming blade at the mesmerized girl.

Unexpectedly he motioned her to him with the brilliant sword and shouted his command. "This way, my young soldier! The battle has just begun!"

Rachel bolted toward her General. The branches withdrew further as she careened through the last of the trees and into the gray beam. She felt as if she was floating as her tired little body passed deep into the light and through to the other side. When she paused to look up she discovered she was standing beyond the grove at the top of the hill. The light that now covered her came from a lantern swinging in her mother's hand.

"Rachel!" her mother beckoned. "Lord, child, you have become a bother. Here, let me have a look at you."

Fortunately, the lantern did little to illuminate Rachel's haggard face. Mrs. Justice brushed away a few twigs from her daughter's clothes and spoke again, this time in a mother's voice. "Come along, darling. It's important we get started." She paused to straighten Rachel's collar and saw the bright blue swatch, but pretended otherwise.

"Sweetheart, I apologize for spanking you," she said very gently. "These are troublesome times, but not of your doing. I am sorry, Rachel. Truly I am."

Rachel heard the words and was warmed by them, but spun quickly to look back at the orchard. Then as quickly turned back to her mother. "Mommy, I saw General Jackson!"

Mrs. Justice leaned into her daughter and hugged her tight. "Yes. Yes. I believe you did. Come," she said as she stood and took Rachel by the hand. "You can tell me all about it on our trip."

As mother and daughter walked toward Colonel and their wagon, Mrs. Justice doused the lantern. Rachel didn't question, but the move brought a gun out of the shadows of the stable.

"Ms. Justice, ma'am'? You ought to keep that torch a burnin'," said a burly man as he struck a match to his own lantern. "There might be trouble afoot tonight. You best not be doin' much movin' lessin' you got yourself a candle."

Mrs. Justice and Rachel stood in the hired gun's light.

"What's all this about?" Mrs. Justice queried resolutely as she pointed to the gun.

"Orders of your husband, ma'am. Too many darkies been runnin' off. He's fixin' to stop 'em. One way," the man said as he tapped his gun, "or t'other."

Mrs. Justice helped Rachel into the wagon then joined her. She tried to turn the man away as she had done Calloway. "Well, I'll not have any firearms around my daughter. You just get yourself over there by the house."

"No, ma'am. This here's my post. If'n I moves off'n her, Calloway said he'd tear up his whip on me. I's a stayin'."

Rachel looked toward the orchard and thought of Calloway's whip as the man extinguished his lantern and receded into the shadows.

Mrs. Justice was nervous. She couldn't wait. If the slaves approached the stable, as they were certain to do any second, there'd be shooting and Rachel could get hit. If she tried to warn the travelers, the entire organization could be exposed. There was no good way out. She called to Colonel and brought the reins down sharply on his rump. The old horse lunged ahead and jerked the unusually light wagon to a start. Behind the cart the man stepped again from the shadows to watch Colonel, Rachel, her mother, and the empty wagon move out onto the road to the Jenson's.

The reins were trembling in Mrs. Justice's hands. Any second she expected to hear the report of a gun. The tension grew as Colonel inched his way up the road and left Providence behind. Any moment now. Certainly any second and men would be killed. Mrs. Justice braced herself for the blast that would now be echoing some distance behind her. "At least Rachel is out of harm's way," she reasoned silently. "But those poor men."

Rachel tapped her mother's arm and the woman jumped, causing Rachel to jump as well. Mrs. Justice smiled weakly and slid over in the seat to be nearer her daughter. "Oh, my! I guess I'm a tad out of sorts tonight, dear."

Rachel knew the cause of her mother's anxiousness, but was unsure how to approach her. Would the tender, loving woman who met her with the lantern be there to listen or would the calloused head mistress of the plantation answer? Rachel cautiously tested the water. "Mother? I saw General Jackson tonight. Down by the orchard."

"You did?" her mother responded with her nervousness unhidden. "How was he? Next time be certain to ask him to the house for tea."

"Awww, you don't believe me."

"Oh, yes I do. I do believe you saw him. It's just difficult to understand how he can be in two places at once. I heard the other day that he was leading his troops into Chancellorsville, but I suppose he is an amazing man."

"He is, mother! He really is!" Rachel exclaimed. "He was on his gray horse, just like in PaPa's painting. And he had a shiny sword and everything! See, I was lost in the orchard and the General, he showed me the way out. He is amazing. And he must have forgiven me too. You know, to help me like that. If he didn't forgive me he wouldn't have helped me would he, mother?"

"I suppose not," Mrs. Justice answered, still listening with one ear for the guns to erupt. She thought to ask Rachel what she sought forgiveness from General Jackson for, but waited instead for the blast.

Rachel sat quietly alongside her mother for a time until she recognized the bend in the road that signaled the approach of the bridge. Her mother was there all right, but still Rachel was uncertain how to talk so openly about such things as Joby, and Calloway, and the men that waited beneath the bridge. Perhaps her mother would not stay. There was no more time to consider a strategy. Colonel's hooves were kissing the worn planks of the bridge.

"Mother, let's stop a minute."

Mrs. Justice was once again drawn from her concentration on the guns.

"What, dear?"

"Let's stop. Let's stop the wagon."

"Why, Rachel? What's wrong?"

"Just stop. We must stop!" Rachel reached over and jerked the reins that rested in her mother's hands.

Mrs. Justice sat in shocked silence. Colonel took advantage of the unscheduled break and rested. Rachel was sitting stiffly, looking forward over Colonel into the dark.

"Mother, do you remember telling me that sometimes you have to do what your heart tells you is right? Even if maybe it means not being a... a proper lady of distinction?"

"Why yes, I believe I may have said that. I don't know if it meant stopping us in the middle of the road, but–"

"Did you tell me that or not, mother?"

"As I said. I imagine–"

"Mother, please. Yes or no."

"Yes. Yes I did."

"And is it true? I mean, is it important to do that?"

"Yes, Rachel, it is very important to follow your heart." Mrs. Justice thought back to the travelers she had helped and the problems it had caused her husband. "Often it is the most difficult thing we do in our whole life, but there are times when we must, even if it's..." There was a slight rustling noise behind the wagon. Mrs. Justice slowed her words and began to turn in her seat. "an... unpopular... decision..."

Without looking, Rachel reached over and gripped her mother's arm tightly.

"It's all right, mother. It's just the dark." Mrs. Justice turned back to the front as Rachel continued. "The dark can play tricks on you, you know. Let's just be on our way."

Mrs. Justice looked with wonder at her daughter, who was still staring straight ahead, uncertain of what her mother was about to say or do. But there were to be no questions that night. Perhaps later, but not now. Instead, Mrs. Justice clapped the reins up and down on Colonel's back and spoke in a hushed voice. "Step up, Colonel."

The quiet horse did as ordered, leaned into his harness and pulled the heavier load off the bridge. A big voice whispered from the rear of the wagon. "Bless you, Missy Rachel." At that, the youngest engineer on the underground railroad ducked her head under her mother's arm and began to cry tears of exhaustion at the day behind her. Mrs. Justice dropped the reins to her lap, leaving Colonel to his own navigations. As the horse walked on steadily, she flung both arms fully around her daughter and hugged her deeply.

"I'm here now. Your mother's here," she said as Rachel nestled deeper into her cradling arms. "Yes, your mother's here. And I'll never go away again."

It was well over a week before word reached Providence that the great General, Thomas J. "Stonewall" Jackson, had died at

Chancellorsville early on the night of Rachel's jump to the Union. Rachel and other soldiers north and south, grieved him at length. Many times thereafter as she traveled to late night meetings with special cargo, Rachel would tell the story of her encounter with the General. On those trips and elsewhere, her mother was always present as she had promised. And often, just into the impenetrable darkness behind their wagon, Rachel would hear the hoof beats of a gray horse.

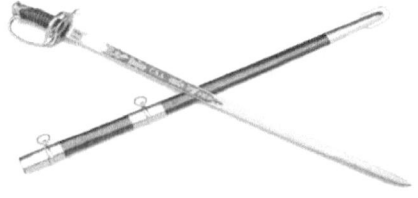

The Jazz Bridge

Downtown has endured many periods of alternating growth and decline. The city's leaders, not really leaders at all, but those who occupied corner offices of the city government building, are quick to point to statistics that seem to justify and clarify it all. There are figures called 'leading economic indicators' which are ambiguous at best and of no importance to the sidewalk walking denizens of the city at worst. Other numbers, like crime rates, have more teeth to bite the trailing leg of the work-a-day public, but those corner office dwellers often put hidden muzzles on these statistics or tease the numbers with a pointed stick – all dependent on what suits them and their hidden agendas. It had much to do with politics, votes, and allocations of dollar bills and little to do with the citizenry who lived, worked, and played in the various districts in the city.

They call them districts now. When the Long Boat River Bridge was built we called them neighborhoods, but things change, evolve. Politicians are fond of calling it growth.

Even the name of that venerated old bridge has evolved. When it was planned before the war it was referred to as the Long Boat River

Bridge Project. Then the war kidnapped the steel. When the bridge project was picked up again, patriotism and recent nostalgia called for the iron blue sign with the peeling yellow painted letters to be cast, "The Veterans Memorial Bridge," which was absolutely fine by everyone. But ask the man fishing from the sidewalk railing that parallels one side of the bridge's see-thru grated steel deck and he'll tell you he's standing on Mel Island Bridge. That common name grew out from the island that splits Long Boat River just beneath the midpoint of the bridge.

The presence of the island was a natural aid to the builders in early spring of 1948 when the first footers were driven down into uncovered bedrock. As soon as the concrete and steel pilings were set on the east bank – the deep city side – hundreds of workers, most in worn Army O. D. green (olive drab) pants fresh from their discharges and long train rides home, scurried over the bank of the river. The strap over Long Boat would grow out from only one side of the river as getting materials to the opposite shore by boat or road and rail proved too daunting and time consuming. So straight out from the heart of the city the steel took aim on Mel Island.

The ex-soldiers were diligent – accustomed as they were to following orders – and the bridge began to take shape. As the distance grew and the height increased, steel workers, Mohawk Indians mostly, came into town on the soldiers' trains or packed in the open backs of rickety pickup trucks with rusted out fenders that flapped in time to the rushing wind. The Indians kept to themselves and worked incredibly hard. They were fearless as they walked the high girders over a hundred feet above the Italian stone cutters who worked the rooted granite blocks. Much was made of it if an Indian drank himself silly after the foreman's whistle blew an end to the day, but in truth, the Italians, the Irish, Catholics, Protestants, unionizers and anarchists, all pulled from a jug, squeezed a grape, or tapped a keg dry with as much efficiency as any other man who worked the bridge. They were all looking for a sort of salve to apply to their cut hands, sore backs, or recent memories of the war. Each one acted as though it might be found in the bottom of a ragged glass, tin cup, or rye whiskey bottle.

Despite the hazards of bridge building and accustomed memories of killing and death still reflecting from the workers, not a single man died in the construction of Mel Island Bridge. A few fingertips fell in the river when steel shifted or cables tightened quicker than the fingers could react, but all in all no one was hurt by the standards of the day. The greatest story that still persists is of the Mohawk who inexplicably fell. He did a wonderful rendition of Johnny Weissmuller and caught a dangling rope about thirty feet later. According to bridge lore, after he stopped swinging some, his friends pulled him back up to the bridge and he never missed a lick of work. His hands were burned by the rope, but that was it. There were over fifty witnesses to attest to the display.

So the concrete and steel stretched out slowly like a wakening child across the Long Boat River to Mel Island. Once there the bridge seemed to rest as building slowed until the following spring. Months later, when the last ice was visible only as a hint of a beard around the island, the ex-soldiers and the Mohawks returned with a vengeance and breathed life back into the construction.

The bridge was completed in the early fall of 1949. And after the last man in old green worn through Army pants swept the road clean at either end, there were ribbons cut and speeches spoken. The speeches echoed down the river from tinny sounding speakers perched on the backs of big trucks who themselves were on the back of the freshly painted bridge. Within an hour the echoes had played themselves out and the speakers had melted away. Then the bridge became more a bridge and less a stage, but it would come back to its birth as a theater when it gained its 50th birthday.

It began as the high school marching band in their snappy black and red double-breasted coats with tails and white pseudo-cowboy hats that fit some well and others not at all. The regimented rows of the band were followed by big shiny red fire trucks whose spinning lights could be heard to grind slowly as they passed by at a crawl.

The big trucks turned into a great mass of boys and a few ponytailed girls in little league uniforms that weren't really uniforms at all. Buttoned up collarless baseball shirts — victims of the recreation department's shrinking budget — had been replaced by simple t-shirts. The move had no effect after a couple seasons as most of the diminutive players had never watched a game. The kids walked in loose teams with baseball gloves but no baseballs and the odd coach tossed in as chaperone. Dotted between the giggling groups of children in their bright colored caps and matching bright shirts with auto parts stores and banks billboarded across their skinny chests, were unknown local dignitaries riding in flashy cars.

The cars were convertibles on loan from the dealerships that sponsored the little league teams and sported temporary magnetic signs on their doors touting the good deals available to the parade watching/car buying public. Between the car doors and the backs of the children, much of the parade assumed the look of a moving advertisement for the moneylenders, car dealers, and the occasional hardware store.

What followed the standard parade fare is what led to the eventual transformation of the bridge. When the last fire truck, a garish greenish-yellow variety – shiny as a mirror with big black tires so clean they looked wet – rolled by at less than idle speed, musicians, in about the same gender proportions as the preceding little league teams, were strutting, walking, dipping, and dancing to their own special blend of music. The notes from the disjointed band echoed off the back of the green-yellow truck and fell on the ears of the parade watchers as jazz.

There were a few trumpets, a splattering of trombones, and a wide assortment of saxophones that ranged from small tenors and a mass of altos to a pair of monstrous numbers whose booming voices provided the bass line for all the lighter notes to ride. All told almost two dozen sparkling horns and a walking percussion section carried on as the whipping tail of the parade – lively and snappy – enchanting the pleasantly surprised parade goers.

The presence of the musicians came about, as most delightful things are prone to do, by chance and happenstance. At the east end of the bridge, where the throat of the span met the city, was a short row of stores that had narrowly escaped the wrecking ball when the original plans for the bridge were passed by the city council in the early 40's. The store fronts had taken up many faces over the years, but the bridge and its ending street, meant to ease traffic and shoppers into downtown, instead came to act as a funnel and things move quickly through a funnel. As the traffic whizzed by, the businesses waned – came and went beneath the passing traffic until years melted into decades. By 1997 all the stores were empty. It was then that the Tombstone Café, thus named for the previous occupant – a headstone carver whose unfinished work remained behind – was born when a small group of local jazz players had an idea.

They had started as three friends enjoying their passion at alternate homes until friends of friends of friends began to test the size of living rooms to bursting. Then the abandoned storefront beckoned and with the support of a two-dollar cover, relieved the strain and parked sax players on partially finished headstones once bound for the peace of a quiet cemetery.

The Tombstone Café grew slowly and slowly intentionally. Players brought their instruments and their spouses, lovers, and friends who in turn brought cookies and coffee. A large white Styrofoam cup became the cash register on the cookie table and as there were no prices posted, everything defaulted to twenty-five cents. But the quarters grew and paid the rent along with the pairs of dollar bills that gained local jazz lovers access to the simple club. Once inside they arranged themselves in the unmatched collection of chairs – straight backs and folders and chrome legged vinyl covered ones that had long been lost to their Formica topped matching tables.

When the Mel Island Bridge's birthday was at hand, a saxophone player, sitting on a headstone engraved simply 'J' at its far left edge had a thought of joining the parade. The stone beneath her was the focal point of the café and the pulpit for ideas and offerings concerning the tiny unincorporated club.

The single letter, the 'J,' had evoked much conversation. Debates raged, albeit quietly, over whether the 'J' was the beginning of a date – June, July, or January – or a name, and then on to a first or last. Quite naturally 'Jazz' was mentioned as a possible candidate, but was alternately embraced and abandoned when the stone was referenced as either a monument or a grave marker.

The jazz players, perhaps because of the spontaneous nature of their souls reflected in their music and the music in their souls, never did petition the city for a permit to follow the green-yellow fire truck, but follow they did. They did little in preparation for the birthday parade and opted instead for a loose play list of just three tunes, knowing themselves full well as they did that one would likely be enough. From one song would spin a thousand notes of music, each built on the one next to it, but more than independent enough to sparkle with its own voice – the wondrous dysfunction of jazz.

When the day came and the fire truck passed, the music began to flow and form from the brass. One song was begun, actually inside the café. It spilled out into the street, took up residence behind that loud colored fire truck with the shiny tires, where it remained in one long lovely, at times boisterous, tune for the length of the bridge.

At the far end of the Mel Island span, which signified the end of the parade proper, the fire truck was finally shifted into a higher gear and roared back to its holding pen where it leaned against the door and waited to be called. In its exit from the parade route's end, the truck belched a cloud of black diesel smoke that had been pent up by the slow speed. The smoke enveloped a number of the still marching, still playing jazz musicians. Perhaps this was as important as anything else in the scheme of what would come next.

The crowd, which had relished and followed the music the length of the temporarily closed bridge, took umbrage against the fire truck on behalf of the players. The musicians, some choked to stopping mid-note, were encouraged by the throng which at first jeered the fire truck until it vanished then applauded the players to begin again. And begin again they did.

The roar of the departing fire truck served as the opening stanza. As it faded, the saxophones, trombones, trumpets, and brushes took up the cause until the collected crowd plugged the end of the bridge. They rested against bright yellow barricades with hastily stenciled black letters that announced, 'POLICE LINE - DO NOT CROSS,' and sat on the bridge abutments and dwindling curbs that vanished into the ground with the end of the steelworks. There was some clapping, but the rhythm proved difficult to follow for the uninitiated and fell away before many bars of unscripted music had been played. But the crowd lingered if the clapping did not and grew as the story goes, "while the band played on."

When evening came, the police did too. They initially came to retrieve their yellow wooden barricades, but when the cops saw they were being utilized as bleachers and leaning posts, most retreated and left just a few wandering monitors of the big crowd. Everyone who had come to see the parade or march in it were gathering – drawn in by a musical show they all assumed was part of the plan. The little leaguers had produced a few secreted baseballs and several bat free, but precarious pepper games were underway in the grasses that monitored the comings and goings of the bridge.

The high school band ignored the morning directive to collect in a weed ridden adjacent parking lot to board waiting yellow school buses with impatient drivers who were having their Saturday interrupted and had missed most of the parade on top of it. The young musicians – masters of the C scale and the one two three four, one two three four marching beat, went like night bugs to a light when the music caught up to them. Some thought it was their friends from Mr. Rosillo's Algebra 3 class jamming. The presence of their instruments granted them immediate access to the ensemble, but the unfamiliar jagged beat and the fact that no one had a sheet of music was daunting. The horns of the more talented juniors and seniors were encouraged by the brassy ensemble to wade in and there were a couple attempts, but mostly the marching band students stayed students, watched, listened, and learned how big the world of music was.

The police and the city officials, back in their offices from their slow rides in the advertising cars, were patient and thought the crowd would head home as darkness slipped down from the lee of the hills and enveloped the bridge. Some parade goers may have thought to do so, encouraged by dinner or the evening news, but when the orange'ish mercury vapor street lights on the bridge began to struggle to life, new hope sprang into the people and the players. In the dying light of the birthday celebration, the bridge took on the warm glow of a first rate night club.

For all his patience, the mayor eventually felt compelled to act. He walked across the hall of the city building to the office of the Chief of Police. They held the briefest city meeting in history and decided on a course of action that would, over the years that followed, prove beneficial to both careers. They would do nothing. The bridge stayed closed. There were more than a few disgruntled drivers – turned away by the throng and backed up by the police department – and one eventual letter to the editor that was trumped in short order.

Meanwhile, the jazz musicians played and the crowd behaved – insuring the longevity of both. Eventually the impromptu concert ended, but it was stopped by fatigue not the police. The crowd, which had dwindled considerably by the late hours, roared its gratitude as best it could and fell into a sort of warm gauntlet at the mouth of the bridge. The weary musicians ambled through the parting old and new jazz lovers, across the length of the bridge and back into the Tombstone Café.

Everything in the café buzzed. The players were tired, but pleased. Their fingers and lips were used, close to exhaustion, but secretly longed to play again already. The parade and bridge had been a marvelous stage. Before the granite 'J' was alone in the café, conversations had already occurred concerning the next impromptu concert, even without the impetus of a parade.

The initial attempts, the first of which was a week to the day after the bridge's birthday, were greeted with a mayor's office far less festive than that exhibited on the night of the birthday celebration inaugural concert. The shows, given in the grass at the bridge's west mouth, were unrehearsed, but far from unattended. The crowds, which had enjoyed the first show courtesy of the street, swelled on the sidewalk and grassy corner until the curb could not hold them. When passing traffic paused to take a breather, the music lovers began to slip into the street.

The movement was not unlike a herd of zebra gathered to cross a river that might split the Serengeti Plain. The cars were the crocodiles and the first zebras, the first adventurous jazz lovers, tested the street as if it were thin ice. They looked for the crocs and seeing none, or perhaps just one a safe distance upstream, stepped tentatively into the street. The crocodile closed slowly, but was soon thwarted as the rest of the herd, emboldened by the brave early jumpers, surged into the stream and clogged it as surely as a dam.

The approaching car slowed to a stop. Then, very cautiously, as if it had become the prey, the croc tried to crawl through the throng of zebras. Eventually it did squeeze through the revelers, as did a few of its compatriots throughout the evening. However, the arriving police saw that soon enough one of the zebras would fall to a croc. They responded by calling their superiors. The superiors called the chief who in turn called his exalted ruler – the convertible riding, anonymous to most, mayor.

It would have been criminal, not to mention politically disastrous to disband the quiet and orderly concert goers with nightsticks and teargas or even to disband them at all with the notes drifting lazily yet happily over them on the softest of summer evening breezes. Instead, the mayor enacted the plan that reassured his next two terms in the corner office.

He first ordered the east end of the bridge closed. Then he went to the west end himself and with arm swinging fanfare literally walked the musicians and their assembly, as attentive as those behind the pied piper, onto the bridge. Once the mass was composed on the deck the mayor promptly shut down that end of the overpass as well. This effectively sealed the concert on the span, much to the delight of the crowd and their jazz players, but to the dismay of a few disgruntled re-routed crocodiles.

In the weeks, months and years that followed, the summer concerts grew some, lost some steam, flourished again and even died entirely for a time, thereby keeping pace with the normal cycle of such things. When the notes settled following the natural rise and fall, the concerts became solos and the solos spread out over the back of the bridge.

Now, Saturday nights throughout nine weeks of the summer, the bridge refuses cars from either end and the jazz players enter in their stead. The men and women, with their myriad of horns, guitars, brushes, and electronic keyboards, drift in ones or twos or threes onto the river's strap and space themselves out in unmeasured distances dictated only by the length a jazz note can travel. The musicians take up spots beneath the bridge's streetlamps to play to walkers and wanderers, music lovers, and hand-in-hand lovers who stroll the bridge. As the concert goers walk, they listen to one piece fall away behind as another stands up in front while their expensive dinners and wines settle or ice cream cones drip down their fingers.

St. Alden's

The evening mist was rolling across the commons, leaving the fresh cut grass damp with what would become the morning's dew. As the velvety fog began to creep onto the stone promenade, Mr. Christian appeared in the doorway of St. Alden House. The old gentleman knew the devilish tandem of cloud and night would bring the things he sought, so he stepped into the collecting haze and allowed the gathering darkness to swallow him. He pushed ahead and soundlessly emerged from beneath the safety and comfort of the gables of the dated mansion. His eyes, well practiced but weak with age, scanned the misty vapor for the signs. In three steps, he saw them. Just three steps tonight and gratefully so. Christian's hand came up nearly to his face. In its grip was a mammoth silver broadsword – not just silver in appearance like polished steel – but a unique silver that was pure, hard, and dense through and through.

Christian's breath showed slightly in the cool air. He allowed himself to glance at the word that came out of his mouth – the word made visible by the evening's chill. "Come," he whispered and watched as the word caressed his hand and the ancient black leather that covered the pommel of the sword. Off in the mist, the sound of rapping clicks, like a troupe of tap dancers on excited heels, answered.

Soon the thick mist that had gathered began to swirl, becoming like apparitions of dancers shooting up and away into the dark. As the fog continued to parade, a low deep throated growl rumbled across the damp flagstone and brought Christian's broadsword to the ready. The sword buttressed all sides, weaving deliberately as its handler retreated in half steps to the relative security found near the alcove of St. Alden House.

The signs that had first alerted him were plentiful now as the fog was being scattered in every direction. Just out of sight of the darkness, snapping jaws held mouths of yellow jagged teeth and loosed a chorus of rising cries. All about him were the growls of the evil, the tortured, and the hungry. Providing the falsetto for the wicked chant was the continued clicking of toe nails and claws on the old and worn grey stones that surrounded St. Alden House as surely as the demons had all but surrounded the aged Guardian.

Then, as suddenly as the first signs had appeared, the howls and sounds of the anxious heels went silent. For a moment there was no sound at all. Even the swirling mist began to settle as if Christian were once again alone. Then faintly, the methodic clip-clop of a single horse's hooves grew in the darkness. The patient and gentle hoof beats came closer, echoing the rhythm of Christian's own heart. In another movement the horse was near, but shielded from Christian's eyes by the night and the vapors. Reined in, the animal was nearly silent, given only to its laborious breathing and the occasional shifting of its feet on the stone. Near the horse, yet still concealed, came again the deep rumble of a haunted wolf's growl. Invisible and unknown to Christian, the collection of the damned began to close tightly on the holder of the silver broadsword.

The morning sun was still low on the horizon as Crealand maneuvered the car along the wandering country road. The long shadows cast by the trees which skirted the route alternated with the sunlight to give the drive the appearance of a nineteenth century flipping motion picture. Crealand shared the front seat with Gel. She was reading. "Something from some exotic branch of science," he thought. The nearly concurrent sun and shadow flashed on Gel's face and reflected off her shoulder length brown hair, which bounced beneath her chin to the rhythm of the road.

Though Crealand had just met her he already thought Gel was stunning. Her face was chiseled like the woman in a painter's eye. She was petite but had inviting hips and curves that couldn't be hidden under all the numbers in her I.Q. But while Crealand considered her beautiful, the world thought her a genius. She most certainly was that and not solely because of her extraordinary intelligence. She seemed impeccably versed in a wide range of subjects and displayed a knack for weaving disciplines in such a way that each was stronger for her consideration. Her academic papers were published automatically and her recent lectures were given to standing room only crowds of intellectuals. She had published two books already though, like Crealand, she was just twenty-two-years-old. The first had been on metallurgy and the other on the application of some ancient mathematics principal. Both were well above Crealand's reach, as he reasoned Gel herself to be. But for now however, they shared a common destination, St. Alden's University, and from there anything could happen.

Reflecting on Gel's accomplishments gave Crealand cause to consider his own – a few published papers on religion and one on philosophy – hardly in Gel's league at all. And yet here they were, both about to attend St. Alden's, the most prestigious college in the world. "Not the country," Crealand heard himself say dreamily, "the world."

"What's that?" Gel asked absently as she glanced up from her reading.

"Oh," Crealand stumbled, not intending on having been heard. "Nothing. Just thinking out loud."

"Hmmm," Gel murmured as her eyes sought their lost place among the complicated language in her lap.

Crealand's own eyes moved from Gel back to the road ahead. In the short trip they passed casually over the rearview mirror. In it he saw Chapin sleeping in the back seat. Chapin was his age, but was a little taller with dark hair and eyes that, like the flashing sun and shade, seemed to move from handsome to foreboding. Crealand was neither handsome nor plain, but his brown hair and hazel eyes were both soft and held not a hint of anything save honesty and trust.

Chapin had been a last minute addition to the trip. He wasn't to attend St. Alden's officially, but rather in a provisional status. Crealand's grandfather, who worked at the university, had asked him to bring Chapin, along with Gel. In the conversation, Crealand had learned that Chapin's father had briefly attended St. Alden's several years ago and as a legacy heir Chapin was entitled to a provisional spot on the university's roster. Crealand's grandfather had also told him that no provisional student had ever graduated from St. Alden's and that most left in the first semester.

This last bit of information concerned Crealand deeply. He himself would be listed as a provisional. His grandfather's position with the university had provided Crealand with entrance to St. Alden's through the back door as it were. He had shared his concerns with his grandfather who reassured him that everything would work out well. Crealand recalled his grandfather telling him that there was much to be gained from St. Alden's besides a sheepskin. Crealand let his mind drift back to Gel and wondered, quietly this time, if one of those things might be a girlfriend.

Chapin disrupted Crealand's thoughts from the back seat. "Hey, where the hell are we? I must have dozed off."

Crealand spoke to the rearview mirror. "Only about fifteen minutes out."

"Hey, Crealand. It is Crealand, right?" Chapin asked. "What's your major gonna be?"

"Oh... I'm a provisional. So I have to get through the first semester in a liberal arts category before I can assume a major." Crealand was instantly upset at Chapin for exposing him as a provisional to Gel. He selfishly tried to counter. "But you'd know all about liberal arts semesters."

"Yea, I do, or rather, I should. I've got a provisional from my old man, but I ain't staying anyway. I'm just here so I can put it on my resume. Give me a week, and I'm outa here. My father did the same thing and his before him. I'm the last though," Chapin said as he leaned back in his seat with a sigh. "After three consecutive provisionals without a diploma, the school pulls your ticket. No more free rides. I guess you could say I'm the last in a long line of dropouts. But, let me add, very well rewarded dropouts. Alden's name alone works wonders in the world."

Chapin rested his tongue a moment then roughly rapped Gel on the shoulder. "What about you? What's your major, or are you a provisional like your boyfriend?"

Crealand felt himself blush at even the suggestion of it. Gel didn't notice or chose to ignore the comment. "My major is actually a dual. One will be engineering with a minor in anthropology and the second will be philosophy with a non-relative minor in metallurgy."

"Those are some strange combinations," Chapin chuckled.

"Strange can be a relative term," Gel answered, still not looking up from her reading. "The anthropology relates to the engineering insomuch as the methodologies people have used, currently use, and will use as they physically, mentally, and emotionally adapt to infrastructures, both ambient and literal, and also to images far less tacit. And the metallurgy forms a bond with philosophy by—"

"Okay, okay," Chaplin said plaintively. "I get the picture."

"I doubt it," Gel said faintly and looked up for the first time to share a clandestine smile with her chauffeur.

Crealand returned the smile and tried to lay the foundation for some mutual interests. "My major will be philosophy after I get this first semester out of the way."

"I assumed as much," Gel replied, buried once again in her book.

"How's that?"

"Your paper on suicide. It was very good. You're on extremely virgin territory in developing your theories of self-inflicted death and religion. I thought it was exceptional."

Crealand was blown away. "Thanks. My research indicates—"

Chapin interrupted by thrusting his head over the front seat. "You know," he said to Gel, "it drives me wild when you intellectuals talk dirty."

"Excuse me?" Gel said as her lips tightened, making no bones about her displeasure.

"Virgin territory. It's such a thin disguise. What can be more suggestive? Freud had your type pegged from the get go."

"Type? What type is that?"

"Sexually repressive. Compensating for physical gratification by hyper-stimulation elsewhere. It's the librarian syndrome."

"Librarian syndrome?"

"Sure. Girls who work at not being sexual and dive into books for their satisfaction. That's why guys love the librarian look – white long sleeve blouse, hair pulled back in a bun, horny, I mean, horn-rimmed glasses. It's all a ruse for sexual suppression. You get a librarian type – a bookworm like yourself – to set aside her book and it's like tapping a geyser. You're a virtual volcano of cooped up sexual aggression. It's a beautiful thing to expose a woman like you to the joys of life."

"The joys of life?"

"Yes indeedy. The joys of life. 'Virgin territory.' It's all right there."

"I apologize for the misconception," Gel said as she smiled away Chapin's discourse. "I was making a descriptive analysis of Crealand's forays into new arenas concerning–"

Chapin turned to Crealand. "She's hot, man. I don't know if it's you or me, but she wants it."

Gel slammed her book. Her face tightened as she began to lace Chapin without looking. "That's one of the crudest suggestions I have had the displeasure of hearing in some time. I'm certain it is simply a reflection of your intellect or shall we say, lack thereof. I will ask you one time to assume some resemblance of decorum. You would also consider modifying your demeanor on the grounds of the university or your stay may be even shorter than you apparently hope for."

Chapin plopped back in his seat. As he did he slapped Crealand on the shoulder as he had done Gel moments before. "Must be you she wants, my friend. It sure ain't me."

"You are amazing," Gel said as she reopened her book and began leafing through it.

"That has been said of me. Several times."

Gel lifted her head and stared out the windshield. Crealand knew she was aligning her words for a full assault. He would have enjoyed the attack, but Chapin skillfully avoided the entire affair.

"So, Crea. How'd you get your provisional?"

Crealand hesitated another second to give Gel a chance for the shot at Chapin she wanted, but Chapin cut in once more.

"So, what's the deal, Crea? Your old man a dropout too?"

"No," Crealand began. "My father didn't attend even though he had the chance. I'm going because of my grandfather. He works there and is awarded a single provisional slot as part of his benefit package. My father chose not to use it, so that's good luck for me."

The crimson that Chapin had brought to Gel's cheeks flowed away as she spoke. "What does your grandfather do at St. Alden's?"

Pleased to be talking to her again, Crealand's words were bright for such simple ones. "Oh, he's the Guardian."

"What the hell's the Guardian?" Chapin interjected. "Like a night watchman or something?"

"No," Crealand continued. "He's in charge of the treasury. They call it the Guardian. I don't really know why."

"The treasury!" Chapin said excitedly as he again leaned over the front seat. "Hey, do you suppose the old geezer would cut me a check? You know, kind of an advance on my expenses while laboring away as a student? Yea, just call it an advance."

"No, I don't believe—"

Gel interrupted. "Chapin, don't you know anything about St. Alden's?"

"Of course. Like what for instance?"

"Like for starters, the St. Alden's treasury does not issue checks. You couldn't get a check for a dollar from them even if they owed you a million."

"Why not?"

Gel spun in her seat for the first time and now looked harshly at Chapin. "You really don't know, do you?"

"Know what? What's the deal here? I think I know all I need to know about a place I'm not staying at for long."

Gel continued. "Perhaps if you knew a bit more, or anything for that matter, about St. Alden's, you'd be more inclined to take full advantage of the tremendous opportunity that's been afforded you."

"Yea, yea, yea. Thanks for the lecture, Mom. Now tell me why I can't get Crealand's father to write me a check."

"Because St. Alden's, and it's his grandfather by the way, deals wholly in precious metal. All debits and expenditures are satisfied with silver."

Crealand drove on in silence, becoming more transfixed by Gel with each word she said.

"Wait a minute," Chapin said as a puzzled expression overcame him. "You're telling me that they don't use checks, they don't use cash, no transfers, credit cards – they don't use money of any kind – they just use silver?"

"Correct," Gel said triumphantly as she spun again to face front.

"No shit, huh?" Chapin mumbled. "That true, Crea?"

"Yes, it is. I spoke with my grandfather about it once. He said that St. Alden's operates at the behest of some humongous benefactor whose principle directive is that the university pays only in silver, just like Gel said."

"That's impossible. Makes no sense."

"Perhaps, but it's true and it's been that way for generations."

"Wow, man. That's too weird."

"And not just any silver," Gel continued. "It's St. Alden's silver. It's the finest silver in the world. Check that – the finest metal period. I've had occasion to study some of it firsthand as part of my thesis. It's incredibly dense, but not brittle. While clearly a metal, it has properties much like a mineral with an organic line in the base structure. Very, very difficult to classify. That uniqueness gives it a value well higher than platinum on the current exchange, minus the market volatility incumbent with most metals. Absolutely remarkable stuff."

"So, it's like, better than sterling silver?" Chapin asked hesitantly.

"Oh, that's not even a question. St. Alden silver is so pure that it has generated a completely new standard by which we judge precious metals. It's really amazing."

"This benefactor guy must be one rich sonofabitch!"

"Chapin, you are so simplistic. Paying encumbrances with silver is scarcely the tip of the iceberg at St. Alden's."

"Chapin," Crealand offered, trying to get in on the conversation and impress Gel at the same time. "The benefactor is so wealthy and St. Alden's silver so valuable, none of the students pay tuition."

"While that's true, Crealand, that isn't what I was referring to. Chapin, listen to me. Do you know what over one hundred of the world's most influential business and political leaders have in common?"

Chapin shrugged.

"St. Alden's. They are all graduates of St. Alden's."

"Knock it off, you two. Shit, you're starting to sound like an ad campaign for the place. But tell me something. Why would all those people want to come here? This place is in the middle of nowhere."

"Different reasons, I'd imagine," Gel answered. "But remember, those people weren't always politicians or business leaders. Most came here as regular as us. It's what they did after St. Alden's that set them apart."

Chapin was momentarily reflective. "Those people did all those things, became all those powerful people, and there's still no tuition? Whoever's running this outfit is dumber than I thought. With alumni like that, they could be charging beaucoup bucks and still be packed."

"That's the point, Chapin. It's not about money."

"Everything is about money."

"Not at St. Alden's. This place is about bringing the finest instructors to one place, adding the most promising students from around the world, mixing them up with the vision and mission of St. Alden's, and watching the results."

"The finest teachers, you say? From all over the world? How do they get them here?"

"The recognition that comes from being a professor at St. Alden's is akin to you wanting to list it on your resume. Plus, and here is where your precious money comes in, they are paid rather unique salaries from what I gather. Isn't that true, Crealand?"

Happy to be back in the conversation, Crealand didn't want to disappoint. "Absolutely! Like everything else, the profs are paid in silver. And, like the students. Everything is provided free."

"By this mysterious benefactor?"

"By the benefactor."

There was a slight pause in the one-sided debate. Chapin soon tried again. "Then, if it's such a great place, why don't more people enroll there? I heard the whole student body is less than a thousand."

Gel turned again. "Chapin, you don't apply to St. Alden's. You are invited to attend. That is why your provisional appointment is such a wonderful opportunity for you."

Chapin had heard enough. He settled back in his seat, folded his arms, and feigned trying to sleep again. "Yea, okay. Have fun kids. I'm doing my week and heading home. I've got bigger fish to fry than spending four years holed up in some musty dusty crusty college for nerds stuck in the middle of the mountains. Goodnight all."

Gel shook her head and dropped her head back against her seat as well. Crealand spoke to the rearview mirror again. "Chapin, I wouldn't be nodding off just yet. We're here."

The entranceway to Crealand's greatest college in the world was a simple narrow paved road marked by a simpler small sign. The sign, silver with black letters, hung innocuously from a fragile looking metal pole. There were no magnificent granite monoliths or ivy covered gates. Chapin was more than disappointed. "Not much of a first impression, is it?"

"Rather quaint I would think," Gel said, though she too was surprised by the very common entrance. "Perhaps the grandeur has been saved for the campus proper."

Crealand turned into the narrow drive. Like the others, he was taken aback by the simplicity of the entrance. When they pulled within sight of the college little changed. The buildings were old and made of dark reddish black and grey stone. Each building appeared elegant in its age, but simple and unassuming – not what any of the car's occupants had pictured – and there was no ivy. Crealand drove through the small campus until he noticed a building with the name, "St. Alden House," chiseled in an arched doorway. He knew from his grandfather that this is where he would find the Guardian of St. Alden's. Crealand parked the car in front of his grandfather's home.

"Well," Chapin said as he looked through the rear window of the car at the plain campus. "I guess we know why it isn't overrun with students. Look at this place! No wonder no one comes here."

Gel spoke for the first time since seeing the tiny university. "Oh, I don't think it's the buildings that keep people away, I think it's the wolves."

"Wolves? Where? What wolves?" Chapin asked as he strained to peer out every window. But his question was only answered by Gel and Crealand's slamming doors.

Mr. Christian didn't wait for a knock at his door. Rather, he bolted outside with the enthusiasm of a youngster in route to a Christmas tree. His face was a smile from brow through his eyes to his chin. He was thin with the wasting common to old men, but nimble and deceivingly fit. His hair was deep grey and as long as Gel's. It flew out around his face as he ran.

"Crealand! I'm so very pleased you've elected to come!" He flung his arms around his grandson and kissed him twice and hugged him with abandon until his wrinkled hands settled on the young man's face. "I knew you would come," he said softer. "I could feel it."

"Why wouldn't I? This is a once in a lifetime chance."

"You can't imagine how pleased you've made this old man."

Mr. Christian leaned back as if he had just noticed the others.

"And this lovely lady must be Gel. I've read much of your work young lady and I must say I am rightfully impressed."

"Thank you very much, sir."

"Yes," Mr. Christian continued, "you will discover that you have fallen on fertile soil here at St. Alden's. I have no reservations that you and she will accomplish many wonderful things."

"She?" Gel said with a quizzical look.

"Oh, she, the University, of course! You will have to excuse the ramblings of an old man. For me, St. Alden's has personality. She has life and gives life to those willing to give it in kind. She has given me life for many, many years. And I give back what I can." Then in a comical hushed voice. "She's a bit of a mistress to me you might say. As much of a mistress as I could endure at my age I'm afraid."

Gel blushed politely and felt the old man take her hand.

"Come, dear. Let me introduce you to the love of my life."

Gel was captivated by Mr. Christian and stepped away with him at one side and Crealand on the other. Only when she turned did she realize she was facing Chapin, who had yet to be introduced.

"Oh, Mr. Christian, this is Chapin."

Gel felt Christian's hand turn to ice in her own. She let go and pulled her chilled hand close to her as she rubbed the coldness from it.

"Chapin. Yes," Mr. Christian said slowly. "Your father was here briefly some years ago. Neglected to stay as I recall."

Chapin thrust his hand toward the old man. "Yep, that's him. I'm next in a long line of quitters, I'm afraid."

Christian took his hand in a grip like iron. Chapin felt a crushing hot pain rocket through his hand and up his arm. The old man merely nodded and spoke softly. "Yes."

Like Gel, Chapin grasped his own hand and rubbed it when Christian gratefully released it. Without looking, Christian gently reached for Gel's hand, took it with care and resumed their walk. Gel felt an intense heat in the wrinkled hand where only seconds ago had been biting cold. She held on as if she had no choice, but instantly felt she wouldn't have released it if she could. Gel did allow herself to look at Crealand and felt a peculiar sense of relief at having him near.

The simplicity the group had seen on their arrival gave way as Mr. Christian pointed out the brilliant idiosyncrasies of the college. Even the flagstone beneath their feet became dimensional as they walked across the wide promenade. The shades of grey and rich black combined to form a vivid texture, sprinkled with short streaks of white which resembled worn scratches.

Running adjacent to the walkway lay the grassy commons which spread out far behind St. Alden House. The splendor of the bright green grass was elevated by a contrasting massive white gazebo, a hundred feet across and two stories high, which rested in its center. The commons had drawn several students who were meandering about on its grassy back or sitting beneath the shade of one of the several large oak trees it supported. A number of people were sitting on benches collected near the gazebo, though none appeared to be inside the monstrous edifice. When Gel and the others walked up to one of four wide stone entrances under ongoing descriptions of the grounds offered by Mr. Christian, they learned why the gazebo was empty.

"The floor, you see, is in need of some repair. It may very well be original. We will replace it soon. Until then we have been forced to temporarily cordon off the main floor for obvious safety reasons. No doubt it would support our tiny throng, but if too many were to gather, I'm afraid she would never stand the gaff. Come, gently, but you can step inside."

"Isn't it odd," Crealand said as he took a tentative step as though testing ice then looked across the hundred foot circle of rotting wood. "The floor has deteriorated while the remainder of the building appears solid?"

Gel looked at the floor and tapped it with the toe of her shoe. "Appears to be basic rot, but it does seem strange that, reasonably protected from the weather, the center would decay at the same rate as the circumference."

"Cheap construction," Chapin blurted as he joined from his place on the stone steps.

"I would doubt that that has been the case, young Chapin," Mr. Christian said. "Rather, it is the result of the water which is under the floor. You see, the entire gazebo is actually a cover for a huge cistern. All of St. Alden's water flows into that nearby reflecting pool then collects beneath us here, under the gazebo."

"Yes," Gel said as she looked out from the gazebo toward a long reflecting pool which held a mirrored picture of St. Alden House. "I wanted to inquire about the water at St. Alden's. A great many scholars have spoken of its almost magical qualities, but I have not been able to locate a single article on the subject."

"And you won't," Mr. Christian said plainly. "The university does not allow any testing of its waters beyond our grounds. And those that have studied it from within have elected not to publish their findings." Christian began to descend the steps of the gazebo as he continued. "But come this way and I shall import St. Alden's waters to bid you a good day."

Again Gel looked at Crealand. They shared a genuine smile and moved off across the wide commons to the reflecting pool which was as large as the gazebo. As they approached the man made estuary, they could see that the water was crystal clear and uncommonly bright. At the far end, a hundred feet away, a simple pipe sent a constant spray of water onto the pool's surface. The reflection of St. Alden House and their faces were as vibrant and clear as if they were being reflected in a conventional land locked mirror. Gel let go of Mr. Christian's hand and knelt down by the water's edge.

"Amazing. Look at the reflection!"

"Yes," Crealand said as he knelt beside her. "Beautiful."

The compliment did not go unnoticed. "Thank you, Crealand, but look. See how clear it is. It's almost like looking in a mirror. This is unbelievable."

Crealand saddled closer to Gel and shared her reflection. Standing above them in their picture was his grandfather and surrounding them all loomed St. Alden House. The three were reading their combined image quietly when a small stone struck Mr. Christian's reflected face and shattered the glassy picture.

"Oops!" Chapin laughed.

"Not to worry," Mr. Christian said. "Good reflections are quick to return to this pool. Watch."

The Guardian was right. Before the stone had settled to the bottom of the pool, only a scant foot away, their images had returned as vibrant as before. The anticipated ripples were small, inconsequential, and slow. Rather than disturb the entire pool, the ripples scarcely spread and were swallowed by the magic water.

"It acts almost like a semi-solid," Gel said breathlessly.

"Like syrup," Crealand agreed. "But clearly it isn't."

"Touch it," Mr. Christian said, as if he was encouraging the couple to open a gift.

Gel and Crealand's hands reached out in unison and cupped the surface of the pool. The water cascaded deliberately through their fingers. "Oh, my," Gel whispered, "it's like... like handling mercury."

Crealand put his arm in the pool up to his elbow, pulled it out and watched in amazement as the droplets fell back to the water. Each one sent a ripple across the length of the pool and back with an unnatural speed and then eased to nothing. "What in the world? Gel, did you see that?"

"I saw it. But I don't believe it."

Chapin squatted down hurriedly by the others. "What is this, some kind of gag?" He slapped his hand in the water intent on splashing Gel. Instead, the surface of the water hardly broke. The water, as it did with the stone, responded with a few shallow waves that traveled only a foot or so. In a second, the water's surface had returned to normal. Chapin stood up and moved away from the mysterious body of water, drying his damp hand on his shirt as he did. "That stuff's got some sort of acidic base. That's what makes it react so weird. Might even be hydrochloric. My hand's hot as hell."

Gel looked from Chapin back to the water with a smile. "There's no acid in this water. I can't explain its responses, but I know the acidity level is probably zero. In fact, it's so cool I'm thinking it's spring fed. Am I correct, Mr. Christian?"

"Yes you are, my dear. It flows right from under St. Alden House."

Crealand was dipping his arm in again. "Gel, watch the ripples." As before, the ripples caused by Crealand's movement shot out across the surface to the other end, a distance of a hundred feet and back before they abruptly stopped. "Gel, the waves. Do you see what I see?"

"If you mean amplitude and frequency, I do."

"That's exactly what I mean. Both attitudes remain constant. The ripples are the same size coming back as they are going away."

"Perhaps even larger," Mr. Christian interrupted. The couple stood slowly and lingered before the Guardian with their mouths open. "Interesting, isn't it? Rather a fine example that what we do, and the attitude in which we do it, can affect a tremendous amount of space. Don't you agree? And further, that those actions can come back to us, with some vigor apparently."

"But what we just saw is physically impossible," Crealand said with no shortage of excitement in his tone.

"This is St. Alden's, Crealand," his grandfather replied. "A great many things are possible from here." Then, dismissing additional discussion on the subject, Christian moved off toward St. Alden House. "Come along, children. Perhaps you would care to see the spring from which all this magic of yours flows."

As Christian walked on, Gel and Crealand exchanged long looks of amazement. Chapin jogged by them and approached the Guardian.

"Hey, Pops," he said flippantly. "What's this about wolves? Gel said something about wolves around here."

Christian didn't stop walking. "Haunted hounds of hell."

Chapin jumped in front of the old man and stopped him. Crealand and Gel soon flanked him.

"Haunted hounds?" Chapin persisted. "What do you mean haunted hounds?"

"Wolves, hounds, dogs, they're really all about the same, aren't they? Canis lupus technically. Comes down to semantics I suppose."

"I don't care what you call them. What the hell are they?"

Christian stepped around Chapin and resumed walking toward his home in St. Alden House. The three students fell in alongside. He spoke very deliberately, keeping his eyes on the house. "When night falls on St. Alden's, wolves have been known to come down from the hills to prey on the unwary." The old man paused to take a deep breath. "Many centuries ago, St. Alden founded his parish on the grounds of what is now our University. His church grew and later boasted a school – the predecessor of this college. As the congregation and school prospered, Satan sent his evil forces against it, trying to stop the good that was coming from St. Alden's work."

Gel and Crealand were mesmerized by the soliloquy. Even Chapin listened as Christian continued.

"One evening just as the sun was setting, a pack of wolves attacked St. Alden as he walked through his young college, just as we are doing now. St. Alden fought the wolves off as best he could, though he had no weapon. But God provided for him a young soldier of the Knights Templar who was visiting the college as a potential candidate. The knight watched in horror as the wolves attacked the priest and dragged him to the ground. With sword drawn he burst in on the hounds, flailing at them with every ounce of his strength."

Christian's hand parried before him as he spoke, mimicking the swordsmanship of the knight from centuries earlier.

"Rescuers pulled St. Alden to safety as the young knight battled the pack." Christian's jaw suddenly set hard and his face reddened with anger. His eyes intensified, but seemed on the brink of tears. "Before the others could return and aid the Templar Knight, he went down to the savageness of the wolves."

After a few seconds, the grandfatherly face returned and Christian spoke gently, almost reverently. "The wolves disappeared immediately after killing St. Alden's first Guardian, who, by the way, is buried on the far side of the commons. Later that night, St. Alden himself died from the injuries he incurred in the attack. Just before he ascended into heaven, he requested the sword of the valiant knight who had fought to save him. It was brought to him as he lay dying in the basement of this very house. The Saint blessed the weapon and began to cry over the death of the knight who had given his own life to save St. Alden. His tears coated the sword and turned it into the purest silver. As St. Alden died he thrust the sword into the stone floor. From that crack, St. Alden's water has flowed ever since."

The group was now at the door of St. Alden House. The younger members were quiet. Christian turned and surveyed the university.

"And after that day, young knights, sent to avenge the death of their brother, have served as Guardians of the college against Satan's earthly Cerberus and his other hounds. But the wolves never again returned by day. Only after sunset do they come, even to this day. Many hunters have tried to kill them – tried to capture them – but none who have sought the devil's creatures after sunset have ever returned. For many years the knights tried to hunt them down, but they cannot be found when the sun is up. After many years the knights were recalled to the east and the college remained under the guard of a single knight. In the evening, the houses were adorned with wolf's bane – ranunculaceae aconitum – to ward off the hounds. Later, the wolf's bane was replaced by something much stronger. St. Alden silver."

Christian's foot tapped the stone threshold at the group's feet. "There's a thin bar of silver in the threshold of every door, and in the sill of every window on the college. Well, at least there was. We have had to remove a few of the pieces for financial reasons, but they will soon be replenished. And the buildings they were removed from are not evening housing units."

"Wait a minute," Chapin said making no attempt to hide his disbelief. "Are you saying that at night wolves prowl around this place and that you keep them away with silver?"

"Yes."

"What is this? Goofy acting water, knights in shining armor, wolves, silver, wolf's bane. Wolf's bane? C'mon. That's straight out of some Dracula movie. I suppose next you're going to tell us there's vampire bats in the clock tower!"

"No. No vampires," Christian smiled. "But I will tell you something very, very important about the clock tower. Do you see the shadow of the tower's spire, just now beginning to reach the far edge of the commons? No matter the season, when the shadow of the spire touches the bell tower on the gazebo, sunset is very literally, moments away. If ever you are out of doors and sunset is upon you, run for the nearest protected dwelling. Run as though your life depended on it. After sunset, the grounds of the university are not safe."

Mr. Christian opened the door to St. Alden House and stepped inside. "Please. Please come in."

Gel and Crealand followed him into the old stone house. As they crossed over the threshold, they looked down for the silver, saw the one inch bar laid in the stone and carefully stepped over it. Chapin followed, but knelt as the others moved inside. He pried at the silver bar with his fingernail, but the bar wouldn't yield. Only then did he step inside, but he looked down with lust at the silver bar as he closed the door.

Once inside the foyer, Chapin realized he'd been left behind and felt uneasy. In his nervousness, he called for the others too loudly. "Hey! Where'd everybody go?"

"We're in here, Chapin," Gel called from an anteroom. Chapin rushed after the voice and as he entered the room, Christian's library, he realized he was almost running. He quickly stopped and faked an inspection of some of the antique books. Gel and Crealand traded more smiles. "What's the matter, Chapin?" Gel chided. "You act like you've seen a ghost."

Crealand didn't notice a reply, though the latter had chosen to ignore Gel entirely and was harassing Christian about the relics which cluttered the old room. Crealand found himself again thinking of Gel and the increasing frequency of her smiles. He was lost in wonder about Gel and his imagined immediate future with her when his grandfather's touch startled him back to the library.

"Crealand? Are you alright, son?"

"Oh, I'm sorry, Gramps. I was thinking of someone, er, something else."

Mr. Christian took the admission in stride and continued. "Crealand, Gel, come with me a moment please. Young Chapin, will you be alright alone for a few minutes?"

Gel laughed at the subtle joke.

"Perhaps the Saints will protect him," Crealand laughed.

"Perhaps," Christian said coldly.

Gel and Crealand followed his grandfather through the downstairs of St. Alden House until they came to a very large dining room. The ceiling was higher in this room. It was more banquet hall than dining room. The sounds of their steps echoed across the forest green marble floor and off the dark raised wooden panels of the old walls. Floor to ceiling windows comprised one long wall and presented a glorious view of the sprawling campus they had not yet seen. Beyond the university were rugged mountains whose tops disappeared in a shroud of mist.

There in the room the couple watched as Mr. Christian pulled a small key from his vest pocket and unlocked a tall antique cabinet. From within the cabinet he removed a glistening bird's eye maple box and placed it carefully on the long carved dining room table. Brilliant sunlight bathed the box from the expansive windows.

"Come closer," Christian said as he opened the box. "I have something for each of you."

The interior of the box was a deep blue velvet which perfectly complimented the two silver objects it held. Christian reached inside and gently picked up a highly carved small silver flask.

"So, this is the liquor cabinet, huh? Are we going to toast our arrival?" Crealand asked playfully.

"No, Crealand," the old man smiled. "This is much more serious." He handed the flask to Gel and she let her hand test its weight in the air.

"This is heavy! It must be St. Alden silver. Am I right?"

"Yes you are, dear. It has to be St. Alden silver as that is the only material that can contain our sacred water and allow it to hold its special qualities."

"Ahhh..., which explains why it is so difficult to study."

"Correct again, young lady." As he spoke, Christian took Gel's hands and pressed them firmly around the silver flask. "Gel, you are a very special person. We have known this for some time. This flask contains water from the mouth of St. Alden's spring. You must always carry it with you. Do you understand?"

Christian's hands were squeezing her own to the point of hurting. "Why, yes. Yes, I will."

"Thank you, dear. Thank you very much." Now the old hands relaxed and patted hers gently. "Please, please do. It is very important."

Gel looked at Crealand, raised her eyebrows, and shrugged her shoulders as Mr. Christian turned back to the box. Both of his hands disappeared for a moment then emerged cradling a sparkling ten inch silver dagger. "Crealand, this is for you. As I asked Gel, please keep it with you at all times. All times."

Christian pressed the heavy knife into his grandson's hands and held it there. Crealand looked at his grandfather and was surprised to find the old man's eyes closed as if he were praying. Crealand sought out Gel for help. She gave him a reassuring look which seemed lovelier to him than anything he had ever seen. Christian opened his eyes and returned to the box. He closed it and placed it back in the cabinet which he locked.

"Gramps, this business about the wolves, isn't that from centuries and centuries ago? I mean, I've heard the story before, but thought the silver and the staying in after dark was like a tradition or something at St. Alden's. Not real. Was all that before just for Chapin's benefit?"

"Unfortunately," the Guardian said as he turned his back to his guests. "Little will benefit young Chapin. He has a very long and very sordid past. St. Alden's will be pleased to see his family's provisionals come to an end."

"I know, but the rest of it. The wolves and the curfew, aren't they just folklore and tradition?"

"No, Crealand. They are not. Few things obtained without sacrifice are of any lasting value. This is especially true of St. Alden's. The sacrifices and conditions are daunting for most, but to those who are selected and those who endure, rewards will come that far exceed their dreams."

"Mr. Christian," Gel asked. "You're suggesting that the benefits outweigh the risks? But the risks seem to present rather drastic if not deadly consequences, if they are as real as you say."

"The risks are very real. Very real indeed. But for most who attend there is no danger. Providing they observe the curfew."

"Is the curfew," Crealand asked cautiously, "why my dad didn't want to come here?"

Now it was Mr. Christian's turn to be cautious. "No. He did want to come."

"Then... why didn't he?"

"He was not selected."

"But you had your provisional spot. Why didn't he use it?"

"Because I wouldn't give it to him."

Crealand was shocked. He stood still and quietly let years of his father's known resentment against his grandfather bear the fruit of understanding. Crealand turned slowly away from Gel and the old man and began walking the length of the dining room table. Gel could only wait anonymously as she witnessed a private family scab ripped off an old wound.

"That's why dad has been mad at you all these years. Because you wouldn't give him the provisional."

"Yes, I'm afraid that's true."

Crealand turned sharply back to his grandfather. "But why? Why didn't you give it to him? You just said he wanted to come, didn't you?"

"Yes I did. He wanted it very badly."

"Then why? Why didn't you give it to him?" Crealand slammed his hand and the dagger down hard on the table. "He's been hurting for thirty years because of that. You don't know what your rejection did to him. Mom's told me about all the second guessing, all the doubts. You wouldn't know. How could you? You were never around. You were always here, tucked away in your precious college!"

Crealand turned his back on his grandfather. Gel walked up behind him and put her hand on his shoulder. Crealand didn't speak at first. Instead he reached over and began caressing the dagger which still lay on the table.

"Gramps, I guess if dad got along without St. Alden's, I can too. I wouldn't feel right about taking the spot that was really meant for him." As he spoke he gently removed his hand, leaving the dagger behind. He turned and looked at his shaken grandfather through damp eyes. "I never knew what it was – what had happened between you two. Now I know. What I guess I'll never know is why – why you'd do that to him. After thirty years, maybe it doesn't matter. I suppose it's between the two of you, but I don't want to profit from my father's pain. I'll be headed home tomorrow. I'll tell Mom and Dad you looked well. Goodbye, Gramps."

Crealand walked out of the house and got in his car. Gel started to follow him out, but Christian stopped her. "Gel, give him some time." The old gentleman picked up the dagger and handed it to her. "Here. You make certain he takes this. Please?"

At that, Chapin walked into the room. "What's going on?"

"Nothing," Gel said. "We'd better get over to the registrar's office. C'mon. Crealand's in the car."

Mr. Christian walked them to the door. "Gel, try to get Crealand to stay. Stop by tomorrow for dinner if you can."

"Dinner?" Chapin pushed his way in. "Sounds great. Count me in."

"Ah, yes. Chapin. You too will be expected," Christian said with hesitation.

"Okay, Mr. Christian," Gel said. "I'll talk to him. Have a good evening. Goodbye for now."

The short drive to the registrar's office was accomplished in silence, except for the repetitive babbling of Chapin. Gel registered, as did Chapin, for the moment at least, while Crealand waited outside. Chapin peppered Gel with questions as they waited in lines with other new students whose dress reflected cultures from the world over. All she offered was a temporary problem with Crealand's provisional appointment. Afterwards, Crealand drove them and their belongings to the main dorm, where all first year students resided. They carried each other's luggage to the simple rooms while Crealand's things remained in the car. He said he would find a hotel for the night though Gel, and Chapin reluctantly, eventually convinced him to spend the night in Chapin's dorm. Crealand relented, but would have preferred to spend the night with Gel for her conversation and comfort. He was leaving, that much he knew, but thought he could at least try to get to know this remarkable girl before he passed the simple university sign on his way out.

After they were settled, Chapin cruised the lounges and the bookstore for co-eds while Gel and Crealand walked the grounds of St. Alden's. Not many steps had passed before Gel took his hand. There was anger and shocking disappointment on Crealand's face, but in his hand, Gel felt the same distinct strength she had felt in Mr. Christian's earlier in the day.

"Crealand," she said as they walked, "I rather obviously don't know all that existed between your father and your grandfather and quite simply neither do you. What is clear though is that your grandfather loves you very much and for some reason, perhaps known only to him, he saved the provisional for you."

"That is painfully obvious."

"All the way here we took turns jabbing at Chapin for not making full use of the opportunity he's been given and now here you are, ready to throw yours away."

"But it's not mine. This chance should have been my father's. He wanted it. And as a result of not getting it, he has punished himself his entire life. Never good enough. Didn't quite make the grade. Always coming up a little short. You can't possibly understand what it's like to watch your father eat himself up from the inside. And made all the worse by the fact that his own father – his own father – could have prevented it."

"But I do understand, at least in part. My father never attended St. Alden's. In fact he never attended college at all. Nor did my mother. Our home was plain and our needs restricted to the very basics. I watched my father labor his entire life striving for something better for his family. And he never quite obtained it. I came along pretty late in their lives. They thought I was a blessing and maybe so. They put everything they had in getting me through prep schools. And now I have no intention of letting them down."

"Yes," Crealand said as he stopped walking, "but I'm here because my father was not. I've stolen his place, a part of what he could have been."

"All right then. But you don't suppose my father went without to put me here?"

"Sure."

"And in a different way yours did as well." Gel took Crealand's face in her hands. "I know it's not the same, but the end result is. You have an opportunity here, given you by your father – suffered by your father. An opportunity he never had has been afforded you at his expense. So you must take full advantage of it for his sake if not your own."

"Those are just words, Gel. His pain was... is real. I've seen it."

Gel leaned close and kissed him. "That was not a word. Please stay. Stay here with me."

Crealand kissed her to make certain he hadn't dreamed it. Then the two embraced and felt Crealand's frustration flow from him. In its stead, they could sense another emotion, much stronger than those that fled. With each touch, each kiss, and gentle caress, a bond took hold, rooted, and flowered. The rest of that afternoon they cultivated their new relationship surrounded by the wonders of St. Alden's. They exchanged stories from their past and dreams for the future. Sunset found them safe behind the silver of Gel's dorm and safer still in each other's arms. Across the campus, Christian endured no such luxury.

The fog over St. Alden's was lighter than it had been on previous nights. Christian stood with one foot perched on the last step of St. Alden House, ready to make good a hasty retreat. Behind him, the silver bar in the threshold glowed brightly in the shadows. Meanwhile, a loose semi-circle took shape in front of him in the form of a dozen monstrous wolves. Their eyes were yellow, deeply set, and focused on the Guardian. Their heads were low to the ground as they trotted back and forth, weaving in and out of each other as they tried to get into position away from the silver broadsword. Occasionally, one would bound toward Christian with ears laid back only to be thwarted by the presence of the saber. Frustrated, the wolves nipped at each other then watched as yet another braved the sword with bared fangs.

Christian was sweating. The broadsword was heavy in his hands tonight. For years he had battled the hounds when needed and had always been triumphant. Now his body and his confidence were failing him. From the mist, deep behind the prowling wolves, a knight clad in black leather sat on an ebony stallion and saw Christian's decay as well.

"Templar!" the dark knight roared and his deep voice echoed off St. Alden House. "Age is your foe, not my wolves. It is time that has sealed your doom, not I. You are an old man. You have been a fine adversary all these many years, but your mortality has betrayed you. Bow to my sword and join me. Be master over the world! Your decision will be made for you soon enough. The time has come!"

"Never!" Christian screamed as the silver slashed at the demons. "As long as one remains!"

The knight bellowed in anger. "Then die in the jaws of my wolves. He is weak. Kill him!"

Several demons yelped and plunged at the old man at once, but Christian could still wield the sword with precision. It raked across the heads of two of the wolves and severed the foreleg of a third. The wolves cried and rolled on the ground in pain as their wounds smoldered like dying fires. Others retreated, well versed in the agony the silver sword could cause. As they regrouped, the knight urged them forward.

"He is an old man, my friends! Take him. Take him now!"

Again the wolves charged. Christian reached out and grabbed the severed paw from its pool of blood on the flagstone. As his hand closed around it, the vise like grip of an enormous black wolf's jaws clamped down on his forearm. He screamed in pain, but practiced habit brought the sword around and down into the head of the beast. Yet another wolf hurled itself from some distance at the injured Guardian. Christian ducked and the flying wolf careened into its comrades sending several skidding on the stone. As the wolves scrambled to their feet, Christian shook the heavy dead animal from his torn arm and, still clutching the dismembered limb of the first wolf, dove across the threshold of St. Alden House and slammed the heavy oak door.

On the outside, the wolves had already turned on the injured of the pack. The dead black wolf was ripped apart and devoured in less than a minute. The wounded wolves ran in all directions, pursued by others. A single grey animal returned to where the severed paw had been and lapped up the pool of blood. After a few minutes the wolves quieted and collected around the horse and rider. The knight dismounted into the pack and knelt among them. He petted the wolves and stroked their heads as he spoke softly. "Be patient, children. Soon. Very soon." As the knight continued to soothe his wolves, a thick fog began engulfing them. Slowly the mysterious vapor continued to rise until the knight and his mount were covered. Then a harsh swirling wind swept across the commons and temporarily scattered the fog. The dark knight and his creatures were gone.

Inside St. Alden House, Christian had stumbled to the basement. In its center was a large stone altar from which a trickle of water flowed. The water collected in a trough three feet wide and a foot deep. The trough was nearly fifteen feet long and ran to a far wall where a siphoning pipe brought the water up to the reflecting pool outside.

The old Guardian leaned heavily against the trough and gripped its side with its free hand. He tossed the wolf's paw down on a bench that ran alongside the trough as he plunged his ravaged arm into the water. The water began to bubble pink with his blood and hiss as Christian bit his lower lip in pain. Sweat continued to gather on his forehead and stream down his worn face into his eyes.

After several moments the bubbling subsided. Christian relaxed and brought his arm up out of the water. The wound was gone, entirely healed. The old man sat down on the bench and breathed a deep sigh as he flexed his fingers, testing the rejuvenated arm. After a rest Christian picked up the severed limb of the wolf and held it over the water. He began roughly massaging the paw until blood started to drip from the neat cut. As each droplet of the wolf's blood hit the water, a rapid hiss and spurt of steam flashed up. Christian continued coaxing blood from the limb until no more fell. Then he reached into the water and pulled out a small handful of solid silver nuggets, commensurate with the number of drops of blood that had fallen from the paw.

Christian weighed the silver in his hand then looked at the grey paw and its forbidding nails. He dropped the bloodless limb into the trough, but there was no splash. Instead, the water erupted into bedlam as bubbles and steam rose with equal fury. As with his arm, the turmoil quickly vanished. And as he had done moments before with the silver nuggets, Christian reached into the water and pulled out a long splinter of St. Alden silver.

Christian turned the piece in his hand and eyed its brilliance. "So little. So little when the need is so great." He lowered his head until it rested on the side of the trough as he took a deep breath. He was very tired. The silver that had been the wolf's paw slipped from his wet fingers noiselessly back into the tank. Christian slumped onto the bench and slept. At the other end of the university complex, Crealand was sleeping in his lover's arms. Dawn would find both men exhausted.

The morning's sunrise and the hours thereafter found Christian and the three newest arrivals at St. Alden's still in bed. The old man was weak and though his arm appeared whole, he knew the deeper tissues were still healing. Crealand and Gel dallied in her bed. Chapin too slept late, as was his custom.

It was noon before all had begun earnest preparations for the remainder of the day. Christian labored meticulously for his anticipated dinner guests. Despite the extra hours of sleep he was still weary. He paused to consider his state, realizing that the water had been imperfect for the first time. To reassure himself, he went to the basement to check the water's flow. It trickled as always and it occurred to him that perhaps the shortcoming was his own.

Gel accompanied Crealand back to the registrar's office and teased him constantly as he signed up a day late. By the time the pair had carried Crealand's things to his new room, it was nearly time to set out for St. Alden House and dinner. Though the afternoon was quickly waning, the new lovers still found reasons to touch and kiss between each box moved. When they finally set the last one aside, Gel checked her watch with a start.

"Crealand! I'd better go get changed. You get ready, then stop by and collect me. How's that sound?"

"Fine, except for the you going part."

She kissed him. "We'll come straight home after dinner."

Crealand looked around his small room. "This is home?"

"No. This is the attic. Home is my room. Downstairs." And she kissed him again.

When their lips parted Crealand breathed a comical sigh. "Home is good. I like home."

"I thought you would. Now get ready." Gel moved to the door and scooped up her purse. Its unusual weight served as a reminder and she returned to Crealand as she fumbled through the bag. Crealand slipped his arms around her waist.

"Home so soon? Oh, sorry. I forgot we're in the attic."

Gel pulled the silver dagger from her purse. Crealand backed away in mock terror. "But Gel, I don't even know the girl! I swear!"

"Funny. Ha ha. Here. Take this. Your grandfather said you should always carry it with you."

Crealand began unnecessarily adjusting some of the boxes. "My grandfather is a superstitious old man."

"Crealand, I think not. At least not entirely. There is something about St. Alden's."

"Oh, no. Not another mystic in the family."

"You saw the water yesterday. How do you explain that?"

"I–"

"You can't. So don't bother trying."

"Yes, dear."

"I'm serious, Crea. Now here. Keep this like he said. Please?"

The humor was off Crealand's face and absent in his voice. "Gel, I'm not carrying a knife with me for the rest of my life. I won't do it. Please don't ask me to."

Gel dropped the dagger back into her purse. "All right." She paused as she headed out the door. "I'll carry it for you."

The door shut behind her and Crealand found himself staring after it. As quickly as it had shut, it reopened just enough for Gel to poke her head through. "When you're finished here in the attic, are you still coming down to the living quarters?"

Crealand walked boyishly toward the door, his arms in an exaggerated swing. "I dunno. Am I gonna get yelled at again?"

"Not if you're a good boy."

Crealand kissed her nose. "I'll be a very good boy. See ya soon." He palmed her face, gently pushed her into the hall, and closed the door. A comfortable coziness neither had known before settled over each of them now on separate sides of the door. Unseen but shared smiles accompanied them as they dressed for dinner. Crealand buffed the tops of his black shoes on his calves as he darted out the door. One floor down, Gel brushed at her black skirt as she wiggled into her shoes. A half hour later they were standing at Christian's dining room table.

"I'm pleased you've come, Crealand."

"I still have questions, but I apologize for getting angry. I'm sorry. I suppose this is between you and Dad, but I feel guilty for taking what should have been his. I'm not sure how to get over that."

"So you are staying?"

"I am, but I'm not comfortable with it yet and I may never be. This was Dad's opportunity. It feels wrong to take what should have been his."

"You have no reason, Crealand."

"I can't help it. I've been afforded this wonderful opportunity at my father's expense."

"It was my decision not his."

"Can you tell me why?"

"Perhaps I can. Might it wait until after dinner? Young Chapin will be along momentarily."

As though cued, the front door to St. Alden House opened minus a knock. "Hey! What's for supper?" Chapin hollered from the foyer as he stared down again at the silver bar in the threshold. He had arrived on a bicycle he had somehow procured and was fresh from spending the afternoon scooting over the college, annoying any young woman he happened upon.

"In here, Chapin!" Gel called.

As Chapin entered he bullishly moved around the elegant table. "I'm not too late, am I?"

"Not at all. I will check on dinner now that we're all present."

"What did you whip up for us, Grandpa?"

The Guardian looked drawn, but was unnerved by his boisterous guest and answered politely. "Lamb, young Chapin. We will be dining on lamb this evening."

"Ah, yes indeed. The proverbial sacrificial lamb. Straight off the altars of St. Alden."

"Chapin!" Gel scolded.

"What's the matter? You wake up on the wrong side of somebody's bed this morning, or should I say, afternoon?" Chapin briefly covered his mouth with his hand. "Oops! Did I let the cat out of the bag? Sorry."

Mr. Christian ignored the intended revelation, stepped through a swinging door into the kitchen and returned just as quickly carrying a silver tray on which a rack of lamb sizzled.

Chapin tried to renew his comical attack on the old man. "Say, Christian, isn't it true that back in the olden days, the stuff the people had slaved over and put on some dumb altar, was just scarfed up by the priests?"

Christian picked up a brilliant silver knife and motioned with it for everyone to be seated. Then he expertly began carving the lamb. "While it is true that the high priests of ancient times did consume food from the altars, if an uncleansed soul were to eat any of the blessed meat, he would die a most excruciating death." Christian laid a slice of lamb over the blade of the silver knife and moved it in front of Chapin as he said with a wry smile. "Care for some lamb from St. Alden's?"

Chapin's face blanched three shades of pale. He swallowed hard as sweat broke on his forehead. "Ahh... Yea, sure..."

The host gently laid the meat on Chapin's plate. "Enjoy."

Dinner was completed over polite conversation about the university's curriculum, its history, grounds, and its architecture.

After dessert Mr. Christian asked his grandson to help him clear the dishes to the kitchen. Gel offered to assist but realized Mr. Christian wanted some time with Crealand so she settled back to entertain Chapin as best she could. Once out of the dining room, the Guardian whispered to his grandson to come with him to the basement. Crealand looked from the basement door to the dining room where Gel waited with Chapin. "She'll be fine," Mr. Christian said. "I want you to see something. We'll just be a minute."

Crealand followed his grandfather to the basement and up to the stone altar. He soaked in the surreal sights and sounds created by the water and the trough, itself a small reflecting pool on which an image of the stone work around it floated. Mr. Christian sat down on the bench as Crealand let his hand run through the waters as he walked along the trough and listened to the whisper of the water mix with his grandfather's words.

"Crealand, I wish to apologize for how I've treated your father."

"Aren't you telling the wrong person?"

"Of course you're correct. I want you to know that I have told the right person – I've told him many times."

"Can I ask why? Why wasn't he given this chance?"

The only sound was the trickling of the water from the spring. As it flowed into the collecting trough it made a sound less like falling water and more like the ringing of a bell. It would have been mesmerizing had the pair of men not been so intensely focused on both the past and the future.

"Your father was and remains a wonderful son. And it's not that he's done something to upset me and given me cause to hold the provisional back from him."

"Then what? I'm at such a loss it hurts."

"As with most things with such import attached there are... there are layers of the decision making process. Yes. Yes, it's true. I could have provided your father the provisional appointment and he would have profited from it."

"Wouldn't you have wanted that for him? I mean, isn't that the goal of parents?"

"And grandparents."

"Okay. But why wait? How'd you know I'd even come along? And it still feels like all this is at Dad's expense."

"I understand. Listen closely." The tenor of the twinkling spring softened and the room was still. "We are all set by God's own hand on the scales of life to be measured. What we are weighed against is God's mystery. It is different for each of us according to His divine plan. Our gifts and talents, our skills and propensities, are all a part of us. You must understand that God often gives to men in proportion to His needs, not necessarily ours. Then, as His plan unfolds for our life and those His destiny compels to cross our path, the endowments manifest themselves and we find we have the abilities to meet the challenges God has put before us. If we choose.

"Of course there is prayer and supplication. God has said He will grant us the desires of our hearts and He will, but there is more to life than our own wants. We are players on the grandest stage. We each have a part to play that influences another person or several, who in their turn, touch still others. We become a ripple in the water – an instrument in God's hands. Through man, God uses the gifts He has bestowed on us to do the thing that must be done to promote good and keep evil at bay."

There was quiet as the old Guardian's words settled around Crealand. After a few moments the gentle flowing sound of the spring returned.

"I follow everything you've said, Gramps, and I agree one hundred percent. Is this why Dad was passed over? Because the scales didn't balance? I don't know how he could be found to be lacking anything. He's such a good man."

"That is the mystery again, son. The endowment is ample for each person. Your father has everything he needs to fulfill God's plan for his life. But you, you have other gifts as your plan is different. You have the gifts necessary for your journey and your journey includes time here at St. Alden's."

"How do you know?"

"The same way you understood everything I said. It is a sense, an understanding. Some would call it a gift. Others a curse. You have it. Your father did not."

Crealand looked at the hand laid stone floor of St. Alden House. "Why me? And why not Dad?"

"Another of God's mysteries."

"And you... Somehow you knew this – that St. Alden's was not the plan for Dad?"

"Yes."

"But it is the plan for me?

"Yes."

"Whoa. Not quite what I expected on my first day."

"I know. It's a great deal to absorb. And it is just the beginning."

Crealand allowed himself a forced laugh. "No pressure," he smiled.

Mr. Christian returned the smile, but it was a veil over an anxiousness he did not hide well. "There is a great deal of effort in being the Guardian of St. Alden's. It is much for a man my age. There is no doubt that I am growing old beyond my usefulness to the university."

"Nonsense, they'll never fire you. You're an institution here as much as this water." Crealand scooped up a handful of water to punctuate his remark. The water fell back to the trough and sent tiny ripples ricocheting around the tank. Beneath the surface of the water, a bright shimmer caught Crealand's eye. As his grandfather spoke, Crealand reached into the water and picked up the piece of St. Alden silver that had once been a wolf's paw.

"Crealand, it's not about being terminated, not by the university at least. It's more akin to—"

"Excuse me, Gramps, but this silver was in the water. What a remarkable piece. Is it yours?"

Christian hardly took notice. "It is God's."

"It's beautiful, but how did it get here?"

"There are many mysteries that surround St. Alden's. For you to understand them all we must spend a great deal of time together. There are things only I can teach you. Things you must learn to master."

Crealand walked to his grandfather's side as he continued to examine the silver. "We'll have time. I'm enrolled. I'm staying. I don't know God's plan, but I trust Him."

"That's marvelous, son," Mr. Christian said as he slowly took the silver from Crealand's hand. "This silver... Its properties are unique that much is true, but its origins are even stranger." He held the piece up to Crealand. "This silver, St. Alden's silver comes from—"

"Hey! What the hell are you guys doing down there?" Chapin yelled from the top of the basement steps. "Hey, Crea? I wouldn't leave my girl alone with someone as dynamic and handsome as me if I were you."

"That young man is a nuisance," Christian said as his eyebrows tightened.

"Hey, Pops!" Chapin continued. "I've got a date so I'm gonna bounce. Thanks for the lamp chops. I haven't keeled over yet so I must be righteous."

Christian suddenly rose to his feet, the angry look replaced by a look of concern. He grabbed Crealand's arm. "He mustn't go! The sun will be setting shortly."

"Oh, Gramps. C'mon. It's just us now. We don't need the ghost stories and what not."

"No, Crealand! He cannot go out at this hour!" Christian broke from Crealand and flew up the stairs. Crealand hesitated and lingered over the water, shaking his head at his grandfather's actions as his hand dipped into the cool soft flow.

Upstairs, Chapin had already left the house. Gel was standing in the open doorway, watching the sun set behind the university's clock. As she looked on, Chapin jumped on the bicycle and pedaled up the promenade. Grey was all around him – the stones beneath his wheels, the buildings beyond, and strangely, the quickly gathering darkness. Christian came up behind Gel and roughly pushed her aside in order to see onto the commons. "Look!" he cried. "The tower spire. Its shadow is on the gazebo bell. CHAPIN! COME BACK!"

Christian shoved Gel inside. He spun and tossed aside an antique coat tree sending Gel's purse and his own bright red blazer sliding across the stone floor. There was a narrow door in the vestibule behind the coat tree Gel had not noticed before. Christian snatched the door of the hidden compartment open and withdrew the silver broadsword.

Gel's eyes widened. "Mr. Christian, what are you doing?"

"I have to go after Chapin!" The old man moved quickly as he stepped out of St. Alden House. "Gel, close this door and do not open it for any reason. Do you understand?"

"But what's going on?"

"Close the door and do not open it. Do you understand?"

"Yes! But, I–"

"And do not let Crealand come out, no matter what he may hear!" With that, Christian slammed the door and began running up the promenade.

Immediately disregarding her orders, Gel opened the door. The campus had grown dark so suddenly it took her a moment to adjust. She saw Mr. Christian, blade in hand, vanish into a peculiar mist that was rolling off the commons.

Crealand came up behind her and touched her arm. She jumped. "Look!" Gel pointed into the wisps of vapor that continued to swirl where Christian had entered it. "And see how quickly it's gotten dark. What is this?"

Crealand took notice of the things she indicated, but something stranger had caught his eye. He tapped Gel's arm a second time and pointed to the threshold beneath their feet. "Gel, look down." The silver bar in the stone casing was glowing.

Further up the wide stone sidewalk, Chapin was pedaling rapidly. He too was surprised at how quickly the light had vanished. As he rode he heard tapping noises in the fog that had mysteriously blanketed the college grounds. He began asking his legs for more, standing on the bike to pump harder as the rhythmic bumping over the slightly raised flagstone promenade quickened beneath the bike's tires. The clicking noise was all around him now in the mist. No matter how fast he pedaled, the noise kept stride. Then the mist to his left parted and a wolf appeared, not looking at him, but loping easily alongside through the nearly complete darkness.

Chapin jumped and almost sent the bike into a spin. His eyes were wide and jumping from the wolf to the mist and the sidewalk ahead. His breath and heart beat were fast and furious. The confirmation of the old man's stories were worse than a nightmare. The beast was huge. Its eyes were yellow-grey. The fur was jet black and long, and even in the poor light it looked coarse and hard, not like a dog's. The wolf was also not panting as it ran. The clicking of its nails on the stone was the only sound.

Chapin worked the pedals with such ferocity that his legs began to scream with pain. Sweat flooded his eyes. He wiped them on his damp shoulders thinking, hoping the things they showed him were only in his imagination. When he dared another glance at the wolf, he learned the truth. It was real and now, there were two. On his right others appeared in the haze, trotting gracefully alongside.

A growing distance behind Chapin, the Guardian had slowed to a jog. He wanted to sprint, but his aging legs told him no. After a few more steps he bent over on his knees, gasping for air. The broadsword rested its razor point on the ground. Night and mist surrounded the old warrior. He realized there was nothing he could do. In a moment, Chapin's screams confirmed what Christian had known from the moment he left St. Alden House. Far ahead of him he could see signs as the mist rose and fell under the thrashing attack. There was nothing left to be done. He turned and began running back for the safety of his home.

Gel and Crealand were still in the alcove of St. Alden House. They had heard Chapin's screams, but were frozen, partially in disbelief, partially in their own terror. The sight of Christian staggering through the mist brought them back to themselves.

"Gramps!" Crealand yelled as he jumped onto the flagstone to the tired and weakened old man. He flung his grandfather's free arm around his own shoulder and began making for the house.

"No, Crealand," the Guardian said with great effort. "Go. Save yourself. You are too important."

Crealand began to answer when a savage blow from a wolf's hurtling body knocked the words down his throat. The two men and the demon crashed to the stone. Crealand was jolted from his grandfather and landed several feet away while the sword had been driven from the Guardian's hand and lay near the steps to the house. The wolf recovered first and pounced on Christian's back. Powerless to stop him, Christian could only arch his neck and scream as the wolf's teeth ripped deep again and again into his back.

Crealand righted himself and saw the horror. Another wolf, and still another, shot from the mist and attacked their long time enemy. A devilish white monster crushed Christian's lower leg in its jaws and began pulling the old man into the mist.

Gel was still on the threshold. She saw the sword at the base of the steps at the same time Crealand did. She took two quick steps toward it, but snarling blood soaked fangs threatened her from just beyond. Gel trembled as her eyes locked with the wolf's. The demon growled low and crouched to pounce. Gel backed up to the door as the huge wolf came closer. It began hovering around the quiet sword as behind him, others tore chunks of flesh from Christian.

"Gel! Close the door!" Crealand screamed, but his attempt to save his lover only reminded the wolves of his presence. As one, several of the hellish dogs turned in his direction.

"Crealand, run!" Gel hollered above the sounds of growls and the ongoing attack on Christian. Crealand saw it was pointless to run. His eyes darted from the closing wolves to his grandfather's sword. Gel saw his eyes on the sword and moved again toward it. As before, snapping jaws told her no. She backed up yet again to the door and noticed the silver bar in the threshold. It was not glowing as brightly. As Gel stared the silver began to flicker and fade.

The sight of the silver caused her to recall the dagger and she leaped back into the vestibule. Gel's purse was on the floor tangled around the coat tree and Christian's red blazer. She was crying and trembling as she fumbled with her bag. In a rage she pulled the knife and turned back into the open doorway.

"Crealand! Catch!" Gel held up the knife so her lover could see it then let it fly. The brilliant blade hit the stone walkway and sparked as it tumbled and slid to within inches of Crealand's feet. He grabbed it and slashed at the nearest wolf all in one motion. The dagger caught the advancing monster across the nose. The wolf leaped and somersaulted as it clawed its own face. Smoke spun crazily from the injured animal's face as it cried in agony. The other wolves froze, captivated for a moment by the antics of their brother. Crealand saw the lapse and bolted through them for the steps of St. Alden House. He lashed out at two more of the wolves, lancing their sides with the dagger as he ran by. The newly injured dogs howled and rolled as if their fur had been set ablaze.

Crealand reached the stairs and stood over the heavy broadsword. He tossed the dagger to Gel and grabbed the handle of the bigger weapon.

"Crealand! Look!"

Crealand looked up at Gel who was pointing to the flickering silver bar in the threshold at her feet. "Something's gone wrong!"

Crealand's attention moved quickly from the threshold to his grandfather. The single white wolf was still pulling the badly injured old man into the mist. Crealand launched himself at the creature and brought the blade down hard on the wolf's head. The animal slumped to the ground without a sound. Crealand grabbed his grandfather's arm and began dragging him toward the house. The wolves were leery of the sword, but closed in for another attack. As Crealand reached the stairs, Gel ran down and began to help Christian to his feet. Behind them, a wolf, with head low to the ground, rushed in.

"Crealand!"

The sword spun with the young man and ran its point deep through the wolf's throat. Blood spewed from its mouth as it stumbled forward and collapsed on the steps of the old house.

The other wolves backed off slightly as Crealand and Gel clamored over the dead wolf with Christian.

"The wolf," Christian mumbled as blood dripped from his mouth. "Get the dead wolf."

"Gel, just get him inside!"

"No. Please, son. We need the wolf. Please... We must get the body."

They all moved inside the house and Christian pleaded again. "Please, Crealand. Get the wolf... Please. The sword will protect you."

Gel already slammed the door and as Crealand stepped toward it she leaped up against it. "No! Are you crazy?!"

Christian spoke from the floor. "Gel, go with him... You are his Guardian... We must have the wolf. Hurry, before they seize it..."

Hesitantly, Crealand opened the door. Gel moved with him as they stepped down to the dead animal. Crealand grabbed the wolf by a leg as he waved the sword back and forth out over its body as Gel wielded the silver dagger. The other wolves prowled and sniffed the ground where Christian had fallen. Crealand muscled the heavy monster up the stairs where Gel grimaced but grabbed fistfuls of fur along with the knife and yanked the carcass into the house. Gel slammed the door, locked it, and leaned heavily against it. Once inside, the wolf lay alongside Christian on the stone floor.

"The basement," the old Guardian mumbled. "Get me to the basement."

Crealand laid the sword on the floor and picked his grandfather up. Gel slipped the dagger in her waist and followed as Crealand maneuvered the stairs into the lower region of the house. Once there, Christian spoke again, though increasingly weaker from the blood trail he had left through the house.

"Lay me in the water."

Gel looked around the basement. "Where?"

"In the water...," Christian said as he feebly pointed to the trough.

Crealand did as the old man asked. Instantly, the water began to send pink bubbles up from Christian's ghastly wounds.

"What's happening?" Crealand said as he held his grandfather's head.

"Healing. The waters... They renew those of us who have been chosen."

"Chosen?" Crealand asked as he watched the water bubbling with blood and tissue. "Chosen for what?"

"To be the Guardian of St. Alden's."

Crealand's fear and frustration came to the surface. "Guardian of what? What is all this? It's like some kind of nightmare!"

Christian's voice was calm and a little stronger. "Guardian of the water. And St. Alden's silver. Guardian of the future and the Good."

"I don't get it! We have to get to the car. Gramps, do you have a gun? A pistol, shotgun – something!"

"No. And it would do no good."

"A shotgun would stop those wolves better than this letter opener," Crealand said as he snapped up the dagger from the waistband of Gel's skirt.

"Crealand, bring down the wolf's body. I can show you better than I can explain."

Gel and Crealand exchanged concerned glances as Gel took Christian's head in her hands. Crealand shoved the dagger in his waistband at the small of his back and vaulted up the stairs and returned dragging the dead animal.

Christian propped himself up in the water, clenching the side of the trough. "Put the beast in the water."

Again Gel and Crealand cast suspicious looks at one another.

"Gel, dear. Help him. Then you will see."

The confused couple took hold of the wolf and carried it further across the room. They struggled to lift it over the side of the trough then dropped the carcass into the water. Steam erupted in a giant plume. The water sprayed and splashed over the sides as the trough around the wolf shook and boiled like a huge churning cauldron. After less than a minute it began to settle. Christian waved his hand for the pair to look into the water. Where the wolf's body had been sat a radiant mass of St. Alden's silver almost a foot thick. Gel reached into the water and touched the silver while Crealand returned to his grandfather.

"I don't understand any of this. I said I knew what you were talking about and I thought I did, but not this. Not this..."

"St. Alden's," the Guardian began, "St. Alden's selects students and teachers that are the purest of heart. Little else matters. Here, the Good element that is in the world comes together. Here it is honed, nourished, and strengthened. Then the Good returns to a thousand parts of the world to work and strive to make it better, safer."

The old man let his words sink in again. Gel heard them and drew up close beside Crealand.

"But the wolves," Crealand asked. "What about the wolves? They don't seem real."

Christian began to slip back into the water. Crealand caught him and once again held the old man in his arms. "If there were no Good in the world," the Guardian said, "who would profit the most?"

Crealand just shook his head.

"The darkness," Gel answered for them.

Christian closed his eyes and shook his head. "Yes. The compliment of Good is Evil. If Good was eliminated or reduced in any way, Evil would rise up everywhere to fill the void. And as we are chosen to protect St. Alden's, there are those sworn to destroy it. As the water is supplied to us to meet our needs and protect us, so the wolves come at the behest of the demons who wish to stop it and to stop us."

Gel spoke slowly. "All this – the wolves, the silver, the university – is about the water?"

"No, Gel. It is about the Good. If Evil can destroy the Guardian, they can access the water and stop its flow. With no water, there would be no St. Alden silver and soon, no university. The silver gives us the ability to bring people together who otherwise could not come and protect them when they are here. Once here they learn the secrets of St. Alden's and the value and power of the Good."

Crealand was overwhelmed. "Gramps. The wolves. The silver." He looked toward the silver at the far end of the tank that had been a vicious monster minutes before. "Is that the only way?"

"Yes, son. The blood and bones of our enemies. Obtained in battle. It is our legacy from the first Guardian."

The old man sighed and his breathing became shallow. He clasped Crealand's hand in the water. "Crealand, your father could not have done what you are being asked to do. He is a fine man, but does not possess the qualities of the Knights. He would have died and all the good in the world with him."

"But I'm no knight. I'm not a fighter! I was scared to death out there!"

"Of course you were, but it is in you. I have always known."

"I didn't ask for this. We have to get out of here!"

Christian grabbed his grandson's shoulder. "You must. You must! Crealand, there is much more at stake here than just you. You will come to see it."

"No, this can't be real. It's like a bad dream."

"Gel, you must help him. Show him."

Gel's face was drawn, but she nodded yes.

"Crealand," Christian said as he dipped his hand in the water around him and rubbed it on his face. "There is so much you need to learn and I won't be here for you." Christian shot a look upstairs. "They will be coming tonight. Many of them, and their master. He will sense my death. Our silver talisman will become weak. The demons will see this and will be made strong and brave by it. They will come to stop the water. You must show them that a new Guardian exists before they are loosed on St. Alden's."

"No, Gramps! No. Stay awake. We're getting out of here."

Christian closed his eyes. Gel started to gently splash water on his face. His eyes opened as though they pained him. "No, Gel. It is too late and I am too old." Outside the house, the wolves began to howl menacingly. "Go now, my children. God be with you." Christian's eyes closed again as he went limp in Crealand's arms.

The water was bloody. Crealand touched his grandfather's face with the water, but the old Guardian was gone. The new Guardian released his grip and Christian's body slipped completely into the water. He floated just beneath the surface as the wolves began howling in a celebration chorus around St. Alden House.

"Crea? Crealand?" Gel said gently as she touched his arm. "C'mon, we've got to get away from here."

"Away? Where? How? How do we get by those things? And what happens if we do? Do you think anyone will believe us?"

"There are others here. Students and teachers. They must know. And we could bring people back and show them the water."

"If what my grandfather said is true, there won't be anyone left alive here by tomorrow. Or anymore water."

"I don't care. I'm afraid. We need to get out."

He took her in his arms and held her. His hands alternated from briskly rubbing her back as though to erase the tension and fear to stroking her shoulders and face in reassurance.

"All right," he said. "We hold up behind the silver thresholds and mantles in the window ledges. We get through until sunrise, then we collect everyone we can find and we caravan out of this place. We'll get help – lots of it – and come back before nightfall tomorrow. Maybe we can build a concrete bunker over this spring so nothing can get at it. We'll seal off access to it. Then we'll move the university to some place safe so its work can continue."

"But without the silver how can it be moved and how can it operate?"

"Tuition. Grants. I don't know. Other colleges manage. One as unique as St. Alden's shouldn't have any trouble. God, it's saving the world! Everyone will want to help."

The howling outside seemed louder and closer.

Gel shook in his arms. "Crea?" She was tearing up and wiping roughly at her cheeks. "It won't work."

"What?"

"This place. This house. They must have thought or even tried to protect it in another way or move it somewhere safe as you said. If it was possible, they would have already done it – maybe even hundreds of years ago. It's here because this spring is here. And it's here because the wolves are here. And the silver. It's all related."

Crealand thought and it was Gel's turn to rub ideas and encouragement into his shoulders and mind.

"You're right, Gel. We can't just run. But we can't fight them off either. He said they'd come tonight – stronger because of his death. How do we stop them and protect this place? And protect ourselves?"

"I don't know, but we have to try something."

"We need a place to think and sort this out. There has to be a way."

"I understand very little of it, but I believe every word your grandfather said." Gel was staring at the water that was trickling into the trough. Outside, the roar of the wolves was getting even louder. Sudden thuds brought confused looks until the two realized at the same time that the wolves were hurling themselves at the house. "What are we going to do, Crea?"

"I'm not sure, but we're not staying here. This is where they'll be coming first."

Crealand took Gel's hand and they ran upstairs. Gel found her purse and took the silver flask out. She also pulled the dagger from Crealand's pants and paced the floor with one in either hand to the cries of the wolves just the width of the outside walls away. Crealand picked up the sword and paced with her. Unknown to them the last light was flickering from the silver that protected the houses and the dorms as the old Guardian's body cooled in the spring that had healed his wounds so many times. Minus the strength, experience, and protection of the Guardian, the silver was losing its powerful influence over Evil. It had served as the conduit for the Guardian's petitions for the power of the Good. Without his earthly presence, the chain had been broken and the authority and protection it afforded was rapidly waning.

Crealand talked in a nervous steady stream as they walked back and forth through the lower reaches of the house until they found themselves in the dining room. "Okay. Think. We've got to get to the car. But if we run, then what? No. We've got to stay. But we need to buy some time. But how can we fight those things?"

Gel interrupted him. "Crea, listen..."

They both stood deathly quiet. In the distance they heard the sounds of breaking glass and people screaming. Crealand and Gel looked at each other and saw nothing but fear. Their minds and mouths came to the same conclusion in unison. "The dorms!"

The pair ran to one of the large floor length windows to see the horror Christian had foretold. Just as they reached the huge window, it crashed down on them, driven in by the force of two airborne wolves. The entire frame and sill careened into the room as shards of glass and teeth reached for the young Guardian. Crealand grabbed

Gel and they both rolled under the dining room table. They scrambled up on the far side just as the wolves regained their balance. The beasts snarled and curled back their lips, baring massive glistening teeth. They crept around the room as they sized up their prey. Crealand and Gel backed up away from the table. Gel still clutched the dagger and flask in her trembling hands while Crealand waved the broadsword.

With no effort one of the wolves shot up onto the table. Gel jumped in fright and unintentionally splashed water from the silver flask at the wolf. A few droplets landed on the animal's rump. Instantly a puff of smoke billowed from the creature's thick fur. The wolf spun and began to bite at its own flank and the burning water. Crealand stepped up and swung the sword at the animal's neck. The slash drew blood and knocked the wolf from the table.

Encouraged by success, Crealand attacked the second wolf. The beast jumped to escape the dropping blade, but Crealand was still able to clip its rear legs. Blood sprayed from the wounds and the animal roared in pain. Both wolves, badly injured, leaped through the gaping hole in the wall that had once been an elegant window. Crealand and Gel followed them to the breech and looked out into the night.

Wolves were running everywhere. The sounds of breaking glass and screams mixed on the commons and echoed throughout the campus. A hundred feet from them stood the dark knight. In his gloved hands he held the back of the necks of two coal black wolves. From his side hung a gleaming black broadsword. Wolves were passing near the smashed out window, but were mindful of the silver sword in Crealand's hand.

The knight yelled to Crealand. "Do you see, young Templar?" The master of the wolves released his grip on one of his pets and pointed across the reflecting pool onto the wide lawn where a young woman was being dragged down by a pair of large grey dogs. Four other animals flew at the screaming girl and tore off her limbs with single bites. Gel closed her eyes as the knight spoke again. "Soon that will be you!"

"No!" Crealand yelled back. "I am the new Guardian!"

The knight laughed as he tossed back his head and heavily patted his wolves. "Not tonight, Templar! You are as weak in your youth as the old Guardian was with age!"

"No!" Crealand cried out again. "You look!" Crealand pointed across the campus to the other buildings, houses, and dorms. The silver talismans were glowing again, though faintly.

The knight saw the returning glow and snapped his orders to the dogs. With his hands he urged the twin black monsters that stood beside him in the direction of St. Alden House. "Kill them! Kill them all, my children! Tonight the world is ours!"

Crealand realized that with the windowsill smashed, the house would be no refuge. He grabbed Gel's arm and jumped through the broken window and hit the ground running. He pushed Gel on in front of him as he slashed with the sword in every direction. "Gel! The reflecting pool! Get in the water!"

Gel ran on with Crealand just behind. They were both stabbing and slashing the air at the wolves that came within reach. Gel stumbled as she reached the pool's edge and fell headlong into the shallow water. Crealand fell over her. Their splashes hit the nearest wolves and sent them scurrying into the night with their coats on fire.

Crealand found Gel's arm and helped her to the center of the pool where they stood, watched, and waited in water a few inches over their ankles. Wolves had gathered on all sides. They sniffed the water and backed away. Some ventured a tentative paw toward it, only to instantly smell the smoke of their own burning flesh.

The knight strode casually up to the water's edge. "You are wise beyond your years, young Guardian. But it is of little consequence." The demon lord walked through his pack until he came to the spray which fed the pool. He pulled his broadsword and struck a savage blow to the pipe. Sparks flew and smoke erupted when the metals collided. The knight stepped back as the smoke drifted off. Crealand and Gel felt their hearts and hopes sink as they saw the pipe had been bent. The life saving water was now spraying harmlessly on the ground. Immediately, the water level in the reflecting pool began to drop.

The knight walked back through his hounds to the edge of the pool nearest the trembling couple. "You see? You cannot stop me. Even now the water drops. Soon my wolves will be tasting your hearts and St. Alden's will become a wasteland!"

Crealand and Gel looked around at the pacing wolves. They looked down to see the water withdrawing from their ankles. Desperately Crealand glanced over the commons until he saw the gazebo. Then he turned and grabbed his lover's shoulders. "Gel! I'm going to make for the gazebo. It's me they're after, not you. If they follow me onto the platform, we might have a chance!"

"No!"

"Yes! There's no other way. If we just stand here we'll be dead in five minutes!"

"Then I'm coming with you!"

"No, Gel! When they take off after me, run to the nearest protected house. If we both die, there'll be no one left. You have to be the Guardian!"

"Crealand, no! Let me go. You were the one your grandfather chose. You're the one who has to make it."

"Gel, it's me they want," Crealand hugged her tight. "I love you, Gel. Now run!"

Crealand pushed away from Gel and sprinted through the two inches of water that remained. He scattered the wolves that were between himself and the gazebo by kicking the last of the water on them. Several were burned and ran. In the confusion, Crealand broke their ranks and ran for the platform. In seconds he hurdled the safety rope and sprinted to the center of the decaying floor. All the wolves had followed him, urged on by the trailing knight.

Gel started to run for safety, but stopped. In her head she heard the words of Christian back in St. Alden House. "You are his Guardian..." She turned back just in time to see a mass of wolves, so large it moved as one, flow up the stairs of the gazebo.

Crealand held the sword in both hands. He spun back and forth, around and around, as the huge pack tightened on him. Soon they were within a few feet. He stamped on the floor. "C'mon, Gramps! You said this thing was weak!"

One of the knight's creatures leaped from the pack and crashed hard into Crealand's back. The blow sent Crealand to the floor and knocked the sword from his hands. The momentum of the attack coupled with the flying blade to send the sword deep into the side of one of the pouncing wolves. The fatally injured wolf fell, but the rest of the pack rushed in on Crealand. As the wolves made their last collective attack, the floor beneath them cracked. In a breath, the center began to collapse. As it fell, the hole radiated out and began giving way like crashing dominos. Before the center had touched the water in the cistern forty feet below, the entire floor had crumbled.

The first wolves hit the water with Crealand beneath them. Several had locked their jaws on his arms and legs only to have the suddenness of the fall and the shock of the water free their intended victim. Crealand felt the water cradle him. He looked up to see huge numbers of wolves flailing and falling all around him. A dead animal hit the water nearby. In its side was his sword. He grabbed it as the beast began transforming to silver and sank.

The entire cistern was boiling as wolves and timbers crashed into it. The demonic wolves were landing in the turbulent water and exploding in a flash of smoke, fire, and steam. Crealand watched from within the cauldron as the creatures became silver right before his eyes. The roar of the waters and the howling was deafening. The claws of the wolves still above him screeched across the tilting floor as they were sent to their deaths. A massive section of flooring carrying over a dozen scrambling demons broke free and came hurtling down at Crealand. He took a deep breath and dove as rotten wood and animals rammed into the churning water above him.

From the nearly empty reflecting pool, Gel saw the gazebo's floor cave in on itself. A lasting burst of steam and spray blasted up from the cistern along with the shrieking of the dying wolves. Without warning the commons became quiet. A few small pieces of tumbling wood splashed softly, making the only sounds and then they too were muted.

"Crealand!" Gel screamed violently as the knight walked to the edge of the pool and pointed at the battered gazebo.

"There! There lies the end of the world as you have known it!"

The knight smiled, puffed out his chest, and laughed. As he did, a few boards creaked from the edge of the cistern. Then a bloody hand reached up and gripped the side. The knight and Gel watched as another hand appeared holding the silver broadsword. Next, Crealand's head popped up. The battle weary Guardian pulled himself over the edge and tumbled down the steps of the gazebo and sprawled on the grass. The knight drew his black sword and set off deliberately for the fallen Guardian.

"I shall end this!"

Gel started to run after him. She stopped and flung the dagger at the knight's back. "You sonofabitch!"

The knight turned and caught the blade for an instant then dropped it as sparks and smoke flew from his hand. Gel ran at him and threw the flask as she had the dagger only to see the knight again deflect it in a shower of sparks. Gel stopped and tried to kick puddles of water on him, but he merely laughed and stepped out of range toward Crealand and the steaming gazebo. In blind frustration, Gel charged him.

Crealand was on his knees. His clothes were soaked with blood and the healing water. He looked up to see Gel attack the knight with her small fists. As Gel swung wildly the knight gripped her throat with one hand and picked her up off the ground.

"You mortals are so weak," he said as his hand tightened.

Gel heard her windpipe being crushed as she felt the pain. Her eyes rolled back in her head and her arms dropped to her sides. The knight merely let her drop to the ground and stepped again to the new Guardian.

As Crealand continued to struggle to his feet, the demon's boot caught him in the face. He fell backwards and the sword dropped from his hand. He reached for it, but the knight kicked it away in another shower of sparks. Crealand rolled and stumbled to his feet as the knight met him with a fierce backhand. The Guardian fell again, but pulled himself up to his knees.

"You are as weak as your mate, Templar," the knight said cruelly as he reached down and gripped Crealand's throat. He squeezed as Crealand's hands tried in vain to grapple with the iron fingers around his neck. "Your mate is near death," the knight said flatly. He glanced over his shoulder while Crealand's bulging eyes followed. "She is suffocating. Would you care to die as she or do you wish me to bring death quickly and sever your head with one swift blow?" Crealand could only gasp for air.

Thirty feet behind the knight, Gel was indeed trying to breathe through a shattered throat. As she thrashed about, her hand struck the silver flask. She fumbled for it, unable to raise her spinning head. After several tries she had the precious metal vial in her hand. She brought the silver flask to her mouth and took in a sip of the water. Her pain eased. She splashed a few drops on her hand and massaged her throat. In a moment she could gasp a few quick breaths. Then she held the flask to her lips as she greedily sucked down what little water remained and felt a strength surge through her.

The knight had grown tired of Crealand. He tossed him to the ground and raised the black sword over his head with both hands.

"Tonight my eternal reign begins, unencumbered by your futile attempts to save this world."

Gel stood to her feet. The silver dagger lay near the flask, where the knight had dropped it. She grabbed it and sprinted toward the knight and her fallen lover. As the knight's sword reached its zenith Gel plunged the dagger deep between his shoulder blades.

The knight screamed. Fire shot from around the dagger's handle and blew Gel backward. Crealand tried to roll from under the heavy black sword, thinking the scream was the last sound he'd hear. Instead, he looked up from the ground and saw Gel falling behind the stricken knight. The Guardian scrambled for his silver broadsword as the knight turned his back to see his attacker. The demon stumbled and the black sword fell to the ground. He tried to grab the hissing and smoldering knife in his back but couldn't reach it. Instead he reached for Gel with both hands.

Crealand hefted his blade, lunged at the knight, and rammed the bright broadsword to the hilt through the devil's own. The black hands dropped away from Gel as the knight clutched the blade coming through his body. Fire and smoke came from his hands as he listed, staggered, then fell to his side. Instantly his entire body began to smolder.

Gel watched the knight disintegrate. She shuddered until Crealand's arm settled around her shoulders. She looked up at him as he dropped beside her. The young lovers clung to one another there on the commons as the smoke from the dead knight drifted away on a soft breeze. A gentle mist was rising serenely from the wreckage of the cistern. Gel saw Crealand's partially healed wounds and pulled the Guardian to his feet.

"Let's get you into the pool. There's still a few puddles."

She helped him across the lawn and onto the floor of the reflecting pool to where a low spot held an inch of the shimmering water. Crealand stretched out flat on the water and Gel quietly began bathing away the last bites of the dead wolves. The water sizzled and steamed on Crealand's skin as the gaping tears began to close. She rinsed her neck and sipped the water from her hand and felt her throat repair itself. After several minutes they were both stronger.

"Gel. We did it. We stopped them."

"We did, didn't we?" Gel started to laugh nervously. "We stopped them, huh?"

Crealand smiled and began to laugh with her. "We did. It's over." He looked around. "What do we do now?"

"I'm not sure."

"Does this constitute our first date? It's going to be tough to top, don't you think?"

They laughed and kissed in the tiny puddle. As Gel hugged him she noticed the worst of his wounds were still open and bleeding slightly. "Crea, let's move over to the fountain. We need more water."

The couple stood clumsily. They were exhausted and both still hurting. Leaning heavily on each other they scuffled across the empty reflecting pool toward the fountainhead near St. Alden House. As they got closer, Gel noticed something disturbing.

"Crea, look. The spray's not working." Sure enough, the water had stopped.

"Probably that whack knocked the pipe out of the trough or something. C'mon. I can make it," Crealand said. "Let's go put it back in. I can heal up in the basement."

They continued around St. Alden House to the smashed window and walked through it into the dining room. Gel helped Crealand over the debris and to the basement steps. As they started down, they heard Christian's voice.

"Is that you, Crealand? Come help me."

Crealand looked at Gel and they both beamed. "It's me, Gramps! We did it!" Crealand yelled as he hobbled down the stairs and into the basement.

Christian was sitting on the bench, resting his arm on the large mass of silver from the tank. His face was pale white. Crealand started to speak to his grandfather again until he saw the old man up close. "Gramps, we..." Crealand's words trailed off. From behind him came his grandfather's voice.

"Oh, dear Gel. I'm feeling a little under the weather. Give us a little kissy pooh and jump start my heart, you sexy bitch."

Gel and Crealand spun around and stared into the shadows where the voice had come from. The point of a black blade emerged into the light. Christian's voice continued, but was changing. "I'm not myself. I'm afraid I might be dead." The bearer of the sword came into full view. It was Chapin and his voice was changing from Christian's to his own. "Yes, I'm sure of it. I am definitely dead."

Crealand pulled Gel behind him. "Chapin! We thought you'd been killed!"

"Oh, you thought right. Tell me, dear Gel, did you grieve for me?"

Gel stepped out from behind her lover. "What happened?"

"Why, I've crossed over," he said as he wandered around the room with the black sword hanging limp in his hand. "I joined the bad guys you might say. It seems a better fit for me."

Gel and Crealand noticed the stone altar at the same time. The stones were in disarray and the water had stopped. Crealand began moving discreetly toward the dismantled source of St. Alden's water. Chapin continued to talk as he began prancing around the room.

"Yep. I'm a knight now," he said as he put his foot up on the chest of Christian's body. "Just like the old man here." Then he spun and thrust the black sword at Crealand. "And just like you."

Crealand froze near the altar. As he spoke, Gel began slipping nearer the trough. "No, Chapin," the Guardian said. "You're not like me. But you could be. Help us get the water flowing again."

Chapin thrust the point of the black blade to within inches of Crealand's throat. "And then what? Be some flunky for you? Be your nit wit sidekick as you take all the glory?"

"No, Chapin. Be equals. Be partners. With two of us, we could do so much good together."

"No. Afraid not," Chapin said as his blade inched ever closer. "I've never been good at sharing." Chapin looked over at Gel who was now standing next to the trough. "No, Crealand," Chapin said with a sneer. "I don't share. Not power. Not women." Chapin's gaze returned to Crealand. "So you, my friend, must go!"

Chapin began to lunge just as Gel splashed him with water from the trough. Smoke flew up from Chapin's back and the side of his face. He waved his sword blindly as he crashed through the basement.

Crealand ducked the black sword, which sparked each time it struck a wall or beam of St. Alden House. Gel and Crealand grabbed for each other and started for the stairs. Chapin recovered slightly and blocked their escape. The skin on his face was smoking and peeling.

"You bitch!" Chapin screamed as he swung the broadsword. Crealand and Gel jumped back and bumped into Christian's body.

Chapin closed again with his sword swinging wildly. Crealand grabbed the lump of silver from the bench and heaved it at the newest black knight. It struck him in the chest and sent sparks into Chapin's face as it fell to the floor. Temporarily blinded, the enraged swordsman stumbled forward. Gel and Crealand ducked around him and made it to the stairs.

They ran up to the kitchen, slammed the door behind them, and leaned hard against it.

"I've got to get my sword," Crealand said, but no sooner had the words been said when the blade of Chapin's black rapier pierced the door between them. They both jumped away as the door exploded, showering them with splinters of wood. The blast blew them both through the swinging door onto the dining room floor. Chapin flew through the dust and debris and stood over them.

"Now you both die whereas I will reign forever!"

Crealand looked up from the floor. "The last shithead who said that is having a smoke out on the lawn!"

Crealand jumped at Chapin's legs and tackled him. As they fell, the black sword tumbled out of Chapin's hand. The two men wrestled on the floor as Gel scampered to her feet and went for Chapin's sword. She reached for the black hilt, but it sparked and burnt her hand.

Gel jumped and ran for the blown out windows. Chapin however, threw Crealand across the room into the same shattered window casing just ahead of her. The Guardian hit hard and slumped to the floor. Chapin retrieved his sword and now too, jumped in front of Gel.

"Going somewhere, my darling?"

Gel looked as if to run, but Chapin cut her off. "It's no use, Gel. I'm too strong." Chapin began walking into Gel until she backed up to the dining room table. "My powers are growing by the hour." He looked back at Crealand, unconscious on the floor. "Whereas his, well, let's face it Gel, you're going strictly second class there."

Gel was nearly lying back on the table when Chapin touched the inside of her thigh with the point of his blade. The blade was hot on her leg but tempered by its master's hand on the pommel.

"You know, you could become my queen," he said as he began sliding the black sword up her leg. "Be careful how you answer. My blade can sear your leg off with a thought."

Across the room, Crealand was coming to. Through blurry eyes, he saw a light flash, flicker, grow dim, and then brighten. He shook his head and blinked hard several times to clear his head. When he opened his eyes again, he saw the silver bar from the broken windowsill peeking out from under the rubble of the smashed windows.

"You go the hell!" Gel screamed.

"Nope. No good. Been there. Done that," Chapin smiled as the sword began to raise Gel's skirt.

Crealand reached out and clutched the silver bar as Gel spit in Chapin's face.

The spit sizzled slightly on Chapin's skin. "Ouch. That wasn't very romantic," the new black knight said through an exaggerated frown as he wiped away the tiny burn. "Now I'm going to have to kill you."

Chapin grabbed her by the hair and pulled his sword back. Gel screamed, swung, and kicked wildly, but it had little effect apart from keeping Chapin distracted from his killing. Behind him, Crealand dove across the room and plunged the silver bar through Chapin's back. It came out the knight's chest and began dripping sizzling black blood on Gel's white blouse. Chapin looked down at his chest and the silver bar coming through it. His wound was hissing and smoking as he dropped his sword and fell to the side on his knees.

Crealand swept Gel up off the table and into his arms. They stood near the dying knight as he slumped over onto the floor and began to smolder. Chapin looked up at the Guardian from the floor and the splintered wreckage of the window frame as he spoke. "You can never win, Templar... Others are coming..."

Crealand grabbed the silver bar and twisted it in Chapin's smoking chest. "Good. We're expanding the college. We'll need the silver."

Workmen were busily replacing the large broken window in the dining room of St. Alden House. Hammers and saws pounded and whirled in the hands of another work crew outside as a new deck began to take shape in the gazebo. Along one edge a small derrick raised chunks of silver from the cistern. The silver was placed on flatbed trucks, covered in old canvas, and driven away. The men stopped work as though they'd been signaled and walked across the crowded commons in bib overalls and sawdust covered sweat soaked t-shirts to stand with select politicos, many religious leaders, and kings of industry from the world over. Countless countries were represented as they weaved by the replenished reflecting pool to pay their final respects at the fresh grave of the knight who had died in defense of St. Alden's.

As the line passed the grave, it ran to Gel and Crealand, who stood nearby dressed in identical red blazers with the university's simple coat of arms embroidered on the breast pocket. The couple was greeted affectionately, often in languages they did not understand. Many of the prestigious guests carried gifts and laid them on a long table as they passed. Men and women in exotic dress, tailored suits, and flowing robes bowed deeply in front of the young couple. As the guests moved on, many could be heard to whisper, "The new Guardians."

A man in a white short-sleeve dress shirt and tie stepped out of the line and stood at the foot of the grave. He stared intently at the grey granite unmarked cross. Crealand moved away from Gel, walked up to the man, and gave him a hug.

"There's no name on the marker," the man said.

"There are no names on any of them," Crealand answered as he motioned to a long row of identical granite crosses that bordered the edge of the commons.

"Seems rather anonymous."

"They are remembered as Templar Knights. That is enough."

"Is that enough for you?"

Crealand examined the sod that had been cut up and replaced over his grandfather's grave. He also thought of the heavy lessons circumstances had forced the old Guardian to teach him so quickly.

"He told me something just the other day," Crealand said. "He said there is more to life than our own wants. We are players on the grandest stage. We each have a part to play. We become a ripple in the water – an instrument in God's hands.

"To be an instrument in God's hands. Can there be anything greater?"

"The answer should be an easy, resounding yes," the man said. "But I don't believe most people have the vision he had to see so clearly."

"It wasn't vision, Dad. It was faith – faith in God's plan. Faith in His mysteries."

Crealand's father looked at him and put his hand on the new Guardian's shoulder. "I understand now. He did the right thing. He made the right choice. I consider myself blessed to have been a link in the chain."

Crealand hugged his father again.

When the embrace broke, the father took the son's face in his hands and kissed his forehead. "I don't know what it might be, but if you ever need someone to help you, please call."

"I will. I will."

"I love you, son."

"Love you too, Dad."

The two men drifted apart as Crealand stepped back toward Gel. His father's hand slipped off his shoulder with a tenderness that was reluctant to let the young man go. Back by Gel's side, Crealand felt her hand rub his back as they both watched his father cross himself and rejoin the line that led away from the grave.

The new Guardians stood for several hours greeting the mourners. Some they recognized from the news. Occasionally, Gel or Crealand would elbow the other and whisper, "Look who's coming."

During a slight lull Gel took Crealand's arm. "We'll be all right, don't you think?" she said.

"I definitely do."

"Regardless, I'd like you to stay close to me."

"You know," Crealand smiled, "the night is the worst. You want me close then?"

"Definitely at night."

"In roommates kind of close? Or, across the hall kind of close?"

"We've been blessed by at least five bishops," Gel said shyly. "So I suppose we could be roomies."

"Hmmm...," Crealand answered. "I was thinking of something more permanent."

"Such as what?"

"Like, will you marry me?"

Gel relished the words. "Yes. Yes, I will definitely marry you."

They turned away from the guests, kissed, and touched each other's face.

"You know, Gel, I think one of those bishops may still be here someplace. Maybe we could get him to perform the ceremony for us. I don't have a ring, but I could get one. What kind would you like?"

Gel opened her blazer and showed Crealand the dagger hanging inside. "Silver," she smiled. "I like silver."

IN HOC

SOGNO *VINCES*

The Junket

A loose fender on the old dark green truck flapped in the forty mile an hour wind and waved goodbye to the welcome sign that marked the entrance to Suttin, Texas. The battered sign, its bright colors long since abandoned to the fierce west Texas sun, trembled slightly under the rush of wind that caromed off the truck. This quiver proved a nonchalant wave of its own – jealous as it was of one who possessed a considerable measure of liberty. In seconds though, the sign collected itself and ceased to move while the fender would shake and quiver all the way through New Mexico, Arizona, and into Nevada.

Behind the wheel of the green truck rode Jonny Archer. His somewhere around sixty-year-old eyes, (somewhere, because he didn't know or couldn't remember his birthday) assumed their usual half-squinting posture while his bony and calloused hands firmly gripped the same worn steering wheel he had handled for the last thirty-four years. Under his easy guidance the truck purred along smoothly. With no snow or salt to wear on the truck's body, general maintenance seemed to insure it would go on forever. As such,

Jonny made yet another quickly forgotten mental note to fix the fender. It never wiggled as it sat in his driveway and without an outward sign that something was wrong he neglected to attend to it and few people ever saw the problem. In this regard, Jonny was much the same as the fender.

As he drove through predawn Texas he adjusted the pillow between him and the sunken seat springs and considered that even with 'general maintenance' he, unlike the truck, would not go on forever. This of course was the reason behind the journey westward. Jonny noticed that movement came a little slower to him. His hands ached often. That trick knee played its trick a lot more than it used to and when it went sideways it wasn't so funny as when people had once laughed at it. Now the trick hurt and made him limp for days after. He didn't want to be called Gimp. He had already been called a lot of names and had no desire for another.

Beside him on the seat bounced a ratty and frayed travel brochure which touted the glamour, glitz, and allure of Las Vegas. The cover was a kaleidoscope of neon lights sparkling to a vanishing point along a wide street above a simple caption which read, "*The Strip*." There were other pictures of gaming tables and slot machines, but they generated no interest. Another, taken from stage level up at the long, high kicking legs of a chorus line, did. The row of dancers, complete with pink feathers, shining tiaras, and scanty costumes, all stacked on those long legs with their seamed hose and spiked heels, stirred Jonny as they must have stirred the G.I.s that catapulted Vegas from a stop over town into "*The Biggest Little City in the U.S. of A.!*" or so the brochure called the place.

Jonny absentmindedly reached beside him and touched the pamphlet. There was a reassurance there. The dog-eared slick paper was his touchstone back to his meager but impeccably neat apartment which had been his home for more years than he had driven the truck. Long ago the county had placed him in the apartment. It had been so long he couldn't remember his world before it. They got him twenty-five dollars a month to boot. A subsidy from the government they called it. "On account of your condition," he recalled being told.

Though he struggled with reading the words in the letters that occasionally came, he had seen the words change; retarded in the 50's, handicapped in the 60's, disabled in the 70's and 80's. In the

90's, he was "mentally challenged," whatever that meant, and now he had "special needs." Jonny didn't allow definitions to use up a lot of his time, opting instead to leave them alone. Whatever the county called him, it was better than back in the 1940's. Then he was just stupid. Jonny never considered himself stupid. He just thought he didn't understand a lot of jokes.

There were many other things he didn't understand. Some could have worked themselves up to be major things, but he wouldn't let them. Still other things, smaller ones, seemed trivial in Jonny's uncluttered mind so he dismissed them without a passing thought. But there was one notion that came up again and again and was not so easily dismissed. It was women. More exactly it was this sex thing. It seemed awfully important to other men. They talked about it, over it, and around it constantly. Jonny had heard some of the jokes so many times he had taught himself to laugh at the right spots. This seemed to please the tellers of the jokes so Jonny was pleased as well.

But apart from smiling on cue at stories, this woman thing had proved to be a bother. It cropped up everywhere. He saw them on TV and heard them in music on the radio. All men wanted one, he reasoned. Some men only wanted them for an hour they said while others wanted one for a lifetime. Jonny thought he should try just an hour first before he went in for the lifetime deal. But for over forty years even the hour had been elusive. He had yet to experience a woman. He came close that one time – teenagers exploring one another, but she made fun of him and called him a dummy. At the time he thought he just didn't get another joke. For all her giggles and squeals there must have been a joke in there somewhere and he hadn't learned yet when to laugh. Jonny thought about the girl, the joke he'd missed, and the word dummy for a long while. Later he decided it wasn't a joke after all, least ways not a funny one, and he swore an oath to himself to not think about this woman thing for a while. It was easier to stay away from thinking entirely as he'd never been that good at it anyway. So the oath took root and turned years into decades as if by magic.

As the labels in the government letters kept pace with the decades on the calendar, Jonny's response to them took on a rhythm he neither controlled nor understood. It came as an after effect that weighed in on him when he had struggled through reading the fairly anonymous memos. There was a gripping pain in all the name calling, not unlike being back in the 40's. On other days the letters were forgotten before the paper stopped rustling in the garbage. Sometimes he would feel the odd sting only to have it pass, perhaps for years. Then it came back – it always seemed to return – and lingered for weeks and months. It stung him like a hornet – buzzing, darting, invisible in its quickness. This was an evasive thing that made children point and adults grow shy or worse. The stares and comments and government name calling reminded him that he was not the same as others. And not the same was not a good thing to be.

Through it all he watched as a chasm grew between himself and the rest of the world. In the early days it was just a tiny split in the dusty ground of his mind, but time fed the growth and soon the gulf was so wide Jonny could not see the other side. Nor, after all these years, could he sense the bottom. He knew it was deep as his lost thoughts sometimes echoed back to him. Lately, the sight of the widening abyss came up in his mind less and less often. When this became clear to him it frightened him nearly as much as the gorge itself.

To help fight the chasm, Jonny stopped cashing his monthly checks. "Normal people don't get them," he said to himself as he tore them up and threw them away. The county and bank responded by depositing them directly into a special account. When the checks stopped coming to the apartment, Jonny was glad. Now he would be normal, but it didn't happen. He still didn't get most jokes.

So Jonny held onto the dishwashing job the county had found for him and stayed away from girls. It wasn't difficult as they seemed to want to stay clear of him too. He obeyed every law, respected the police, and was painfully neat and polite. But the days were lonely and without knowing, the lonely days had conspired with the calendar to become lonely years.

The highlight of his life it seems had already come. It happened all in one month and started when he landed the job on the oil rig. It was only maintenance, pretty dirty stuff. It was the jobs no one else wanted to do, but to him it was nicer than washing dishes. He was outside and not enslaved to a sink. Jonny stayed with the rig and the general maintenance, just like his truck. He lived simply, worked always, and saved his money for unknown reasons. Shortly after he'd started on the rig the Vegas tri-fold brochure came in his mailbox. It was beautiful. The ladies were beautiful. It had been a great time. That was fifteen years ago.

He could have driven to Galveston, or any city where street corners served as front offices for girls working the night, but it didn't suit him. He was nervous enough as it was. The chance of being seen was appalling. The jobbers on the rigs would laugh. It would be better to go out of state. The Vegas pamphlet provided a perfect little yellow map in a small square on the back cover. It looked to not be a far drive, but it was two states away. No one would know him as he sorted through this woman thing at last.

Until then there were always the things a man could do by himself. But again it didn't suit him. He had no strict prompts. Any incentives he may have needed came on television or printed advertisements. Jonny had seen the magazines in the stop-n-rob gas stations, but to get the magazines you had to ask at the counter – far too embarrassing. He once opened a *Playboy* in the bathroom on the rig and snapped it shut. The ladies were completely naked. That was wrong. That was why they called them dirty books. The men on the rig used to tape centerfolds on his work locker until, like school children, they grew bored with it and moved off to something else.

The movies the men traded and talked about from the book store across the tracks that didn't have a single book for sale (Jonny had checked) were worse. The kissing and carrying on was between the two people on the screen. To Jonny it was none of his business and he thought it was like being a peeping-tom. He did toy with the idea as a teaching tool but gave up on it when he didn't have the right tv or machine to make them play.

The Vegas dancers though, danced in public for everyone to see and enjoy. Plus, they were pretty and smiling under their heavy makeup. Some years ago a man on the rig had called hookers "painted ladies." Jonny's Vegas girls had painted faces. It must be the same thing. And they always smiled.

Texas was extinguished in the rearview mirror. New Mexico would not go away so peaceably. It seemed to scratch and claw at Jonny, the truck, and his dream of the dancing girls, as if by its shear width it could discourage him into turning back. It could not. Jonny's patience was sixty something years old. The blowing sand

and tumbleweeds would prove no deterrent. He watched them skip across the road in front of him or race through the high desert beside him, trying to catch him, until they, like New Mexico, finally gave in to the Arizona state line.

After considerable time the truck gained a foothold in Arizona and was soon making strides, though only hitting fifty miles an hour on long gentle downhill slopes in the heels of the Rockies. Together, Jonny and the truck counted down the miles to the Petrified Forest, the Grand Canyon road signs, and eventually Mt. Tipton. There were three stops for gas and sour coffee from stained Pyrex glass decanters. After seventeen hours of driving, I-40 finally released Jonny and the green truck as it melted in the heat waves behind them.

Near the Nevada border the twilight sky to the west appeared to grow brighter as the sun, already out of sight but still stretching its arms, welcomed the Texas visitors. The light wasn't neon, but Vegas was now only a stone's throw down the road. From the metal and concrete strap on the back of the Colorado River, Jonny caught a glimpse of Lake Mead and made one of his quickly forgotten mental notes to return to see it in earnest after the real purpose of the trip had been satisfied. Almost without warning the fender grew still as the truck slowed and rolled into *"The Biggest Little City in the U.S. of A.!"*

A parking lot obligingly snapped up the truck and left Jonny walking toward the strip as the truck's engine clicked and pinged the refrain of the overheated as it rested. It was a longer walk than he'd planned as he'd stopped well south of the strip, but it was a pleasant enough walk as he was near one of several golf courses that blossomed in the city. The fairways were empty in the collecting darkness and brought to Jonny's mind a cow pasture instead of a city of dancing girls. As though looking for reassurance that he hadn't taken a wrong turn, his eyes and fingers flipped through the tattered brochure and back out at the acres of grass that was quickly giving up their green for gray at the end of the day. Though his steps were determined, they faltered slightly in the shadow of the golf course and his recollection of cows.

A reprieve flickered from the north. The night was busy wrenching control from the day and it gave the twinkling lights of the strip the strength they needed to reach down Las Vegas Boulevard South to Jonny. When they caught his eye a sharpness entered his step. His chest encircled a rhythmic beat that quickened as his eyes widened. In minutes, neon giants clamored for Jonny's attention as he walked down the widest sidewalk he had ever seen. He held his dated brochure out in front of him and let his eyes jump back and forth from it to the street ahead, to the side, across, and up as he searched out the picture in his hand and in his head. The landscape had changed dramatically in fifteen years. This was something he had not considered. As he stood in the flashing red shadows the impact of the passage of time was something he did not fully comprehend.

Increasingly perplexed, Jonny moved further along. He had covered more than a mile and a half without finding the reality captured in the picture. He stumbled a few times, not watching his step, as he scanned the neon stars for a point of reference. In his increasing confusion, he bumped into a red haired hooker who, with another like minded lady, was busy guarding a corner and trolling for clients from the heavy traffic in the streets and on the sidewalk.

"Hey, Pops! Watch where the hell you're going! I don't mind a lil' bumping, you know? But don't damage the product."

"Oh... Pardon me please," Jonny said embarrassed.

The years had taught him to excuse himself and back away whenever he caused a problem, but in doing so this time, he only succeeded in running into the second working girl on the crowded corner.

"Whoa, take it easy!" she screamed. "This is my best outfit!"

Jonny spun, excused himself again, and backed up – right into the first hooker.

"C'mon, sweetheart," she cooed quite sweetly. "Whatsa matter? You been in the sauce? Why don't you stagger your old ass right down the strip there. Okay? Before you hurt yourself. Go on now," she said as she shook her breasts in his face. "You don't want none of this."

Jonny was overwhelmed by the flashing neon around him and the hustling girls. As if in self-defense, he thrust out the old pamphlet.

"I'm looking for these."

The hooker looked at her companion and slipped the brochure from Jonny's hand. She opened it and glanced at the pictures then turned it over and pointed out the copyright date to Jonny. "See this date, Pops? This thing is over fifteen years old." She flipped the aged paper around again and hastily pointed at the dated photos.

"This building right here? It ain't even standing no more. They tore it down to make room for a bigger casino. Most of this stuff isn't even here anymore." She abruptly turned on her tall heels and shot a look up the strip. "Nope. I don't think any of them places are left."

Jonny was dejected. He ploddingly took the precious brochure back and leafed through its pages. "They're gone?"

"All gone."

Jonny held the picture of the chorus line up too close to the hooker's face. "Even these are gone?"

She pulled back and looked at the picture. "What? Chorus lines? I dunno. Gone, I think. Why, you wanna see dancers?"

Jonny, crushed that his dancers had gone, lowered his head. "Painted ladies. I thought I'd meet a painted lady for an hour or so," he said as he tossed the pamphlet back and forth between his hands.

The hooker bent over and stared up at his downed turned face. "You got any money, Pops?"

"Yes..."

"Well then," she said as she righted herself and lifted Jonny's chin with a dingy hand topped with fake long nails painted gold and green. "You come to the right place after all." She spread out her arms to Vegas. "You're surrounded by painted ladies! But here now, I seen you first."

"You're a painted lady?" Jonny said somewhat incredulously as he looked back and forth from his pamphlet to the hooker.

"Honey, I am painted from head to toe. Look at this face," she said as she jabbed her nose at Jonny's. His eyes bolted wide open and he jerked his head back as the two faced off. "Look at these eyes," she continued. "Hell, them's not even my real color. I got tinted contacts. And these lips," she said as a coarse tongue flicked out like a snake. "That's high-gloss-cock-suckin'-resistant-red. Like it?"

"It's bright," Jonny said shyly.

"I even got paint on my toenails in case you're the kinky type. You the kinky type, Pops?"

"Umm... I dunno."

"No, I don't imagine you do and you don't exactly look like a high roller neither."

Jonny looked down at himself. He wasn't certain what a high roller was or if he even wanted to look like one. He had worn his nicest twill pants and his short sleeve plaid button down was faded but clean. "I just wanted to meet a dancing girl," he said after the quick survey of himself.

"I thought you wanted a painted lady?" the hooker grinned as she winked at her friend. "My specialty is being a painted lady but my girlfriend here, now she's a dancing girl! You want her instead? Here, Chloe, show Pops how you dance. Shake them tits for him real good."

The friend began to squirm and wiggle. Jonny stepped back from the show. The first girl reached over and pulled Chloe's top up and exposed her breasts. "Here, Pops! Is these a set of dancing tits, or what?"

Jonny stumbled backward and bounced off a collecting crowd of girls and their patrons. As he teetered a few feet away, the hooker ran toward him.

"Hey! You change your mind about the dancing girl? You want your painted lady back? Here I am! Everything painted, just like you wanted. Hell, even my hair is painted. See?" With that, she grabbed her own hair and neatly pulled off her glowing red locks. Beneath the wig was a tight dirty tan scalp cap held in place by countless bobby pins.

Jonny froze at the sight of the woman holding her hair a foot above her head. The wigless hooker burst into uncontrollable laughter and was quickly joined by the others on the corner. Jonny turned and ran up the street. His face was flush and he was breathing heavy when the laughter finally quieted in the distance. Around him, the swarming tourists had swallowed him up.

He walked on at a pace out of sync with the crowd. His hands, and his beloved brochure, were buried deep in his pants pockets. His rapid steps soon took him far away from the corner hookers and placed him beneath the brightest lights of the city.

"Them weren't no painted ladies at all," he mumbled as he walked. "They was mean and rough as cobs. They wasn't the same at all." The words echoed through him as he pulled out the crumpled pamphlet. He looked again from it to his surroundings. Nothing was the same anymore. The buildings were all gone. The signs were different. And his special dancing girls had become banks of hissing neon and twinkling lights. Everywhere he looked, his eyes were invaded by tubes of bright colored light. The hooker was right – everything had changed.

The dream inside him flickered like a dying light bulb. There were no dancing girls anymore. And no more dream to quietly sustain him. The vision of the high kickers he had cherished for so long abruptly faded. There on the sidewalk of *"The Biggest Little City,"* Jonny let his dream die. He wadded up the Vegas brochure and looked around one more time in hopes of seeing something he had missed. When nothing returned, he let his longtime touchstone fall weakly to the sidewalk. The paper struck the ground accompanied by an odd crashing noise as the chasm in Jonny's mind widened considerably.

The rumbling in his head lessened as did the street sounds around him. The glare of the neon also dimmed as his senses took leave. Lost in possession of a broken dream, Jonny moved feebly through the throng in the wrong direction. The abandonment of his quest left him confused and prompted him to walk steadily away from the green truck and away from the high end of the gaming district onto a side street off the strip. In two blocks Vegas was transformed from glitz and glamour to sordid and seedy.

Half a block further up the street, a commotion which began in the bar of the Paddock Room Club & Lounge – a small casino and club whose heyday had long passed – was trying to spill out onto the sidewalk. The object of the fuss was reluctant to move, hence the spilling was incomplete. As it was, two burly plain clothes security men were trying to evict Arlene Tremble, forty-nine-years-old going on seventy, with as little fanfare as possible. In her present condition, alcohol having taken a strong effect some time before, Arlene, Arty as she was called, opted instead for as boisterous an exit as possible.

"Get your filthy hands off'a me, you perverted sonsabitches!"

"C'mon, Arty, cut us some slack. You're wasted. Go home and sleep it off."

"Sleep?" she said, suddenly docile. "Like in a bed?"

"Yea, Arty. In a bed."

"So you're trying to get me in bed, huh?" Arlene stiffened against the guards' bum rush. She raised her chin with an air of absurd dignity. "Well, I'll tell you this. It'll cost. I've been working this town since you two pimps were in diapers. Hell, I probably banged your fathers. But that ain't gonna count for shit now. I don't give out no family discounts. If you want a piece of the Queen of Vegas, it'll cost. Plenty!"

"Are you kidding me, Arty?" a guard said as he winked to the other. "I couldn't keep up with you. Word is you were the best hooker on the strip."

Arlene relaxed and slid easily through the door of the club, greased by the compliment. When the past tense of the remark finally struck her she spun on the security men. "Whadaya mean, 'were?'"

The two mean each held an arm of the departing bar fly and effortlessly moved her onto the wide sidewalk. "Let's face it, Arty. You're a couple a days past your prime, don't you think?"

"Not a day, mister. Not one damn day."

The guards had successfully deposited their problem on the curb. As they stepped back toward the small casino, they continued the tongue in cheek conversation. "How old are you, Arty? Seventy? Seventy-five?"

Arlene clumsily kicked off a worn shoe then staggered and fell to her knees when she tried to pick it up. The men were laughing as she wound up and threw one half of her only pair of shoes in the general direction of the mocking. Surprisingly, to both Arlene and the men, the shoe found it's mark and clipped one of the bouncers on the shin.

"There, you bastards!"

Jonny had just come near enough to see the splendid pitch and hear both the thrower and the guard yell.

"You old bitch! I ought to slap the shit out of you for that!" the victim snapped as he rushed back at Arlene. His partner tried for his arm to stop him, but missed. Arlene was still on her knees while Jonny and others were being drawn toward the whole mess.

By the time the bouncer reached her, Arlene was trying to scramble to her feet. The awkwardness of wearing just one heel, coupled with the effects of several bummed and bartered high octane drinks, combined to push her back to the ground. Jonny came alongside her as the guard started in.

"Listen to me, you crazy old worn out whore! Stay outa this club! We're sick of hauling your busted ass out every night! Nobody wants you around so stay the fuck out, you stupid bitch. You hear me?"

Jonny often heard loud talk on the oil rig and knew nothing good ever followed. There was a thought of leaving, but instead Jonny reached down and helped Arlene stagger to her feet. He was more than a bit confused by it all, but the word 'stupid' caused him to sympathize with this haggard lady.

The second bouncer stepped in front of his outraged partner and tried to talk him down as Arlene looked at Jonny through bloodshot and blurry eyes.

"I was only trying to order a drink," she said plaintively. "Then these two punks commenced to beat on me."

The quiet guard looked to Jonny and spoke as though answering unasked questions. He didn't realize the questions would never come. "We work security for the casino."

"Policemen," Jonny thought and unconsciously straightened a bit.

"Your friend here," the guard continued, thinking Arlene and Jonny were acquainted as Jonny still held her arm and her hand was gripping his sleeve to both hold herself and drive home her plea. "She's had a couple too many. You and I both know she's not a bad egg when she's straight, but the booze brings out the rough side of her. Why don't you take her home. Okay, pal?"

"Home?" Jonny said with shock. "But I live a long way away."

"No. Her home. Will you do that?"

Jonny took the suggestion as an order. "Yes, sir. I will."

"Thanks, bud. Arty. You go along with your friend here and I'll see you in a couple days. Okay?"

"Go fuck yourself, copper," Arlene grinned as she stared down the guard.

He ignored her and concentrated on Jonny. "Just get her home. Can you do that for me?"

"Yes, sir," Jonny repeated.

The guard collected his still agitated partner and walked back into the club leaving Jonny still gently holding Arlene's arm. Jonny was looking at the club door when Arlene jerked herself away.

"Get your hands off me!"

Jonny stood dumbfounded.

"What are you looking at?" Arlene snapped.

Until then Jonny hadn't been looking at anything, but she brought him to focus on this disorderly and disheveled woman in front of him. He guessed her to be around sixty, near his age. The truth was kinder, but the lifestyle Arlene had trapped herself in the last twenty years had effortlessly heaped on the extra mileage. Her face was covered in heavy, crudely applied makeup and her hair was a slightly disjointed platinum wig, which caused Jonny to reflect on his encounter with the earlier hooker and her removable hair.

Jonny took note that Arlene's dress, a simple cotton print number, was well faded and thread bare throughout. The short sleeves were frayed and her pantyhose had tears at the knees, a result of the most recent tumble. Her bare arms and legs were rail thin. As Jonny continued to survey her, Arlene grabbed his eyes with her own.

"Hey, mister? You see something you like or you just window shopping?"

Her voice brought Jonny's attention to her face where he stared into bloodshot eyes partially hidden behind the makeup. Deeper into her eyes, unconcealed by the distended blood vessels, caked powders, and sloppy liner, paced something he recognized instantly. It was a fear – the almost unseen tightness and twitch the eyes carried that held a crying anxiousness like an animal's eyes in a cage. The eyes flashed a warning that there was great risk here. There was danger inherent at being too close to the bars that loosely held a frustrated and hurt creature. Claws of self-protection and fangs to deliver pain for pain could lash out and lead to a blind rush to escape or stand and slash until exhaustion overcame the thing and it slumped back into its cage with sweat and blood covering its face. Yes, there was reason to stay well clear of those trapped and in pain.

But as clearly as the pain revealed itself, Jonny saw another thing. It was his reflection coming back to him from Arlene's eyes. The likeness suggested his own fear – fear at simply being.

"Hello?" Arlene said loudly. "Anybody in there?"

"Uhh... My name's... My name's Jonny," he said as he extended his hand.

Arlene clasped the hand affectionately. "You're all johns to me, honey. What would you like?"

Jonny's stammering was caused by Arlene's gravelly voice. He was surprised to find her hands so warm and soft. "May... maybe a cup of coffee?"

"Look, sweetie," Arlene said as she released his hand and motioned around them. "This ain't no roadside café and I sure ain't Daisy Duke from Dixie. You looking for some lovin' or not?"

As ever, most of the slurring conversation went over his head. Jonny listened as best he could, mustered up his confidence, and blurted out his next words. "What I was really looking for was the dancing girls, but they told me there weren't no more of them around. I guess everything changed."

Arlene flashed a conniving smile. "You kinda old to be doing much dancing, don't you think?"

"No, ma'am. I was... I mean, it weren't really dancing I had to mind."

"Ohhh, so you're looking for somebody special, huh?"

"Special? No, just somebody for an hour. Like the guys say."

"Okay, honey. I got it. You're looking to get banged, but you're a tad shy about it. Am I right?"

"I guess so," Jonny offered reluctantly, thinking Arlene was as far from his vision of the dancers as the first hooker.

"You ain't too old for humping are you? I mean, you're a step or two past your prime, don't you think?" she said, mimicking the bouncers from a moment ago.

"I don't know."

The last of her drinks kicked in and Arlene teetered. Jonny caught her arm again and helped right her.

"Whoops!" she said as she pushed someone else's hair from her face. "Little outa sorts tonight."

She started to walk with only one shoe on, Jonny at her side, then stopped suddenly and spun toward him. "You know, I'm a professional!" she blurted. "It takes a real man to keep up with me." She reached down and grabbed the crotch of Jonny's pants. "You better be harder than Chinese arithmetic when you take me on, mister, or I'm apt to tear you down!"

Jonny's jaw went slack and his body went rigid. Before he could respond, though he had no idea what he would say anyway, Arlene was again leading him up the street. Jonny dashed back and retrieved Arlene's shoe missile then caught up to the still talking, still walking, wobbling, self declared Queen of Vegas.

As the pair stepped through the crowds they were quiet, save for Arlene's mumblings as the alcohol wrestled to take full effect. By the time they reached her two room apartment, several blocks from the strip, Arlene was scarcely able to walk.

The apartment was on the first floor of a semi-functioning battered warehouse half-way up a dimly lit alley. Jonny was hesitant, but moved in step with his drunken guide. Her door, wood with peeling gray industrial paint, had a piece of discolored water stained plywood screwed over the upper half where glass panes had once been. Arlene fumbled with a single key tied around her neck on a long dirty white shoelace. After turning the tumbler, Arlene automatically kicked the sticking door and it lurched open to a darkened room. Jonny stood in the doorway while Arlene patted the wall hard until she stumbled across the light switch. A single bulb came to life in a plain ceiling fixture that was minus its shade. A second dead bulb in the light was half black and covered with dust.

Jonny scanned the room around his host as he stepped deeper into Arlene's place. Clutter was everywhere. It wasn't garbage, near as he could tell, but it sure looked trashy. On a low coffee table, covered with water stains, burn marks, and old magazines, stood an air freshener that had long ago surrendered. Some clothes were strewn across a tattered couch that seemed to be in a competition with the table for most stains. Across from the couch was a lawn chair with frayed alternating green and white webbing. On its seat was a dirty plate, fork, and a coffee mug.

In a far corner of the smallish living room/kitchen combination, sat a large brown clay flower pot holding the unrecognizable carcass of a long dead plant. The carpet, which stretched out from the plant and around the worn couch, coffee table, and lawn chair, was stained in several spots and worn to the padding in a path from the door to the second room, Arlene's bedroom. To the side of the living room in the kitchen area, Jonny saw a sink full of dishes, a two-burner grease covered hotplate with dirty pans collected nearby, and an ancient rounded refrigerator with a huge latch that resembled something from a barn door. The refrigerator was humming loudly.

"Soo...," Arlene slurred as she snuggled up to Jonny. "You coming in?"

Jonny realized he was still standing just inside the open doorway. He stepped inside and closed the door behind him. The door didn't fit the casing well and he had to push the bottom with his foot – the opposite of Arlene's practiced kick to open the door.

His host staggered and bumped the back of the couch as she tried to saunter back across the disheveled living room. Arlene put her arms around Jonny's neck and pushed herself into him.

"So, baby. You wanna some a this?" she stumbled. Her head dropped down on Jonny's chest and she went limp. He caught her for at least the third time since they'd met.

"You okay, lady?"

Arlene stayed as she was, but mumbled a soft reply. "I'm fine, but I ain't no lady. I ain't no lady."

"Sure you is," Jonny said as he hesitantly patted her back. "You just a might down on your luck. Things'll pick up. In no time at all you'll be back on your feet."

"Shhhit. Only thing I'll be on is on my back. Ha!"

"Go on now. Bet you got a nice job coming 'long and then there you'll be."

Arlene picked up her heavy head and struggled to hold it steady as she examined Jonny's face. "Honey, I got a job. I'm one of your dancing girls. Used to be anyways. Business ain't been too good lately. Lately. Like the last fifteen years..."

Arlene was blacking out in Jonny's arms. She'd slump for a moment then regain her senses as Jonny lifted her.

"Here now," he said as he half dragged, half carried her toward what he assumed was her bedroom. "You just needs to lay down for a spell."

"Yea, always layin' down for a spell. That's me. Ha!"

The bedroom was dark except for the sparse light that filtered in from the bare bulb in the outer room. Jonny didn't take notice of the clutter in this room and instead brought Arlene to the bed and sat her down. "There you are now. You get some sleep and you'll be right as rain. Go ahead now, lay on down there."

Arlene flopped over on her side. Jonny hesitated as he had never touched a woman's legs, but gently and carefully took hold of Arlene's ankles and brought them up on the bed. Arlene struggled to prop herself up on an elbow and addressed her intended trick. "Hey. You're a pretty good fella. What's your name again?"

"Jonny Archer."

Arlene collapsed again on the bed. Her mouth was half buried in her pillow and partially muffled her voice. "Name's Arlene. Peoples call me Arty... Just think if we was to get married. I'd be Arty Archer. Ain't that rich?"

"Kinda rhymes, don't it?" Jonny said thoughtfully.

"Yea... Rhymes..."

Jonny reached across the semi-conscious Arlene and pulled the comforter back over her. "You're a good guy, Archer," she muttered.

"Thank you, ma'am."

"Yea..., some good guy," Arlene said with short lived enthusiasm. "Inside of fifteen minutes I'll be waking up to you humping the ass off me..." Then she faded fast. "Maybe this time I won't wake up... Would... Wouldn't that be grand?" And she passed out.

Jonny stood over her for some time, staring at the first woman he'd ever seen in a bed. Arlene was breathing heavily and her wig was askew on her head when Jonny whispered good night, tucked the comforter in around her, and backed out of the room. He silently eased the bedroom door shut and turned into the front room.

As he crossed the room to the door, his truck, and the highway home, he instinctively picked up a dirty glass from the coffee table and placed it near the sink. He continued on, but stopped again and knelt down to straighten a pile of old newspapers that had fallen over near the door. The papers straightened, he opened the door. The deadbolt lock caught his eye and he realized he had no way of locking the door behind him. He thought back to the key on the dirty shoelace, but shook his head no at the notion of slipping it off Arlene's sleeping neck.

"I'd wake her up, sure as anything. Then she'd think I was just trying to get at her," he said out loud to the deadbolt. He closed the door. He couldn't leave her like this. He'd have to wait until morning. It was that simple.

Jonny stepped with a sense of purpose across the dirty carpet and sat down on the couch. He was put off by the stains and clutter all around him. His hands came to rest on his knees, but stayed there only a moment. In less than a minute they abandoned the clean safety of his pants and busied themselves aligning the dated magazines and scraps of paper that littered the coffee table. Before long, Jonny was up and in full swing around the room. By midnight, the living room was as spotless as he could make it, the dishes were done and put away, the hotplate cleaned, and the refrigerator freed of its unrecognizable holdings. By one am Jonny had stretched out on the old couch and was asleep beneath a multicolored afghan. It was the first time he had slept away from his apartment in forty years.

The sun had slowly snuck up on Jonny's face by late the next morning and woke him rather rudely by pinching his eyelids. He stretched like a waking cat and sat upright before he glanced at his watch. It was nearly nine o' clock. This was the latest he had slept in many, many years. As he folded the afghan and lay it across the back of the still exhausted couch, he considered that the entire trip had been one first after another, but the thought didn't last. His stomach reminded him that it was also well past his usual breakfast time.

He left the apartment and the still sleeping Arlene under the protection of the daylight and ventured out in search of a grocery store. Arlene's shelves had little to offer and much of what they did hold was unappealing, even after the winnowing Jonny had accomplished the night before.

On his purposeful constitutional, Jonny discovered that his truck was waiting not three blocks away. He cheerfully slid into its cab and found a comforting dose of reassurance he had not noticed he needed. Reunited, Jonny and the truck made a brief sojourn off the comparatively quiet early morning strip and found a grocery store in a sprawling plaza. When he had picked up the breakfast items and resigned them to the care of the truck, he strutted into the woman's clothing department of a nearby store and bought a short sleeve gingham dress in a size guessed at by holding it at arm's length. He surprised himself by moving through the checkout line with a quiet confidence that would have led a bystander to imagine he'd been buying gifts for years. In truth, this was his first. Another first, he thought, but there was no time to dwell. In short order he was back at the apartment.

Jonny parked the truck in the alley and walked to the door holding the dress in a dangling bag between an armful of groceries. There was more than enough food for a quick breakfast – a thank you he reasoned for him spending the night on her couch. A hotel would have cost much more and then there was also the matter of the unintended savings he had incurred by not finding the proper painted lady. But all that would come another day. For now he felt he had to give a little something to this lady with the terrified eyes.

Jonny knocked softly and listened for signs of life. Nothing came. He slowly turned the knob, but the door resisted and waited for Arlene's kick. Jonny felt the door stick and gently nudged it with his shoulder until it obliged. With his face stuck just inside the door, Jonny half whispered. "Miss Arlene? You up?"

The apartment was as quiet as when he'd left. He crept in and closed the door as it occurred to him that perhaps now he was a burglar and not an invited guest. This dilemma passed as quickly as most thoughts. It was put out of his mind completely when he began to fix breakfast. "No burglar would fix breakfast for the folk he was robbing," he confided to the bacon and thus convinced himself he was still on the right side of the law.

Meanwhile the other room was watching Arlene creep back to life. As she stirred, her headache reminded her of the previous night's drinking. Her mouth was bone dry and her dress had slipped sideways. Her shoes and her wig had come off beneath the comforter.

As she slipped away from the comfort of the bed and moved to the tiny adjacent bathroom, the smell of bacon frying aroused her otherwise dull senses. Her stomach flipped between being repulsed by the breakfast smell and relishing it. For now she made her way to the bathroom, content to leave the scent of breakfast to the neighbor, who she assumed was the morning chef.

Jonny had heard Arlene get up as assuredly as she had smelled his cooking in her kitchen. When she opened the bedroom door and the two met face to face, Jonny, somewhat startled, quickly withdrew his hand from a plate full of eggs, pancakes, and bacon he had just set on the table for her.

"What the hell?" Arlene said dryly.

"It's breakfast," Jonny stated proudly.

"I know what it is. What I want to know is who the hell are— Ohhh...," Arlene trailed off as recent events flooded back in her mind. "Why you still here?"

Jonny was taken aback by the whiskey coarseness of her voice, not to mention the very real and very unruly mousey brown hair with gray roots that had replaced the platinum wig.

"Umm... You was sleeping last night, so I figured–"

Arlene bolted across the room and yanked back the flimsy curtain which shielded the kitchen from its only window. She squinted hard at the bright sunlight. "Well you figured wrong! See this? That's the sun. And when the sun's up, I don't go down. Not on my back, not on my knees, not nothing! Got it?"

"O... Okay," Jonny said hesitantly, the stammering caused by the reference to sex. He bailed himself out by pointing at the plate of breakfast and the plastic bag on the table. "This here breakfast is for you. You was looking a might poorly last night so I figured you–"

"There you go figuring again. I don't eat breakfast."

He hesitated once more then reached for the bag. "This here parcel's for you too." Jonny shook the print dress unceremoniously out on the table. "I hope it fits. I don't know about sizes and all."

Arlene glared at her new benefactor and spoke slowly. "Just who the hell do you think you are, mister? You can't come in here and just carry on so. What? You think you're gonna get something for nothing? You think you can get a piece of me for a plate of eggs and a four dollar cinchy dress? What are you, stupid?"

That word again. After all these years. And from her. "No, ma'am. I ain't stupid," Jonny said as he lowered his head.

"Damned if you don't act stupid. And you talk sorta stupid too."

Jonny didn't answer. In the vacuum created by the word, Arlene looked around her place and took note of the tidiness and cleaning that had been performed as she slept. She was as confused as Jonny, but while Jonny masked his confusion with silence, Arlene hid hers with venom. "Hey. You do all this?" she said sharply as she motioned around the apartment.

"Yes, ma'am."

"Stop calling me ma'am," she barked. "And why'd you do all this?"

"I, umm... I was here and the place was in a bad way so I figured, I mean, I sorta took hold and went to cleaning some."

"What the hell's wrong with you? You don't go poking through people's stuff like that. You crazy or something?"

"No, ma'am, er... I just don't get jokes like most folks do. I'm sort of men-tal-ly challenged, they said."

"Holy shit," Arlene said slowly. "Ten thousand johns on the strip looking to get laid and I gotta bring home Forrest fuckin' Gump!"

Jonny just continued standing with his head down. Arlene let her features relax and she laughed a little. "Look, buddy. That was real sweet of you to clean up and fix this breakfast, but I ain't running no shelter. You probably took a little taste last night when I passed out, or felt me up or something. We'll just call it even. So why don't you hit the road. Deal?"

"Okay," Jonny said without looking up. As he shuffled off toward the door Arlene crossed her arms, leaned against her clean kitchen table, and watched him closely.

"Hey, mister. By the way. How come you stayed here last night anyway? Ain't you got no place to go?"

"I gotta place," Jonny said without turning around. "But I couldn't lock your door. I didn't want to leave you like that."

"Leave me like what?"

"With the door unlocked after dark and all. I didn't think you'd be safe."

Arlene started to soften. Her own head dropped a little then came up and scanned the neat apartment and the prepared food. There was a strange feeling welling up inside her. She hadn't felt it in years and it frightened her. The weakness that was in her throat was not a safe thing here in her world. She grabbed it and forced it back down. Frantically she looked for some of the old callousness to replace it.

She lunged forward, snatched the dress off the table, and wadded it tightly in her hands. "Hey! And I ain't no charity case! And this ain't exactly skid row. Sure, it ain't no Waldorf Astoria, but it beats a blank. Least I ain't running around in the middle of the night sleeping on stranger's couches. Like some kinda bum!"

The outburst made her feel protected again. Her shield was back in place as Jonny turned and stared at her sympathetically.

"I know why you're mean," he said gently.

Arlene was shocked. "Huh?"

"You're afraid."

Arlene spun, opened a kitchen drawer, and yanked out a large carving knife. "Afraid, am I? Afraid of you? Like hell I am!"

Jonny took no notice of the toothless threat and pointed calmly to his heart. "No. I mean afraid... in here."

Arlene threw the dress at Jonny and it caught on his still pointing hand. "Here you crazy sonofabith! Get outa my house! Get out!"

Jonny and the dress exited silently and closed the sticking door behind them. The truck started as ever and backed out of the alley and moved off in the direction of west Texas. The fender and Jonny's lower lip each began to quiver.

In her shabby apartment, minus Jonny, Arlene could loosen her façade. It fell away in a sudden rush of tears. She sobbed against the counter for some time, her body lurching against the thrusts of a thousand remembered hurts and as many unwanted lovers. As tears eroded her anger and fear, a new regret rose to take their place. She lifted her tear stained face and looked longingly with red and swollen eyes at the door.

"Dumb old bitch. First person to do something nice for you and you go and throw him out. So typical, Arty. So, typical..."

As she talked she ran her hand across the shiny countertop and over to the table. She laboriously lowered herself into her chair and looked at the untouched breakfast. At the other end of the table was a second plate, still empty. "God, that looks good," she whispered. "Two plates instead of one. That looks so good."

As she poked at the cooling food, the sound of a truck pulling in the alley brought her head up and momentarily her spirit. She jumped to the window and brushed aside the curtain again. In the alley was a delivery truck. No Jonny Archer.

"Probably headed back to where ever he's from by now."

To further insult her, the delivery wasn't for her. The truck was merely turning around. Her heart sank as she let her hand fall away from the curtain. She returned to the table and her breakfast for one. Even cool the food tasted good to her though each bite was seasoned with the pain of a lost chance.

Eventually the plate, with much of the food, found its way into the sparkling sink. Arlene left it there as she returned to the bedroom. She threw the bed together and made her way into the bathroom where she fumbled with a bottle of aspirin. Two pills were tapped into her hand and she looked at them for a moment then dumped the entire bottle into her palm, spilling several into the sink in the process. The rattling pills instantly combined with the sounds of a gentle rapping at the apartment door.

"Shit," she said, as though she'd been caught in the middle of a crime. She hurriedly poured the pills from her hand back in the bottle leaving a few others still careening around in the bottom of the sink. The knocking at the door had stopped before Arlene had time to primp her hair and sprint through the front room.

She grabbed at the doorknob and fell backward as her hand slipped off. Then she latched onto it with both hands and jerked it hard. The door stuck some as always, but gave way to Arlene's excited pull with a loud rattling snap. Beyond the annoying door, Jonny was stepping back into the truck. Arlene fairly glowed.

"Hey, mister. Where you going?"

"West Texas," Jonny said seriously.

Just then Arlene noticed the dress folded neatly at her feet. She bent quickly and picked it up. "You forgot this," she said as she held it out.

"No," Jonny lied for the first time in memory. "They umm... The store wouldn't take it back. I thought maybe you'd still like it a little bit."

Both of them, conscious they were still strangers, looked at each other across the alley and across the years of loneliness and heartache. Their eyes held one another for some time – Jonny, not knowing enough to look away and Arlene, afraid that breaking the stare would prompt another regrettable goodbye. With tentative steps Arlene moved away from the accustomed safety of the dreary apartment and rather playfully swinging the dress stepped in the direction of the truck.

"Hey, ah... You know your plate is still empty in there. Could I offer you a bite of breakfast before you start out? Least I could do, know what I mean? For the dress."

Jonny was cautious, but stepped away from the truck and met her halfway. He remembered the big knife, but more so, Arlene's cutting tongue. "I was fixing to stop at this little restaurant I seen coming in," he said as Arlene's hopes shook within her and she unconsciously began twisting the dress.

Jonny saw the flickering light begin to fade in her eyes, being replaced again by the fear he himself knew so well. While his last words hung in the air, he took a deep breath, lost his thoughts yet again, and leaped into the chasm.

"But maybe you'd like to come along," he said through a soft smile as he pointed to the tightly clutched gingham. "Maybe even wear your new dress there."

Arlene's grip on the dress relaxed. Her heart soared and spilled over into the first honest smile she'd had in years.

"We wouldn't sink a passenger liner…

Would we?"

Forever Beneath the Celtic Sea

"We're coming up on periscope depth, Captain."

"Very good," Schwieger said as he eased through the few steps to his station at the periscope of U-20, his German submarine. Experienced, calloused, and confident hands gripped the well balanced instrument and effortlessly hefted the boat's clandestine eye to its maximum height. As the thirty-year-old Captain pressed his own eye to the viewfinder, the lens above him broke the surface of the windswept Celtic Sea just off the south east Irish coast and west of Germany's English enemy.

"Bearing!" Schwieger barked as he spun himself and the periscope to catch sight of a ship nearly two thousand meters out on the horizon.

"Nineteen degrees ea' nor'east, Captain. And steady."

"Speed!"

"Eleven knots, sir. She's making a run."

Calmer now, the Captain questioned his first officer. "What is she, Commander?" he asked as he gave way to let his second view the quarry.

"Looks to be a freighter, sir."

"Agreed," the Captain said as he again took hold of the periscope and resumed studying the grey silhouette. "And her destination?"

"I'd say given her heading she's bound for the yards of Liverpool, sir."

"And from there?"

"Sir?"

"Her cargo. What is its destination? Given the God-awful state of Europe."

"Ahhh. Yes, sir. Munitions and supply for Flanders Fields, I would venture."

"Flanders Fields? Indeed." Captain Schwieger said as he continued his own study. "You'll have to go elsewhere for argument."

Around the tight confines of the sub's conning tower and below throughout the wider body, nose to tail, the crew waited to execute with well oiled precision the orders they knew would come.

"Helmsman?" Schwieger said in voice that was more request than order. "Lay in a course to intersect. Heading two eight seven. Bring us around. Commander? Arm torpedo tube one."

"Arm torpedo tube one!" the Commander echoed, as his own words bounced from man to man along the sub.

"Range?" Schwieger asked no one in particular.

"Sixteen hundred meters. Holding at eleven knots, Captain."

"Open outer door on one."

"Open outer door on one!"

"Open outer door on one..."

"Stand by to fire."

"Stand by to fire!"

"Stand by to fire..."

The command was relayed through the boat to the forward torpedo room, a cramped and clammy space where extra torpedoes hung from the already low, rounded grey ceiling. Seventeen-year-old seaman Guenther Stroehmann heard the reverberating order and grabbed the simple lever that would launch havoc with the wake of the torpedo. His hands were glistening under a sheen of dirty oil and grease. He had spent most of the day cleaning and preparing the loading mechanisms for tubes one and two. The forward torpedo bay, integrated into the bow of the submarine, had a mirror of it facing aft in the stern. The second firing station gave U-20 two more torpedo tubes that could be armed and ready for Schwieger to spin the sub or fire in another direction depending on the location of the target. The two identical stations, fore and aft, lent itself to competition between the crews. Cleanliness and mechanical preparation ruled the day and young Stroehmann wouldn't let his post be beaten. He was young – one of the youngest on the thirty man crew – but his work ethic was solid and his devotion to his captain and to Germany unshakeable.

Back at the periscope, Schwieger watched, waited, and gave the order. "Fire one."

As before, the words passed from mouth to mouth, careening with the ease of water flowing in a pipe, bolting through the boat's narrow corridors until they reached Guenther. He twisted his right hand down hard and yelled at the top of his voice, "ONE AWAY!" Beside him he heard the torpedo come to life and felt the lurch as it rocketed from its bed.

Guenther automatically placed his hands on the forward wall of the cramped room and waited to feel the detonation of the explosives and the death throes of the freighter. The sub itself barely breathed as nearly a minute passed in total silence with Guenther's palms pressed against the hull and in the attack room, Schwieger's eye pressed against the periscope.

Under his breath Captain Schwieger counted down the stopwatch that ticked in his head. The seconds and the distance ran together while, invisible to him, the torpedo crept through the cold water. Schwieger counted softly to himself. The torpedo crashed against the hull of its target on cue. A monstrous blast no one on the U-20 could hear sent men and metal over sixty feet in the air above the stricken ship. The sub felt an unmistakable shudder caress her. All who felt it recognized the tremble as the tell-tale sign of a hit. A slight smile of satisfaction came to Schwieger's face. "There she goes men. Prepare to surface."

In the forward torpedo room Guenther clapped his hands when he felt the wave of the explosion pass around the submarine. He pulled his lucky deutsche mark from his pocket and tallied another scratch on the grey wall with the multisided coin. The number of enemy ships he had sunk now totaled seven. He ran his hand over the scratches, brushing away the loosened flakes of paint. When he returned to Hamburg he mused, he would be a hero.

The rest of the submarine was darting sailors as the men prepared to surface. A machine gun crew stood at the hatch ready to man the 37mm gun that waited on the sub's deck. Other men had lighter machine gums over their shoulders. Captain Schwieger and his officers waited as well. When the cry came that they had breached the surface a seaman unbattened the hatch, thrust it open, and jumped aside as the gun crew scampered up the ladder through the sea spray that showered down through the open portal. In seconds the entire collection of men stood on the deck and packed the tower, cheering as the last vestiges of the freighter slipped beneath the waves.

The captain, over continuing shouts of celebration, ordered his boat ahead at quarter speed. In short order the sub was cruising through the floating remains of its victim. Boxes and bundles floated everywhere. Men, dead and dying, were bobbing in the bitter water. A few clung to pieces of freight and were summarily executed or left to die in the cold sea. There were orders to the contrary – orders to surface and call for all hands to abandon ship before launching a torpedo. This directive was often followed and often not. This was war, perhaps the biggest the world had ever seen. Surfacing near a ship presented a real risk of being rammed and run down as there was bounty money levied on each U-boat.

U-20's executive officer made notes on the debris, placing stars next to entries of "food stuffs" and "diesel oil," much of which burned on the surface around the creeping sub. While the commander continued jotting his notes, the communications specialist took advantage of the surface time to check radio traffic otherwise out of reach when the boat was beneath the waves. He reported up the conning tower to the captain that he had monitored lagging transmissions surrounding an SOS from a freighter called *Centurian*, apparently torpedoed thirty miles south of St. George's Channel, U-20's present location. Later, Schwieger would log the *Centurian* sunk on 6 May 1915.

The submarine remained on the surface a scant twenty minutes. All the members of the crew, including Seaman Stroehmann, scrambled out the hatch as they rotated among themselves for a few minutes of fresh air. Soon however, all the men had returned to their posts and U-20 had returned to hunt the Celtic Sea.

The following morning broke slowly, hindered by dense fog cradling Ireland's southern shoreline. Schwieger utilized nature's cloak and cruised openly at thirteen knots on the water's back. With a trail of sunken ships behind her, the U-20 was making for home to refit before joining a wolf pack bound for the North Sea. As the hours ticked away the fog melted and forced the boat to seek the shelter found in the depths. When the submarine dove, Guenther was writing another letter home. The letters were more a journal of the mission than true letters as he wouldn't be near a postal pick up until he was back on land at the submarine's lair. The writing took a pause as the sub nosed down. Guenther was accustomed to the changing pitch of his bunk, but momentarily held the rail of his narrow bed to keep from sliding. Even though the letters wouldn't be read for some time, he picked up his writing as the U-20 leveled off. He recounted the recent sinking of three ships in two days, forewarning his hometown that a hero would be returning.

Once his command was settled beneath the waves Captain Schwieger traversed his boat. Each step was surrounded by the quiet hum of the electric propulsion motors. He paused near the torpedo loading hatch amidships and gently touched a small wooden cross that was fixed to the curved hull of the submarine. In a vessel as confined as the U-20, this tiny space served as the crew's church. Schwieger had long known of the cross and how, during inspections in port, it mysteriously vanished, something he appreciated as most ranking members of the military could be counted on to take exception. But the cross, and the two square foot sanctuary it carried with it always materialized as the sub left port for the sea. Schwieger smiled as he thought of the symbol and its innocent game of hide and seek, but the smile quickly faded when he considered for a moment how he and his boat played the game on a grand scale. With the war back on his mind he petitioned for a continued good hunt and a safe return then eased his hand away.

The captain had just stepped from the small chapel when a seaman's head poked through an open watertight doorway in front of him.

"Captain, the Lieutenant Commander says there is a ship on the horizon."

Schwieger moved quickly. He grasped the header of the doorway and vaulted through feet first. Once inside the control room he rapidly ascended the short ladder into the attack room within the conning tower of the sub. His commander was peering through the periscope but stepped aside as Schwieger entered.

"I thought it was a convoy at first. It's hard to say what she is, but it's big."

"Destroyer?"

"No, sir. Bigger."

"Battleship?" Schwieger asked, obviously excited as he pulled himself into a tight embrace with the periscope.

"I can't say, Captain. She's a long way off."

"Helmsman," Schwieger ordered. "Lay in a course to intersect. Bring us hard about to starboard. Bearing twenty-two degrees. Let's get a closer look."

Over the next hour and a half the two vessels drew closer to one another – one knowing, the other ignorant they were being shadowed. Schwieger and his commander took turns at the periscope, relieving each other and their eyes as they struggled to examine the hulking shape in the distance. Finally the commander saw something that disturbed him. It was heard in the tenor of his voice.

"Captain, she's got four funnels."

The senior officer assumed the watch and saw four thick smokestacks on the horizon. As he continued studying the intended prey growing in his lens, he noticed that not all the funnels were spewing smoke which told him the huge ship was running under partial steam. Behind him his commander silently mouthed the word, "Liner," to others nearby who in turn passed the information quietly on to their shipmates. The word rocketed through the boat as quickly as the order to fire, but in jetted whispers no one except the next nearest man could hear.

The captain spoke from behind the periscope without looking up.

"Commander, arm torpedo bays one and two and open outer doors."

The commander's eyes jumped in their sockets beneath a brow that was instantly furrowed. His jaw slackened and he turned his head as though to adjust his hearing.

When the captain's second didn't instantly relay the instruction, Schwieger looked up from the picture of the monstrous ship in the lens.

"Commander? Did you hear the order?"

"Yes, sir," the commander said as he tentatively pointed to the periscope. "But I believe that is a liner, Captain."

Schwieger put his hands behind his back and stepped the short distance to his commander until the two mariners stood nose to nose.

"That, Commander, is a ship operating in enemy waters. As you are aware, our directive is to attack all vessels which sail within our reach."

"Yes, sir. I understand, but—"

"Speed!" the captain snapped as he spun back to the periscope.

A voice rang from the control room below. "Seventeen knots, Captain. We'll range to seven hundred meters on our current course."

"Steady as she goes then. Commander, arm torpedo bays one and two and open outer doors."

The commander's eyes stayed on the captain as the latter resumed his post at the periscope. His repeating of the order was barely audible and slow. He hadn't quite finished before a sailor in the control room snatched up the order out of the air.

"Arm torpedo bays, one and two, and open—"

"Arm torpedo bays one and two and open outer doors!"

The order reached Guenther just behind the news that the vessel they'd been stalking was a passenger ship. He mechanically armed the torpedoes as his eyes looked through the hatchway toward the command room as though his eyes might find justification appear before him. While his eyes searched, his ears listened for an order that would belay the one that moved his hands over the launch levers. All while his mind was racing above the surface to the mammoth target.

"We're not going to fire on an ocean liner," he said to no one present. "It must be a battleship or something. Or maybe a liner converted to a troop ship."

As Guenther continued to reconcile himself to the order he hurriedly cranked open the doors of chutes one and two then retreated to his station over the firing handles. He closed his eyes and literally shook his head in an effort to clear his mind free from beneath a weight he had never felt before. The stealthy killer he worked and slept in had no need to attack a civilian passenger liner. "What reason would there be?" he heard his voice say to his ears only.

As his words fell aimlessly to the floor others bolted into the room.

"FIRE ONE!"

Guenther's hands were suddenly gripped by shock. Hesitation froze them as they attempted to engage the firing mechanism. It was hard to push. Was it stuck? He had done the maintenance himself. They were spotless – oiled and greased – and had moved as smooth as a summer breeze. A quick burst of sweat bled out across his forehead and ran into his eyes in less than a heartbeat. As it burned he felt the handle give way. The lever started to begrudgingly descend while his hands still begged retreat. He hunched his shoulders up over the firing panel and forced the lever completely down.

"ONE AWAY! he screamed.

As before, Guenther heard the relayed acknowledgement fade as it race down the sub and up to the attack room. As the words vanished he found himself staring at the reluctant firing lever. His hand touched it as if the machined metal might break under his hand. Guenther tested the drop of the handle and it moved as effortlessly as ever before. His hand dropped away and picked up his chin as he wiped the sweat off his mouth. Still staring at the firing panel, habit made him absently reach out and place his hands on the forward hull of the submarine. The coolness of the steel brought his attention to his hands. Only then did he realize that just his fingertips were touching the sub's skin. The reluctance at the firing had been in him, as it was now. A tremble within his mind trickled down to his fingers as he now openly hoped no shudder from outside the U-20 would reach him.

In the conning tower Schwieger was watching the ocean liner in his view finder. Breathless seconds passed before the torpedo sunk its teeth into the starboard side of the great ship. The blast was predictable, but almost immediately a second much larger explosion nearly ripped the gargantuan liner in half. The U-20 shuddered roughly, trembling in the cold murky depths beneath the weight of what it had done. Captain Schwieger stood at the periscope staring at the destruction as his command crept closer and waited for the order to surface.

The crew's actions were as always – the gunners were assembled by the hatch – but an unspoken dread, shared by some in tight glances through pleading eyes, began to seep from man to man through the sub's watertight doors. The shouts of victory were absent. They were replaced by the distant screams of men and women alike who were driven from the stricken ship into the frigid water above the submarine. The men of U-20 would never hear a sound. Two hundred meters away, the huge liner and over two thousand passengers and crew were going in and under the water. The giant ship was being taken down bow first and Schwieger was watching.

For the first time since his torpedo struck the mark, he stepped back from the periscope and motioned to his commander who had been examining a book of black silhouettes used to identify potential ships in the area. As the second in command stepped to the lens he spoke to the captain without looking at him.

"Most likely the *Lusitania*."

"It is. I recognize the colors of the Cunard Line."

No sooner had the commander assumed the lens then simple words escaped his heart and mind and passed his lips. "Oh my God..."

The captain looked around the small attack room. "Pass the word among the crew. Anyone who wishes to see the *Lusitania* sinking has permission to come to the attack room, but do it quickly. She is listing hard to starboard and I believe she will be down in twenty or thirty minutes."

An impromptu but orderly line formed and the men of U-20 took fifteen second stints at the periscope. Guenther was one of them. As the crew passed by the captain some men uttered soft congratulations, but most said nothing.

"Fine seamanship, Captain."

"Great work, sir."

"Well done, Captain."

Guenther's voice was softer yet and his comment had less to do with the privilege of using the periscope for the first time and more to do with an education and enlightenment regarding war he had not anticipated. "Thank you, Captain."

When the last seaman cleared the attack room Schwieger went back to the periscope and watched the final thrashing of the drowning *Lusitania*. He could plainly see the cold water was alive with victims as hundreds – a thousand – toppled from overturned lifeboats and leaped from crashing decks. So many people were in the water it would seem one could walk on them to the Irish coast.

"Sir, tube number two is stilled armed. Do we send it?" the commander asked.

"No," Schwieger answered without looking up. "I cannot send another into this mass of humanity. They have put children in the life vests incorrectly."

"Captain?" the executive officer asked. "Incorrectly?"

"Yes, the vests should be much higher for children."

"I don't understand, sir."

"Higher! Higher! The vests should be higher – above the shoulders."

"Sir?"

Schwieger came away from the periscope and rubbed his eyes as though they pained him. He spoke with them closed beneath his massaging hands. "A child's head is heavier than his legs. In the sea, a vest slung around the chest will cause the child to tip upside down, weighed down by his head." He opened his eyes and pointed to the periscope. "I see children's legs. Hundreds of them. Growing still as I watch. They are tipping upside down – drowning before the boats can pick them up."

The commander looked at the periscope and envisioned the horror above but could not bring himself to take to the lens.

"Bring us about and lay in a course for home," Schwieger directed. "We will refit. You have the boat, Commander. I will be in my quarters."

The captain was lying in his bunk within his tiny cubicle when the first officer sought him out. The pair exchanged blank looks as the commander tossed a single paper on Schwieger's abbreviated desk.

"It's the communications log," the junior officer said coarsely. "The floating antenna was able to breech the surface. We picked up lingering reports of an SOS from the passenger liner *Lusitania*, just off Kinsale. The local fishing fleet is launching a rescue."

Schwieger nodded his eyes.

"They won't make it in time," the commander continued. "The water's too cold."

The captain didn't speak as the lecture continued.

"She was probably crossing from New York to Liverpool."

"Yes," the weary captain said as he swung his feet off his bunk and reluctantly picked up the radio report.

"Certainly there were Americans on board, Captain."

"Quite probably."

"And, quite probably, you've just given the Americans an excuse to enter the war."

Schwieger jumped to his feet and aided by the tight confines of his quarters found himself face to face with his commander for the second time that afternoon.

"The Americans have been in the war! Who do you think is supplying the British if not their English cousins in the United States?"

"That may be true, Walther," the commander said, ignoring protocol. "But the *Lusitania* is... was a passenger ship. Those were civilians," he said as he pointed up through the steel hull of U-20 to the surface, cluttered with debris, bodies, and those waiting to die. "Women and children. You said so yourself."

"Yes!" Schwieger shouted. "There were children on that ship. And we warned them not to travel. We placed notices in their newspapers telling them these ships are traveling in hostile waters. Notice not to sail! Did the British and French bomber pilots tell the people in Cologne and Düsseldorf they were sending planes to bomb them? No! Do the bombers avoid German cities because there are children sleeping there? No! War paints with a broad brush, Commander! A very broad, very ugly brush."

Without another word, the commander wilted and withdrew from the barrage. He made his way back to his station where he sat for hours contemplating his views on war and collateral damage. Tucked into the far reaches of the bow, Guenther was doing the same.

The disillusioned sailor sat at his torpedo launching station and studied his hands. He looked them over, front and back, examining each finger then did it all again. There were few pauses in the strange review and then only to stare at the firing handle and his tally marks scratched on the wall.

After several quiet minutes, Guenther bent over to reach a small cabinet welded into the wall of the sub beneath the firing mechanism. He moved as though it hurt him to do so. A dented paint can, with dried grey streaks on its sides identical to the walls of U-20, waited for him. The can came out in his hand and settled between the young sailor's knees. Once again Guenther pulled his lucky Deutsche mark from his pocket, except this time he used the versatile coin to pry off the can's lid.

Amidships, Captain Schwieger was standing in the submarine's small chapel staring intently at the small wooden cross as if he full well expected it to move. He stood motionless for some time while the hum of U-20's electric motors whirled and carried him into the Atlantic.

Several minutes later a motion stirred him and he turned to find Seaman Stroehmann walking up behind. The sailor was whipping splotches of grey paint from his fingers. As the captain watched, Stroehmann stuffed the oily rag and his hands deep into his pockets. The young man's shoulders were hunched over and he was walking with his eyes fixed on the sub's grated steel floor.

Guenther's thoughts consumed his senses. He didn't notice the captain until he was nearly on him. Startled, the low ranking seaman quickly saluted. When Schwieger returned the salute Guenther slipped his hands back into his pockets and began to move away, anxious to disappear, but abruptly stopped.

"Begging the Captain's pardon, sir. May I ask a firm question?" Guenther's words were strong, but his tone was nearly reverent.

Schwieger looked at him from beneath the brow of a coarse German mariner, but his place in the boat's chapel and the events of the afternoon had dulled his edge. "Yes," is all he said.

"Sir, was that a passenger ship back there?" Guenther looked over his shoulder, back toward the Celtic Sea. "The *Lusitania.*"

Schwieger returned his gaze to the cross and resumed his study. "It was."

"But I heard there was a big explosion. Bigger than my torpedoes can make. And some of the boys said they saw bales of rubber floating. Was that rubber for England's armies?"

"Without question," Schwieger answered with no vigor.

"Sir, were there other things, because of the explosion – ammo and guns maybe – in her hold?"

"No doubt she was laden with armaments destined to be exercised against your homeland, young seaman."

"And sir, I know we've had a good round out this cruise. We've sunk a lot of ships. Someone must have warned a ship as grand as the *Lusitania*."

"I should think so, yes."

"Yes, sir," Guenther said faintly as he nodded and dug his hands deeper into his pockets. He hesitated over his next words then proceeded cautiously. "Captain? Sir? Do I kill people when I fire our torpedoes?"

Schwieger's gaze didn't flinch. "People die. Yes, they do."

"I mean... do I kill them by sending them out from the boat or am I just following orders?"

The Captain pulled his eyes away and looked compassionately at his young charge. "Are you asking am I the one who kills them by giving the order, or you by triggering the mechanism?"

"Um...yes sir. I guess I am."

The captain's brow wrinkled in thought before he answered. "We all take orders from someone, seaman. I believe we all share in both the triumph and tragedy of death."

The two men allowed their eyes to drift to the wooden cross. After a still moment, Guenther spoke again. "It's our job, right, Captain? Sinking ships?"

"No," Schwieger paused. "It is our duty."

The words took their time sinking into each man. When they had reached the heart of both, Guenther asked a question from deep within. "Sir, if it is our duty, why are you here, in the chapel?"

Schwieger sighed heavily and looked at the ceiling of his command, only a few inches above his head. His eyes were blinking rapidly, trying to fashion a bulkhead against tears. "I am here," he said as he swallowed hard. "For the same reason men the world over go to chapel."

Compassion and embarrassment combined to pull Guenther's face away from the straining officer though his own legs trembled. As the hum of the motors steadily droned on around them, mocking the noise in their heads, Guenther nervously shifted his weight and absently examined the shine on his shoes. When another quiet moment had slipped by like the water beneath their feet, Guenther looked back up the cross and posed a final question.

"Captain? Does God make allowances for soldiers and sailors?"

Schwieger lowered his chin. Unimpeded, the water in his eyes cascaded down his cheeks. "I hope so, son. I hope so."

Captain Walther Schwieger went on to sink many more ships in the fulfillment of his duty. The toll included another passenger liner, the *RMS Hesperian* sixteen months after downing the *Lusitania*. *RMS Hesperian* was carrying 1,114 souls, yet only 35 perished as there was no secondary explosion caused by munitions. The *Hesperian* took over a full day to sink whereas the *Lusitanian* went down in less than twenty minutes.

Captain Schwieger was killed one year later in the North Sea when the submarine he was commanding, U-88, struck a British mine. All hands were lost and Captain Schwieger's body was never recovered.

In another accident, the U-20 was grounded on the Danish coast and scuttled by her crew. Eventually she was scrapped. The conning tower, deck gun, and one propeller were recovered and are now on display at the Strandings Museum, St. George, Thorsminde, Denmark.

Captain Walther Schwieger was posthumously awarded the Pour le Merite, otherwise known as the Blue Max, the highest decoration in the German military, for his service during World War I.

The truest history is lived.

The History of West Texas According to

HENRY BRASS

Recounted by Dr. Whitten Tines, L.A., Calif.

"I have a favorite sound," he'd say. "It's been with me a good long while. It fits in my ear so well I can hear it in my sleep. Most folks dream with their eyes, you know? They see things – a grizzly, the business end of a gun, themselves falling down the face of a plateau, blizzards – all manner of tight spots.

"I'm not like that. I'd hear this sound. And I just drift on off to wherever it was my dream was taking me. But it seems I don't dream much anymore. Reckon I'm dreamed out. I don't remember but one anyway, but I do remember that sound. There was always a reliable comfort in it. I'd just settle in," he said with a weak wave of his hand as if shooing a fly that he didn't care lingered or not. "And go with the dream. It works like that when I'm awake too. Or it used to. There'd be my sound, see? And I'd settle in and go with it. I near always have."

"What sound was that, Mr. Brass?"

Breathing was hard for him. I could tell. No one knew how old he was, not even him. His look might have said twenty years older, but if the stories were any judge, his fifty or sixty some odd years had been hard ones and it showed on his face and in his hands.

"Just Henry," he said, reminding me.

"Yes, sir."

"And leave that 'sir' buffalo chip in the tinder box next time you're in. I can't move my legs. It's commencing to get hard to breath. I could wake up in hell the next time I close my eyes."

"Or heaven."

"Yep, or heaven. I don't suspect I done too much to get turned away at the gate."

"No, sir."

His eyes darted toward me and narrowed as if he were looking down the sights of a rifle.

"Sorry. I mean, Henry. And even if you have done some things, God still loves you."

"Oh, I know that. Hell, He set me down in West Texas, didn't He? And, face the facts — West Texas is the prettiest girl at the dance."

Looking back, at the time I didn't have a lot for comparison, but if Henry was wrong about West Texas he didn't miss by much. This was beautiful country. Henry was right about God putting him in a special place. With few exceptions the entire country was represented outside any door and captured in any vista. The sweeping prairies of Henry's high country stretched out in front of your eyes until you couldn't see any further. Shift your gaze and you'd pick up the soft rolling hills that would drop off and signal the distant descent to the coastline. Look the other way and you saw the Franklin and Hueco Mountains and further north, the grand Guadalupe Range — the dying southern end of the great Rockies. Over your shoulder was a different place entirely — the belly of the Chihuahuan Desert. I've never seen it rain over the desert, but I've only been in El Paso a few years. Henry would know better than me, but he hasn't always been here either.

West Texas skies were blue and the summers unmercifully blazing. Droughts were common and crops and animals suffered in the heat. In winter, winds with teeth of ice raced off those monstrous frozen peaks to the north and blasted across the high country plains, pulling tears from eyes blinded by the cold and instantly froze them on rosy cheeks. But somewhere in between was Henry's gift from God.

He had a dog trot cabin tucked in a valley that was thick with willow trees and juniper. It was on a small creek that eventually gave itself over to the Pecos River. Henry rotated out of the cabin and out of his valley between wars to trek south along the Pecos to trap and hunt in the winter. Come spring, he'd swing wide to the east and trade in Austin, or hopefully before, if he could find what he needed. Otherwise he had to press on to the more populous towns where he had to trade a measure of his comfort for the opportunity to barter for the few things he needed to see him through another year.

Henry would be back in his valley by mid-spring and spend a few months tending to his place and preparing for the summer season. When the heat came, he went north into the Rockies to hunt. The big mountains held lots of game in its rugged arms and his pack horse was weighed down when he returned. Following these summer hunts he followed the Pecos south and veered away only long enough to trade with the United States Military at the Forts in Stockton or Davis. If the trade had been weak or his energy high, Henry would amble to the northwest and empty the last hides at Fort Bliss – the most western outpost in Texas. When he added this portion of the trip, he made certain he had left time to visit nearby El Paso.

This simple background came from Henry with no prodding. It was a good, honest life that met all his needs and then some. He always traded for a few pieces of gold in his seasonal rounds then secreted them away for another time when age had stolen his strength and his mountain and river hunts were lost in days past.

Now, sitting in a nicked up old chair that was missing a few spindles from the back, I was at the edge of his cot inside a threadbare white tent on the slope of Franklin Mountain outside of El Paso. I looked at this man with the simple life and wondered how West Texas had turned on its most devoted son and had locked him inside a flapping tent he would likely never leave alive.

"Ain't it kinda funny how most people's dreams is really what you might call nightmares?" he said one day. "Now don't think I don't know a good nightmare when I'm in one. I had one once where this big ol' she wolf had her choppers locked right down on the back of my front. When I'd try to turn with my skinner to make her leave go, why she'd just whirl around me, like I was a cat chasing its tail. And all the while her kin was circling and growling and nipping at the rest of me. By God that'll make you sit up in your bed roll at night. Make a strong man throw a few extra sticks on the fire too."

Henry's stories could be like a fire started with oak. It was sometimes hard to get started, but when it got going, it would really burn. Yet the talking was always slow – as slow as I write or more. What he said had an ease that doesn't come across in reading. It was a pliable noise, like a smooth hum made out of mud. Writing doesn't do it justice.

"Here's another thing you'll find right interesting. All these nightmares people have – bears, wolves, getting shot, trapped on a rock face in a blizzard? I've lived 'em, not dreamed about it, but faced them down, eye to eye. But I never thought of them as terrible, awful things. Certainly not nightmares. In West Texas these things just sort of happen. They come on you or you onto them and you make due.

"Mind you I said West Texas. Some people call it the high country. It's not like East Texas. If you do enough easting, you can run right into swampland. If you're in a swamp, you ought not to be calling it Texas at all. I don't know where the line between East and West is, but I suspect anything near Austin on is East.

"I've been there, but it ain't for me. Austin's a nice enough spot and I even been north to Dallas just to say I been there. Good trading in Dallas. I made Houston once. A bunch of sickly people living in a swamp, just like I said. I wouldn't take Houston if it came with a side of biscuits and beans."

There'd be a long gap as he caught his breath and caught up with his story. His eyes would rest a minute then look around as he concentrated and searched for his next turn.

"There's lots of people in East Texas. That tells you about all you need to know. If there's a lot of people living somewhere, chances are the living is a might too easy for real Texians. There's trading posts to fetch food from, a smithy to fix your tools if they give out on you, no Indians looking to lift your hair, even big game that in West Texas would sniff you out as a meal, has been drove out.

So you get folks moving in that are a bit soft the way I measure. And soft people ain't my kind of people. I hear there's even a mess of Yankees living in East Texas. Yankees wouldn't make out in the high country. The trail can be a might steep and a bit rocky. A hearty way of life separates the wheat from the chaff. If you look around and you see a passel of Yankees, you're in East Texas."

I laughed out loud at that and I could tell it pleased him. His eyes eased shut so slow you could see every bit of the movement. It was like watching a child go to sleep. He seemed to try to pull in a deep breath as if it was the end of a long day, but he couldn't do it. Instead it choked him and made him cough. His cough was a harsh, raspy cough like when the breeze suddenly changes and you get a lung full of smoke around a fire. At least this time. Maybe he was running low on parts to hack up, but other times I saw him ease his hand down in exhaustion after a coughing spell and he'd be so tired he wouldn't even try to hide the fistful of blood that dripped through his fingers.

The other men nearby coughed as well – all the time. I was there from early summer to almost Christmas of 1878 and I never recall a quiet time – day or night. Someone was always coughing, and I mean coughing hard. So hard they would faint. Some fainted and never came to. They just died right there on those simple cots with straw stuffed pillows, if they had pillows at all, inside those little white tents.

The tents were somehow compliments of the Army. The ruling fathers of El Paso had set them up outside of town in the lee of Franklin Mountain when it became clear the boarding houses on the back streets weren't up to the task. But it had less to do with space and more to do with sickness. These men all had consumption, or tuberculosis as it was called in less polite or maybe more medical circles. It was in various stages from man to man. I had it too. No one in their right mind would work here who didn't already have it. But I was twenty years old and immortal, as most twenty year olds deem themselves. Plus I was making the same money as some poor well digger or cattle puncher. Being young and strong, I could also ward it off pretty well. I never did become one of these 'lungers' as they were called, who coughed and spit up blood into already soaked rags few people would touch.

In El Paso they started calling this collection of tents 'The Sanitorium.' It was an official sounding place and later several towns and every bigger city had one. North, in Las Cruces, it really took off and they built a nice place that I heard did everything they could for people suffering – for several dollars a week. Only the rich lungers went there. Others came to the tents where there was lots of dry fresh air, the only treatment. But credit the townspeople of El Paso – they didn't run these poor bastards out of town like some places. Well, I guess maybe they did, but only as far as Franklin Mountain and then they hired me and people like me, to feed them and make them as comfortable as we could – comfort coming in ample supplies of whiskey and laudanum with some quinine and cod liver oil from time to time. El Paso's use of Franklin was the right thing. If they hadn't gotten those Army tents, chances are all of El Paso would have coughed itself to death over time.

Henry knew the cards he'd been dealt. As he would say himself, "This is West Texas and things just sort of come along and you make due." He was making due.

"Henry?" I said gently, as though I was waking him.

He didn't say anything, but his opening eyes and steady gaze was sufficient.

"You didn't tell me about the sound."

"No?"

"No," I said then let it hang there in the air, begging to be picked up again.

"You have a horse?" he finally asked.

"Yes."

"What kind of horse?"

"I'm not sure. I never thought of what kind of horse he was. He's brown."

"Brown?" He seemed quite agitated. "Brown's not a kind of horse! Brown's a color, it ain't a kind. Where'd he come from?"

"I got him up in Oklahoma territory."

"What were you doing way off up there?"

"I come of age in Oklahoma."

"You Indian? Don't look it."

"No, I was born in Kentucky."

"By God, you're a world traveler, ain't you?"

He was making a joke, but I was still flattered. "No, I was just born in Kentucky."

"How did you end up picking up a brown horse in Oklahoma?"

"My father struck out for Colorado with my mother and a wagon full of us kids sometime in the 60's to do some mining. We made it out along the Cherokee Strip on the Kansas side and held up while my mother was to get over a bout of fever. She never did get over it. My father buried her and most of my brothers and sisters.

"There wasn't much work and so we came down into Texas. I got my horse along the way."

"Your family in El Paso?"

"No. We worked our way south for a while then a couple of years ago my father decided he wanted to head east toward Nacogdoches, but I wasn't too set on it so him and my sister – her and me are all that's left from that wagon full of kids, went to have a look. I decided to head to California to see if there was any gold left. El Paso is as far as I've gotten."

"You could have made out worse. And you're young yet. You can strike out again."

I thought about my sister for a minute and all those graves I'd helped dig. Then how I had only made it to El Paso and I was still digging unmarked graves. I was thinking I hadn't come too far when I startled myself out of my own thoughts.

"Why'd you ask me if I had a horse?"

He seemed to think seriously about it, as if I'd said something profound.

"If you have a horse, you probably own a saddle," he said as his eyes eased closed in the same dreamy motion as before. Before I could say anything, his chest rose in a slow breath, not as deep as before, and the coughing didn't come. It was a breath born of a welcome resignation. He talked for the next several minutes in that methodic manner of his – slow and easy, deliberate, pacing himself, with his eyes closed, as if he would talk all day if only his body could keep him propped up.

"When you take hold of that saddle in the early darkness, it makes a sound like a woman saying good morning as you wake up next to her. It's a muffled, creaking, gentle sound. The leather yawns and stretches, saying good morning to the day and to you. It wonders out loud, like you do to yourself, what lies ahead. In the easy popping sound of the leather, the saddle settles on your horse's back and creaks and moans its way into the day. Sometimes it almost sounds like it's crying that it has to move at all – like a youg'un you have to roust from his bed to do his chores.

"Then on other days, there's no good morning at all. As the horse stands there on three feet, resting that fourth one and easing from one to the next, the leather snaps out reveille as sure as the horn blower in Fort Stockton. It's a beautiful sound every time, but when it blows that leather bugle, my blood begins to race. I'd hear it and I'd know I'm about to do something more than look through the brush for longhorns."

"Your favorite sound is your saddle?"

His eyes opened for the first time in several minutes and he looked as though he felt sorry for me for not understanding.

"It's a lot more than just the sound of a saddle, young fella. It's a sound that is whispering to you, but most folks don't know the language. It's like learning Mexican talk at first. Damned if I know what they're jibber-jabbering on about, but then you start picking up on a few words – hopefully enough to keep from getting bushwhacked or your throat cut. That sound is the same.

"'Where you off to?' it says. 'Going to see a lady,' says me. Then it sings with every step of my horse, every movement in the saddle causes that leather to sing out and it's like you ain't even on the ground no more.

"That sound can be damn near anything – a call to arms, like when I let myself get pulled into some war. Damn, that sound almost hurt my ears in those days – endless riding, circling, jumping Mexicans – that leather crying as I whipped that horse into a lather to get as far away as fast as I could.

"That sound meant it was time to run and hide, or run and fight. And when the fighting was over, it sighed and said, 'Let's go home.' And that's what I done."

Henry's eyes slipped shut again. I let him rest and he let me soak it in. I don't know that I could hold it all, but I understood it meant a lot to him – this sound that had signaled so much and accompanied him throughout his life. He might have been touched in the head for all I knew, I was no doctor, but remembering that sound brought him comfort, and there couldn't be any harm in that.

I was back the next day and Henry took his quinine and a glass of weak whiskey and water and settled back into his blankets and his story as if only a few minutes had passed.

"It played reveille for my father back in '36 when I was just a sprout. He didn't say much when he got back home, but in the spring of 1846, me and him rode down toward San Antonio way with about every man from the high country to have another go at the Mexicans. Well, I guess I was old enough to stomach it by then or maybe it was because we were about to set against the Mexicans like he had done ten years before, but whatever the reason he talked almost all the way.

"He wasn't at the Alamo in the early spring of '36 and anyone what says they was is like as not a lying sonofabitch."

Henry shook his head and waved at the fly again as he rested for only a moment. "Oh, there was a few what slipped outa that slaughter house – and the women and children got turned loose in the end. Someone had to tell the tale.

"People forgot right quick that there was a pretty long siege – probably a couple of weeks at least as my father told it – before Santa Anna's boys really got down to it. And we sure couldn't count on that murdering bastard to tell the truth. And I don't call him a killer for what he done at the Alamo Mission in San Antonio de Béxar. That was battle. But what he done in Goliad a month later was no battle. My father's partner got caught up in it. Name was Giuseppe Pietas, but everybody called him Joe Pete."

It was March 19th, 1836. The dispatches recounting the battle of the Alamo Mission in San Antonio de Béxar only two weeks before had continued to trickle into Fort Defiance in Goliad, Texas. Joe Pete heard the stories of the Mexican Army raising a blood red flag before the fighting which meant no quarter would be given. And they were right. When the Texian hold outs were over run, only the women and children were spared. Even a young boy was killed by soldiers blinded by bloodlust when he made a move they thought resembled a Texas rebel.

With this on the defenders' mind, the order to pull out and retreat to Victoria, Texas, and meet up with General Houston's force was not unwelcomed. If Joe Pete, short, stocky, dressed in worn clothes from his home in Tennessee, would have known what the next few days would bring, he'd have lobbied to stay behind the protected walls of the Presidio La Bahia. The Presidio was what Fort Defiance had been called before the Texians took it by force in the early days of the rebellion against Mexico. But now Joe Pete blended in perfectly with the other men – rough looking men, mercenaries and farmers drawn from all across the south to a fight they thought worth fighting or worth the money – as they formed up in loose companies to abandon the fort.

The retreat to Victoria began early on the 19th under the cover of a heavy lingering fog, but with no haste. The commander of the Fort, Colonel James Fannin, didn't believe the closing army of Mexican General José Urrea would pursue the retreating Texians or if they did, wouldn't present much of a battle. But he didn't see the size of General Urrea's army or more importantly, the teeth of the President of Mexico, General Antonio Lopez de Santa Anna, when the Colonel set out with over three hundred men, including Joe Pete.

"How far to Victoria?" a member of the Kentucky Mustangs brigade asked Pete.

"About twenty-five miles."

"Can we cover that today?"

"I don't think so," Pete answered as he pointed. "Them oxen pulling the carts are in bad shape. We need mules or horses on those wagons to make any time."

The carts Joe Pete referenced were carrying a half a dozen small cannon. Other artillery had been buried at Goliad to keep it out of the hands of the closing Mexican Army. Additional carts and supplies to maintain a garrison of three hundred men for very long had been left behind – Colonel Fannin thinking they would be re-supplied when they'd covered the relative short distance to Victoria, but then an axle broke a mere two hundred yards from Fort Defiance.

It took several hours to get it fixed and the column underway again. In minutes they hit the San Antonio River and lost more time in the crossing. By then the fog had long lifted and General Urrea's troops were hot on their trail. Late in the day he came upon the Texians when Fannin had, against the wishes of many of his officers, stopped to rest the beleaguered oxen. In minutes, the Texas collection of soldiers was over run and in a pitched battle with the Mexicans.

"This ain't no good," Pete said to the Mustang trooper as he looked around to the wide prairie the Mexicans had chosen to attack them on. "It ain't but four hundred yards to them woods," he continued as he motioned to a thick patch that made up the tree line near Coleto Creek.

"We might make it if we can hold out until dark."

"Maybe," Joe Pete said as he lined up a shot, fired, and dropped his musket to reload. "Problem is everybody on this field is looking at them trees yonder."

"Including the Mexicans," the Mustang answered as a rifle ball whistled by his head and hit one of the oxen behind him.

"Yep. Including the Mexicans," Pete said. "If we can keep them off us with our cannon, we should be able to hold out a bit, but I don't think we can get to cover unless we get some help outa Victoria."

But reinforcements never came from Victoria and they couldn't keep the Mexicans off. Joe Pete and men like him turned back several charges and delivered horrific casualties, but a simple commodity brought the Texians to their knees and forced their capitulation. Water.

As the sun set on the 19th, sixty some men around Joe were wounded and there was precious little water and no medicine to treat them. As the dying men cried out in pain, the morale of Pete's fellow soldiers waned hard. Pete wandered around the square encampment and tried to rally his friends.

"We did good, fellas. Tomorrow we'll cut through a corner and make for them trees. There's plenty of water there and just beyond is General Houston and the Army. We'll make out, boys. Keep your heads down, your powder dry, and your chins up."

He had his own head down in the dim light of dusk and was hustling toward one of the corners of the square the three hundred men had fashioned in the grass. His latest friend from Kentucky was laying down a stone's throw from one of the cannon in the corner checking two muskets he'd been alternately firing during the day.

"It's getting dark, Joe. Why you ducking? It's over for the day."

As if on cue, a report rang out and a soldier, who a moment ago had been walking slowly around the oxen, trying to make the weak cattle comfortable, dropped his musket and fell over without a sound. A sniper's bullet lodged in his brain.

The Kentuckian looked up from the ground, shocked and embarrassed.

"It'll be like that tonight," Joe Pete said. "They'll use their snipers until they can't see no more. Then they'll shoot into us most anywhere – just to keep us awake and nervous. Keep your head down."

"Probably touch off their cannon a few times to keep us guessing," the Mustang said. "I even heard them to have their bugler sound charge, so we can't sleep."

"It's not their cannon what troubles me – it's ours."

"How so? Near as I can see we've got powder and canister."

"It ain't that, Mustang," Joe Pete said, looking very grim for the first time that day. "We're about outa water. I see them rationing it to the wounded. If we're rationing water to wounded, that means we're low. I don't think we have enough to clean the barrels and keep them cooled down in a fight. They'll misfire or blow and kill us instead of them."

"That true, Joe?"

"Sure as I'm standing here."

"Then what, Joe?"

"Colonel Fannin will make a pact with General Urrea."

"Surrender?"

"Either that or get cut to ribbons on this field. I figure General Urrea hasn't left himself so short as our Colonel. He could probably melt those cannons down turning this patch of prairie into a big hole in the ground. If we run for them trees, his snipers and cavalry will take us down. If we stay put, maybe we die of thirst first. I don't fancy any of those options. Our Colonel and his captains will be thinking the same way."

"Damn, Joe, that's mighty bleak."

"Sorry, Mustang, but it's pretty clear. Either General Houston comes riding out of those trees at daybreak, or we surrender to the Mexicans by noon."

Joe Pete didn't miss by much. The terms for surrender were sent to the Mexican Army and accepted, though their guarantee was less than resounding. Colonel Fannin had requested fair treatment of his men and medical attention for his wounded. He also requested parole of his troops to the United States Military.

Under the guise of accepting the terms, the Texians were summarily marched back to Fort Defiance. Though the mood was grim at having been caught in the middle of an open field and having suffered the loss of several men, the soldiers were happy to be alive and thought they would be freed in short order.

Joe Pete and the member of the Kentucky Mustangs walked along together, unarmed, but alive and unwounded as the Fort came in view.

"Well, Joe, we're near back home!"

"I guess we'll be sleeping in our own bunks tonight."

"Maybe we'll have to share them with a Mexican."

Joe Pete laughed. "My bet puts us on the parade ground. If we get a blanket, I'd say we done good. The Mexies will hole up in our barracks and the officers' quarters. But it won't be more than a few days and they'll have a trade worked up with General Houston to get back some of their own men."

Joe Pete was close – he did sleep on the ground that night, and the next, and the one after that. A week later, the Texas prisoners were in rough shape. Food, water, and sleep had been slim and there was no protection from the spring weather as it alternated from thrashing driving cold rains and a pounding early summer sun.

"How much longer, Joe?"

"Not sure. I seen some other fellas brought in. There's more than enough for a trade. I don't understand the hold up. I know Houston wouldn't leave us here."

Joe Pete didn't know it wasn't his General, it was the Mexican General and President, Antonio Lopez de Santa Anna. He had issued a decree that all Texians were to be classified as pirates rather than prisoners of war. The distinction by definition allowed pirates to be executed and not afforded the protection of 'civilized warfare.' General Urrea was busy writing letters to Santa Anna asking for leniency for the captured Texans, but the Butcher of the Alamo gave no ground. "Kill them all!"

General Urrea responded by moving a substantial number of his troops to the northeast and left the Fort under the control of Colonel José Nicolás de la Portilla with strict orders to treat the Texans properly as prisoners. No sooner had General Urrea crossed the San Antonio River and disappeared over the horizon then a dispatch arrived at Goliad from Santa Anna. "Execute all pirates in accordance with Mexican law."

The next morning, March 27, 1836, was Palm Sunday morning. Joe Pete and nearly three hundred and fifty Texians were marched out of the citadel.

"Finally, Joe. Looks like the Generals have come to terms. We'll be back to fight with this bunch again."

The pair slapped each other's shoulders, smiled and walked out beyond the heavy wooden gate. Joe Pete's eyes suddenly fell to the ground and he looked sad.

"What's on your mind, Joe? We're headed back to our lines. Cheer up, like you're always telling us."

"It's not that, Mustang. I got a partner with Houston. We been riding side by side since we was wet-nosed kids running a trot line together. He's going give me a going over for getting caught up by these Mexicans."

"It wasn't our fault, Joe. Hell, we was caught in a bare field with no cover or water, you said so yourself."

"I know, but he'll ride me over hard for giving my bunk to a Mexican whilst I slept outside in the dirt!"

"Ha! I get it. He's that kind of friend."

"He is, and I'd give to him twice as bad if it were him."

The Kentucky Mustang soldier laughed again. "It's a good thing to have a friend like that. I have a few guys here in the Mustangs like that." He put his hand on Joe Pete's shoulder. "And now I got a Texas regular to call friend. I appreciate you looking out for me, Joe. I don't forget a good man when I meet one. Even if he ain't from Kentucky."

Joe Pete didn't have time to answer. His eye caught the rising of a rifle barrel behind his new friend and heard several reports fired in unison. He and the Kentucky soldier were driven into each other by blasts from either side of the column. They, along with hundreds before and after in the lines, spun and were thrown to the ground as musket balls hit them at point blank range.

Pain held Joe Pete down. His backbone held the slug and he couldn't move from his chest down. The pain moved quickly upward and he cried out without thinking. The Kentucky soldier had been hit beneath the arm and the lead had nipped his heart. He was bleeding to death and would be dead in a minute.

"Joe? Joe? What'd they go and do that for?"

Joe Pete couldn't answer. He writhed in pain, unable to move most of his body. He twisted as best he could and flung his arms at anything and nothing. Mexican soldiers came up on him and stuck him with repeated bayonet thrusts in his chest and neck. The bleeding quickly calmed his body and he was gone. Beside him, the soldier of the Kentucky Mustangs suffered the same while ahead and behind on the columns, all the soldiers not killed in the first volley of Mexican bullets were stabbed and hacked to death until the Mexican's arms were tired.

After a breather, half of the Mexicans piled over three hundred bodies and put a torch to them to hide the crime. Others returned to the Fort and executed the wounded Texans who had been unable to walk. Only then did they kill Colonel Fannin and toss his body unceremoniously on the fire of burning bodies.*

Henry Brass closed his eyes as if the memory would disappear. I let him lay quietly and wondered about the story of the Goliad Massacre — were there that many men? Was it that cold blooded? And Fort Defiance — had the Texians really set out from there one morning only to be corralled home there that same day as prisoners? I didn't know at the time, but Henry was incapable of lying when it

---

*Colonel Fannin made three requests before he was the last to die. 1) That he be shot in the chest and not the face, 2) that his property be returned to his family, and 3) that he be given a Christian burial. Colonel Fannin was shot in the face, his property looted, and his body burned.

came to these types of stories. He had relied heavily on his father in the senior Brass's telling of this story in their ride south together to take up arms against the Mexicans ten years later in the Last Mexican War. I suspect Henry's father was cut from the same cloth as he was.

His eyes opened, but appeared focused on the past.

"I remember Daddy saying they was butchered on Palm Sunday. Shot them down like dogs then burned the bodies. He was further northeast at the time – caught up in the Runaway Scrape when he heard of it. You ever heard of the Runaway Scrape?"

"No, Henry. What was that?"

"After the Alamo and the massacre at Goliad, General Sam Houston took his boys and made out like they was high-tailin' it outa Texas altogether. They were headed east for Louisiana. That sonofabitch Santa Anna was right on his ass thinking he was about to end the Revolt once and for all.

"Ol' General Sam was gathering up all the settlers in Texas he could to protect them from the Mexicans so between the homesteaders and the retreating Army of Texans, they called it the 'Runaway.' The 'Scrape' part was a passel of fights they had on the way as they was beating out a hasty retreat.

"Lots of men were learning about Alamo and Goliad and went to join up in the Runaway Scrape. By mid-April or so, General Sam come across a great spot of land for a fight – right near the San Jacinto River. He moved on about four hundred yards or such a manner, just enough to let Santa Anna's fat ass get comfortable on that patch of nice ground and then Sam asked my father and about nine hundred other fellas to turn around and run right into almost fifteen hundred Mexican soldiers. They never saw what hit 'em. They were laying about in their afternoon siesta. Daddy said some was actually caught with their britches down as they say! General Sam turned hell loose on 'em.

"Inside twenty minutes around six hundred Mexies was dead. Our boys was screaming, 'REMEMBER WHAT THEY DONE AT THE ALAMO AND GOLIAD!' and kept shooting and hacking their way right through their camp. They found that murdering bastard Santa Anna in a private's uniform hiding in a swamp like a little girl, the spineless coward. My father and some of the boys from the high country wanted to stake him out and skin him Apache style, but General Houston said they needed him alive to sign the peace.

"I remember Daddy saying, 'We woke up on April 16th, 1836, in Mexico on the run, but went to sleep that night as new citizens in the great Republic of Texas.' So that was that. New citizens. We had our own country."

Henry tried to prop himself up, but the telling had worn him out. I eased out of my chair and adjusted a rough blanket he'd been using for a pillow.

"Henry? You want me to see if I can find you an extra blanket to sit you up some?"

He took a breath — a little too deep — and launched himself into a coughing spell. His face contorted and reddened as blood and spittle came up into one hand while the other held him up and off the cot enough to be as comfortable as possible without falling. His legs not working made everything tougher for him. The doctor that flew through every two weeks or so said that the consumption could get to a person's legs once in a while. It didn't happen all the time, but in the end, people couldn't get enough air to walk even if their legs worked and had no strength to try.

When the coughing eased he collapsed onto the cot. "If you run across a halfway clean one, I'd be much obliged. But don't slip nothing away from any of these other sorry sonsabitches."

"I wouldn't do that, Henry."

"No," he said as he recovered from the spell and looked at me thru eyes that were bright red around the edges. "No, I don't believe you would."

"Maybe I can bring one from town."

"That'd be real nice. I'd like that. I ain't no daisy, but some of these boys is a might rank. I figure when they pass over, you rinse their blankets in the creek and give them to the next sick bastard. I wouldn't know how to act if I had a fresh blanket to put my head on."

We both smiled.

"Let me see what I can do."

"Thank you. Thank you. That was a bit of a rough one for me," he said as he wiped the blood from his hand. "It's hurting in my chest here. Suppose you could draw me up a thimble of laudanum?"

"Sure thing, Henry. Be right back."

The doctor and everyone who worked the tents were liberal with the laudanum, whiskey, and even morphine. It was kept locked up in a thick, heavy trunk where the workers congregated. If it was open, lungers who could walk were prone to snatching a bottle or more. More than one had killed themselves, accidentally or otherwise, by drinking laudanum like it was whiskey. They went to sleep and never woke up.

I gave Henry the laudanum and I wasn't too shy with it after having just watched him choke up a fistful of blood. I sat a few more minutes with him and he started to fade to an uneasy sleep. He asked me if I remembered his special sound and I said I did.

"What is it?" he asked as though testing either my memory or my truthfulness.

"Your saddle."

"Half-right."

"Okay. Not your saddle, but the sound it makes."

"Better."

There was a still shallowness in his breathing and I knew the laudanum was taking hold.

"What a beautiful sound. Soft, like a woman breathing in your ear... That Joe Pete was a wonderful man. Awful what they done to him... He brung me a piece of maple sugar candy when he come to see Daddy." He was tired. "It was maple candy once..." He mumbled something about Santa Anna and smiled in his near-sleep then was quiet.

I slipped away from his cot and hustled to do the things I'd traded for the story of Joe Pete. But that night and for days after I listened when I saddled my horse. Sure, I could hear that leather bending and creaking, but I didn't hear it say anything. In the morning I'd ride out until those white tents started to come into view as gray ghosts in the pre-dawn light. The brown horse from Oklahoma would be put on a tie line between a couple trees and the noisy saddle would get dropped far enough away so the horse wouldn't step on it and get tangled in the cinch strap. Throughout the process, repeated day after day after day, I never heard a word.

I walked by one day and saw Henry was lost in his thoughts. I wasn't certain he had even seen me as I wondered what was behind the faraway look in his hazel eyes, but decided to slip away and let him rest.

"Where the hell you off to?" he spit.

"Nowhere."

"You got to shovel dirt on some sorry sonofabitch out back?"

"Not as far as I know."

He motioned to the little chair.

"Sit with me a few more minutes, will you?"

I couldn't have refused even had I any inclination to not sit and listen. He was talking before I was settled.

"I remember you saying how you 'come of age' in Oklahoma, where the brown horse come from."

"Yes."

"I was dwelling on that some and it come to me that I come of age in a brand new country. Republic of Texas. We weren't tied to Mexico no more and the United States was off to the north and east. Them was heady days as I grew up. People were talking about the Republic all the time. They was saying we were gonna stretch west clear to California, but I suspect the Mexicans would have had something to say about that.

"It was rough going sometimes. Blizzards in winter. Droughts in summer. Rascal Comanche could really raise hell, but they didn't bother most of the folks I knew of in West Texas. Truth is, I never seen them bother no one who didn't bother them first and that's the God's honest truth. My family traded with them quite regular. I did the same for years. Hell, when I headed south for another go around with the Mexies in '45 or '46 I had a whole Comanche family move in my place. My father had a bent back from the rheumatism and had a hard time getting around. They was a great help to him. My sister had gone way north not long before the war commenced. Her man and some other cowboys had a mind to start a ranch somewhere up in Nebraska, I think it was. They done real good too. Had trading relations with the Cheyenne and when the Army come in chasing the Sioux, they sold them beef and horses."

He smiled slyly to the side and his eyes sparkled. "That was the Texas in her and her man. Work hard. Treat people fair and trade with all comers – red, white, outlaw, or lawman.

"That's my point I suppose. People is people. The Comanche didn't trouble us. We was fair with them and them with us. There was parts of the big mountains we didn't trap or hunt because they asked us not to. Simple as that. Respectful people. You can go a long way on respect in West Texas."

"I can't disagree, Henry. You get back what you give out, don't you think? I mean, if you treat folks right, like as not they'll treat you right. Love your neighbor is what the Book says."

Henry twisted his head a little and looked at me out of the side of his red sunken eyes. "You a preacher?"

"Nawww," I laughed. "They'd never have me!"

"Doubt that. It'd be their loss if it were true."

"I'm just headed for California. Need a little stake and I'll be on my way."

"I hear there's a part of California been cut right from the Devil's hind foot. They could use a good preacher man with sand and some sense in his head out there. Most preachers I runned across is sissy boys raised in New York or Boston – Yankees who can't cut the mustard around here. You can."

"I ain't got no Bible training."

"Hell, ain't no one born with it, but 'spect they teach it somewhere."

"Yes."

"You could go learn on it and then go to California."

"I ain't a preacher."

"Not today maybe, but you've got the ears for it," he said.

"The ears? Preachers need a good head for learning and converting sinners. They gotta know the Bible front to back."

"You're a smart young fella. You got them other preachers knocked already and it's because of your ears. Come here a minute," Henry said as he motioned me over closer to his cot.

"A ain't knowed a lot of preachers, but the ones I did know that was worth their salt had what you have. They could listen. People don't always go to a church house to get read the scriptures and be told they'll burn in hell if they look at the ass on their neighbor's wife. They need to be lifted up. What's the word for it? You know the word..."

"Encouraged?"

He slapped his hands together. "That's it. You're damn right! Encouraged. Most of these sorry sonsabitches want to be encouraged."

"Oh, I dunno—"

"Bullshit you don't! You're always taking to fellas here, helping them feel better, listening to them as they struggle agin' dying. Listening to them tell lies or listening to them cry. You're good at it and you need to keep on with it. Long after this sickly place blows away and these old tents with it.

"You're the best thing these boys have for a preacher. I think you should fire up a Sunday service. I'll come!" He looked at his worthless legs. "I mean, I'll come if'n it's right here!"

We were both laughing.

"How about it? Give her some thought. I'll put in a word with the doctor. I know him right well. He swings by my place ever week or so." We laughed again but this time it was too hard and he slipped into a coughing fit.

By the time it ended, I was standing at the cot with the laudanum. All he said was, "Thank you. Thank you." And he rested.

I slipped away and tended to the affairs of the tents. It hadn't been much over an hour and I was back by his cot.

"I needed a little rest for a minute there I reckon," he said as he struggled to ease himself up a bit on a worn, but clean blanket I had brought him. "I got all fired up about you taken the vow or whatever it is they do for a fella who's commencing to be a minister."

"Damn, Henry, if you haven't got my life planned out for me!"

"Go easy on the language, son. I don't recollect most folk would take to a preacher who cussed."

I laughed all the louder. Henry only smiled.

"Okay. Now that my future is laid out, without any training or what not, would you mind going back a little? When your sister went north, you went south—"

"Had to!" he interrupted, something he rarely did. "We had to put an end to them Mexican bandits trying to take back a sizeable part of Texas for theyselves. As I recall they had in mind to push the border up from the Rio Grande, north to the Neuces River. Damn, that was some awful fighting. I was about your age, maybe a might younger.

"It weren't easy and I knew better what my father had gone thru ten years afore. We'd be see-sawing back and forth with the Mexicans and then that sound of mine would signal a counter-attack coming from some band of Chiricahua who was raising hell along the border. Smart bunch, them Chiricahua. I think they knew the borderline better than us or the Mexicans. If we were hot on their trail, they'd duck over down Mexico way, and if the Mexican Army was after them, they'd slip away up here. And if the Texians and Mexies was squared off in a pitched battle, the Comanche or Apache would be nearby – not picking sides – just waiting until it was over then they'd come swooping in to pick up any spoils. It was a risky game. Those braves would ride on into a battlefield thinking they'd just pick up some boots and clothes, maybe a rifle if they was really lucky, and both armies would open up on him and shoot him full of holes for his trouble.

"It was hard for all sides. Hell, none of us boys cared where the line was drawn. It weren't more than a few miles as the crow flies in either direction the way we figured it.

"All the killing that went on – I look across that big river and it don't look any different. I don't think the Rio Grande gives a damn who's drinking it, fishing in it, crossing it, or pissing in it. I suppose it's about the water and the land. Some government wants to say they own it. I don't imagine they care about the pissing part. I've heard that now if you do cross it you have to ask permission to come back. Damnedest thing I ever heard of.

"By the spring of 1845 I was going pretty well heeled* on account of Daddy's stories of the Revolution, the boys' gallant fight at the Alamo, and the butchery at Goliad. It all formed a stew that just sat and simmered in every young man's belly across Texas as we growed in our new country while the Mexicans were getting their nerve up and their Army ready to try us again."

While Henry was talking, I poured a good shot of whiskey in a tin cup and splashed some water down on top. I moved the cup in a tight circle a few times to stir it, knowing Henry could care less if he got a mouth full of whiskey or water.

"When was that, Henry?" I asked as the cup changed hands.

"Well," he said with that molasses slow delivery. "I was riding somewhere in that scrape through most of '46 and '47. I believe it was fall of that first year when I was somehow attached with a group of Rangers. I wasn't no real Texas Ranger, but I had met many of

*armed with revolvers and rifles

them trading so I just begun tagging along with them you might say. Damn savvy Indian fighters which, when you added the experience the older Rangers had against the Mexican's in my daddy's war, made them a good bunch of men to ride with.

"Santa Anna was back in the saddle running the show in Mexico again. It made Daddy spit whenever he heard about it, knowing they could have killed that murdering bastard way back at San Jacinto."

Henry stopped for just a minute. I thought then and still do that he was thinking about his father, but we never got back to talking about him.

"Us Ranger types was running with a battalion of regular army boys and pushing hard into Mexico. We'd crossed the Rio Grande some time before, but it wasn't no big event. We barely got our pants wet. Wherever we were, the water was real low and wide — ankle deep most of the way across. When we cleared the bank on the Mexican side someone said we had to report to Mexico City and turn ourselves in to President Santa Anna for trespassing! We had a good laugh over that. I remember Daddy pointing over his shoulder telling me that on this side, the Mexies called the river the Rio Bravo. Remember it like it was yesterday.

"Whatever we called it, the short of it was we didn't have to go clear to Mexico City to meet Santa Anna or his boys. We hit the first of the worst of it in Monterrey. Am I sick?"

"Yes," I said, caught off guard in the middle of the story.

"Hell, I'm as right as rain compared to some of our bunch on that trek south into Mexico. Boys got the dysentery so bad they couldn't walk, let alone fight. They died right where they fell. We buried them in that sand and shoved on.

"When we got to Monterrey, the dying really started. Them damn fool officers we had in the regular army had their boys marching right into town in lines — waves of soldiers to be shot down. Made no sense. Them Mexies would be behind them thick walls of their houses and just kept shooting. We lost a mess of good men.

"We fired some artillery into the town but it didn't make much of a dent. So Daddy and some of the old Texas boys, who had done this thing a time or two in the Revolution, showed the Army officers how you had to dig through the roof or outside wall of a house at one end of town and dig from house to house thru the walls and roofs right up the street. We called it 'mouse-holing.' You got in the middle of them then behind them.

"It was impossible to go up a street and go in a door or window. They had their muskets trained on every opening. Stepping into a doorway was like walking into a cross-cut saw. They shot you in half before you took a step.

"The rub was that inside them houses was some of the worst fighting of the war. It come down to hand to hand – kill or get yourself killed. I remember one tough sonofabitch. I dropped down through a hole in the roof and scurried toward the doorway of this upstairs room. I damn near run smack into a Mexie outside the room. We both fired and both missed. He come at me with his bayonet and I dropped my rifle and grabbed his blade in both hands – damn near cut my fingers off. But it worked. Threw him off balance some. He was still holding his gun shoving it at me. I turned loose of that blade and hit him in the face as hard as I ever hit a man. He staggered and dropped his rifle but didn't go down. He lunged at me and we went tumbling – both of us trying to knee the other.

He had one hand on my face and the other on my throat. God he had a vicious grip. I just gave up my throat and put both thumbs in his eyes – buried them up to the palms of my hands. Lord, did he scream. He sort of rolled off, out of instinct I think, and I pulled a skinner from my waist and introduced it to the underside of his ribs. He flopped around yelling in Mexican, but he was squirting blood from his ribs and some other stuff from his face. It wasn't long before he quieted down but, and I'm being honest here, I didn't wait around to watch him die. As soon as he was off me, I was up and going. Mouse-holing left no time for sitting still, but it worked.

"Most of Monterrey was taken that way – mouse-holing from house to house. Helluva tactic. I know they didn't teach that one in that fancy-ass West Point. Maybe they do now, I don't know, but if they do, they learned it from Texians in the Mexican War."*

Henry was proud of that trick, I think more proud of showing it to the United States Army than the fighting or victories his Texians

* 'mouse-holing' was the first application of urban warfare tactics. It has evolved to the use of breach explosive charges to enter buildings, but the brutal hand-to-hand combat can be much the same as it was in 1846.

won because of it. His voice tightened some whenever he referenced the United States in his stories. I wasn't certain yet if he'd gone east to fight in the Civil War, but if he had, I was pretty certain he'd ended up fighting for the Confederacy.

He rested a few minutes and I filled in the gap.

"You know what, Henry? I've been listening to my saddle – listening for your sound."

"Any luck?"

"Nothing. Not a word."

"They ain't exactly words."

"Right, but even the leather creaking isn't meaning anything."

"Give her some time. I don't recollect when it started coming to me. Maybe it'll take a while yet."

He was quiet again, but it didn't last long. Henry started to smile and it grew into a wide grin that erupted into a silent laugh. I could tell he was struggling to keep it stifled. His eyes were clenched tight shut and the corners of his mouth nearly touched his eyes. It was only a moment more and the weight of the laugh burst the dam on his face and he laughed out loud, but it was short lived. In a painful flash, the laughter morphed into a horrendous coughing spree that went on way too long.

While he was in the throes of it, I abandoned my post in the rickety chair for the laudanum. I brought it back along with another two shots of whiskey and one of water. As soon as his body let him out of the spasm for a moment, he gulped the odd mix of medicines.

The cough picked up again, but less violent and slowly eased its grip on Henry's throat and chest.

"Give me a minute, partner. By God that was funny."

"What was funny?"

"We was..," Henry said softly, and breathed through his nose as if it'd help ease the coughing. "We had pushed south, deep into Mexico. This was maybe, oh, six months or so after Monterrey. Santa Anna hisself come outa Mexico City to welcome us. We met around the port of..., damn... the port down there... Just north of the Yucatan. Veracruz! Port of Veracruz. There was this little place nearby there called Cerro Gordo."

He started to laugh again and worked hard not to.

"No laughing," I reminded him as I tried to help.

"Right. The fighting sure wasn't funny. But there was two different things I recall about that battle. One wasn't funny at all – just so damn odd. But that last bit was just funny as hell.

"Anyway, the damnedest thing. Probably a year or so before, a bunch of Irishmen showed up in Galveston Harbor, looking to sign on with the army and fight the Mexicans. I guess whoever was doing the recruiting said the more the merrier and drafted the bunch on the spot. Well, hell, you could count the number of weeks they was in Texas on one hand before them Irish deserted and took to fighting for the Mexies! Now don't that beat all?"

"Does seem right odd. What would make them switch colors? They get captured or something?"

"Nope. Had it planned all along. Turns out they were all members of the Catholic religion faith. They thought we were roughing up the Mexies because they was Catholics too! Couldn't have been more off.

"Well, in Cerro Gordo, those Irish lads got cut off from their Mexican Catholic partners, and they fought like hell because they knew the hangman's noose was waiting for them as deserters and turncoats if they got captured. And that's just how she turned out. We weren't happy at all having to hang those fellas, but we had to – we knew it and they knew it. Captured 'em and hung 'em. Just like that. One of the strangest things I remember about that war."

"That is awful strange, Henry. But damn if I don't see much of a joke in it. What was the second part?"

He immediately started to laugh and just as quick started to cough. The laudanum wasn't working as well as it had. I thought about another splash of whiskey, but he bid me wait with a wave of his free hand. After another minute the cough passed.

"No, you're right. Hanging those Irishmen was no pleasure, even though they were deserters. But before the battle was over in Cerro Gordo we were laughing – and I mean laughing out loud even as the bullets were still flying by our heads."

"So," I said, slower than he talked. "Hanging Irishmen wasn't funny – I understand that – but getting shot at makes Texas Rangers laugh? They might have been stranger than the Irish. Had you been into the mescal?"

"No, not that time, but I'd be lying if we didn't generally have some handy, mostly for medicinal purposes. It'd make a fella kind of sleepy before they cut a bullet out of his ass or sawed off a mangled up leg or arm."

I considered my work here at the little white tents. If this was an Army field hospital instead of a place for dirt poor lungers to come to die, I imagine my days would be much different. Henry made me begin to think.

He was smiling broadly again and more importantly, his eyes, still ringed in red, were twinkling. Despite what the story would do to him, Henry was more than willing to suffer through it for the pleasure he was finding in the telling.

"It had been a stout fight. And, as back in Daddy's time when Colonel Fannin decided to rest those damn oxen and got Joe Pete butchered for his trouble, Santa Anna was worried about his men getting some rest and a few good meals in them after humping from Mexico City clear across country to the Port of Veracruz and having to face down some real wild men in the Texas contingent such as myself.

"Us younger fellas were fairly tight, and not just from a few swigs of mescal. We had fought well in Monterrey and elsewhere coming south, but we wanted a shot at Santa Anna and here he was – the symbol of cruelness and tyranny. When he turned his regulars to face us, his citizenry of Veracruz were as excited as we were.

"He had appointed hisself the new Mexican President, again, and he was in a damn good position. On a lesser day he would have whipped us, should have whipped us. But not that day.

"There was a pass outside of Veracruz that was the one decent way in or out if you wanted to get to Mexico City – and that is just what we had a mind to do. And wouldn't you know that pass happened to be Cerro Gordo. And that bastard got his troops there before we did. When we showed up, Santa Anna had over twelve thousand soldiers jammed in that pass and on the overlooking hills. I remember looking down into that valley and not being able to make out the road. The bottom of that ravine was just a mass of soldiers – so many jammed in they looked like ants crawling over one another. The hillsides weren't much better. Everywhere you looked there was vast spreads of white and different colors – Mexican Army regulars and conscripts, moving slowly into firing lines behind natural and man-made fortifications. The distance made them appear to move slow, but when this thing jumped off, and you happened to still be alive when you got there, it would be happening faster than a hummingbird beat its wings. This was a killing zone and a damn big one. If we had to go in the business end of it like as not we weren't coming out the other side."

Henry closed his eyes, tired from the memories and the telling of the tale like before, but I have to admit I hadn't heard the funny part yet. Or if I had it didn't sound funny to me. Maybe I just missed it entirely.

"There was a bunch of young captains and lieutenants around that war – people whose names are apt not to be forgotten for a good long while when folks talk about this country. Probably not so much for what they did in Mexico, but for what they did twenty years later in the Civil War. Like a lot of us young fellas, them Civil War Generals cut their fighting teeth on Mexican blood. The shame of it was when we was done in Mexico, they commenced to killing one another. Helluva waste of good men and good sense."

"No argument, Henry. But was that the funny part? I still don't–"

Apparently I'd given him another reason to laugh. As he did, he choked out words between the laughter and hacking coughs.

"Hell, no... we aint'... we ain't got to... to the funny... part yet!"

He was recovering again so I slipped off to the medicine tent and brought him back a cup of the special brew. He took it with thanks and settled back onto his cot.

This second round hit the spot better than the first. It was pretty common with lungers toward the end that it took sizeable amounts of whiskey, laudanum, and even morphine to ease the consumption. After a time at the tents, I could almost predict the days a man had left in this world based on the amount of "medicine" he was ingesting each day.

When the second dose had quieted Henry's affliction, he picked up like it had been me that had broken off the conversation.

"So, there we sat, looking at Santa Anna with his ass dug in the ground like a badger – perched in that draw and covering the approaching hills with blankets of troops. If we attack – we're dead. If we wait in a siege, we never get to Mexico City and putting down the Mexican invasion comes to a stalemate.

"This young Captain of ours, he stands there looking out over the Mexican preparations for better than two hours. I don't think his eyes ever came away from his spy-glass the whole time. Finally I see him lower his glass and commence to rub some life back into his eyes. He don't say a word to nobody, just mounts up and rides about three hundred yards northwest of that big gully. He don't come back to the main camp for at least two more hours. Then in he comes, real quiet and slow like.

"That's the kind of guy he was – quiet, but a helluva soldier. The kind who knew his way around a battlefield. The kind you applauded for when they promoted him. Name was Lee. Robert E."

"THE Robert E.?"

"One and the same. Smartest damn soldier ever took a breath of life. Jeff Davis seen it too, but that comes later. Most all the good soldiers, both sides, come up out of the Mexican War.

"So Captain Lee, like he was explaining 'rithmatic to a little boy, proceeds to tell the commanders about a trail he has mapped out to flank the entire Mexican Army. And he's right – right as rain. They sent most of us boys in on Captain Lee's say so and Santa Anna gets overrun so fast the entire lot of Mexicans don't know if they's afoot or ahorseback! They were scrambling like rats when you carry a lantern into a corncrib.

"And when I say the Mexies were moving, I mean moving! Santa Anna himself was hustled out of his tent so fast and so near to getting kilt, he didn't have time to strap his fake foot on. See, the Mexicans had a spat with the French after we run them out of Texas in '36 and them Frenchies shot Santa Anna's foot off in Veracruz for his trouble. We found the wooden fake stump – boot and all, still in his tent!

"We poured into that gully and all there was was Mexicans running out on all sides. We routed them, plain and simple. After that we walked right into Mexico City. Except Santa Anna – he didn't walk nowhere, because our boys kept his foot! The last I heard they had hauled it all the way to their regimental headquarters in Illinois. Can you imagine that? Santa Anna's phony foot sitting in a glass display case somewhere in Illinois. And the cruelest bastard to ever draw a breath of life hopping on one foot screaming at some poor cobbler to whittle him out another stump leg. Now, you chew on that and tell me that ain't funny as hell!"

I stood up and swung my chair out of the way near the head of Henry's cot and started hopping on one foot yelling, "Bravo para México! Viva la Mexico! Viva la Mexico!"*

Henry was laughing too hard and the cough came back on him like a thick dark cloud's cold shadow in front of a weak winter sun.

I patted his shoulder to reassure him before I went for more medicine. It was then that I felt his bones sticking through his clothes. He was as skinny as a rail fence. It didn't show through the layers of clothes and blankets. I gave him as much laudanum as I dared.

I don't really remember what happened the next few days, but I didn't get back to my chair and Henry's cot for some time. The men in the tents were getting worse, as everyone including themselves knew they would, and needed more care. Others died and new men took their place. It was a busy time I guess.

I stopped at his cot one afternoon carrying an armful of filthy sheets and blankets destined for the burn pile. Henry was so still. He looked like he might have been dead.

"Henry?" I whispered. "Henry?"

One eye cracked. The other looked held down – almost glued shut. It took him a moment to focus and another one to recognize me. He spoke, but never moved.

"Death will have you by the throat carrying that pile."

"Headed to burn it."

"Don't let me stop you. Get away from me with that. I don't want to get sick."

One edge of his mouth slipped up in a tired smile. The eye fell closed and I walked away quietly.

Late in the day, I went back to see him. I brought a shallow pan of water and a towel that was as clean as any I could find. He was resting as before, but I came prepared with a strong dose of the laudanum regardless.

*Santa Anna's prosthetic leg remains on display at the Illinois State Military Museum in Springfield, Illinois. The Mexican government has repeatedly asked for its return.

"Henry?"

The eye didn't even crack open, but he answered.

"Hi ya, Whit. You ready to go fishing?"

I wasn't certain if his mind was gone or he was dreaming.

"I can't just now, Henry. I've got to work."

"Never let work interfere with a good time. Life's short, as well I know." And the crack of that lone eye opened. "Had you going, didn't I?"

"You did, at that. How about a shave, Henry?"

"You think I'd let you near my gullet with a knife? I'd sooner do a jig on a bear trap."

"I'll be careful."

"No, sir. I'll be dead quick enough without you laying my juggler aside with your saber."

"I didn't take you for being scared of a shave."

"I ain't scared. Just don't need one, is all."

"Make you feel better. Freshen up and look decent."

"Only thing will make me feel better is a visit from the Grim Reaper. Keep your skinner in your pocket, barber. And you ain't no prize yourself. I seen horses that been rode hard and put away wet look better than you."

"By God you are sassy today."

"Speaking of my maker, I suspect He will recognize me right off when I stroll in the pearly gates without no shave from a wanna-be Saw Bones."

"I never said I wanted to be a doctor."

"Probably why you want to cut my throat – just to see how it works inside."

"Who told you I wanted to be a doctor?"

"None of your business."

"Who?"

"I got eyes, you damn fool. You said you weren't up to snuff when it come to preaching, so it has to be doctoring."

"What has to be?"

Henry's hand came out from beneath the blanket as if in slow motion. He waved it casually around the tent just an inch off the cot. I could count the bones in it.

"Why you work here."

"I get paid good."

"Bullshit."

"I do!"

"That ain't why you're here. You know it same as me."

His hand was already settled back on the green blanket. I wasn't going to argue and risk a coughing session.

"No shave?"

"No shave. But I ain't scared. A list of the things that scare me wouldn't fill a very big book. Hell fire, I once lit out after three Apaches armed to the teeth and I was riding a camel!"

I spilled the water on the cot as I lurched forward laughing.

"Henry! Three Indians armed to the teeth and you on a camel! Bullshit! You're gonna make me think all your stories are whoppers."

"It's true!"

He was trying to sit up in bed, but he didn't get far or resist when I put my hand on that boney shoulder as though to hold him down.

"As sure as I'm lying here, it's true!"

"Stop it, Henry." Now it was me that couldn't breathe for the laughing. "I'm gonna bring up my supper. On a camel! I can picture it."

"Sonofabitch... Let me get my wind. I'll tell you. Laughing like a damn yapping coyote. And here I lay on death's doorstep. You heartless bastard. Some doctor."

"Henry, come on. That's flat unbelievable. Funny as hell, but unbelievable."

"Let me know when you're done gabbing."

I did take another minute to catch my breath. Then I let him go.

"Okay, Henry. Let's hear it, but I haven't quite gotten over Santa Anna and his missing fake foot. This camel tale is going to be a tough one to swallow."

"When you get to your fancy ass doctoring school, take five minutes and study your history learning. I ain't told you a thing that ain't the God's honest truth and I ain't changing horses mid stream now."

"What'd you say about doctor school?"

"Never you mind that now. Listen to what I'm telling you."

I was still chuckling, even though his reference to 'doctoring school' had sobered me some.

"After we got home from Mexico City and Santa Anna was corralled again, I went back to running my trading route – summers in the big mountains north and winters trapping along the Pecos south. I don't recollect the year exactly. Let's see... the Republic went under the Stars and Stripes in 18 and 45. I come back across the new border after the war... and the Great Compromise was in '50... Had to be the late 50's. Lord, time has got away from me. Call it 1857 or 58.

"Lieutenant Ned Beale – least ways he was Lieutenant to me – was going to make out for a new southern trail to California. Somebody had the idea that as we had to cross the deserts of Chihuahua and Sonora country, Beale should use desert critters, them of course being camels."

"Is this a joke, Henry?"

"I'm telling you. I was there. Seen it with my own eyes. I have rode a camel," he said proudly.

"I'll be damned."

"I doubt that, but when I signed on with Lieutenant Beale to make for California we had a mess of camels with us. The government had gone clean to Egypt or China to fetch 'em. And they brought back some Greek boys to do the wrangling because a camel don't wrangle like a cow or a horse. Not even close."

He rested again and I let him. Though he was quiet, I handed him the tin cup. He hadn't asked and didn't thank me. He just swallowed the laudanum and whiskey and closed his eyes to rest. His breathing was raspy, like wind whistling at a loose window. At length he spoke again following a shallow breath.

"A camel is the orneriest animal God ever give life to. You ever see a camel, Whit?"

"No."

"They're kind of... Well, it's like the Almighty couldn't quite make up His mind what He was after. Maybe He started out with something like a horse, but give 'em big feet so could stay afloat in sand. Then He had to make it so they could go days without water and live off scrub weeds a goat would pass on, so He had to tweak their innards some. It must have been in doing that, He had to give up any decent disposition at all. A camel is so cantankerous that wherever they piss nothing will grow for forty years and that's been wrote down.

"Damnedest animal. One minute you can lead them just like they was a dog walking down main street. The next minute, it's like you had a holt of a rank longhorn's tail. And when a camel sets his mind to do something, or not do something, you might just as well settle in for the ride. You can hit him right smack dab in the head with a rough cut plank and he won't even blink.

"But, I'll tell you something, a camel can carry three times what a Army mule can. And do it on no water, no rest, and cactus for supper. If a camel can get his mouth around something, he'll eat it."

"So you rode a camel from Texas to California?"

"Almost. We had our horses, and the backside of my frontside has always been partial to my saddle, but there weren't no saddling no camel, not like we do anyway. Plus the horses were scared to death of them. Someone trailed the horses a long ways off. We ended up on the camels through the toughest going because the horses couldn't make it."

I could see Henry was tiring.

"We followed Lieutenant Beale clean through though. He had to been some sort of awful smart man – plugged us on so straight and true you could have stretched a piece of yarn from here to the ocean and it wouldn't have bent ner touched the ground. He had been a Navy man at some point I do believe. He could steer a wagon by the stars I reckon."*

"Did you ride a camel back to Texas?"

"Only way to get them varmints back. They done a helluva job, but it was tough on them. It seems our desert ain't like them Egypt and Chinee deserts. Ours is too rocky, not enough plain sand. They come up lame a lot. And they're so dad gum nasty. You know how you can pet your horse and stroke his neck almost like he was a woman? You can talk to a horse and he'll listen as you curry him down at night. There ain't no petting or talking to a camel. A camel plain don't give a shit what you've got to say."

---

* Edward Fitzgerald "Ned" Beale's Expedition became the 1,000 mile southern wagon route in 1857-59 and has been calculated to follow almost exactly, the 35th parallel. It would one day become the foundation for the Transcontinental Railroad, the famous Route 66, and currently, I-40. The camels were eventually abandoned to the deserts of the southwest where sightings continued until the 1930's.

For reasons long forgotten it had been a very quiet stretch of days. I had just dug two graves, though no one had died. It was something to do to pass the time. When I walked into Henry's tent he looked at the dirt on my hands.

"Lose another patient?" he said as he weakly flicked a finger to point at the dirt.

"Not yet."

"Not yet...," and he smiled for one of the few times I'd seen it in recent days.

Henry's face was a strange mix of pale colors. His eyes were bloodshot and sunken into his head. His cheekbones were scarcely being held in place by gray skin. Both lips were bluish and cracked with dried black blood at the corners.

I crossed the simple hospital and pulled up the chair that had kept a constant vigil at his cot.

"How are you holding up?"

"Fit as a fiddle and ready to dance."

"Sure."

"How about, as healthy as a horse?"

"Whatever you say, Henry."

"Your horse – the brown one. He a good animal?"

"Get's me around," I said. "He's not fast, but he does show up for work every morning."

Henry snorted a short laugh. "Shows up for work."

We sat there noiselessly enjoying one another's company as the coughing rose and fell around us. Henry was very still.

"I never had a fast horse," he said. "Never was an issue. I was prone to strong steady ones who could work the mountains or the trap sets. I generally had a good mule along too. I had a matched pair all through the war. They served so long, they was made sergeants."

The black blood cracked in the corner of his mouth as that half smile of his rose up at his own joke.

"Names was Tom and Bill. Good names for mules, don't you think?"

"Fine names. Original."

Henry started to continue then stopped when he caught the brunt end of my gag.

"Oh, now that's right funny. Spoke like a man who's never drove a team a mules. You needs short sharp names for mules. Otherwise they don't know who you're talking to."

"Do they ever?"

"Damn right they do. I could ask Tom to step up and ask Bill to hold, and we could turn a wagon in a circle within the length of itself. Mules is a helluva lot smarter than horses. They just ain't so pretty ner as fast."

Henry was breathing heavy and as though he had to think it through and make himself pull in hard then force the air back out.

"When Texas throwed in with Jeff Davis and the Confederacy, me, Tom, and Bill went to sign on together. None of the three of us ever fired a shot the whole of the war.

"After my cameling experience with Lieutenant Beale, I went back to my trot cabin. Daddy had passed. I took up with my regular routine of hunting, trapping, trading, and keeping my place up between. I had come across Tom and Bill around San Antonio on a trading run. Instead of packing a single mule, I took to packing a wagon. It wasn't long and I had a bit of a carting business between the high country, El Paso, and San Antonio. When the war come on and I went to sign up, they took one look at Tom and Bill and had a whole new plan for us.

"Right off, I took to hauling supplies from West Texas up a backdoor run near Dallas over to the Red River at Arkansas. I'd trade out my wagon full of supplies for bales of cotton smuggled across the river. Then I'd turn around and roll them down to the Mexican border to be sent off to the French or parts over yonder.

"At the border towns, I'd get loaded down with whatever the boys in Louisiana and Alabama needed, and off me, Tom, and Bill would go again. We made maybe forty or fifty runs. We never even seen a blue coat for over three years. We had to watch out for Comanche in the south and lost Jayhawkers down from the north, but other than that, we just kept our heads down."

Henry closed his eyes and rested as best he could. His breathing was painful for him and his stories had worn him out. I didn't say a word, but went to fetch him a stout cup of the medicines. I don't know what I put in that cup, but it was almost full when I brought it back. As had become his practice, Henry didn't say a word. He just took the cup and drank. This time though, he stopped as though to save and savor the last half a cup.

"I run mostly medicines," he said with his eyes closed. "Quinine and such, same thing you give me now. And whiskey. A lot of whiskey. I suppose it was just another medicine or good as money. With both sides printing paper money that folks was mighty skeptical of, a pint of whiskey was like gold for trading. I always thought it was mighty odd I didn't hardly ever make a run of powder and shot. From what I hauled, you'd say there was more sickness and dying than fighting going on in that war. I didn't cart much food either. I remember hoping those boys had grub coming in from somewhere. From what I hear, it was pretty slim pickings.

"That was an awful war and I know I didn't see none of it but the ass end of Tom and Bill. The boys that come straggling back after was in rough shape."

He opened his eyes and took a shot from his cup.

"What happened at the end was the only time I ever been put off by being Texian."

I was surprised to hear him say that.

"Why, Henry?"

Though he was always a slow talker – delivering every story in that methodic rhythm that was mesmerizing – he didn't come back, slow or otherwise. It made me regret the question. While I was thinking of a subject to jump to, Henry was in the tin cup. He didn't down the mixture though; he was sipping it, as if he'd acquired a taste for the whiskey, laudanum, water, and morphine.

"It's alright, Whit," he said as he read my face if not my mind. "I been in a lot of wars and seen lots of folks pushed to near madness by it. People can be cruel and, like a herd of cattle, if a few turn in a direction, the whole herd will follow like as not. In Galveston, most of the herd went in a piss poor direction. I was there. I seen it. I ain't proud of this, Whit, but the only men I killed in the Civil War was likely Texians. They wasn't Union. They was Confederates, same as me."

It was clear this was a torment for him. While he returned for another comforting sip from his cup, I tried to relieve him of the burden of telling it.

"Henry, I was telling some of the other men your story about those damn camels. They laughed like hell. Do you mind if I do that? Tell your stories? That camel run really puts a smile on them."

His gray lips came away from the cup.

"No, it ain't no bother. But if you want to be fair with them, you'd better tell them about Galveston too. Life ain't been all camel stories. You know what I'm getting at?"

I did indeed. Thanks in large part to my time working the tents. I could only nod.

"Me, Tom, and Bill had been making the Red River run for years. We were in the south, having just dropped a half load of cotton, which should have tipped me off. I generally didn't make a run with just half a load, but I had and now I had an empty wagon. We had been told to run east to Galveston to meet up with a good-sized boat that was running the Union blockade to get supplies into port. It was late spring of 1865 and I was hole up in a stable near the Galveston docks with my team waiting on orders. Instead of hearing who, what, and where, I hear General Lee had surrendered. God damn that was desperate news.

"Soldiers began just walking away right then and there. I recall a few speeches like, "Rally and fight on," sort of bullshit, but when General Robert E. Lee says throw in your cards, by God it's over.

"A few weeks later is when it went real bad. You had half a Army just been told they were beat. It didn't go over good and they had no pay, little provisions, and damn little leadership. The folks who lived in Galveston were in it too. As the fortunes of the Confederate Army went, they went too.

"First thing to go was the quartermaster's office. People needed supplies and food. And it went downhill from there damn quick. I commenced to hitching up the team to get the hell out of Galveston as quick as I could. I believe people would have put Tom on a spit and ate him if I'd stuck around much longer.

"It weren't but a few days and everyone had just run amuck. The army was disbanded. People were robbing and looting every store and warehouse they could find. It come right clear that it wasn't just stealing food to eat or a coat to keep warm. It was stealing to steal. There weren't nothing going on but out and out stealing and killing over stealing.

"Three fellows came in the stables I was at and began carting off anything that wasn't nailed down. They were looking hard at my team until I run them off at the business end of my rifle. When I pulled outa that yard I ran right into hell.

"People were running around carrying off anything they could lay hands on. Soldiers were fighting each other in the street over an arm's full of dry goods. You'd hear a pistol crack and people would hold fast for just a second then rush on. Between the pistol shots I could hear glass breaking, doors being kicked in, and people yelling."

Henry pulled the cup to his mouth again, took a swig and seemed to rinse his mouth with the brew. He rubbed his chin and dry mouth. Not once did he look up at me.

"I cleared that stable at a firm trot. When we got to the main street, men started to jump at me – trying to get to whatever was in my wagon. I had leveled my rifle at a few and they backed off, but soon I heard a clamoring behind me and turned to see two fellas right in the bed of my wagon. They was apparently disappointed to see I was empty so turned their likes to the wagon itself. I leveled my rifle and told them to get the hell off right quick. They told me they were gonna eat my liver. That's just what they said. Like crazy people. They both made for me and I shot the nearest one right off the wagon. The second one didn't break stride. I pulled my pistol and shot him too.

"Tom and Bill never broke stride neither. They jumped into a gallop and we headed for the hills. As we passed the docks, I saw the ship I was supposed to hook up with, the *Lark*, she was called. Awful. Her deck was awash with soldiers and town folk fighting and shoving their way to clean out her hold. All I could think of was how them sailors and that ship had run the Union blockade to help these people and now they was raping her."

An odd look came onto Henry's face that rose and fell as if a wave from Galveston Bay was still crashing on his mind. It flashed from anger, to a grimace, to fear, to sadness in as many beats of his heart. I felt each emotion and I hurt inside for him.

He returned to the cup, but held himself to a mouthful.

"I stepped up the team and we was running hell bent for election. But men would see that wagon and rush me. Like before, when they seen she was empty each one looked to me and the team. And each time they moved, I shot. I had the boys pull us right over three strap lads who thought they could just grab a hold of the harnesses and bring the team to a stand. Tom and Bill only knew my voice. I felt the wagon wheels pitch over two of them fellas, soldiers they was. I suppose they might have lived. The wagon was empty and not too heavy. Maybe got a snapped leg or arm for their trouble, but they could of gotten a helluva lot worse.

"When we cleared Galveston, both Tom and Bill was soaked in sweat and had white froth scrapping up beneath their harnesses. Damn, they was a good team. Them mules should of been promoted to Captain easy for saving our lives.

"When our own little Runaway Scrape was over I pulled the boys in just long enough to throw two dead men out of our wagon. Whether it was my shooting or the pitch of the wagon, two saddle tramps had fallen right when they was hit and was dead before they hit the floorboards. Those dead thieves got a free ride outa town then a quick boot in the face off the side of our wagon."

Henry stopped again, clearly getting tired more easily. He drained the last of the cup, but seemed to be feeling well – the intoxicants coming into play, I'm sure.

"We lit out for the high country and never looked back. It were quite a spell before folk stopped looking sideways at each other. Everybody was wondering who or what you were up against. Made for rough times. Me and the team worked our way west. We steered clear of the cities, towns, and most roads. Didn't have any real trouble – nothing of the likes of what we seen in Galveston."*

Henry stopped for another moment as if to let the air clear of that story. There was a swallow left in the cup and being a man given to willful waste and the inevitable willful want, he wasn't about to waste it. He slurped down what he could then ran his finger around inside the cup as if wandering up strays.

"I'm tuckered out, Whit. You took me for all I had tonight. I'm about ready to hit the sack. Tomorrow's another day."

---

* Soldiers began openly pillaging the Galveston quartermaster's stores on May 21. Several hundred civilians sacked the blockade runner '*Lark*' when it docked on May 24, and troops sent to pacify the crowd soon joined in the plunder. Riots continued in the city until May 26. In Austin, the state treasury was raided and $17,000 in gold was stolen. By May 27, half of the original Confederate forces in Texas had deserted or been disbanded, and formal order had disappeared into lawlessness in many areas of Texas.

"Yes it is, Henry. You need anything before I head out?"

I was asking him if he wanted another cup to see him through the night, but he turned me away.

"No, I believe I'm alright. I'm carrying a pretty full load and I want to be in good form tomorrow."

"What happens tomorrow, Henry?"

"Never you mind. Just important affairs to tend to. I'll be needing a piece of paper and a sharp pencil first thing tomorrow if you can manage them. Then you can mind your bed pans." He tried to be serious, but he choked out a laugh and me with him.

I only knew another day was coming that carried jobs, work, decisions, responsibilities, and the memories of things heard an evening prior which could not have been learned in a textbook. At twenty-one, surrounded by the living dying at the tents, I had come to hold a greater appreciation for life and what we could do and should do with this little sliver of time allocated to us. Henry was thinking the same thing – sliver of time – and how much he had left. I had been in the tents long enough to know that when men began asking for writing tools, you could count down the days. They wanted to write letters while they still could. Those that couldn't write asked for help with no shame taken or given. I penned a lot of those last letters. Most of them were pleas for forgiveness after being swept away by a war, a woman, or a dream.

I was surprised how many wrote of having consumption, as though it was a battle wound. Perhaps it was, but the enemy had been life itself. When Henry comes to mind, and most of the others, I must say I have never seen a country bite its children so hard. They were tough men, reared in tough times on a hardscrabble plain called West Texas. I was young and strong and determined to stay that way. I knew I had a touch of the consumption, but was planning on warding it off. If the tide turned against me I believed I had the strength to suck a shell out of my pistol. I didn't want to die on a cot under a white Army tent.

The next morning, Henry thanked me for the brown scrap of paper and the rough cut pencil, though he promptly returned the pencil and asked me to put a keener edge on it. He watched closely, but didn't comment as I raked the soft wood with my knife. I gave it back without a word to a thorough though silent inspection.

"You need a hand, Henry? I'm pretty fair with words."

"No, thanks. I got her from here. Swing back after a bit. I'll be in need of a favor."

After so much time together and so many stories, I was disappointed to be left out of any role in the last one. I took a couple steps back as though leaving the presence of a king then fell off to the side and went on about my business. Henry never looked up except once toward the cloth ceiling of the tent as he searched for a word there or in his mind to translate to the paper. I secretly watched him for several minutes, but he was very deliberate and seldom seemed to be at a loss.

When the day had nearly retired, I picked up a heavy cup of his medicines and went to Henry's cot. As I slid my chair over and held out the cup, he reached in his shirt pocket and pulled out the folded brown paper and the scruffy pencil. He handed them both to me as he reached for the cup.

"Trade."

"Okay," I said as I began to unfold the paper thinking I could now help with words or spelling.

"Hold on, Whit," Henry said, trying to have the crack of a whip in his voice, but he was far too weak.

"What's the matter?"

His hand came over mine and his letter. "Ease that down some."

His hand was cold. It was shaking and had the feel of dried out leather.

I took the letter to be private words for his family or a wife or lover he had yet to speak on. "I'm sorry, Henry. I'll just look quick and see if there's anything I can help with, then I'll fold it right back up to go to the post."

His strength had gone and this wonderful story teller was down to single sentences and worse. Sometimes he just nodded his tired head.

"No. No post."

"Who do you want me to give it to, Henry?"

He pointed one boney finger at me.

"Me?"

The finger fell with his eyelids as he nodded yes.

"This letter is for me, Henry?"

"Ain't no letter."

Reflex brought me eyes to my hands and the paper as he continued.

"It's a map."

His breathing was really taking effort.

"Take a look. But keep it down some."

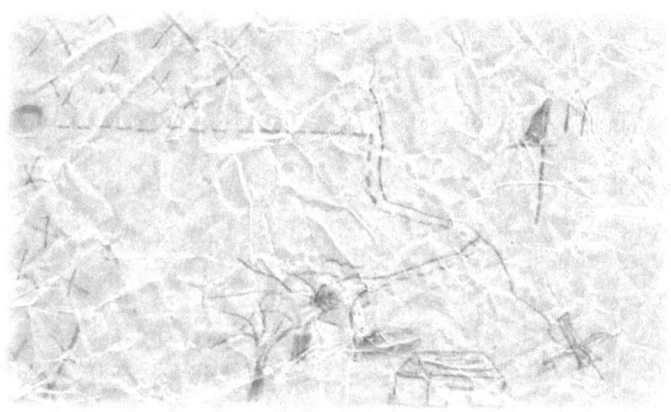

Henry's Map

I unfolded the paper and turned it to align a single arrow indicating north. It wasn't very elaborate and the 'N' for north was the only word or letter. The rest was different lines for rivers and creeks, small 'x's I took for mountains, a few big dots, some scribbled pictures of trees and a trot cabin.

"That blot near your left thumb – that's us. El Paso."

He sighed and it sounded as if he wanted to breathe out more, but there was nothing there.

"The blot by your right is where... where you're going... That's my cabin drawed up there."

"Henry. I'm sorry, but I don't think I can get you there. I don't think you're quite up to it just now."

He was already shaking his head no.

"Not me. You. That chicken scratch to the north is the Guadalupe Range. Keep that in sight on your left and go direct east... You'll come to the Pecos River... Don't cross it. Turn south... The first creek you get your... your britches wet crossing is Toyah Creek. If you come up on Horsehead Crossing, you... gone too far south."

He was wheezing, trying to get it all out as I followed along on the little map.

"Turn up Toyah. You'll be coming back west. Stay on the south bank. Turn about south again up the second draw... Little canyon there a way... Couple a big trees. Used to be a big nest... Eagle nest. You'll find the dog trot."

"Henry, I really appreciate this, but you know I'm trying to get to California."

"I know. To doctoring school. Am I right?"

"I'd like to try it, but I've got to work up a stake."

"That's why... That's why you gotta make this run first."

He motioned me closer. His face was so drawn I could see the blood just beneath the skin around his eyes. His beard was scraggly and gray and his breath was sour from the drink.

"I used the south cabin of the trot for Tom and Bill in winter when we weren't on the southern trail. There's a box stall in there. And about a foot of horse shit they always left behind."

Henry's breath was about gone. He was as close to dying as any man I'd ever seen before or since.

"In the southwest corner, you need to dig down some... Through the old horse shit... and a foot or better of Texas. There's a cast iron strong box. You go get it. Promise me you'll... Promise me you'll go."

He descended into a coughing fit and tried to take in some sips from the medicine cup but was spilling most of it. I took hold of the cup and steadied it. He fainted and swallowed involuntarily. I tried to bring him to, but he couldn't stay. When his eyes lolled in their sockets and he moaned, I was quick with the cup until it was nearly empty. Henry was hurting bad. It showed on his weathered face.

I settled back into the chair and Henry slipped into a deep sleep from which I didn't believe he would ever wake. As I sat there, I reflected back on the stories, the laughter, and the sadness he had shared with me since we'd met in the white tent. This was goodbye. But I suddenly felt that despite the "ears" I provided him, I hadn't given Henry much in return.

The cup went to the ground and I stuffed the paper in my pocket as I jumped up. The chair went over backwards and was still moving after the flap of the tent had watched me race by.

I ran to my brown horse so fast he was startled and pulled back against the tie line. But nothing was after him, least of all me. I grabbed something else.

In the same flash I was back at Henry's white tent. Two fingers circled the horn of my saddle as it hung down my back. The cinch and back strap were dragging and flopping and catching on everything nearby as though I was hauling a schoolboy to the woodshed for a whipping. I had to stop to free the twisted back strap from a short hewn table leg, but gave up in less than a second and jerked the table over and cursed the strap that was slowing me down. I vowed that if I missed Henry's passing I'd come back and burn that table and the back strap for the witches they were.

My foot caught my flipped over chair and tossed it near upright. I grabbed it with my free hand and set it right next to the cot and Henry.

I put the saddle on the chair with the horn pointing down into the seat and the back of the saddle sticking up along the broken spindle back of the chair. With feet and hands I slid chair and saddle so close to Henry's head that a lot of the saddle was on his cot. Then I stood behind the chair and leaned heavy onto the saddle back and coaxed Henry's song out of the leather.

I heard the saddle's voice right away and so did Henry. That creaking pop of leather ran across the cot looking for those old ears. The sound still fit. The comfort was there. The countless messages only Henry could decipher had reached him.

I kept easing up and down on that old saddle and watched its music wash the pain off Henry's face. In a minute it was entirely gone. His breathing was shallow and halting. This wasn't going to save him, I knew that, but it was working just the same. His eyes opened for only a moment and I don't know what they saw, but the comfortable sound in his ears was reflected in his eyes. They slid closed and never opened again. His breath came less and less — a coarse, raspy rattle as weak as a pup. Still, he wasn't in pain in his body or heart. I was the one hurting — I couldn't stop the tears pouring out of my eyes. I continued prodding that saddle for his favorite sound and watched the life ebb out of this proud son of Texas. West Texas he'd say.

Then I heard him whisper, "Let's go." And Henry Brass breathed his last.

The sound from the saddle grew still. I dropped to my knees by the cot and put my hand on Henry's forehead. "Have a good ride, my friend. No more pain. No more pain."

I buried Henry that day through blurry eyes. The next saw me resign my position at the tents and saddle my horse, listening for the sound. I headed out for the Pecos River. The trot cabin was easy to find with Henry's map and directions. When I was digging through Tom and Bill's old shit I laughed out loud.

There was a strong box, rusty and brown, right where Henry said it'd be. Inside was an old Colt pistol soaked in oil, packed in grease and wrapped with several layers of oily rags. It would clean up nicely.

Beneath the pistol were several greasy pouches. Inside were gold pieces of every description. There were coins of all sizes. When I rubbed the grease off a few I noticed the dates — literally a few coins for every year of Henry's life from the time he'd 'come of age.' This was to have been his rainy day money when he could no longer support himself. Instead he gave it to me.

Henry's gold, his pistol, and most importantly his stories, made it to California, but not before stopping again in El Paso and visiting Franklin Mountain.

When I left, there was a bright white limestone marker at his grave. It read —

Here Rests
HENRY BRASS
Soldier, Patriot, and
Loving Son of Mother Texas

I pushed out of El Paso headed west. I looked for lost camels the entire way and smiled often. No camels crossed my path, but I reached Los Angeles on Lieutenant Beale's road. I ended a few hundred miles north, in San Francisco at the Toland Medical College.* Henry would have been proud. The weather aggravated my consumption, but I toughed it out for what I could gain before moving south to dryer country where I hung out my shingle. While I learned much of medicine and anatomy, I like to think I've helped people with my ears, as Henry said. And when called to perform a surgery, I often smile as my scalpel nears the patient's skin, which seems to unnerve my staff. They don't know I'm thinking back to Henry, as I often do, and his refusal to allow me to shave him for fear I wanted to open his throat up, "just to see how it works."

*Dr. Hugh Toland opened Toland Medical College in November of 1864 in San Francisco with a class of eight students. Two four-month classes cost $130. In 1873, Toland Medical College joined the University of California.

Dr. Whitten Tines worked tirelessly toward a cure for tuberculosis, but did not live to see the advent of antibiotics and the curtailing of the disease. With few minor flare-ups, Dr. Tines's own tuberculosis remained dormant throughout his life. He died September 20th, 1929.

If you enjoyed these stories, please help promote

The Cats of Savone by sharing with family and friends

and posting a review @ Amazon.com &/or Goodreads.com.

Thanks so much,

David-Michael

Novels by David-Michael Harding

How Angels Die

Cherokee Talisman

Available at Amazon, Smashwords, and Barnes & Noble

Find free reading excerpts, preview upcoming
novels, and check out the author's blog at -

DavidMichaelHarding.com

www.ingramcontent.com/pod-product-compliance
Lightning Source LLC
Chambersburg PA
CBHW050924120626
46552CB00001B/29